My Lord Bag of Rice

My Lord Bag of Rice

New and Selected Stories

Carol Bly

MILKWEED EDITIONS

© 2000, Text by Carol Bly
(800) 520-6455. www.milkweed.org
Distributed by Publishers Group West

Published 2000 by Milkweed Editions
Printed in Canada
Cover design by Big Fish, San Francisco
Cover painting by Bruce Crane (1857–1937), "Snow Scene," watercolor and gouache
    on blue wove paper. The Metropolitan Museum of Art, George A. Hearn Fund,
    1968. (68.40) Photograph © 1980 The Metropolitan Museum of Art.
Interior design by Elizabeth Cleveland
The text of this book is set in Old Style 7 and Wade Sans Light
00 01 02 03 04   5 4 3 2 1
First Edition

Milkweed Editions, a nonprofit publisher, gratefully acknowledges support from the Elmer L. and Eleanor J. Andersen Foundation; James Ford Bell Foundation; Bush Foundation; Dayton Hudson Foundation on behalf of Dayton's, Mervyn's California and Target Stores; Doherty, Rumble and Butler Foundation; General Mills Foundation; Honeywell Foundation; Jerome Foundation; McKnight Foundation; Minnesota State Arts Board through an appropriation by the Minnesota State Legislature; Norwest Foundation on behalf of Norwest Bank Minnesota; Lawrence and Elizabeth Ann O'Shaughnessy Charitable Income Trust in honor of Lawrence M. O'Shaughnessy; Oswald Family Foundation; Ritz Foundation on behalf of Mr. and Mrs. E. J. Phelps Jr.; John and Beverly Rollwagen Fund of the Minneapolis Foundation; St. Paul Companies, Inc.; Star Tribune Foundation; U.S. Bancorp Piper Jaffray Foundation on behalf of U.S. Bancorp Piper Jaffray; and generous individuals.

Library of Congress Cataloging-in-Publication Data

Bly, Carol.
    My lord bag of rice : new and selected stories / Carol Bly. — 1st ed.
        p.   cm.
    ISBN 1-57131-031-2 (alk. paper)
        1. Minnesota—Social life and customs—Fiction.   2. City and town
    life—Minnesota—Fiction.   I. Title.
    PS3552.L89 M9 2000
    813'.54—dc21   99-047930

To Mary, Bridget,
Noah, and Micah Bly

My Lord Bag of Rice

Introduction

I first came across Carol Bly's *Backbone* some twenty years ago and made myself a nuisance in my admiration for it, pressing it on friends, then checking up to see which stories they'd read and whether their own enthusiasm had reached satisfactory heights. This collection—her first—became a favorite in the courses I taught on the short story, and it has lived on vividly for me in that place of memory where our own past gets tangled up with the truest stories we've heard and read, so that we can hardly tell one from the other. And so too with much of the work that followed over the years.

What was it—what is it—that I like so much in Carol Bly's stories? Their art, first and last, the sure way she has with this exacting form. An example: One of the hardest things to do in a short story is change point of view from one character to another without losing velocity and focus. The usual effect is a dizzying kind of Ping-Pong, the perspective shuttling so nervously to and fro that we begin to wonder just whose story we're reading, and finally cease to care. For that reason most writers in the form stick to a single angle of vision. But in "Chuck's Money" and other pieces collected here, Carol Bly manages to see from the eyes of different characters without any disruption in our sense of a unified, purposeful narrative.

She has her own way with the form, yet never for the form's sake alone. As with her language, the aim is to clarify our view of her people and their lives. Here—from "The Last of the Gold Star Mothers"—is a characteristic moment: "When Mary Graving was sober, her face was too decided and twitchy to look good with the large plain earrings she always wore. She thought she was generally too grim looking, and her earrings looked too cheerful at the edges of her face. Now that she was drunk, though, and wearing a red dress, her face felt hot and rosy. Her smile stayed stuck on, and she knew that the earrings—a new pair, especially cheap, not from Bagley's in Duluth but a product of the Ben Franklin store in Rachel River—looked fine. She was not beautiful but she was all right." A certain world is given to us here, not only a specific regional and social world, but one where people can know themselves without despair and, even drunk, face life on their own terms, with the materials at hand. The language is unobtrusively honed, and though it has a colloquial tincture drawn from Mary Graving's internal diction, it also keeps a certain distance, reserving its essential objectivity for other perspectives and shifts of tone. This seems to me a model of description, smart without condescension, efficient without being cool or brittle, telling us much without any show of effort or haste.

Carol Bly brings her Minnesota world to life in the names

of places and people, the resolutely nice, optimistic rhythms and inflections of their speech, the sad distant sense of the land and what it has meant to these folk even when that meaning is frayed or lost. Her stories are as particular in their settings and culture as those of Turgenev and Joyce and Flannery O'Connor, and as far from being simply regional. At bottom, her work is about responsibility, and she does not rope off the problem of political responsibility from the personal varieties that concern most writers of fiction. Can you be a producer of chemicals used in weapons and still be a good man? Does loving-kindness and generosity to friends, family, town, and church cover your complicity in, or your failure to resist, distant wrongs? Carol Bly's fiction will not be found guilty of that timidity; she is manifestly determined to create an art that is fully responsive to the evils done in our name and with our tacit consent.

But in the end it's the people I remember: Mary Graving making peace with the knowledge that she's been cheated by an old friend, Harriet White going AWOL from the old folks' home and walking through the snow to the farm where she'd raised her children and known her purpose on the earth. These are people who think and speak and act in complicated, unpredictable ways. They often surprise even themselves. They have moral nature and the power to stifle it. They see their choices and they make them, for good or ill. They have, the best of them, *backbone*. Great word, backbone. There's a strong one running right through this book.

TOBIAS WOLFF

My Lord Bag of Rice

STORIES FROM

Backbone

Gunnar's Sword

As she climbed the hill to the Home, Harriet White felt the town falling away behind her. She usually despised the town in a casual, peaceful way, the way adults sometimes despise their parents' world once they've left it. The mind simply remembers it as something unpleasant, but dead. Right now she felt annoyed with the town in general because she had begun a quarrel with the Golden Age Auxiliary women about the quilts they were making: they were using old chenille bedspreads for centers, since the center can never be seen, and then doing elegant patchwork covers. The pastor had held the quilts up at service and praised the ladies. These quilts, which looked cozy but didn't keep out the cold, were then sent to the Lutheran World Relief. Harriet was irritated by these women's ethics, which were like a mix of local pastors' remarks and the inchoate philosophies of their husbands in the VFW Lounge.

She had lived all her adult life with her husband and son on their quarter section, where a half mile in every direction was theirs: when she came to the Home, she had somehow to shrink it all to the size of her room. Some people managed that by stuffing all the furniture they could bring from their old houses into the tiny rooms of the Lutheran Home; Harriet managed it by working away at her pastimes with a fury. The crafts room was full of her output; she was like a factory: she turned out more sweaters and afghans than twenty residents together. But when it snowed, even during the tiresome snows of late March, she felt a settling inside her, as if her mind lowered and glided outward, like the surface of a lake. She would fetch her coat and overshoes and walk about the ordinary, dreamless town. She felt lost in thought like someone who has been dealt with cordially.

Harriet's neck was ropy and knotted, in the way of old people who have got thin. She forgave herself that. As a little girl, and later as a young woman, she had feared the degradation that age might bring. She remembered watching the hired girl, who had cared for her over weekends when her parents went to their club, pulling on her stockings. Above the knee, Harriet had seen the white meat of the thigh swelling and she had sworn, I shall never let my legs look like that! And later she had sworn, I shall never let my chin sag like that! Or, I shall never lower myself to that! Now, as she swung fairly easily up the hill, she thought she was less discontented with her body, and self, than she had been at any time earlier. She was eighty-two, but kept a jaunty air, some of which was gratitude when her right ankle didn't act up. She climbed firmly, noting how soundless the cold air was, except for traffic in the town below. The elm treetops were broomy and vague; the smoke from

Carol Bly

the Home power plant piped slowly straight up. She hoped it would snow.

On the upper sidewalk at last, she saw Arne, the Home's driver and man of all work, helping Mr. Solstad, the mortician, wheel a casket out of the east entrance. Harriet paused, partly for the flag that lay over the coffin, and she knew it was the body of Mr. Ole Morstad, whose funeral was to be down at the church that afternoon. She was not sorry that he was dead; he had been taken up to the third-floor infirmary more than three years ago. Then, rather than now, they had recognized his death; her roommate, LaVonne Morstad, had cried and Harriet had held her shoulder and hand. "He will never come back down onto second!" cried Vonnie then. And so he hadn't.

Arne and Mr. Solstad eased the casket off its wheeled cart into the hearse. Then Arne came over to Harriet, with his workingman's sidewise walk, blowing on his hands. He smiled at her. "Morning, missus," he said respectfully, as he always did. Residents who were very feeble or not very alert he tended to call by their Christian names. "Will you be wanting a ride down to the services this afternoon, Mrs. White?"

"I'll walk, Arne—it isn't so cold!"

"Not for you maybe," he said admiringly. "But some of 'em, they wouldn't go if they had to walk."

"I bet you won't be taking down storm windows today after all," Harriet said, remembering an announcement over the public-address system that morning.

"Feels like snow," he said, swinging his head northwest,

where the tiny cars ran along on the cold gray highway. "Weather don't seem to scare you none though."

They both paused as the hearse drove by them carefully— and then they gave each other that farm-people's signal as they parted. It was a slight wave with the right hand—half like a staff officer's from his jeep, half like a pastor's benediction. Harriet went in.

She avoided the reception entrance, with the residents sitting about looking hot and faint, and the few children inevitably hanging around the TV sets instead of going up to the grandparents they'd been sent to visit. She marched straight off to the back, where the crafts room was, and had the good luck to find Marge Larson, the therapist, there. The room was full of half-finished products at this end—but at the other end, screened off by a Sears Roebuck room divider, was the "shop," where the finished hot pads, napkin holders, aprons were on sale. The Golden Age Auxiliary members came by regularly and bought. Harriet's work was known because it was fair isle knitting, in western Minnesota called Norwegian knitting. Not everyone could do it. Harriet also helped Marge with other people's unfinished work, or work that needed to be taken out and remade, which she kept quiet about.

Together they discussed some of the projects lying around on tables. Some weren't any good. An old man was in the room, too, but it was Orrin Bjorning, who could not hear and could not work. He sat utterly still, and the dull light came in off the snow so that the skin on his forehead and cheeks looked like a hood—as if a monk sat there frozen—instead of like a face. He insisted on spending whole mornings in the

Carol Bly

crafts room, his fingers bent around a piece of 1 x 1. He never stirred. When the PA system announced dinner time, he would shake himself and slowly leave, never speaking.

Harriet and Marge walked around the room, touching and lifting Orlon, felt, acrylic, cotton. Harriet promised to return in the afternoon and work a little on Mrs. Steensen's rug. Mrs. Steensen had started braiding. Marge often placed new lots of nicely stripped wool in the woman's lap, and Mrs. Steensen always looked up and said energetically, "Yes—good, thanks then, Marge!" in her Scandinavian accent. *"Ja—*I've been needing just such a blue—now I can get on with my rug!" And then all morning her hands made little plucking gestures at the rags in her lap. Marge and Harriet together worked up two or three feet of the braid from time to time, and Mrs. Steensen seemed not to notice. "Rug's coming along pretty good!" she would shout, when Marge came by.

At ten Harriet left. She still had her coat to hang up, and she had to write a short speech. Later, she would have to help Vonnie Morstad dress for the funeral.

But she stopped at the second-floor landing because Mr. Helmstetter and Kermit Steensen were sitting by the elevators.

"Thank you very much for that little rabbit favor, missus," Helmstetter said. "I gave it to my granddaughter—the one they called Kristi. Kristi is for Christine, that's her aunt on the other side, then Ann for the middle name. I suppose it's for someone. She was very pleased."

"Ja, I suppose you told her you made it, huh," Kermit said, one of the Home wits.

Helmstetter blushed. "She wouldn't have believed that, I guess. Where you going in such a rush?" he said to Harriet. "You're always rushing. Chasing. This way, that way. Such a busy lady."

"Busier'n Jacqueline Kennedy," Kermit said.

Harriet sat down beside them and they all faced the aluminum elevator door. "I can sit down a moment."

"Work'll keep," Helmstetter said.

"Work don't run away," Kermit Steensen said in a witty tone. Again they all laughed, all of them more heartily than they felt like, but they all felt pretty cheerful for a second. Harriet rose to the occasion.

"Well, how's *Edge of Night* coming?" Harriet asked them. She knew that they all listened to television drama serials during afternoon coffee in the coffee room. In the morning the sun didn't come in the coffee room, so it was empty save for the candy stripers' carts and a slight odor of dentures. In the afternoon, however, the lace curtains were transformed and a light fell on the people as they were served their "lunch"—the western Minnesota word for the midafternoon snack. Sometimes the sun was so gorgeous that they had to squint to make out the dove-pale images on the TV set. Helmstetter and Steensen and a couple of other men—and nearly all the second-floor women—kept track of the dramas. From time to time, Harriet asked them about the plots.

"We don't watch that anymore," Kermit told her. *Splendor of Our Days* is what we're watching now."

"This young fellow has got an incurable disease and he is trying not to tell his girl about it, but she knows. She wants to talk it over with him so she can help him."

Carol Bly

"Oh, that isn't the point!" Kermit said sharply. "The point is he doesn't want her to find out he's scared to die. He wants to keep on laughing and joking right up to the end. She belongs to the country club that his folks want to get into."

"There's an old Viking story like that," Harriet put in. "Do you remember that old legend about how the Vikings believed you must make a joke before you died, in order to show Death you were better than he is?"

Letting the *Lutheran Herald* sag on his knees, Helmstetter said courteously, "How'd that hang together then?"

Harriet said, "There was a particular young Viking and he and his friends had a grudge against a man named Gunnar. So one day they decided they would put a ladder up to the loft where Gunnar slept, while he was away, then they'd hide in there and then kill him when he came in at night. So the friends helped the young fellow put up the ladder, and up he went, with his knife between his teeth. Just as he was heaving himself over the windowsill, however, Gunnar, who happened not to be away after all, leapt off his straw bed and ran his sword right through the young Viking. The Viking fell off the ladder backward. His friends raced over to where he lay, with the blood coursing out of his chest.

"'Oh—Gunnar is at home, then?' they asked with astonishment.

"'Well now,' the young man said as he died, 'I don't know if Gunnar is home, but his sword is.'"

Helmstetter and Steensen hesitated: they weren't sure they got the point of the story, yet they felt moved. "Pretty good, pretty good," they both murmured. There was a polite pause, and then Kermit Steensen fidgeted and brightened and said, "Not to change the subject, you see this girl belongs to the country club, but the boyfriend isn't interested at all, but all the time his parents are anxious for him to belong and they keep throwing him together with this girl."

"But she's really interested in that other fellow—the doctor fellow!" cried Helmstetter with a laugh.

"She isn't either!" said Steensen. "That was all over weeks ago. In fact they've dropped him; you don't see him anymore."

"I seen him on there just yesterday!"

"You see lots of things!" Helmstetter said.

Harriet rose after a moment, and said, "Are you going to be in the dining room at eleven?"

"What for then?" Both old men were very anxious not to be forgetful of any part of the Home schedule.

"We're having coffee in honor of Marge Larson, you know, the woman who helps us with crafts? It's her birthday. We'd do it this afternoon but there's the Morstad funeral."

"Oh, *ja*, then," the men said. When Harriet left, they fingered the church magazines on their knees in a distracted sort of way, and Kermit began deliberately snapping over the pages.

Harriet looked forward to getting to her room. She not only had two books going at the same time but she also had one small bit of knitting—a complicated sweater for little Christopher. She had not used a pattern, but had counted the stitches there were to be across the shoulders, at front and back, and then, using the same number of squares on light-blue-inked graph paper, she had made up her own pattern.

Carol Bly

She blocked in the colors with crayons, trying different combinations. It was immensely satisfying, because she not only had the problem of what colors and shapes would look well in wool, but also she wanted, if possible, to make up a pattern that would incorporate the different colors in any one row at least as often as every fifth stitch. If a row were to have blue and white, for example, she made sure the blue yarn was used at least as often as once in five—or the white, conversely. This way she prevented "carrying" yarn for more than an inch in the back. Long, carried yarn tended to get caught on buttons and baby fingers. Harriet laughed at herself for her love of knitting—You are simpleminded, she told herself—yet it sustained her in a way that would have surprised her years before. For example, during meals—as in most institutions, meals were a weak side of life at the Home—she could keep cheerful, and even hold up a sort of one-handed conversation, by reminding herself that the orderly, beautiful knitting lay waiting upstairs. Sometimes the thought of her knitting even came to her during Larry's visits. I do hope, she told herself, I won't get so my own son is overshadowed by a pair of worsted mittens. She felt certain that the best defense of one's personality, against everything—senility mostly, and worse, later—was one's humor. And hers was intact. Or at least, so people assured her.

"You have a wonderful sense of humor, Mother," Larry had told her on one of his visits from Edina. "When did you develop it? Was it when you married Dad and went into farming?"

She opened her top bureau drawer to take out the lined paper to write the speech for Marge on, and found Larry's

Gunnar's Sword

last letter. "I'm hoping to get out to Jacob over the weekend, hopefully Saturday," he wrote. Ghastly usage, Harriet thought affectionately. "I'll call Saturday around noon if I do. Are you having a cold horrible March? The city is a mess—mud and melting snow. I don't know why we Minnesotans complain about winter, spring is what's horrible. See you soon. Love from us all, a kiss from that wonderful little Christopher—Larry." Harriet read it over again, and then laid it under her notebook.

She began work on the speech. "We are gathered here this morning in honor of Marge's birthday," she began. "But it seems to me it would make a lot more sense if she were gathered here in honor of *our* birthdays—we've had so many more of them." She sat back, staring at the smudgy storm window that Arne had not removed. "What drivel," she thought, glancing at her speech again. She crossed it out. Even first-rate jokes didn't work particularly well at the Home—and second-rate jokes went very badly. She visualized the dining room—the bleached foreheads, held motionless over the plates full of desserts; the stately, plastic flowers. She bent to the job again, forcing herself not to hope that Larry might offer her a ride out into the country to look at the farm. She worked away at the speech, finished, shortened it, and had just thought to check the time when Vonnie came in.

The young girl volunteers called candy stripers had put curlers in Vonnie's hair for her. On the first floor was a shampooing room, where once a week a few members of the Jacob Lutheran Church—the Golden Age Auxiliary—laid their heavy coats on the steel-tubing chairs, and washed and set the hair of any of the women who cared to come down. In

Carol Bly

between those Tuesday afternoons, the candy stripers would sometimes do it. The residents preferred the services of the Golden Age women, most of whom were in their fifties and could remember how hair "should be done nice"—meaning, with bobby pins screwed to the head, dried hard, and then brushed and combed, leaving discernible curls. The young girls, on the other hand, believed in either back-combed hair—or more recently, in simply straight "undone" hair. Vonnie came into the room scowling, and Harriet supposed she wasn't pleased with the way the candy stripers had done her.

"Shall we lay out our clothes for this afternoon?" Harriet said, closing her notebook.

Vonnie grasped the arms of her rocking chair, got ready, and then jammed herself down into it. "You lay out *your* clothes!"

"Can I help?" Harriet said gently.

"I can lay out my own clothes; I can get into my own clothes. Next thing you'll want to rinse my teeth!"

"Going to the dining room for the birthday coffee for Marge?" Harriet said after a pause.

"To hear your speech you mean!" snapped Vonnie. Her cheeks shook.

"Vonnie!"

"Oh, *ja,* Vonnie! Don't Vonnie me!" cried the woman. "I am sick of you doing everything like you were better than everyone else. Speech for Marge! Why couldn't we of got a printed card like everyone wanted? A nice printed card, with a nice picture, a photo of some roses on nice paper with a nice poem on it, they got hundreds now, at either one of the drugstores—you're always going on them walks, you could of walked to the drugstore and you could have got it and you could of read it aloud to us, and then we would have the cake and it would be real nice. But oh no, you got to do some fancy thing no one ever thought of—oh, *ja,* it had to be something— a speech!"

"Ridiculous," Harriet said. "A woman like Marge gets a hundred cards like that a year. The idea is to do something more personal."

"Whose idea? Everyone else thought a card would be real nice!"

Vonnie turned around and faced Harriet, the day's full light on her stretched forehead. "And I got something else to say to you also! My knitting! You can just keep to your own and leave my work alone! When I want your help with my work, I'll ask you for it."

"Oh, Vonnie," Harriet said, "all we did was take out back to the row where the increasing was supposed to start, and do the increasing every second row—and then you take over again from there."

"Don't you have any of your own to do? Why don't you do your own increasing and your own decreasing and leave mine be."

They both stood up and stiffly began taking fresh stockings, their better shoes, their dark print dresses out of their closets. If they dressed now, they wouldn't be caught dressing later when LaVonne's relations began coming in to pick her up to go down to the church. They had a half hour before the birthday coffee for Marge.

When they both were dressed, there was a pause. There

Carol Bly

was a problem they simply had to solve: Vonnie's hair. Harriet finally took the lead. "Vonnie," she said as efficiently and impersonally as she could, "let's get your curlers out now—because now's when we've got time to get it combed out before LeRoy and Mervin come."

The widow grumbled, but let herself down in her chair, with her eyes pointed coldly into the mirror. "I don't want it brushed out too much. I don't like the way that one candy striper girl does it. No sense of how hair should be done."

"The one called Mary?" Harriet asked. Standing behind Vonnie, she began gently taking out curlers.

"*Ja.* Now that other one's a real nice girl. Friend of the Helmstetters. My Mervin married a Helmstetter." Slowly the curlers came off—LaVonne Morstad kept one trembling wrist raised, to receive them one by one from Harriet. Talking to each other in the mirror, the two women pulled together again, a little.

The chaplain's voice now came over the PA system: his voice was rusty and idealistic. In his Scandinavian accent, he said: "If everyone will please come straight down to the dining room, we will be having a coffee hour in honor of Mrs. Marge Larson. If everyone will please come down to the dining room, we will be having a coffee hour in honor of Mrs. Marge Larson. *Vil De vaer så snill å komme til spisesalen; vi skal ha kaffe . . . ,*" continuing in Norwegian. He did not give his announcement in German, for in the Jacob area most of the German-Americans were Catholics. There were only a dozen or so in the Lutheran Home.

Harriet left Vonnie muttering over the funeral programs.

The widow had the conviction something had been printed incorrectly, and she kept running her big finger across the lines again, pronouncing the names, the thous and thees, in a hoarse whisper.

Harriet found Marge and Arne dragging the PA system hookup over to the standing mike, near the diabetic table. Now the younger residents came in briskly, glancing out at the snow-lit window, nodding to one another. The more aged people followed, looking like the wooden carvings of Setesdal Valley and the Jotunheim. Over the shuffling slippers, the stooped backs were immobile; you were aware of the folds and creases of sleeves, the velvety skin coating elbows that looked sore, the huge blocky ankles of the old, like knots of marble. Harriet listened, a little nervous as always before she addressed a group, aware of rayon rubbing, now chair legs being dragged out. Finally everyone was seated— even old Orrin Bjorning sat gazing at his right hand cupped over his left. Harriet was delighted to find Kermit Steensen and some of the other men sitting where she could see them; if you had just a face or two responding, you could carry the others.

"Harriet," Marge said, "would you read off the birthday list for this month? We were going to do it for Golden Age this afternoon, but since most of them will be down at the funeral, we thought we'd better do it this morning."

Harriet flattened the typed yellow sheet over her clipboard, rapidly checking the names for those she might not pronounce right. Three were crossed through—she recognized the names of two men who had died in the past few weeks, and of a woman whose relatives had moved her to the

Carol Bly

Dawson Nursing Home. Mr. Ole Morstad's name was still on. "Shan't I pencil through this?" Harriet asked, pointing.

"Oh my goodness—thanks!" cried Marge, leaning across Harriet to run her ballpoint through it. "I'm glad you caught that!"

They stood together, planning the next few minutes—odd, Harriet thought, this stupid fifteen-minute affair, a two-minute speech for a birthday, and yet it had all the trappings of the hundreds of meetings she had presided over. It had also the old lilt to it—the sense that she herself was exciting, someone who could bring off things, someone to be relied on; if little difficulties arose, she could back and fill. She was a leader. Color came up into her face and she knew it.

As Arne knelt at her feet tinkering with the extension cord, Harriet thought, I used to believe that as I got old I'd feel closer to people of all sorts of backgrounds. I thought there was some great common denominator we'd all sink to—and I'd feel *more* affectionate toward clumsy or inexperienced people. But it hasn't worked out. I don't! I am perfectly resigned to being among people who never read or reflect on anything, but I don't feel close. And less than ever can I understand how they can bear life with one another. She looked out, now, over the whole dining room because Arne was through, and her birthday list, touching the mike, gave a hoarse rattle, showing the current was on.

"Good morning!" she said, remembering not to duck to the mike. "We are gathered together this morning in honor of someone who means a great deal to every one of us." She went on, faces turned toward her. Quietly, at the edges of the room, the kitchen staff with their red wrists carried in coffee urns and set down plates of dessert. Harriet noticed with the speed of eight years' residency that the dessert was sawed slices of angel food with Wilderness Cherry Pie filling and Cool Whip on it. She was aware of Marge herself, modestly perched on a chair at the diabetic table. When the speech was over, and the gift received, Marge would be off again—flying around doing the dozens of chores she somehow accomplished during a day—pushing a wheelchair to the shampoo room, helping a church women's group plan their surprises for the infirmary trays, even helping to tip the vats of skinned potatoes in the kitchen. Harriet mentioned some of these tasks so graciously done—and she heard the warmth fill in her voice. It had its effect, too: she had the people's attention. The moment she saw that, she felt still another warmth in her voice: the warmth of success. So she wound up with some lilt, made Marge stand, handed over the gift, excused the roomful of people from singing "Happy Birthday" because she knew they hated it— the sound of their awful voices—and she read the birthday list, after which everyone clapped. Then she said to Marge, "We all say, bless you, Marge," and retreated from the microphone.

Harriet settled herself in a folding chair by the maids' serving stand to hear Marge's thanks, but Siegert, the head nurse, was bending over her shoulder: "It's your son, Mrs. White. He's waiting for you in your room. I said you'd come up, but surely you can stay and have your coffee . . ."

"No, no!" cried Harriet. "I'm coming! Larry! No, I don't want any coffee! Thanks, Mrs. Siegert!"

The nurse smiled. "Tell you what, I'll bring up some of the dessert for both of you—and some coffee, how's that?"

"How nice you are," Harriet cried, and hurried out.

Carol Bly

She wanted to go the fastest way, which is to say up the staircase, but then she would be short of breath when she arrived and then Larry would worry. So she pressed the stupid bell and waited for the poky elevator to sink all the way down from the infirmary on third.

She found room 211 full of Morstad men. They were milling about in the tiny space—between the bureaus, the two rocking chairs, the beds—in heavy dark overcoats flung open in the hot air of the Home. They were shaking hands, in turns, and then prowling about the room, trying not to bump into one another or the radiator. Vonnie herself stood rummaging in the top drawer of her bureau. Her rocking chair kept rocking as one man or another struck it with his ankles. Harriet paused a moment, daunted by the crowd, and then entered and shook hands with each person separately. They were in their good clothes. "I think I ought to know yer face . . . Mervin Morstad's my name. My brother LeRoy, Mrs. White. He's from the Cities—over in Edina. Well I guess you know our mother all right." (Sociable laughter.) ". . . Deepest sympathy." "Oh, thank you now. . . . Yes, he was. He sure was—a blessing in a way, if you get how I mean. . . . Here—mother, never mind—it don't matter. . . ."

But Vonnie was furious. "Don't matter! I'll say it does. Look, right there, in print, and we paid for it, too!"

Both her sons, Mervin and LeRoy, huge men with gleaming, round cheeks, tipped their gigantic shoulders like circling airplanes over the card she held. She handed it to Mervin, and he read aloud: "Olai Vikssen Morstad. Born 14 April 1886, Entered into Eternal Rest 9 March 1971. Eighty-Four Years Ten Months Twenty-Four Days!"

Gunnar's Sword

"Well, it ought to be twenty-three days, shouldn't it?" Vonnie shouted.

"Oh, Mom, it doesn't matter," the son called LeRoy said.

"Oh doesn't it! Well, people will just sit through the services, you know what people are, and they'll count that up and they'll see just as sure as anything someone didn't add straight. There'll be talk."

"Come on, Mama," Mervin said. "Here's your coat . . . hat." Harriet found and gave him Vonnie's black bag, her gloves. "Come on, Mama," Mervin said, helping her. "They've got a real nice dinner down at the church—and Corrine's are all there already and they want to visit with you. And Mahlin's— all except Virgil, he's away at school yet. . . ." And gently he went on, listing the various relations who had come for the old man's funeral and now were being served a hot luncheon by one of the church circles. The big men followed poor Vonnie out of the room—Mervin taking her arm in the doorway. LeRoy hung back a minute and said civilly, "I know what you done for our Ma, Mrs. White. All these years. She wouldn't get by near as good without you being so good to stay by. So thank you then!" A final view of his huge blushing face.

"Oh, Larry!" Harriet cried. "It's so good to see you!" For her son was there: all that while, he'd been waiting in that crowded room, quietly sitting on the edge of her bed near the far wall, glancing through her books.

They hovered a moment, hugging each other, in the middle of the room. "Mama," he said delighted, like a boy. "Look what I brought!"

There was a huge bundle of what looked like used clothing on her bed.

Carol Bly

"You can hold it if you're good!" Larry laughed. He picked up the clumsy package, unwinding some of the clothes.

Harriet darted over without a word. Trembling, she undid the rest of some old padded jacket the baby was wrapped in, loosened his knit blanket—not without noticing through her tears, though, that it was one she had knitted. She carried Christopher to her rocking chair, and sat down. For a moment baby and great-grandmother made tiny struggles to get sorted. Harriet had to get her good foot, the left, which never gave her trouble even recently, onto the ground, to use for pushing to make the chair rock. The baby had to move his tiny shoulders as though scratching an itch, but in actuality he was finding where and how this set of arms would hold him. He didn't pay much attention to what he saw out of his eyes: he saw only the dull whitish light off the snow, smeary and without warmth. What he felt in his shoulders, behind the small of his back, under his knees, was the very soul of whoever was holding him; it streamed into him from all those places. He stilled, paying attention to it, deciding, using shoulder blades, backbone, and legs to make the decision whether or not the energy entering was safe and good. Everything now told him it was, so in the next second, he let each part of his body loosen into those hands, and let his feet be propped on that lap, then let his chest be lifted and pressed to that breast and shoulder—his colorless, rather inexpressive eyes went slatted half shut. He made a little offering of his own; he let his cheek lean on that old trustworthy cheek, and then, with a final wiggle, he gave himself up to being held. All she ever said to him was, "Christopher, precious!" but that was nothing to him—that was just noise.

Gunnar's Sword

Larry had stood up and gone over to the doorway; someone was conferring with him. He returned with a tray with two cups of coffee on it, and a plate with some white cake with inevitable Wilderness Cherry filling on it. "That was your head nurse—Mrs. Siegert, isn't it?" he asked, proudly keeping track of the Home staff.

He sat down on Vonnie's rocking chair, with the tray; he shoved Vonnie's Bible over. The lace bureau cloth immediately caught in one corner of it and wrinkled up, and the program for Ole Morstad's funeral, a paper rabbit candy basket, and a tube of Chap Stick fell on the floor.

Larry, sipping his coffee, told his day's news. It hadn't been a bad drive out from Edina, although Evelyn had sworn he would run into snow. One hundred and fifty miles with very few icy patches—not like last year at this time! "Met some of your menfolk here, in the hallway, on the way up," he added conversationally. "I told them who I was and they said, 'Oh sure, we know your mother! She's a real alert, real nice lady!'"

"I'm a regular Miss Jacob Lutheran Home!" Harriet said.

They both laughed, and he told her Evelyn sent her love. He told her about bringing Janice, his oldest son's wife, out to see her folks in Boyd, and how he begged the baby away from her on condition he wrap him up well.

"What farm business did you come about?" Harriet said, meaning to ask intelligent questions, although in truth she was only holding the baby.

"Oh that—" Larry said, frowning. "Before I get to that, there's something we've been over before, Mother, and I want to say it all again."

"Yes—all right!" She laughed at him ironically, mainly

Carol Bly

because it felt so marvelous holding the baby. His little eyes were half open, but she held him so close, up to her cheek, so that the eye against her cheek was of course out of focus and therefore only a dark blur: she thought, I shall never forget that look of a baby's eye when you hold him too close to see—the dark, blurry, soft fur-bunch of his eye!

"You know that Evelyn and I have plenty of room, Mama. We want you, Mama. This is OK"—he gave a kind of wave at the tray of Marge Larson's birthday cake and Vonnie's mirror—"but, Mama, we want something different for you."

"You're right," Harriet said gently, "we *have* been over this before. You know how touched I am you feel that way, Larry. You and Evelyn."

She imagined again their house in Edina. It was one of a Cape Cod development—white, but with the green-black shutters hung behind, rather than hinged on top of, the outside woodwork, and therefore straightaway visibly fake. But they had some marvelous rooms in it—a kind of library with a wood-burning fireplace and a Viss rug with a light blue pattern, and the dining room. The other rooms had somehow soaked up the builder's ideas, and they all seemed to wail, Edina! Help! Evelyn had done what she could, but the built-in hi-fi cabinet in its fake Early American paneling suffocated the walls.

This wasn't why Harriet didn't go to live with them, but she conjured up the picture anyway.

"I know perfectly well you moved in here because that was the right thing for Dad," Larry was saying. "That was *then,* Mama. True, he would have been a burden on us—you never said that, but we knew that's what you thought.

Anyway it's all different now, and I want you to reconsider. Very carefully."

"There's still your dad to think of, you know," Harriet remarked.

Larry put down his cake. "I don't know if that's true or not," he said. "I mean I don't know if that's the right thinking for you or us to be doing at all. I can't think it would make any difference—and meantime I've got a mother 150 miles away from me that I'd like to have living with me if you don't mind." He spoke a little feverishly—which Harriet understood as slight insincerity on his part.

"I don't know how to thank you," she said. She squinted hard into the baby's sleeping shoulders. His woolly sweater and the upper lip of his blanket she felt clearly on her eyelids. "I expect I could thank you by knitting baby blanket number 234 for Christopher here?"

They both laughed a little, but Larry let the laugh fall and quickly took up his point again. "And Evelyn feels the same way, too, Mama."

Harriet was thinking as fast as she could. She had to think: why was Larry feverish? He must be talking excitedly because he didn't really feel so enthusiastic about her moving in with them as he wished to show. Or, that he felt enthusiastic about it now, but that the offer really—very deep within him—was good only so long as his mother was sprightly, alert, a little witty, and so forth. And that he was not giving her the profoundly felt invitation—which would be an invitation to live with him and Evelyn when she might be incontinent, irritable, afraid, or even demented. And perhaps she, like Einar, would have a bad stroke.

Carol Bly

As Harriet went through this in her mind, being as systematic about it as she could, she felt this last was the real explanation of Larry's nervousness. It reassured her in her refusal to live with them: even if she should choose not to consider Einar, and went to her son, she would still have to adjust to the Home later—to this one or to an unfamiliar one.

Having thought this through to the end, she gained her poise. She said kindly, "I know Evelyn feels that way. And I know you do, too—both of you—well, you're marvelous children. I'm going to stay put, I think, though. You know I thank you very much."

"Well, there's another reason, Mama," Larry said.

Harriet looked up, still feeling the new sense of control from having thought through the whole thing.

"You see, Mama, I've actually sold the farm. That's one reason I am out here this weekend."

She felt damaged. This piece of news was like an actual danger to her body. The trouble with being at the end of life, Harriet thought, is that body and mind get too close together: that is, when the mind takes a blow—such as from Larry's selling the farm—the body takes the blow as well. You feel the thing physically. Other times, she had noticed, it worked in reverse. When she had originally tripped over Orrin Bjorning's bird-feeding station he left on the floor of the crafts room—a good five years ago now—not only had she hurt her right ankle and toe, but she had felt a kind of damage to her soul. Tears of hurt feelings had come, she remembered. Senility, she suspected, arrived the day you forgot to laugh at these incidents.

Rapidly she now went over Larry's actual words. If he

hadn't literally sold the farm, she might convince him not to. But she thought she could still hear his voice saying he had already done it.

He hadn't asked her. She didn't expect to be begged for advice, but it would have been lovely, really lovely, if he had let her in on the various stages of the dealing. He could have told her, I'm beginning to consider offers on the farm, Mama. Or, Well, Mama, two of the buyer prospects look pretty good.

No doubt he had sensed that she would try to talk him out of it! In any case, she gathered herself carefully, meaning to have nothing of the wounded about her.

"You ought to sell the farm, my dear," she said smoothly. "You can't manage a piece of real estate properly unless you're right there, available, when things come up—and goodness knows, it doesn't look as if you and Evelyn are ever going to farm—and certainly Janice and Bob aren't moving in that direction. And I can't really think any of you would want to *retire* to the farm. No, that was probably a good thing!"

Larry gave her a sharp look but she gave away nothing— he surely saw only half old-woman-being-sensible, half great-grandmother-holding-the-baby.

"I don't want you to get around me this time, Mama," Larry said. "I want you to come live with us. We have all that room now. And time. And there'd be congenial people for you to meet. We're not country club people you know! Look, Mama—you've spent your whole life out here!"

The loudspeaker made its electric whine, and the pastor's hoarse, nasal voice came on with the table prayer. *"I Jesu*

Carol Bly

navn går vi til bords, å spise og drikke på ditt ord. . . ." It was dinner time at the Home—and the only sound on the second floor was the soft rub of nurses' shoes, as they moved about their duties.

"Let's go to lunch!" Larry said, standing. "Which one of the marvelous French restaurants of Jacob, Minnesota, shall we take in today? McGregor's Cafe or the Royal?"

"Neither for me," Harriet said. "Give me ten more minutes, dear—and then you go because I've got to go to that funeral this afternoon—and I just had cake and coffee. I don't want more now."

On a scaffold outside, Arne was manhandling a large screen frame. Apparently he had decided to start with the taking down of the storm windows after all. Both Harriet and Larry watched him a moment, in the way people who have done a job many times can't help pausing to watch someone else tackle it. They nearly felt the weight in their hands of the storm window coming off—they knew which snapholders had been loosened first; they knew the instant the weight of the glass and wood dropped into the vault of Arne's palm.

"You don't feel bad about the farm then?" Larry said, still looking out the window. Arne's shadow kept sliding back and forth in the room.

"No, dear. It was a good idea. Probably, you should have done it ages ago."

"You used to like it when we drove out there and checked out the old place," he said. "You'll miss that."

"Nonsense. There're hundreds of places I enjoy driving past."

"If you won't come to lunch, Mama, I've got to take that baby back to his mother, I'm afraid. You're sure you won't come?"

Christopher had wet through his clothing a little; his blanketed bottom was moist and warm, but Harriet, whose arm had ached the past half hour, couldn't bear to part with him. This moist, hot weight seemed like a part of her—she dreaded handing him over. She dreaded it. Yet, a minute later, when Larry carefully reached down, she managed a social smile up. Suddenly her breast and lap were cool. She felt abominable, never to nurse or hold a baby again. Her heart turned really black; she felt her whole body was like a cold andiron.

Larry promised to write, to repeat the invitation. They kissed and he left, saying he'd go see Dad on the way out.

Harriet waited until from down the hall she heard the elevator doors open and close, then she hurried out herself.

"Oh, *ja!* there she goes!" cried Helmstetter, sitting in his usual place at the landing. So everyone was up from dinner already.

Now there were four other men taking up all the chairs there, or she'd have joined him. They all looked especially fragile and pale because they had now put on their good suits; the corrugated necks were so thin, they touched their white collars only at the ribby cords. They were all ready for the funeral.

The two candy stripers were approaching the elevators from the new wing; glasses and pitcher tinkled like little bells on their cart.

"Hullo, Mrs. White!" they both said.

"Hello—DeAnn . . . Mary."

Carol Bly

"Oh my," the one called DeAnn said, cocking her head at the men sitting about, "aren't we dressed up all fine and nice! Everybody looking so nice!"

"They're going to a funeral," cried the other candy striper.

DeAnn swung the light cart about. Mary had to step back, so it could enter the elevator when the doors opened. "Well, they all look real nice," DeAnn sang. She pointed her arm at full length to press the elevator button, and turned her firmly permanented head to the men. "Mr. Morstad was a real fine man," she sang to them. "And he looked real nice, too, for the services."

"I didn't think he did!" said Mary in a low tone to Harriet, dodging close to make room for the head nurse, Mrs. Siegert, who came up to wait beside them. Looking younger than fourteen and very exposed, Mary seemed to gather her bravery and she blurted out, "I didn't think he looked very nice! He looked so tiny and brown and . . ." Her voice faded in terror, for the head nurse, as well as DeAnn, who no doubt despised her, and the four old men in the lounge chairs, now were staring at her.

"And dead," Harriet said, helping. "I agree. But then, the funeral had to be the fourth day instead of the third so the relatives could get here—that's why." Harriet brought out her best, sensible tone: "I remember on the first day he looked rather like himself—only asleep. The second day he began to look diminished, somehow. I remember thinking, That face wants to *leave*. The face is begging us to let it go—like a guest on the porch trying to get away from an officious host. . . . Then, yesterday, I remember—I happened into the chapel coming from my walk, and he looked simply like a dead man—he had lost all distinction. It wasn't that he wasn't pre-served or anything like that—but just that he had got gener-alized—he had become a sampling of death."

The candy striper's hands came together. "Oh yes!" she cried. "Yes—exactly—that's how he was!" Still the elevator hadn't come down. The light showed it was on three, and they could hear metal scraping and men drawling instruc-tions on the floor above.

The young candy striper whispered, leaning over the cart toward Harriet, "I even noticed a tear under his eyelashes, Mrs. White."

"Oh for goodness sakes!" the head nurse snapped.

"That happens," Harriet said. "I know what that racket is," she said to Mrs. Siegert. "I bet Arne's stuffing storm win-dows into that elevator—"

They had still to wait, half-listening to the scraping noises upstairs as something was fitted into or out of the elevator.

"You girls hold back with that cart," Mrs. Siegert said, when the elevator came. "Let Mrs. White get in first." But when the tall metal doors had slid open, no one could get in, for the elevator was full of men and a stretcher—Arne, now in his good dress suit, and Mr. Solstad, the mortician, both men standing soldierly beside a stretcher cart. The significant mounds and hollows under the white sheet told the mind *A body is lying there*, but such an observation was only aca-demic. Harriet couldn't seriously believe in a human being under there. "We'll be done with the elevator in a moment," Arne said. The doors closed again. Harriet, Mrs. Siegert, and DeAnn watched the first floor light come on, and they all had to listen to the elevator door springs downstairs, being struck

Carol Bly

open twice. Harriet unwillingly imagined the body on its tray being nudged and guided out.

Harriet and Mrs. Siegert walked down the third-floor new wing. The infirmary rooms ran along the north side, so they were walking along in direct light from the tall windows facing south. In the middle of the corridor, Ardyce, a very, very old person who had been incontinent for over a year, stood urinating on the rubber runner. Feeling the hot liquid course over her great ankles, she had begun to cry. Her bony, caving body gave this shriek like some poor sort of violin.

Mrs. Siegert was not an easily likable nurse, but she had her strong side; swiftly she got to Ardyce and had the limp elbow and said, "Don't cry, honey—I'll take you. We'll get cleaned up OK—don't cry." They wobbled together to the old woman's room.

Two younger nurses were guiding a white-curtained screen out of number 307 on little metal wheels. "Oh . . . it was Mr. Kjerle?" Harriet asked.

One of the nurses bent to wipe up the urine from the corrugated rubber mat, and in a moment all was quiet again. Only mysterious breathing came from some room or another, and a cough like small twigs rubbing from some other room.

Harriet put her head into 307. She had meant to do whatever it is we intend in a place where someone has just died. She meant to give some honor or to wish Mr. Kjerle luck flying off the earth; she meant to help to lift him far off the curvature of the earth by evening. She wasn't clear about it but she felt somehow obligated. She crept into the room, if only to sense his possible presence. In any case, Harriet had expected the room to be empty. Everyone knew Mr. Kjerle's relatives never came to visit—only a retired piano teacher from two miles west of Jacob used to stop in sometimes. The piano teacher's visits weren't much. He really only prowled aimlessly about the infirmary room, not really visiting the old man, at least not keeping up a conversation. Whenever Harriet was up on the infirmary floor, he would waylay her, talk to her eagerly; sometimes, leaning in the doorway of 307, he would tell her it was cruel the way some of the residents never got any visitors.

Harriet was brought up short to see a woman sitting at the bare little desk under the window. She sat so still, and wrote with such concentration, that in the indifferent northern light she looked positively spooky. She wore an elegant knit dress of dark lavender—for a second Harriet felt pleased, as if at a glimpse of the *grand monde*. Harriet received three impressions in rapid order: first, that this elegant figure writing was the spirit of the dead man; second, that it was some beautiful creature of society set here like a statue, just to give pleasure; and third—she smiled with simple happiness at this—that it was the doctor.

Dr. Iversen didn't wear her medical jacket; like the other two doctors in Jacob, she avoided looking like a physician when she went to the Home. If you carried a medical bag, the old people snatched at you, telling of new sets of aches or about old prescriptions that didn't help anymore. Right now she had been called to the Home to "pronounce," that is, to legalize, a death. She had been sitting quietly, therefore, making out the certificate.

"Hullo," she said courteously, as she saw a resident pause in the doorway. Then, with the instant calculation, the mental

Carol Bly

sorting of people that she exercised every day in her job, she added, "Mrs. White. Hullo, Mrs. White."

"How are you?" Harriet said, coming in, shyly. "I'm sorry, I didn't know anyone was in here."

"No, of course not," the doctor said. She had not quite finished, but without showing any haste, she quickly picked up the sheets, placing the printed side that read Minnesota Department of Health, Section of Vital Statistics, inward, against her hip. She rose. "How is that painful foot, anyway?" she asked.

"It isn't very painful," Harriet told her, gratified to be asked. "When it is, I take those gigantic tablets of yours any-way, and can't tell left foot from right!"

"Most of them," the doctor said, "wouldn't admit that a prescription ever did any good. I wouldn't dare ask how their foot is."

"By most of them I gather you mean most *old* people." Harriet laughed. "Don't talk so quickly! I shall be like that someday—and so will you. In fact, it's too bad you're so much younger—we could sit in our rocking chairs and tell each other what ached, and neither one of us would pay the slightest bit of attention to the other one. In fact, maybe you'll be worse. You'll be tired of listening to other people complain."

"No change, I suppose?" the doctor inquired, nodding to-ward the wall between the room they were in, number 307, and the next, 308.

"I haven't been in today—I'm just going now," Harriet said.

"It is hard, isn't it?"

"Yes—and I feel so sorry for him," Harriet added, not having planned to say anything like that.

Room 308, like 307, faced north, the cold light seeming simply to stand outside. There was the same little window desk, whose purpose was simply to be a piece of furniture for a sickroom. There was a high bureau, on which stood favors sent up from the public school children. At Christmas there had been paper reindeer with sleighs made of egg carton sections. Now there was an Easter bunny, stapled to a bit of egg carton, in which one or two of the hard candies that must have filled it remained. Harriet supposed the staff took a candy now and then, just as they gradually were taking the bureau space. In the top drawer were the clothes Einar had worn when they brought him up. But in the other drawers were odds and ends, a few more added right along—a small plastic bag of curlers, some lip moisturizing cream, two magazines read by the candy striper who spoon-fed patients, half a box of tissues. More and more that had nothing to do with Einar seemed to sift into the room; his small influence, like a little scattering of pebbles, was being buried lightly under other influences.

Harriet spent a second by the desk, her eyes on the fields, plowed black, and to the north the semis moving like little blocks on U.S. 75. Then she straightened and went back over to the bed.

"Hello, dear," she said. She pulled the white-painted rocker over and sat down to talk to him. On the good days, he gave a sound, as well as he could, to recognize her; on the other days, no particular sign. Today—nothing, so she settled to talk to

Carol Bly

him. "A little news for you, Einar," she said. "Larry's selling the farm—probably a very good idea," she went on. "And considering the condition of the buildings, he did very well I think. There's no doubt that was the right idea—selling the farm."

She paused. She pulled herself together again. "I gave him the go-ahead on that. . . ." She was trying to remember other things to tell; she remembered in the crook of her elbow, with the palm of her hand, the feeling of Christopher in her arms, but the memory was still too personal. In fact, it was not yet a memory, but still part of herself and therefore couldn't be told. "I gave another speech this morning," she went on cheerfully. "Anyway"—she smiled—"the speech went off all right. About the only other news is I've fairly well planned little Christopher's sweater now, so I'll start the knitting of it soon. Oh yes—and the men said to give you their best. That Helmstetter whose first name I never can remember—and Kermit—they both said to greet you. They were telling me about television. They don't watch *Edge of Night* anymore, they said. They watch something called *Splendor of Our Days*. It sounds dumber than the other one, but I expect if you kept track of it all the time, it would begin to seem real—you'd begin to care what happened to those people. . . . But those television characters don't seem like real people at all—and you know, they never show where the people are—they're always in a room somewhere—you never see a real place that counts, like a farm or anything like it— it's as if none of them had any place to belong to. Did I tell you, Larry sold the farm, Einar? Yes—very good idea, too!" She talked to him some more, and then rose, saying, "I'll be

Gunnar's Sword

back at five again to help you with your dinner, dear," and she went out.

She had spoken truthfully to the doctor in saying her right foot was not painful. When she finally got outside with her hat and scarf and gloves, she swung along well, and drew deep breaths of the cold, burdened air. It definitely was going to snow. She lightly dropped down the hill to the traffic circle, noticing all the cars and the hearse parked in the church lot. She turned west on Eleventh Street and was still moving freshly and gladly when she came to U.S. 75, with the closed Dairy Queen building and Waltham's Flower Shoppe.

When she turned north, on the right-hand shoulder of the highway, the wind struck her forehead. It wasn't bitter, but it was colder than she had hoped for. She turned away from it, long enough to pull her scarf up about her neck better, and now the buildings of the town, even the hasty gimcrackery of the Dairy Queen, looked protective and familiar. Well, I don't have to walk all the way to the farm on the ugliest day of spring, she told herself wryly, but she turned into the wind again, bending her head. Under her feet the dozens of pebbles on the road's shoulder underfoot looked shrunken and abandoned. She tried to set up her walking motion into a kind of automation, the way she and Einar and Larry had done for years and years when they were tired from the farmwork. At first you grew tired, then you grew so tired you felt you might cry, and then, by not feeling any pity for any part of your body, by not weakening those parts, that is, with pity, you actually exacted from them more character; once the ankles, back, shoulders, wrists, learnt to expect no mercy of you, they began to work as if automated. Then you weren't exhausted

Carol Bly

anymore, and you could sift fertilizers, or lift alfalfa, or shovel to an auger for hours and hours, until, with the head-lights glowing like tiny search beams, coming out of the fields as if out of the sky itself, the tractors came home with the men who had been hired—and everyone could quit. Thus the tiredness could be held back until you all leaned over the salmon hot dish, and reached for the bread.

Harriet did the same thing now, looking up only once really—taking in a field of corn that someone hadn't gotten plowed, or even disked down at all. It'd do it good to snow a little, she thought of the scenery critically. So she was de-lighted like a child when the first flakes blew at her, around three-thirty.

It took her another two hours to get to Haglund's Crossroads, and a half hour to the farm from there. This last half hour was the township road running east, however, so the steady snow, that had been hurting her forehead, now struck only her left cheek, and she took her second wind cheerfully. When she reached the corner of her farm, she felt surprised: her old land, not ten feet from her now, across the ditch past the telephone company marker, looked just like all the fields she had been walking past. When she had sat on the porch in the hot evenings, all the dozens of years she and Einar had had the place, she certainly never would have thought those particular sights—Elsie Johnson's barn with the louver-window towers, Vogel's run, the Streges' line of cottonwoods to the south—would lose their distinction. When Larry had taken her out for rides, she always knew the place. Yet now, this late afternoon, she felt no particular recognition.

"Well, but the house will make the difference—when I can see the house," she said. Because the driveway lay another quarter of a mile to the east, she decided to cut across the plowing instead. She paused and then went down into the ditch, some pebbles falling into her boots, and then slowly up, and began working along the headlands of the field. Her forehead was tight and silky now with cold, and the skin gave an unpleasant sensation of not being close to her head. Harriet moved carefully, not just because she was exhausted, but because it was borne in on her that she was a very old woman and she would make a fool of herself if she fainted out here in the middle of nowhere, with night coming on.

The plowing was coarse, and from her height—as she imagined herself an airplane passing over it—it became a chain of harsh, tumbled mountains, with peaks turning floury, but the smooth sides, scoured by the shares, still gleaming black. At last the farmhouse, or at least some dark, square, blessedly man-made shape, stood out one hundred yards ahead. Its lightless windows, broken, and its tumbledown porch seemed friendly and very memorable. It had been a marvelous idea to come—marvelous!

Harriet's fingers, particularly on the right hand, were starting to freeze, but she put them in her coat pocket and went forward quickly. She also planned ahead, using her common sense: she would stay in the house or around it, but not for more than half an hour. She wasn't a fool; it would be difficult to explain why she'd come, but if she left soon and got home, she might even not be missed.

The rough plowing ended; she stepped into the spineless pigeon grass, and emptied her boot. The snow stopped, but

Carol Bly

enough was down so the farmyard, with the L-shaped old house on it, rose a pale, glowing mound. Harriet went happily up.

The front door was half ruined and stood open. She decided that it would be depressing inside the house, so she sat down gratefully on the edge of the porch, feeling sorry for its beautifully milled railing posts wrecked and lying in the snow. She crossed her hands in her lap—a trick she had had all her life—in order to think deliberately, and get things right.

Immediately her mind and body seemed to have opposing wishes. Her mind wanted to go over favorite memories—it wanted to swoon, to graze, to be languid, and to rove over things that are delicious, such as her old loves. Her own mother and father, for example, whom she visualized dancing in their club, or drinking with faces yellow from the firelight at home. The mind wanted to go over how she loved them although she had despised their shallow, rich, greedy life; how much she loved her parents and would like to know what they were thinking now. . . . It wasn't a new line of thought but her mind wanted so very much to go over it again. But her body, or her soul, whichever it was, was thoroughly excited and seemed to be urging, Something very strange is about to happen! It was alerted like an animal—it refused to let her dream along the old intelligent reflections— it wanted to get the scent of something, it seemed to send fingers out beyond the broken porch. Oh—she thought, holding these two parts as well as she could—it is definitely something spiritual, something about to happen! And not from inside me! All these years I assumed it was all inside me—but apparently it isn't!—and I am afraid! In any case, it was in the outer circle of darkness now, rising over the Haglund Road maybe; anyway, it lay outside the farm, and was lifting and falling, coming in closer, without any excitement of its own, simply waiting, not crouching nor threatening—something calm, but mortally large. She needed to invite it, Harriet felt, if it was to come in any closer.

Then a third thing happened: headlights were moving along the snowy road to the south, going east the way Harriet had come, and then going past the place where she had turned up through the field. Now the invisible car presented its red taillights for a moment but then, in the next, the headlights swung left and were quartering on Harriet. So they knew she was gone and had figured she might do just this—walk up here; and they were coming, to save her from the cold and dark. Her hand, particularly the fingers, hurt enough; she nearly leapt forward gratefully.

Wait a moment, she thought, sensibly: there are three different things I can do. I can still run behind the house—it isn't too late—they would call about a little here and there, but they wouldn't think of the old chickenhouse we had used for lawn mowers. Then, whatever that part of her was that wanted to invite the huge mortal thing outside, would have a little more time to do it in. But no, Harriet thought, as intelligently as she could, they would see her foorsteps in the snow and she would be tracked like an animal, and she would never recover her pride—not ever, after that. Now the headlights were fully turned in her direction, and as soon as the car tipped up to make the rise, the lights would flood over her, as the lights of all their visitors always had, blinding anyone

Carol Bly

on the porch. It was going to be unpleasant, whatever happened. She tried very hard to think of some little speech to give that would not let them find her old and out of her wits—something to pass it off lightly—but how? For she didn't feel she had any light touch at the moment at all: more and more, her soul was being engaged by the gigantic, mortal thing waiting in its wide arc outside. One minute it seemed to offer to go away, and leave her with her ordinary life in her hands again. This she couldn't bear, not now that she'd once seen it; she had a taste for it now. The next minute, however, she found she was still unready, too frightened by far, and she would agree to marry any sort of dullness rather than to join whatever that was. She couldn't toss off anything with a laugh now. If she herself were so deadly serious, how could she hope to make whoever was driving up in this car take the whole thing lightly?

Now the headlights were brilliant on her, so she had to look down at the wrecked railing and posts, which lay like a ladder thrown down in the snow. The headlights came no closer: the car must have stopped, and she heard the incredible confidence of an American automobile engine idling in neutral. Doors clicked open and shut—men were tramping in the darkness behind the headlights—someone in a low tone could be heard saying, "It's her all right!" Another voice—"You all wait. I'll go up!" Then a gigantic black profile of someone came at her, shielding her from the beams.

"Hi, Mama," the man said.

In a flash Harriet was angry at this grown Larry—a shallow thing he seemed, no matter that he was her son, no matter he was being dear and dignified and not talking at her, helping her step over the smashed banister in the snow. But she thought, How different he is from the baby he was, with the dark, blurry eyes so close to her face, for now he was only a grown son—predictable, and wrapped around with his health and sense.

Other people sat in the car. As Harriet got into the front seat, she saw all their faces in the light from the car's ceiling—Arne, it was; Larry; Siegert, the head nurse; some other nurse she had seen but didn't know—and she felt comforted, partly, by this lighted little circle. Outside the car, in a much wider circle, the mortal presence still wafted lightly. Harriet felt very definitely that it was offering to lap forward toward her again. She felt she could rally it and offer to go out with it, like something bobbing on lumpy, stale seawater in the darkness; she felt it wouldn't take her quickly. It would lap forward and receive her, but for awhile it would let her look back to the tiny car, with the tiny circle of human beings. But they were all she knew, so she fled into the front seat, and let herself be walled up with Arne's shoulder on one side, moving as he went into reverse, and Larry's great shoulder on the other side. And from the backseat came low, special voices—the nurses talking to each other professionally. Harriet hoped she had not lost individuality from their point of view: now she was a woman who wandered off from the Home and had to be brought back at a good deal of inconvenience, and on such a busy day. She must be very careful to be light and sociable. "So good of you all," she murmured. "It was very cold."

She was very grateful for losing the sensation of God being close—or perhaps she had made up in her mind the

Carol Bly

whole impression of something in the darkness. In any case it didn't matter. She hadn't the slightest curiosity to think it over, for something much worse occupied her. Squeezed between these kind men, with the car heater blowing hot breath into her face, and with her eyes—full of dancing needles and blue tiny fires—on the dashboard, she was sharply aware that she wasn't safe with these protectors. Her hand was in great pain now, from the freezing: but suppose all of her were in pain, and suppose death did come, and not some death she chose to conjure up and call upon, but plainly Death himself, the real one—she would flash down like silk between these men, past the glittering dashboard, without leaving the slightest impression, the way pebbles in the road were blown off by the speeding car. I'm simply not going to be able to do anything about it, she thought with surprise.

They were driving rapidly down the Haglund Road—she felt the millions of pebbles of gravel that had always lain there, unwrapped, which no one pays any attention to, all the millions of things that lie about unbound to the millions of other things. With a tremendous burst of humility and joy Harriet thought: What a tremendous lot I have failed to think through! Yet I always thought I thought through things so well!

From a mile and a half north, the Jacob Lutheran Home suddenly stood up, with its three stories of lighted windows. It was difficult to visualize the shuffling heels moving about near bureaus, or to believe in the cartful of magazines parked idle for the night in the coffee room. The Home looked at least like a mighty office complex where far-reaching decisions are made that affect common people without their even knowing it. It was difficult to believe in Einar up there, lying lightly gowned in white, scarcely touching, like a bit of string, as he had lain for fourteen months. Harriet thought, And I shall lie up there, too, and from month to month, because I will no doubt get less amusing and I will get more frightened, there will be fewer and fewer visitors, and even this huge man next to me, Larry, my son, will come much less often, and perhaps my death will rock forward and backward on its heels waiting a long time, and I shall be so diminished by the time it comes even the staff won't feel anything personal. There will be none of the old recognition . . .

They were approaching the confident little town. Harriet was very surprised to find that she hadn't spent eighty-two years in love with all there is, with tiny things like pebbles, which were in some strange way her equal; pebbles were her equal; she was astounded she had missed it! Now she needed every possible second, even if it were to be spent in a daze. How could she ever have said, "It is cruel that so-and-so's life drags on like this!" or, "It is a blessing that death came to so-and-so!" Or, "I certainly hope I shall go quickly when I go"— as if it were a question of being fastidious.

The heat of the car did not help her frozen hand. The pain was frightful—but her thoughts seemed so much more frightful to her that she deliberately gave in to the pain. From the backseat came kind voices: "Soon there, Harriet!" and "You're not the only one to go out walking, you know," and "We all do it, Harriet . . ." And in he front seat, her son's shoulder jerked a little next to hers and he stared ahead, silently, through the windshield.

Carol Bly

When they were up in room 211, the doctor examined her fingers carefully. "We'll have you knitting again—it won't be long," she said. "She can have something to help her sleep," she said pointedly to the head nurse, who paused in the doorway.

Larry sat on Mrs. Ole Morstad's bed, with his knees spread, his hat thrown up on the pillow. He was turning over Harriet's alarm clock, and he looked very tense and bored. Harriet, too, felt very strained and bored.

"If you would *please* reconsider, Mama," Larry was saying—still asking her to go live with him. A second ago her heart had leapt—but only for a second. She would love to leave this fate! She would love to go to him! Again she imagined his house, the flowery rug with its wide edge of sky blue that looked like a cool, ancient summer all the time, and the marvelous tone of the Vivaldi on his record machine; Janice would come on weekends, perhaps, and bring the baby, and Harriet would rock with the baby, and look at all the woolen yellow flowers in the rug.

Larry was making the offer, but she heard a new apprehension in his voice. I am a very old woman apparently, she told herself, and I've wandered off in a snowstorm, but I'm not going to add this to my other sins. As she turned him down, she smiled quite genuinely, because the pill she'd been given was taking effect—her hand no longer hurt—and everything looked peaceful and colorless.

From time to time, the upper echelon of the staff and residents looked in and greeted her—Marge Larson, the therapist, even stopped a moment, Kermit Steensen nodded from the hall—the candy stripers had long since gone home or she knew Mary would have greeted her.

Gunnar's Sword

Tomorrow morning, word would have got around the whole community, and the simpler, the very aged, or the less acquainted people would take to hobbling by room number 211. They would want to have a look at someone who had stirred the community by getting a notion to go back home. From their flagged, lifeless expressions it would be hard to understand that actually their hearts were rather aflutter with this Harriet White's doings—the way the hearts of young women feel roused, and unstable, and prescient, when the first of their friends is going to marry.

Carol Bly

The Last of the Gold Star Mothers

On a windless early evening in October, almost the best time of day of the best time of year in Minnesota, no one was standing on the escarpment path in Rachel River County Park, where you can look out over the fir forests toward Lake Superior and the distant glow of lights of West Duluth. The park was deserted, in fact—no one was leaning on the old WPA-built wall to watch the Rachel River falling perfectly from one black stone to the next, eventually to find its way down the escarpment to the place where it joins the St. Louis River. People in Rachel River keep busy, and sometimes they seem too distracted to see things. No one, for instance, had noticed a battered safe, which sat in the bed of the stream in the park. It had been stolen from a Union 76 gas station a month earlier, in a celebrated local crime. The thief had been found out and caught, but the safe, torch-cut open and dumped right in the middle of Rachel River, still lay among the rocks, and the slight, spindly water fell on it without variance.

On this particular evening, a Tuesday, most of the regular

people—that is, not the Duluth airbase personnel and their wives, who don't count, but the *regulars*—were down at the Rachel River VFW Lounge. Drinks, for once, were at half price, in honor of Mr. and Mrs. Kevin Ohlaug's son, Curt. Everyone explained to everyone else that Curt Ohlaug had been in the service in some native place called Engola or Angola, no one knew in what branch of the service, but, anyway, now he was back, and drinks were at half price. The local radio-news lady, a thirty-three-year-old divorcée named Mary Graving, sat in the best corner booth of the VFW Lounge. She was celebrating something secretly. From the beginning, she had intended to spend the whole evening there, so she had had the foresight to prop herself up in the right angle between the back of the booth and the wall. By her elbow, someone had scratched on the wall a suggestion to the IRS about what it could do with itself. Mary had arranged a smile on her face quite a while ago; now it was safely fixed there, and she herself was safely fixed, and although she was immensely drunk, she was not so drunk as the others, which meant she counted as dead sober.

When Mary Graving was sober, her face was too decided and twitchy to look good with the large plain earrings she always wore. She thought she was generally too grim looking, and her earrings looked too cheerful at the edges of her face. Now that she was drunk, though, and wearing a red dress, her face felt hot and rosy. Her smile stayed stuck on, and she knew that the earrings—a new pair, especially cheap, not from Bagley's in Duluth but a product of the Ben Franklin Store in Rachel River—looked fine. She was not beautiful but she was all right.

Carol Bly

She was crowded into the booth with seven local people whose familiar faces were getting blurred. One was LeRoy Beske, the sheriff. Each person had a hand around his glass, and their fingers looked silvery in the nightclub lighting. The fingers were numb and stiff with drink, as silvery and thick as fingers on the empty suits of armor in city museums. No one is shallow and vulgar forever; sooner or later the whole species likes to be profound. Now, after everyone had pleased everyone else by adding comments to the IRS graffito, a moment came when LeRoy Beske was profound. The others could take it from him, the sheriff explained, that all of culture—all of American culture, and that went for the Europeans, too, who weren't any better—was getting more and more slovenly and cowardly and uniquely filthy. The sheriff repeated the last phrase clearly, as sonorous as John Donne. "Yes," he said, "uniquely filthy." In 1946 he had stood on the Boulevard Saint-Germain with his buddies, and he could assure them the French, too, like everyone else, even the French with their fancy Paris, were uniquely filthy. Everyone in the booth marvelled at every remark. A hundred philosophies brimmed wonderfully in their heads.

That was Tuesday night. At nine-thirty the next morning, Wednesday, the dispatcher's room in the Rachel River jail was softened by sunlight that slanted through the barred horizontal windows. Kristi Marie, who covered the radio, was filling out court forms at her desk under the two radio speakers; a deputy named DeWayne Sorkelson sat at another desk, idly making throws onto the blotter from a dice cup. The sheriff himself leaned by one of the windows, watching for the other deputy, Merle Schaefer, to come in. Everything was as usual, but the team was a little nervous this morning, because Kristi Marie and DeWayne knew that LeRoy Beske was going to put the scare into Merle whenever he showed up. Now and then, while they waited, a message came crackling in on the radio; Kristi Marie replied, and a voice would say "Ten-four," and the radio went off again.

Kristi Marie was on the two-way for the forenoon, but she had told them plainly that someone else would have to cover in the afternoon, because she and five other girls were going in a car to Duluth, to an art gallery. A member of their study club had suggested that with the world getting the way it was in so many places, it was a shame to throw away the cultural opportunities they had, what with Rachel River being only eleven miles away from Duluth, so Kristi Marie was going.

Now the sheriff straightened up. Merle had appeared outside the jail, where he paused on the concrete steps and gave a languid smile to a little boy named Gregsy Hanson, whose face shone up at him. Poor kid, the sheriff thought. Gregsy Hanson's dad sold him out for the bottle, and his mother sold out everybody in town. When she went down the aisles in the Super Valu she even sold out her baby as he sat in the cart, explaining his faults to everyone in the produce section. And now, the sheriff thought, even this cop that Gregsy admired wasn't much good. Merle came in the jailhouse door, and Gregsy stood one-legged on the concrete, with his other knee thrown over the seat of his bike, as he watched him go. The *Duluth Herald* bag lay, caved in, in his bike basket.

"Turn on the radio to KTRW, so we get the Rachel River program when it comes on," the sheriff said to Kristi Marie. "Turn it low until she comes on, though."

Carol Bly

Merle came in, raising a hand to his glossy thick hair. He was having an affair with a woman named Verona McIvor, in Floodwood, and whenever he looked in the mirror of his cop car he saw a man involved with a woman, and with women generally—a gigantic man hopelessly wrapped in physical satisfactions, his own desires, women's desires for him. When he walked, there was a lunge about his walking, as if he carried several women on his shoulders, clinging; they clung all about him, and his walk supported the great weight of them.

"All right, Merle," the sheriff said.

He's going to bust me for seeing Verona, Merle thought, instantly noticing that no one in the room would look at him. I don't want no counterculture job selling auto parts to farmers, he thought. I want this job. I want the uniform. His quick glance out the window showed him that that little kid, Gregsy Hanson, was still standing there waiting to look at him, Merle.

"OK, Merle," the sheriff said. "We live in one lousy, slovenly time of United States history, but there is one lousy, slovenly thing that's not going to happen again in Rachel River County. OK? OK. Labor Day you were in charge of the Gold Star Mothers' car in the parade, right? OK, the parade forms in front of the Vision Avenue Apartments, where you pick up the Gold Star Mother, the only one we got left, and then everyone marches and drives to the cemetery where they have the doings. I got two complaints on you. First, you stuffed our one remaining Gold Star Mother into the car so mean she got bruised. She brought a charge. But that isn't all. Then you got to the cemetery, and I suppose I ought to be grateful you didn't run down them Rachel River Saddle Club horses on the way. When you got to the cemetery, what'd you do but get out and turn off the ignition, which means the air-conditioning went off. You left the windows rolled up and you left the Gold Star Mother in there. Mrs. Lorraine Graving is not a young woman; it was a hundred and five Fahrenheit. She could have died in there. I would like you to know that she is a symbol of our whole national honor. Without her we wouldn't be the kind of country we are today. Now, if we're not going to have any respect anymore, it'll be the end of the Gold Star Mother program completely."

Merle was so relieved it was not about this woman that he was seeing in Floodwood that he had to work to keep from smiling. He would not lose his job over stuffing a Gold Star Mother into a Ford.

He said, "Yes, sir," in a tone he had heard on a police program on TV.

"And there's another thing," the sheriff said. "You regard yourself as this big hand with the ladies."

"No, sir," Merle said with great dignity.

"Well, since you're such a great man with the ladies," the sheriff went on, "I've got something you can do today. You know her—it's Mrs. Blatke, that widow of that guy committed suicide. Well, I want you to find her, and then you make it clear to her she doesn't call the police anymore. I know she's upset. I know her husband robbed the Union 76 station and we caught him, and I know he killed himself. I took that refresher course on police psychology and I know she blames herself or something, but that don't mean she can go around town getting in fights with everyone all over Rachel River

Carol Bly

and then call the police. OK? And I don't want you to tell her mean. Tell her nice but firm. And don't make a pass at her."

"You got to be kidding!" Merle shouted. "Make a pass at Mrs. Blatke? Listen, nobody would serve as a pallbearer at her husband's funeral, and who volunteers but me, and I got the five others, too!"

"Yes," the sheriff said. "And then later that night you called her up and word is you made a pass at her."

Kristi Marie waved one hand at them and turned up the volume on the speakers. "And now," the radio announcer's voice said, "we go to Mary Graving, in Rachel River, for the Rachel River County news. Good morning, Mary!"

"Good morning, Bert!" said Mary. Her voice sounded a little husky, because it was carried by telephone from her house at the south end of Rachel River to the Duluth studio and then the eleven miles back again by radio.

"Today is the Feast of St. Maurus," Mary said. She did not sound very hung over.

"Gee, she's got a nice voice," the sheriff said. "I'm glad she took that job, since she had to get a job. Is it true she's got nerves?"

"I don't know," Kristi Marie said. "I heard that, too. But she always seems real cheerful." Kristi Marie tipped her plump face up toward the loudspeaker over her desk. "She never forgets anything, either," she added. "She had it on five times to remind people to bring potluck to the St. John's annual meeting, and that's not even her church, she didn't need to have." They all listened to the radio over the quiet whine of the jail fan. The sheriff and the other officer had begun casting the dice to see who paid afternoon coffee.

"Although today is actually the Feast of St. Maurus, we haven't got any reliable information about his life, and for a very special reason I'd like to tell you, instead, about St. Alban," the radio said.

"But she shouldn't have religion on the radio," Kristi Marie said. "Last time they had religion on, we got seven phone calls from Lutherans saying they didn't want that Catholic crap on the radio, and nine calls from Catholics saying they wanted equal time if they were going to have that kind of Lutheran crap on."

"Speaking of religion," the sheriff said. "Do you remember when that occult group cut up all those cattle, over toward Perham?"

"I remember that," Kristi Marie said.

"It is too bad that St. Alban isn't better known," Mary was saying over the radio, "because we have a man in Rachel River with a birthday today, who is here, alive, able to celebrate that birthday, just because of people in France who did what St. Alban did long before that. St. Alban was the first martyr in the British Isles. During some persecutions, Roman soldiers were going around picking up Christians to torture them, and a legionnaire came to Alban's door and said, 'We are looking for a certain escaped Christian.' Well, this Christian was hiding in Alban's attic, and Alban had traded clothes with him. 'Yes, I know,' Alban said. 'I am the one you are looking for.' 'You don't look like him,' the soldier said. Alban said, 'Look at my clothes—look at me. I am the one you want.' The Roman soldier was stubborn, however, and said, 'Somehow, you don't look like the right man.' But then he thought, I've got to bring in somebody, and it is getting

Carol Bly

late, so finally he said, 'All right, all right'—whatever the Latin or Celtic for 'All right, all right' is—and he took in Alban, and they killed him.

"During World War II," Mary's radio voice went on, "underground forces in occupied Europe faced the same sort of thing Alban faced. It must have been terrifying to have someone knock at night and explain he was an American flier or an underground intelligence agent, and could you hide him? You always knew that if the Germans caught you, you would be tortured for information and then likely killed. Well, Mahlon Hanson, of Rachel River, who gets our radio birthday greetings today, is alive because somebody was brave enough to risk self and family to hide him, thirty-four years ago, and help him reach the Channel. And, speaking of help, what better help could you expect than to have your next winter's furnace costs cut in half—that's right, cut right in half. You couldn't do better than to plan now, because if fall is here, winter can't be far behind, and Merv Skjolestad is carrying a line of wood-burning stoves that can make hundreds of dollars of savings for *you*."

When the program was over, Mary replaced the telephone receiver in its cradle, turned off the power box, and unplugged the cassette player she used for taping town council notices. The Duluth station had set up this radio-telephone hookup for her in her own basement. To Mary, the program meant a tiny, unfailing income, with the marvelous virtue that she could be home when her children, Will and Molly, got home from school every day. The other end of the basement was reserved for her toy-making business. Between the radio program and the toy making, Mary spent many hours every day in the cool, brightly lighted basement. The old cellar shelves were soft and grainy with rot; the previous renter, an AFDC mother, had left loops of rusty Kerr-top canning rings there, but Mary had scrubbed off the space she needed, and spread out the tools of her trade there—a dish of chuck keys, a small sabre saw, two sizes of nail sets, all her lacquers, a mitre box, her power saws and sander. The place reminded one that generations of women had stored home canning there and had filled and emptied laundry tubs into the sump hole; there was an aura of domestic bravery and domestic squalor about the place still. But now the basement had some glint and bustle, too, which came from Mary's shiny, imposingly modern radio equipment on the desk, her squared-off drawings on the steel table, and the bright orange electrical drop cords curling everywhere. In the middle of the room, and in the space where a washing machine had recently been before the men had come and repossessed it, there stood several half-finished castles and Norman keeps and three-storeyed dollhouses, all smelling beautifully of AC ply.

On school-day afternoons, the children would burst into the house above her; the old farmhouse shuddered when they struck the door with their knuckles and books. Mary would climb the basement stairs dazedly, and in the shabby living room she and Will and Molly would drink cocoa, sitting in front of a print of two sailing ships over the mantel. The ships were heavily square-rigged. They tore along in the lunging, green, tremendously deep Atlantic. The children loved to say, "Just think what would happen if a man fell overboard into the sea!" And Mary usually assured them solemnly, "It must

Carol Bly

have been nearly impossible, in those days, to put her about to pick up anyone." Sometimes Mary explained as much about the rigging as she understood. They all drank their cocoa and speculated silently about a man overboard treading water in the deep sea and watching his ship grow smaller as it sailed away and left him. Then, on most days, the children went outdoors to play, and Mary went into the kitchen. Little by little, the hours of silent work in the basement would sift from her mind, until soon her supper making seemed perfectly practical, perfectly pleasant, in the way that hobbies are pleasant when you get your mind off your life work. If they were having pastry for dinner, she gave it her attention and got it right.

But just now, in October, Will and Molly were spending a week at Pike Lake with their father, Cordell. As Mary worked on a bookcase she was building as a surprise for them, she kept track of the quarter hours as she waited for the time, arranged with Cordell, when she would telephone and talk to them. The calling hour was agreed on for midday on Wednesday, since school would be closed then for a teachers' in-service. Across from where Mary sat stood the old, red-painted steel table, on which she kept her drawings of toys and her general accounts. In her childhood, in Duluth, there had been metal furniture in two places in her house — in the maids' room in the basement and out on the shaded, north-facing terrace. Every spring, the terrace furniture was repainted by the hired man and then set out on the stone flagging. All summer, it never seemed to lose its chill. Mary had been expected to take part in her mother's teas out there, when she had to listen to her mother's friends and their little quarrels about books. They sat on the painted metal in their silk dresses, and responded to one another in flurries. "Oh, but Julia," they cried, "can you really say that with impunity?" Mary sometimes found herself staring down, past the terrace ferns, into the window of the maids' room in the basement. She could see the two iron beds there. Her own basement, Mary sometimes felt now, was not unlike the maids' room.

Sitting by the unfinished bookcase, Mary fitted new paper into her sander. At the same time, she was estimating her income for the current year. The bookcase was to have a lever on one side, which opened a secret vertical shaft that would run from the top to the bottom of the case, at its back. On the opposite side, the left, there would be a fishing reel fastened to the case, which was to operate a miniature dumbwaiter inside the secret shaft. She meant to make a tiny velvet-covered chest to fit in the dumbwaiter, in which the children could keep their treasures—whatever they liked. She was not building this bookcase to be sold, and for this reason her face was mobile, nervous, and sometimes smiling as she worked. Her facial tic was not so bad as it was sometimes. The other toys standing about—the apartment-building dollhouses, the sixteenth-century half-timbered dollhouses, the castles, and the puppet show—were all parts of her business. They sold at prices from sixty-five dollars to four hundred dollars each.

Before she became self-supporting, she had never imagined that one tends to do major economic calculations over and over again in one's head, as if the figures might improve with repetition. She knew that her total intake this past year would be $11,300, but she kept refiguring it. Now she added

Carol Bly

things up again while she carefully drilled a hole for the fishing-reel cable to run through. The twenty-minute radio program, five days a week, brought her five hundred dollars a month, which was six thousand dollars a year. If she got orders for four large castles at $350 each, that would be fourteen hundred dollars, which made a total so far of seventy-four hundred. Ten medium-sized castles would bring in fifteen hundred dollars more, making a total of $8,900. In the first year after he had left her, Cordell sent her eleven out of the twelve agreed-upon monthly child support payments; in the second year, he sent ten. Now she figured he would send an average of, say, eight payments per year for another year or so. At $150 per child, that brought the total to $11,300. It was not really enough.

She worked at the children's bookcase for an hour, getting used to the pleasure and irritations of the task. She liked to work fast, watching her hands touching things gently. She disliked her habit of sometimes carrying pencil or nails in her mouth. Presently, she went over to the radio table and telephoned a farm-equipment dealer named Merv Skjolestad to suggest that she write him an ad for his Patz manure movers, which she could alternate with the ads she now read over the radio for his Schweiss wood-burning furnace. She could alternate the ads—Monday-Wednesday-Friday and Tuesday-Thursday. Merv told her that wasn't all he had. He had a whole new line of grain-storage bins and some brand new milk-house equipment. She took down the sizes and prices, and told him she could do the furnaces on Mondays, the grain and milk-house line Tuesdays, and the Patz equipment and furnaces by turn on Wednesdays, Thursdays, and Fridays.

She eased him off the telephone in time to call the children at the prearranged time.

She listened to the telephone ring twenty times. Then she decided she might have misdialled, so she called again and let it ring ten more times. After a while, she went upstairs to wash her face, which looked awful. She was a person whose eyes puffed up quickly.

She gathered her sheets and clothes from a basket and drove to the other end of town, to the laundromat. She was very sorry to find a woman she knew named Mrs. Blatke in the laundromat, sorting through a pile of unclaimed clothing. "Why, hello," said Mrs. Blatke, in a false tone. Mrs. Blatke's voice was not perfectly respectful, because although her husband had been caught knocking over the Union 76 station and then had felt so bad that he couldn't support her and their kids that he had committed suicide, at least he had been a faithful husband to her, and this Mrs. Mary Graving might be a big shot, with a big-shot job running the radio program from Rachel River and selling fancy toys to big shots in Duluth, but the fact was Mrs. Blatke's husband had died and Mrs. Graving's husband had just up and left her. Mrs. Blatke, therefore, did not move over enough to let Mary Graving get her laundry bag between the folding table and the line of machines. Mary, on her side, knew that Mrs. Blatke stole people's dryer loads if they were not watching, so she did not say "Excuse me" when the laundry bag hit Mrs. Blatke's leg, with the sharp edge of the Cheer box inside the bag doing the hitting. Then Mary thought of something she must have forgotten in her car, and she went back out and came back in and squeezed by Mrs. Blatke again and hit her legs all over again.

Carol Bly

"Funny a lady like you having to use the laundromat," Mrs. Blatke said after a while. "I've heard if you miss one payment on a washing machine, they will repossess it, these days. But I wouldn't know. I was never one to buy stuff I couldn't afford and then have to have it repossessed."

Mary looked thoughtfully out the window. "I doubt if that cop is coming to look for me," she said aloud. "I never have had cops coming after me in a laundromat. Maybe he's got something to say just to you? I could step outside."

Mrs. Blatke jerked around and peered out the steamed window. "That's a no-good cop," she said warmly.

"He isn't much," Mary said.

They gave each other a quick look and then Mrs. Blatke said, actually in a kindly tone, "He did volunteer to be a pallbearer at my poor hubby's funeral, though, and no one else would, because . . . because."

"I know," Mary said. "And I'm sorry about your husband, too."

Outside, in the autumn sunshine, the policeman leaned against his car, idly smoothing his glossy black hair.

Mary didn't wait to dry her clothes, but took them wet from the machine and got into her car and drove away from the laundromat. In the rearview mirror, she saw the policeman—whose name she now remembered: Merle—amble into the building.

She had an appointment with a man named Fran Paddock for three o'clock at Ye Olde 61—a kind of roadhouse dinner club, which he and a partner, who did some sort of cooking for the place, had recently bought. Now they were going to keep it open in the afternoons, too, in order to sell quality tourist items. The club stood halfway between Pike Lake and Rachel River, on a bypassed highway that supported a sprinkling of businesses that had been thrown up in the last few years where there had once been endless jack-pine forest. There were still patches of forest here and there, but as one drove along one saw the high domes of oil storage tanks among the trees, and sometimes whole vistas of new, barrack-like housing opened out. There was a turmoil about the landscape, as if it might all turn into a single giant shopping center by morning.

Mary walked into the orange, varnished-log building. In the dining room there was one table, over by the window, that didn't have chairs placed on top of it. A youngish man with sandy hair came out of the kitchen, opening his palms in an apologetic gesture.

"I'm Fran's partner," he said. "I can't shake hands, I'm baking—but at least I set up someplace for you two to sit."

They both looked out the window next to the table. "I'm feeding bears out there," he said. "This time of year, sometimes three or four come lumbering up."

"Bears-shmears!" a cheerful voice said behind them.

It was Fran. Long ago, he and Mary had gone to school together in Duluth. Looking at him now, in the shadowy restaurant, Mary could see that he had changed less than she had in the past fifteen years. He still had the undeniably comely looks and extroverted expression that had never caught her interest when she was a girl. The basis of their friendship was not their few dances together at the Northland Country Club in the summers but their nerveless and violently

Carol Bly

competitive dinghy racing at the Duluth Yacht Club, on Lake Superior. They had both won a lot of races, and Fran had probably beaten her a few more times than she had beaten him; the Coast Guard had had to bring them in out of trouble more times than all the other Duluth sailors put together.

"I see you've introduced yourselves," Fran said now with his old grace. "Mary's an old friend—and a great sailor too."

He sat down; Mary sat down. Fran's partner hovered for a moment, and he and Mary exchanged a glance. They hadn't introduced themselves at all, and now Fran was still talking about sailing in the old days. Mary understood that he was probably being extra gregarious in order to assure her that even if they were meeting on business he did not discount his old association with her. He was trying to lessen the tension of one person being there to sell the other one something— telling her that he knew she was not trading in on old ac- quaintance for commercial use—or that if she was, he was not offended.

"I still say there's nowhere you get that sense of reality that you do sailing," he said. "Hiked way out over the side—close to the water like that—you're touching down on reality. . . . But why should I tell that to you, of all people?"

"I haven't sailed in years now," Mary said with a smile.

She noticed that Fran immediately looked away when she said this, the way rich people sometimes do when they are afraid that a friend is about to explain that he or she has had to retrench.

Fran's partner wandered back into his kitchen, and Mary and Fran began to talk business. From time to time, as they discussed orders and discounts, she heard the baker slapping dough in the kitchen.

"There won't be any plastics," Fran said. "Strictly good things. What we're dealing with here is the guilty father. The children have been with him all weekend, say, and now it's Sunday afternoon, late, and they've been cross and that made him cross and he got sharp with them, but he doesn't want to deliver them back to their mother with them remembering that, so he stops in at Ye Olde 61, and buys them these very good toys. It'll work, Mary. When the kids get home, the mother turns over the toys, looking at the labels, checking to see if they're just strictly airport, but Ye Olde 61 toys won't be airport—so Dad will end up way ahead. OK! Let's see what you have, Mary. One of my real resources, is what you are."

She showed him drawings and descriptions and Polaroid pictures of her work. She saw he could tell that the things she had made were really first class—especially the French townhouse, with its blue-green mansard roof and the tiny sign painted on the smudgy cream outside wall: DÉFENSE D'AFFICHER PAR LA LOI DE 1881.

Fran laughed. "We need a tiny wooden toy dog out there peeing on that lamppost," he said. "It would be a great selling point. The French are great on peeing."

The moment Fran said this, Mary knew he was going to cheat her clean. In the next few minutes, he did make an unfair consignment offer for her major toys, and said he would not handle the small ones. "What you really need are stuffed animals made with art fabrics," he said. "Or, you know—that quilted sculpture. Can you come up with a line of that?"

"Kids hate those art toys," Mary said.

"Yes, but they're very counterculture looking, and that's in," Fran said.

He glanced out the window. "Hey, one of your bears has come in!" he shouted toward the kitchen.

The baker hurried in and bent over their table to look out the window. His arms, sanded all over with whole wheat flour, were very near Mary's face. Mary and Fran and the baker watched a huge bear moving things around outside, lifting garbage, studying it.

"They're like dancers, compared to how dogs move," offered the baker.

After a while, Mary got up. "I'll get back to you on the consignments," she said to Fran.

"Remember, Mary," he said. "This is big. The guilty fathers, the classy toys, the grimy, whining kids *wanting* something. And don't forget to glue a dog onto the French apartment-building one. And how about a trademark, like *La Vraie Chose*. That could be your mark, Mary—*La Vraie Chose* on all your toys. It's a terrific idea!"

She smiled. He wasn't mistaken. It was a sound idea; his shop was a sound idea. As she drove home, she felt so low spirited that she forgot she was secretly celebrating, last night and today, and was not going to be sad.

Back in Rachel River, she had one more appointment. She drove to the Vision Avenue Senior Citizen Apartments, where Mr. Dahle, the manager, said it was nice of her to come on time because it made him just so nervous when people weren't punctual. He expected punctuality of himself, he said; he expected it of others. "The problem is Lorraine, your mother-in-law," he said. "Or should I still call her your mother-in-law?"

"I guess she still is my mother-in-law," Mary told him.

"It's been five months since the rent was paid," Mr. Dahle said, holding his palms upwards. "Now, I have discussed with Mrs. Graving—Lorraine—would she go on welfare. That is a practical move, you know, and there is no disgrace to it. She told me her son Cordell would pay the rent. I said, 'Well, he hasn't paid it for five months now.' Then she said I was lying and trying to cheat an old woman out of the rent, and she would call Cordell and he would drive over from Pike Lake and show me a thing or two. So I said, 'Well, you might as well call him, because if he comes in I can ask him in person will he pay the rent or not.' Then she grabs her Gold Star flag off the window and shakes it at me and says, 'You see this Gold Star? If you treat me wrong there's a lot of people who are going to remember what this stands for, and they won't like it.' I told her I am not treating her wrong, I am trying to get the rent paid is all."

"I'll go up," Mary said.

Her mother-in-law, Lorraine Graving, was crouched by the window, lifting the Gold Star flag up so she could see out. She was stooped but full of spring. "Ooh, did you see that!" the old lady said. "My, but there's a fight going on down there! Look at that—that grown woman grabbed that boy's bike and threw it right down on the sidewalk! Crazy! And she's left her car parked right out in the middle of the street!"

She turned and looked at Mary. "*Ja*, I know why you're here," she said. "Now, you listen to me. I'm not letting that Dahle push me around, and I'm not going to let *you* push me

around. You never gave Cordell the least bit of love and support. I always helped him and he always said, 'Mama, I'm
going to take care of you when you're old.' Well, now I'm old
and he is taking care of me. He was always an affectionate
boy, Cordell was. I can't say the same for his brother Emmitt.
Emmitt's the boy I lost. I don't suppose you ever met Emmitt.
During the war, you know how people went around showing
you all the letters they got from their sons, with those APO
numbers, and *reading* you the letters, too? Well, we never got
any from Emmitt—not a one. He seemed to be just as glad to
be away from home. We was running forty head of cattle in
those days, and they never took both boys off a farm. One
would get drafted, one could stay home. So I said to Emmitt
right out, 'Emmitt, you better be the one to go, you're always
so restless anyway, driving around fast cars and all.' I told
him a good joke that I thought would make him have a sense
of humor about it. I told him, 'Join the Navy and See the
World!'"

Mrs. Graving paused to let Mary laugh, but Mary was
hung over and had laughed at jokes all night at the VFW
Lounge, and a childhood friend had tried to skin her in business, so she decided she didn't have to get up a laugh.

"Anyway," her mother-in-law went on, "he may not have
had much sense of humor about going into the Navy, but he
really enjoyed it once he got in. He must have, because he
never wrote any homesick letters. He didn't ever write at all.
Home never meant anything to him, like it did to Cordell.
Cordell always had more plans, anyway. Dad and I helped
him. We helped him buy all that lake frontage and that resort
in Wisconsin that you were so set on having."

"I never heard of any Wisconsin resort," Mary said.

"I'm tired of people lying to me," Mrs. Graving said. "First that manager, Dahle, and now you. We paid all your doctor bills, too. All them bills, and there was never anything the matter with you that I could see."

"I never had any doctoring bills," Mary said. "I never went to a doctor, except for when the children came. You're probably thinking of Cordell's ulcer treatment."

"I gave my son," Mrs. Graving said conclusively.

Outside the glass doors of the Vision Avenue Apartments, Mrs. Blatke and Gregsy Hanson, who had once been a Faith Lutheran Church release time student of Mary's, were shouting at each other on the sidewalk. Mr. Dahle stood by, wringing his hands. An interested circle of elderly residents had gathered. They murmured "Ooh!" and "Goodness!" from time to time.

"Oh, hi, Mrs. Graving," Gregsy said, breaking off.

"Oh, so it's 'hi, Mrs. Graving,' is it?" Mrs. Blatke screeched. "But when I want to park my car in the parking place, he won't move his damned bike. Well, I'm asking you, 'Mrs. Graving,' since he seems to like you so much, who is that boy? I'm calling the police."

"Yeah, and I won't tell you," Mary heard herself saying.

"You going to take up for some kid who busted one of my headlights, are you? You going to take up for some kid against me?"

Mary said to herself, I might as well get into a fight as not. I really might as well.

"He's a friend of mine," she said aloud. Then she said,

Carol Bly

"You owe him an apology, too." She watched the woman's wrath with satisfaction.

"Apology? *Apology?* Me apologize to that crummy kid?"

"You threw his bike down on the sidewalk," Mary said. "I saw you."

"Well, did you see what he done to my car?"

It was bad. Gregsy Hanson or somebody had thrown a stone right into the left front headlight. For some reason— from pure force and accuracy, probably—the stone was still stuck in the shiny reflector of the light.

"You tell me the kid's name, or I'll call the police!" cried Mrs. Blatke. "They'll make you tell."

"They won't make me do anything," Mary said. Suddenly she felt very hung over. She said, "Maybe your other head-light will get busted by somebody."

"Ladies! Ladies!" cried Mr. Dahle, grasping one earlobe desperately. "Please—I've called the police—they'll be here— please, *please!* Here they come now!"

It was Merle Schaefer. Mrs. Blatke ran over to his police car and shouted that Mrs. Graving had just threatened to break one of her headlights and that kid there had already busted the other one.

"What kid is that, then?" Merle inquired, getting out of the car languidly.

The three of them turned and saw Gregsy Hanson now pedalling up Vision Avenue, away from them, and throwing rolled-up copies of the *Duluth Herald* at doorways as he went.

"And anyway, she's crazy!" Mrs. Blatke shouted, pointing at Mary. "I know she's crazy because she goes to them people at the Lutheran Social Service on Thursdays. Everybody's seen her."

Merle looked at Mary thoughtfully and then he turned to Mrs. Blatke. "Funny—I already told you, just today," he said. "You don't call a policeman, remember? You forget awful quick, Mrs. Blatke. Now, you listen to me. When you get home this afternoon and you see a big ape there, two storeys high, and this big ape climbs in your living-room window and swipes your TV and then it goes in your refrigerator and eats everything you got there, including the ice cubes, *you don't call a cop!* You understand that, now? You will get me in trouble yet."

Mr. Dahle now held up his hands in a position exactly like the framed "Praying Hands" picture that hung in his office. "I think we can all go back in now," he said in a high, gentle voice. "I think the show is over." He giggled.

Nobody who came to the Faith Lutheran Church to see a counsellor or therapist on Thursdays parked their car in the church parking lot. They parked across the street by the hospital, at the "Visitors" sign, and then walked over to the church. It didn't do any good. Everyone knew exactly who had nerves and who was crazy in Rachel River. It didn't matter about the wives of Duluth airbase personnel; no one cared if they were crazy or not. But everyone knew exactly who the others were. Anyone who used the visiting psychotherapeutic services offered once a week by Lutheran Social Service was crazy or nervous. If they had a decent job, they had nerves; if they were on welfare, they were crazy. Mary Graving was just nerves, they guessed.

Carol Bly

Now Mary sat, facing north, in the Sunday-school room where she had taught release time religion, years before. The window faced the forest, where there were still wild animals living. One spring, twenty years ago or more, when men who had come back from one war or another still felt purposeful when they were gathered in groups, someone in town had spread it around that you would get a bounty if you went into those woods and brought out two fox's feet. All that summer, people killed foxes; there was near and distant firing almost every day, and traps set everywhere. Men referred to the animals—as people always do, for some reason, when they intend to kill a lot of them—in the collective. "There's a lot of fox in there," they remarked to each other on Main Street. "A lot of fox and some bear, but not so much bear as fox," instead of saying "A lot of foxes and some bears."

"I want to tell you something," Mary said to Jack, the therapist she saw every Thursday. "But before I tell you that, thinking of bears—out there—reminds me of something else I'll tell you."

She told the therapist about the young man baking bread in the Ye Olde 61. She described his strong elbows and his arms, how they smelled of whole wheat flour, and how he braced them strongly on the table so they were next to her face, while they all looked out the window at a bear. She told how she had sat there talking business with the other man, and this man had come and leaned over their table, and how all of a sudden there was this tremendous, irresponsible, un-accountable, absolutely unforeseeable desire, all because of this man leaning over while they looked at the bear. She told Jack how they all looked at the bear, which wasn't really that interesting but they quit talking and watched it, and then suddenly this man with his arms covered with bread dough—a man whose name she didn't even know—said, "Do you see how when a bear moves it is more like dancing than when a dog moves?"

"Well," Mary said now, "well, when he said that—well, the way he said it—well . . ." She went on explaining, failing to explain it. "That part about the bear," she said at last, "that *dancing*—that finished me off!"

They both laughed, but then the therapist waited, deliberately making a pause too serious to be filled with conversation about bears.

"Well—and then I lied to you last week," Mary said. "And this is what I am celebrating. I told you I would not commit suicide because of the children. That is not the reason I won't commit suicide! I was wrong. I won't do it because of this thing I am celebrating. You see, I thought all life was of the creature, life of the body, and I felt I am dead in my body—yet I am not dead. So therefore I thought I would do a test. I would see if life is all life of the body or not. So I took nearly all the week and went back over, in my memory, all the body life I have ever had. I went back over how it was with every man I could remember—well, at least, every time I could remember!"

This explanation seemed grandiose, and Mary became anxious because she knew that patients waste half the time in sexual bragging, so she said, "I went over some of the times, anyway, and I made myself remember everything, just as if it were now. I went through the births of the children all over again. Exactly as if it were happening now. I remembered

Carol Bly

every detail of the labor and the delivery—and oh, after the delivery!—of both children, and of beginning to nurse them in the hospital, and singing to them. 'Annie Laurie' I sang— not the first verse, which is dumb, but the other two—remembering to sing very quietly because you can tell a baby's ears are not yet spoiled by bad sounds. You can tell by that nearly mashed, delicate-looking way the ears lie close to their heads. The way they lie mashed back against their heads like that, you can tell they have heard only the most wonderful sounds, like sounds from underwater. . . . So I went back over all that, and it was awfully sad. My God, it was sad. But it was not what I was grieving for. It wasn't!

"I felt sorry for myself and for everyone else in the meantime, because if it is physical delights we live for, we certainly don't get to spend our time in very nice places. We are always working in the basement, or drinking in the VFW, or washing things at the laundromat. The rich are the only ones who sail on beautiful lakes—and they call that 'touching down on reality.' Just yesterday, someone told me sailing was 'touching down on reality'—and all the while he was skinning me clean on a wholesale offer! Suddenly I realized I wasn't staying alive for my children. I was staying alive for something I haven't even begun to do yet. So I stopped being altruistic as if I were some saint, giving myself up for others. And I stopped thinking my whole life would be different if only I could live in a cultivated place. Why do we praise children when they are willing to go into museums? So culture is nothing, I found out this week—nothing. It isn't why we live. And animal life—all that body stuff—that isn't it, either. It is something yet to do, something we're supposed to be doing in the future! But that's as far as I've got—I haven't looked at it any closer. I was simply so excited that I wasn't going to die, and that animal life is not all there is, that I went to the VFW Lounge to get drunk and celebrate. And in there I listened to the men talking. They're in worse shape than I am, even— they thought World War II was sort of a suit of armor, and now they don't know what they ought to be doing. Do you know that whenever I mention World War II on my radio program five or ten of them, in this one little town alone, call me up and tell me things from their lives?

"And yet I had a terrible day, yesterday. Because I didn't know what life will be, and animal life has been taken away, and then even the new life, my life of thinking about suicide, was taken away. I was so empty then. I was horribly empty! So I got into a coarse street quarrel with a woman over a little boy. When he called me up later and said, 'Thank you for standing up for me,' it was as if somebody who was not anybody had stood up for him. I was simply emptied."

"But this week?" Jack said. "What about the suicide?"

"It's gone," Mary said. "But, do you know, I used to make special toys for the children—I still do. I am making a bookcase with a secret compartment. When I was sewing for them, or building something, I used to think, Well, then *this* is life. And I was wrong about that, too. Life for others isn't anything, either. Just as the rich are mistaken in thinking there is reality in sailing, the rest of us are mistaken in thinking there is reality in carpentry.

"So I think it is something we have to keep an eye out for— what we're supposed to do, why to stay alive. Do you sail, ever? Well, if you know small boats you know about keeping

Carol Bly

an eye out for the darker place on the water to windward, because the darker place, which keeps getting close, is what tells you how to trim differently. . . . Well, that's enough!"

She stopped. Her facial tic reappeared now, and she controlled it.

"But it is wonderful, *wonderful,*" she said, "to come here and tell you depressing stuff. Every day, I am cheerful on the radio, and people come up to me in the Ben Franklin and say, 'Oh, you cheer us up so on the radio!' And my friends who are happily married come up and say, 'You do a terrific job of taking on that toy business so cheerfully!' We must be living in the most cheerful-minded century in the history of the world, even though the sheriff says the whole race is uniquely filthy!"

Mary and the therapist both laughed, and then they did serious work for the remainder of the session. She was not allowed then to divert from this serious work by telling stories about coarse women, or any of the other supposed facts of her life.

The Dignity
of Life

Two people stood quarreling in the casket showroom. They were a sixty-three-year-old man named Marlyn Huutula and his unmarried sister Estona. She was so angry that she bent toward him from her end of the coffin.

"You really ought to keep your grimy hands out of that clean quilting!" Estona told him in a ferocious whisper. "As if you owned the place! As if Svea weren't lying dead this very minute, right here in this very building, and you showing no respect!"

Jack Canon, the funeral director, had been hovering near them. Now he gave a swift glance over to see how grimy Marlyn's hands were. He would let this grown brother and sister quarrel a moment; he meant to leave this end of the long showroom so that they would not feel self-conscious as they whispered furiously about prices.

Marlyn and Estona were buying a casket, and the service that went with it, for their aunt, Svea Istava, an old woman who had come down in the world. Svea had died alone in her

79

wreck of a place just north of St. Aidan, Minnesota. From the time she moved there in 1943, until she died in February 1982, she had always had a few faithful visitors. They would pick their way through her sordid front farmyard, avoiding the wet place and the coils of barbed wire. Her place was what was called "inconvenient": that is, it had no water up to the house. But whenever someone visited—Mrs. Friesman to leave her idiot son Momo, or Jack Canon, the funeral director, or on Sundays during the football seasons, her nephew, Marlyn Huutula—Svea filled their cups with smoky coffee.

Her most frequent visitor, Momo Friesman, found her dead. Next morning, people sitting around the Feral Café traded information about Svea, making her a kind of random liturgy. They told one another how Svea had taken better care of that dog, Biscuit, than she took of herself. They told each other it was certainly hard to believe that Svea Istava had ever been the wife of a lieutenant colonel in the 45th Field Artillery, whose body had not been sent home because that was during World War II, not Vietnam. Mrs. Friesman had seen his Bronze Star and his European Theatre of Operations Ribbon Bar hanging on cup hooks in Svea's smudgy cupboard. Finally, people in the café settled to the most interesting thing about Svea: they said she was worth half a million dollars. In one booth, the sheriff was talking about her to the state patrolman who lived in Marrow Lake. The Marrow Lake man went past Svea's place nearly every day and had never seen such a dump. But the sheriff said that you could tell the true class of a person, though, by how they treated a dog. He himself had a handsome white shepherd bitch; that Biscuit, now, originally was a runt from one

Carol Bly

of his litters. He had taken it over to Svea because he knew she would make it a good home, and so she had.

Everyone thought that Svea had left the whole half million (if she had any half million) to her nephew Marlyn instead of half and half to Marlyn and his sister Estona. Marlyn visited her once a week for years, whereas Estona talked mean about Svea. Estona, who ran the Nu-St. Aidan Motel, was always roping in total strangers, finding out what they did, and then asking their advice. With both elbows on the sign-in counter, her eyes trying to read their bank balances when they opened their checkbooks, her wrists supporting her cheeks, she would say, "So you're a sales representative? As a sales representative, would you please tell me if this sounds right to you? I mean, you're in a position to know . . ." Then she would explain about Svea's money going to her kid brother because he was a man and made up to her on Sunday afternoons. Recently, she had said to the new adult education teacher who stayed at the motel on Wednesday nights, "You're a humanities consultant? Now that sounds like something that has got to be about how people treat each other! Fairly or unfairly? Well, would you tell me, as a humanities consultant—would you call it fair that this old woman, who keeps her place so bad it is amazing they don't get the countryside nursing people in to spray around, do you think it is right she would leave all that money to my brother and not my half to me?" Estona regarded the humanities consultant as another middle-aged woman like herself, who had to have picked up some sense somewhere along the line. "I don't know if this is in your field or not, but just looking at it humanly, can you tell me that he is making any big sacrifices for his aunt when he can check on his Vikings and Steelers bets as good on Svea's eleven-inch black-and-white as he could on his own remote control at home? Or maybe it's just me."

As Marlyn and Estona stood around the casket show-room, Jack Canon thought of everything that had happened since Svea's death. Her body had been discovered by Momo: Jack had quickly gone out to fetch it. He knew Momo as well as Svea, because Momo liked dead bodies. There was scarcely a wake or visitation in the past ten or fifteen years at which Jack hadn't had a word with Momo—that is, he had had to take him firmly by the elbow. Then, after he took Svea's body to the chapel, twenty or more youngsters went out to her place, apparently, and dug great holes all over the yard. By the time the sheriff reached the place, the boys had tipped over Svea's outhouse and were prodding the hole, looking for money. Another boy and girl had got hold of power augers and were drilling into the frozen ground, like mining prospectors, among the stacked snowtreads and fence-wire wheels. The sheriff pulled them all in on Possession and Vandalism and then let them out again. He called Jack and said he was going to ask the state patrolman to help keep an eye open these next days. "If we are going to have any trouble," Jack told him, "it will be during visitation days, not at the funeral itself." The two men talked to each other quietly on the telephone, in the special, measured way of people holding the fort for decency and dignity—while all the others give in to some horrible craze. The sheriff said with a sigh, "Well, we'll manage. I've got to locate that nephew of hers now, wherever he is." Jack felt the respect the sheriff had for him, a funeral director, and the disrespect he

Carol Bly

felt for Marlyn Huutula, who never had steady work in the wintertime if he could help it. Like half the men of St. Aidan, Marlyn kept a line of traps somewhere out east along St. Aidan Creek. Once he had tried to bribe the sheriff out of a speeding ticket while the sheriff stood at his car window, writing. Marlyn had picked up the rabbit lying on the passenger side and passed it up to the sheriff. The sheriff had been busy writing, so he didn't look carefully: all he saw was white fur and a little blood. At home, his shepherd had just had new litter of white puppies, so he mistook this animal. It was a full minute before he saw it was a rabbit, not a puppy. He had been writing a warning; now he tore up the yellow card and gave the man a citation instead. All day, as he later told Jack, his stomach churned. Then he blushed. "I don't guess that would bother someone . . . in your line of work," he added.

"Yes, it would bother him," Jack told him.

"I never had much tolerance," the sheriff said.

Jack Canon felt less tolerant every day now. He had started an adult education course two weeks ago; he thought it would give him perspective, but it was just the opposite. Now he minded remarks he heard that previously he would have passed off as "the kinds of things people say."

He frequently thought of his crimson vinyl notebook that lay on his office desk. It was labeled: HUMANITIES: ST. AIDAN ADULT EDUCATION PROGRAM — MOLLY GALAN, INSTRUCTOR. Jack had never been a man who took notes on his life as it went by. Yet now, several times a day, he said to himself, sometimes even aloud, since he was a good deal alone, "I ought to put *that* into the red notebook!" or *"That* ought to go into the red notebook if nothing else ever does!" And he looked forward to Wednesday night, the night of his class.

Tonight it was to meet in his office, as a matter of fact. That had come about because two weeks ago, on registration night, only one student had shown up to sign for the humanities course—Jack himself. His teacher was a spare, graying woman with a white forehead, who was unlike anyone he had ever known. He glanced over her head, her figure—her long hands with thin, unremarkable fingers, trying to say "It is in the eyes," or "It is the hands," or "It is how she *carries* herself"—but he knew all his guesses were wrong. She leaned against the second-grade teacher's desk, and Jack sat cramped before her in a desk-and-chair combination comfortable only for small children. They waited for others to appear. Through the schoolroom doorway, they heard shy voices, calls, remarks—people signing up for Beginning Knitting Two, a continuation from the fall semester.

No one else came at all. Presently, Mrs. Galan explained that the guidelines of the course would allow the class to meet in private homes, if the class so chose. The following Wednesday, there was a blizzard, but Mrs. Galan made it on I-35 from St. Paul to the Nu-St. Aidan Motel, and to the schoolbuilding. This time she read off to Jack some of the course subjects approved in the guidelines. They might choose among Ethnicity, Sources of Community Wisdom, Ethical Consciousness in Rural America, Longitudinal Studies of Human Success and Failure, Attitudinal Changes Toward Death, or simply Other. They agreed that the following Wednesday, since no one had shown up again this time, they might as well meet in Jack's office. He explained to her that she should walk round to the back of the chapel, where the back door opened onto a concrete apron. It was kept clear of snow, he told her.

In his years and years of single life Jack had noticed that lonely people were either carefully groomed or remarkably grimy. He himself had to be immaculate at all times. It was a habit by the time he was fourteen—along with learning how to cover the phone. He would push his arithmetic problems against the chapel schedule board, keeping the phone where his left hand could raise the earpiece on the first ring. Then he spoke immediately and courteously into the flared mouth. By the time he was a senior in high school he was used to nearly all the work of the chapel: he knew how to lift heavy weight without grunting, while wearing a white shirt, tie, and suit jacket. He learned to keep longing or anxiety from showing on his face. One October day, in 1936, he was sitting on the football bench at St. Aidan High School. The big St. Aidan halfback sat down next to him, for just a minute. Jack had been sitting there, knees together, chilled, for an hour. The halfback, a great tall boy named Marlyn Huutula, dropped down beside him when he was taken out to rest a minute, and his body gave off heat and the glow of recently spent energy. It was nearly visible like a halo—that great hot energy field around the boy. Jack knew enough not to look at Marlyn for more than a second; he must not let himself be mesmerized into staring like a rabbit at a successful boy, the way he had seen others do. So Jack had given Marlyn a casual grin, and both of them turned to watch the field. Then the coach snapped his fingers at Marlyn, who jumped up right in front of Jack. The coach's arm went around the leather-misshaped shoulders; Jack overheard the friendly growl of instructions. The coach pointed into the field with one hand, slapped Marlyn's buttocks with the other, and the halfback swung away toward the players, his socks sunk below his calves, jiggling in folds around the strong ankles. For the thousandth time that autumn, Jack expressed manhood by not letting his face look sad.

But the next Thursday afternoon, just as he was helping his father transfer a casket from the nervous pallbearers into the hearse, Jack recalled the bad moment on the football field. His face jerked upward in embarrassment at the memory. When his father had closed the hearse doors, he pulled Jack aside. St. Aidan Lutheran's two bells kept tolling so the sound rang down nearly on top of them: the sidewalk was white and cold with afternoon sunlight. "I'm going to tell you this just once, but it is very important," Jack's dad said. "Do not put on a fake sad look—the way you did just now when we were taking the casket. Get this straight: they don't expect you to look sad—just professional. Just keep your face serious and considerate."

Jack became more and more carefully gauged in his appearance: he controlled his face, he maintained his grooming. But Svea Istava, whose body now lay in his operating room, had turned dirty as she aged. When Jack first knew her in 1943, she was a handsome woman of thirty-nine or so. She told him she had to give up the St. Paul house that her husband's officer's pay had been financing. She asked Jack if the World War II dead were going to be returned to the United States. Next month, she bought an old, very small farmhouse on an acre of scrubland, about a mile past St. Aidan.

The first time Jack went out there to visit, his eye passed

Carol Bly

over the turquoise-painted, fake-tile siding. He saw the string of barbed wire that someone had hitched to one corner of the outhouse and then stretched over to the cornerpost of the house itself. He supposed that Mrs. Istava would gradually have trash removed from the farmyard. He hoped she would find enough money to put in plumbing. He imagined the huge shade of the oaks darkening not these piles of rejected auto batteries and other trash, but new lawn. There was a distant view of both church spires, and to the north lay the pleasant, spooky pine forest.

To his surprise, Svea didn't remove the barbed wire; she took to leaning things against it—first a screen door that warped and she couldn't repair, next a refrigerator that stopped working. Its rounded ivory corners and its rusted base grate seemed natural after a while; Svea tied a clothes-line length about it so that Momo Friesman would not climb inside and be killed. Sometimes she stood the way poor rural people stand, elbow bent, one hand planted on one irregular hip, and the face gazing vaguely past the immediate farm-yard, as if to say, "There is life beyond this paltry place—I have my eyes on it."

In those days, Jack sometimes thought he would save Svea from all that. He imagined himself, in a square-shouldered way, driving out one miserable winter night, when the sky would be black and the ground-storming of down snow nearly blinding. "Oh, how did you ever make it on such a night?" she would cry, and he would say briefly, a little sharply, "Come on—we're going to town! We're going to be married!" He imagined the reliable Willys pushing through all that dark-ness and whiteness.

It never happened. Svea never called a junk man to pick up anything in her yard. Instead, more junk arrived. Jack had to pick his way to the doorstep over corrugated-tread wheels of broken lawnmowers. Often, Momo stared at him from a pile of rubbish near the tipped refrigerator. He knew the child trapped mice and then buried them in a distracted, faithful way among Svea's onion sets and carrots.

As the years passed, a rumor grew up that all this while Svea Istava had been and was still worth five hundred thousand. The more unlikely her person and possessions, the more entrenched the myth.

Meanwhile, gradually, Jack began to lose confidence. He began buying more and more expensive clothing. By the 1960s, even his garden gloves were from L. L. Bean. He was the first man in St. Aidan to have a wool suit after a decade of Dacrons and polyester. By accident, he found out what was wrong with him. One evening, he sat with the sheriff down at the station. It had been a bitter February day, as it was now, and the sheriff was saying that the bad news in St. Aidan County was the rising crime rate but the good news was that more and more uranium leases were being let out around the area. Jack listened idly, leaning comfortably against the iron radiator, watching the heat move the window shades a little. The sheriff held several puppies on a pillow in his lap; his hands kept passing over the little dogs and the dogs kept re-arranging themselves in a whining, growling, moving pile of one another. As Jack looked on, he felt that he was losing confidence because he wasn't touching other live bodies enough; he watched in an agony of envy as the puppies wandered with their fat paws into one another's eyes and ears and

Carol Bly

stomachs—he got the idea they were gaining confidence from one another every time they touched.

The next day he walked into the Feral Café to have lunch with the new Haven Funeral Supply salesman, Bud Menge. Haunted by the revelation of the puppies, he sensed that women looked up at Bud Menge as he went by, and re-arranged their buttocks in the booths.

Bud was friendly, right from the first. After a year of their acquaintance, Jack said, "Couldn't you ever stop and let me buy you lunch without you trying to sell me something?"

Most dealing in St. Aidan took place at either the Men's Fellowship of St. Aidan Lutheran or at lunch in the Feral Café. Bud's face grew grave and considerate. "Listen, Jack, how would you like to discuss something that is absolutely new and different and will revolutionize your whole approach?"

In ten minutes, Bud sold Jack an industrial-psychology program that he had used ever since. The Casket Showroom Lighting Plan, like all of Bud's ideas, was disgusting from the outset. "That's really revolting, Bud. Let's face it, Bud," Jack had said, "That is just about the worst taste I have ever heard of!" Jack had often made such remarks during Bud's first year as representative for Haven Funeral Supply. Later he was slower to speak. Bud never presented him an idea that was not absolutely profitable.

The first aspect of the Casket Showroom Lighting Plan was simple: You lighted only those caskets you wanted a client to inspect. You placed small wall-bracketed lamps at six-foot intervals along the two long walls, and across one short end-wall of the showroom. These lamps had either rose or cream shades: you lit only those you wanted on each given occasion. Jack generally lighted the caskets that went with the fifteen-hundred-dollar service, the twenty-three-hundred-dollar service, and the four-thousand-dollar service. No one in St. Aidan ever bought the four-thousand-dollar service, and in fact, it was not for sale.

This four-thousand-dollar casket was an elaborate part of Bud's Lighting Plan. Jack saw that it was lighted, and left its cover up, but did not lead clients over to it. Bud explained the procedure: people shopping for caskets feel that they are likely to be cheated by the mortician. Even if the mortician is a fellow small-town citizen whom they have known for years, they still feel they must watch him like a hawk now that they are buying from him. They know perfectly well that their own harrowed feelings at the time of a death are the funeral director's pivot. They are on tiptoe against his solemnity. Therefore, Bud explained, clients want to wander around the showroom on their own: they feel they are getting around the funeral director if they look at caskets other than those he seems to want to show them. They want to be shrewd. Eventually, Bud explained, because it is lighted and open, the four-thousand-dollar casket catches the client's eye. He goes over, and, wonder of wonders, finds this casket to be noticeably more elegant than anything the funeral director has shown him so far. Immediately, he thinks that it is probably priced the same as the caskets he has been shown, but simply is a better buy. He suspects it is being kept for some preferred customer of the funeral director, and that a comparative lemon is being pawned off on him at the same price. Bud told Jack, "You follow them over to the four-thousand-dollar casket, but stay behind a little—as if you didn't really want to go over

Carol Bly

there. 'How come you never showed us *this* one?' they will ask. 'How come you never showed us this one when it's just beautiful?' they will say. So then you tell them, 'You're right—it is the most beautiful one, by far. It is the best casket we have ever had at Canon Chapel.' Just tell them that much at this point. Let them hang a little. Sooner or later the client will stop staring at you and will say, 'So how come you didn't show it to us?' Now here is where you pull your act together," Bud told Jack. "You tell them, fairly fast, 'Because I don't want you to buy that casket, is why.'" Bud begged Jack to pause again, right at that point. "Stick with the pauses, Jack, I'm telling you. Pause right there. Every single client—I don't care if it is the middle-aged mother of an only son who just died—every single client will say, 'But why don't you want me to buy it? What does it cost?' Now you go right up to the client and say, 'Because it costs four thousand dollars. I know you can afford four thousand dollars, Mrs. So-and-so, I know you can easily raise that amount. Money isn't the problem. The reason I don't want you to buy it is that I'd a hundred times rather that you bought the twenty-three-hundred dollar casket and gave the other seventeen hundred to church or charity in memory of'—and you insert the deceased's name here—'I'd a hundred times rather you'd spent the seventeen hundred extra that way than on a casket.' OK, now, Jack, here is the third pause—don't make it very long—just a short one. Now you say, 'Or does that sound crazy, from where I'm supposed to be coming from?'"

Bud was right. No client ever said, "Yes, it sounds crazy." Men gave Jack a warm look and sometimes slapped his arm. Women sometimes came around the four-thousand-dollar casket and hugged him. Everyone said, "Thanks, Jack, for being so square with us." And just as Bud had prophesied, not one of those clients ever bought the fifteen-hundred-dollar casket: they all bought the twenty-three-hundred-dollar one. The whole point of the Lighting Plan was to switch people from the fifteen-hundred-dollar to the twenty-three-hundred-dollar casket. During the whole sales procedure, Jack never had to lie. After explaining the plan, Bud had paused briefly, then looked very straight at Jack across the strewn café-booth table, with the chili bowls and paper sachets of coffee-whitening chemicals that both men had pushed away so they could lean forward on their forearms. "Some of them," Bud said, "I wouldn't bother to explain they don't have to lie—they wouldn't care. But with you, Jack, now that's a major thing."

The last point of the Casket Lighting Plan was to have one end of the showroom nearly dark. Jack made use of this point right now: he broke into the quarreling between Estona and Marlyn Huutula.

"Folks," Jack said loudly, "I am going to look over some odds and ends of paperwork. I'll be down at the other end of the room, so when you want me, give a call."

Clients needed the sense of quarreling privately. They needed to confer over how little they could spend without causing talk in town—talk about how cheap they were, after all that *he* or *she* had done for *them,* too. Jack always left people to have this quarrel, but he stayed within earshot so he could return at the right moment.

At a tiny writing table at the dark end of the room, just behind the county casket, Jack looked over an eight-page

Carol Bly

booklet showing full-color photographs of funeral customs all over the world. The photographs were on the right-hand pages, the "Discussion Questions" on the left-hand pages.

"What's the good of it?" Jack had said in the Feral Café, when Bud passed him the booklet across their coffee cups.

"It's the most practical thing we have come up with yet," Bud told him with his frank smile. "It solves the problem of the local necrophiliac. And every town has one."

Jack said, "I wish you wouldn't use that word in the Feral Café, Bud. In fact I wish you wouldn't use it at all. And besides," he added in the no-nonsense tone he used when he had to, his mind picturing Momo Friesman, "we haven't got anyone like that in St. Aidan."

"Every town has one," Bud said. "If you haven't got him today you will have him tomorrow. When some funeral director tells me his town don't have one, I look at the funeral director himself. Ha, ha! Just joking, Jack."

Bud opened the booklet to a page called "Funeral Practices of the Frehiti People." "OK," he said. "Here's how it works. Your man shows up at a visitation or wake,"

"And who are the Frehiti People? What do we care!" said Jack.

Bud grinned. "How should I know who they are? They don't live around here anyway. Anyway, they're somebody. Some sociologists or humanities people or somebody did all the research—we know it's OK. That's a point I'm glad you asked about, Jack. You know, the research in this booklet didn't come from our publicity department like most of the stuff. This is the real thing—you can be confident when you use this. Anyway, your guy comes up at the wake so you go

The Dignity of Life 93

up to him and you put your arm around his shoulder, the nice, teaching way a football coach throws his arm around you and you feel good because you know the coach is taking you into his confidence. OK? Didn't you say you played football for St. Aidan High? OK—then you know the way I mean. Now, with your free hand, Jack, you flip open this booklet. It is easy because they put this Frehiti People discussion at the center where the stapling is, so it naturally opens right there. So you keep your other hand on his shoulder, see, and you show him this picture, the one you see there, with the jungle huts in the background, and them carrying the corpse in a kind of thatch-covered chair with the feet hanging off like that, toward us. And the discussion questions at the left. So you don't have to tell this person, 'Look at the terrific picture of a dead body with the feet hanging off that kind of coolie chair or whatever it is.' What you get to say aloud is, 'I wonder, so-and-so—you want to use their name as much as you can, Jack, as you know— 'Hey, so-and-so, I wonder if you'd look through this new book and read these discussion questions. Maybe this is something that would help families get through grief— would you look this over and then tell me what you think?' And Jack, all the time you are saying all this, his eyes are glued onto that picture and his mind is thinking—if people like that think—There are other full-color pictures in the book, too, and I want to see them all! Then he hears you offering to let him take the booklet home with him. Now all this time, you are pushing him along right out of your funeral chapel and he is halfway home before he realizes he is no longer at the visitation. And that is fine with you. The last

Carol Bly

thing you need is someone trying any sensitivity games at a visitation."

Bud gestured toward the booklet in Jack's hand. "That little item may not have a lot of class like our bronze desk accessories and all, but it is one hundred thousand percent effective."

Now Jack sat at the dark end of the showroom, looking at the dead Frehiti in the photograph. The man's feet, whitened in the foreground, in sharp focus, were separated from the gloomy jungle village in the background; the feet had come to meet the viewer; the straw hut roofs, the gnarled equatorial trees, the smudgy broken grass of the village street—all that receded and lowered behind, like a cloud departing.

Jack heard Estona Huutula's voice rise in fury. He was used to family differences in his showroom, but this one was especially nasty. He listened, trying to decide when he should break in.

"I don't see how you can be so uncaring," Estona was shouting. "You know that when they open up that will, there will be a half million for you—probably for you, alone, too; you won't even have to share it with me, since you did such a good job making up to Svea all those years! You know what people will say, Marlyn! They'll say that there that nice aunt left him a cool half million and all he would buy her was the county casket."

"I never said I wanted to bury Svea in the county casket!" Marlyn shouted back.

The casket they referred to was a narrow, light blue coffin that St. Aidan provided for welfare clients when the family could afford nothing else. It was nicely made, but most funeral directors, including Jack, made sure it was locally referred to only as "the county casket" so that no one would contemplate buying it for a loved one.

"All I meant was," Marlyn said, "why go to twenty-three hundred when we can get the same service and a perfectly nice-looking casket for fifteen hundred?"

Jack rose from his small desk.

Estona said, "That's going to look just fine, isn't it, when you get all that money? I call it downright cheap!"

Marlyn grumbled, "We don't even know if Svea had any money anyway."

"All the worse for you then!" cried Estona with a slashing laugh. "All those Sunday afternoons you put in for nothing! Sitting there in her filthy kitchen letting her tell you how Chuck Noll should do this, Chuck Noll should do that, and how old age comes even to football players, and how Cliff Stoudt was a fool to hurt his arm. That one time I was there, you must have said it twenty times if you said it once: 'You may have something there, Svea!' I nearly puked. And 'Everything that goes up has to come down, I guess, Svea— even Lynn Swann!' If you weren't the sponging wise nephew of the sports-expert aunt! And the two of you drunk as lords before three in the afternoon, too! I nearly threw up listening to you—I'd say 'puke' except we're in a funeral chapel!"

Jack generally let relations quarrel until both of them had turned their irritation, by mere exhaustion, from each other to him. As soon as he felt all the anger coming toward him— none left for each other—he would spend a minute deliberately hardselling a coffin he knew they didn't want. Then they would concentrate on outwitting this awful funeral director

Carol Bly

for a minute or so. He let them outwit him. Then he decided which coffin they would really like, and usually wrapped up the sale, including choice of remembrance folders, in fifteen minutes. The clients left in harmony with each other, which was good: the moment they left Canon Chapel the elation of having stumped the mortician would die and they would notice their grief again.

"And another thing!" Estona cried. "You know, if you had *really* respected Svea's dignity in life or death, you wouldn't have been out tomcatting the very night after they found her, would you? There we were, the sheriff and I, trying to figure out where you were, with all those kids having dug up poor Svea's yard and all! Do you know that the sheriff sent the deputy down the river because they thought you were checking your traps? Finally Mrs. Friesman said she seen you driving somewhere with that Mrs. Galan from the adult education. 'Oh,' I said, 'he wouldn't be with her. She always stays with us at the Nu-St. Aidan Motel.' Well, yes, she saw you though, she said, so what could the sheriff do; he drove back out to your house and there you were in the middle of the night, the both of you! Of course I'd made a fool of myself, telling the deputy I knew you wouldn't be running around with her because she seemed like such a nice widow lady and very intellectual."

Jack now made his way slowly from the dark end of the room, like someone a little off balance. He approached the brother and sister standing under the yellow wall lights and took Estona by the elbow. He explained that they would now go into his office and have a sip of something that he kept, which sometimes helped people in times of grief. He led them

The Dignity of Life

around behind the chapel, past the door leading to the operating area, and into his office. Sunlight poured in, dazzling after the draped and shadowy showroom. Jack seated Estona on the couch; he put Marlyn in the conference chair, and opened a bottle of pinot blanc. Although everyone in St. Aidan knew that Estona Huutula turned on the NO part of the NO VACANCY sign at the motel each night around ten and settled down with a whiskey, Estona said, "I don't use much alcohol, Jack, but a little wine *would* help me, I think."

Estona then allowed they ought to get the twenty-three-hundred-dollar white-lined casket instead of the fifteen-hundred-dollar tan-lined one because it would be more cheerful for Svea to look out of. Both men looked out through the faint window curtains when she said that. She added, "Or maybe that's just me."

In the normal course of things, Jack would have let Estona sell Marlyn on the more expensive of the two caskets, but now he wanted this old high-school classmate and his sister out of the office so badly he would have sold him a co-op burial-club service with a pine box for $34.50 if they would just get out. So he took it into his own hands. Ignoring Estona, who was tapping her glass for a refill, he spoke to Marlyn in a man-to-man tone, making fast explanations. He filled the man in on some of the side services provided in a funeral, such as getting police cooperation in case there was further trouble, or unwanted crowds to see the body of a simple old woman worth five hundred thousand dollars. He explained that his own man, LeVern Holpe, would park cars, assisted by the chapel man from Marrow Lake.

Marlyn responded exactly as Jack wanted: he tried to be

snappy and intelligent too. Marlyn never mentioned the fifteen-hundred-dollar casket again. Then, just when Estona was beginning to look as if she felt neglected, Jack passed her the new remembrance format that Bud Menge had brought over only the week before. Gone was the twenty-third psalm in old English eleven point on the left-hand side: instead, there was a passage from *The Velveteen Rabbit* in a modern face without serif. Jack said to Estona, cutting Marlyn out of it: "Estona, I want your honest opinion of these. If you don't care for these new-style remembrances, say so, and we will have the others printed up for Svea."

At last brother and sister were gone. Jack telephoned LeVern to say that he could come over and work any time now. He himself would have a catnap. He lay down on the small office sofa.

The winter sun, very bright and low at this time of year, sent its long webby light through the glass curtains. Jack fell gratefully asleep, still wearing his suit jacket. Sunlight fell onto his desk with all the accessories Bud had provided him—the bronze-tone plastic paperweight imprinted CANON CHAPEL: CARE WHEN CARE MATTERS MOST. The sun fell onto his red-covered humanities notebook, too. It fell onto his own face, and made his white hair nearly transparent and his skin luminous. Once during the following hour and a half, his young assistant, LeVern, looked in soundlessly and thought how sad the human face looks asleep; he decided that Jack Canon, in his opinion anyway, led a very crappy life. LeVern decided he could manage the job without waking the fellow, and called Greta at the beauty parlor when he was done to tell her she could come over and do Mrs. Istava's head now or whenever she was ready.

In his dream, Jack went to spend the weekend in a motel north of St. Paul. He was to meet a woman there who had exclaimed, "My God! I think I am falling in love again! I love you, John!" So long as Jack still believed she would show up, he patrolled the motel room, swerving round the ocean-sized bed and rounding the television set like an animal. Once he had decided she was not going to show up, he took to rereading all the materials in the desk except the Bible placed there by the Gideons. Everything he read swam and enlarged and darkened in his eyes. Everything had color swimming at the edges; even the papers he held were yellowed like church windows on Christmas cards. He read through the room service menu with its appalling prices and his eyes swam with tears. He read the daily cleaning services options with his eyes silvered with tears. He was reminded of something that someone at a Minnesota funeral directors' convention had once told him: the man had said that when he became born again, for the first few weeks, whenever he opened up the Bible, no matter at what place he opened it, his eyes would fill with tears. Jack was thinking that over, in his dream, when he waked to LeVern's tapping on the office door.

LeVern put his head around the door. "All set now, Jack," he said. "I'm going home now."

"Oh, then, you're ready for me," Jack said, trying not to sound slowed with sleep.

"No, it's all done," LeVern told him. "Greta's here working now."

Jack lay vulnerable in the huge sadness of his dream. The day was nearly over. All morning he had longed for the day to

Carol Bly

be over, because it was Wednesday, the night of his class. Now the joy was gone out of it.

Eventually, he rose and bathed and shaved and put on the best sports jacket he had. He looked at his gray eyes very carefully in the mirror, but it was OK: none of the dream or his own feelings showed.

He locked the front door of the chapel, making sure the twin lights for visitations were both turned off; people understood by that that Svea could not be viewed until the next day. Then he went round and lighted the rear yard light, which fell upon the private entrance to his office and the garage. At nearly eight o'clock, the bell rang. Jack cried to himself, "She came after all, then!"

He swung the door open to the cold night. Outside, Momo Friesman stood on the garage cement, his bulging eyes bright from the overhead light.

"I came to pay my respects to Mrs. Istava," Momo said quickly, "and don't you turn me away, Jack. I got a right. She was neighbor to me and my mother, and I was friends. She had me come keep her company once a week and I got a right to mourn her as good as anyone else."

"Visitation isn't until tomorrow, Momo," Jack said.

Then he recalled Bud Menge's little book of photographs and discussions. "There *is* something you could help me with, though, Momo. Do you have time to come in a minute?"

Momo's eyes shone. "I can help you in the lab, Jack!"

"No," Jack said firmly, "not in the operating room—but wait." He started to go to the casket showroom for the booklet, but then remembered he couldn't leave Momo alone or the man might leap through the office door toward the operating room. So he put his arm around Momo's shoulder and led him to the sofa. When he saw Momo was all the way seated, he left.

Momo had the face of a twelve-year-old; he was forty-three, in fact. Every morning in the summer, his mother drove him into town and Momo went to all the trash disposal cans in St. Aidan, recovered *Minneapolis Tribune*s from them, and sold them up and down the one street of town, shouting, "Paper! Paper!" All the businesspeople sent some-one out, a receptionist or whoever was nearest the door, to give Momo a nickel and take a paper. When he had gone the whole length of the street, from the Canon Funeral Chapel at one end to the Rocky Mountains Prospectors' office at the other, he would find more papers lying on the top of the trash cans, so he sold them again—this time to the other side of the street. At noon he waited among the boxes that came into the Red Owl on the truck; the owner would shout, "He's here, OK, Mrs. Friesman!" when his mother came to pick him up. Once a week she took him over to Svea Istava's place across the road, and Svea would let him dig in her piles of orange crates and used winter tires.

When Jack dropped the booklet into Momo's lap, it opened as Bud had promised, to the photograph of the dead Frehiti man in his grassy chair. Jack thought to himself, It is five after eight now. She hasn't shown up. She is not going to come. Well, he went on to himself, everyone has to have some kind of memorial made in their honor. We shouldn't any of us die without someone's doing at least *something* in our honor. Jack looked down at Momo, who was bent over the photo-graph. Well, Momo, Jack thought. You're it. Svea let you into

Carol Bly

her place all those years. Tonight, then, I will let you into mine. You can sit there and gloat over that book for two hours if you want. Jack went and sat down at his desk. He said in his thoughts, I don't suppose you'd understand, Momo, if I tried to explain to you that Molly Galan was supposed to be sitting here where you are sitting, not you. Well, anyway—it isn't her: it's you. Jack remembered how Svea remained kind to Momo even when, two weeks after her dog Biscuit died, Momo found the grave, despite the rusty refrigerator grille Svea had laid on top of it in hopes he wouldn't notice. Momo dug up Biscuit and brought the body into the house and laid it on Svea's oilcloth-covered table. Biscuit looked bad after two weeks in the earth. Even then, Svea did not lift a hand to Momo. She only telephoned Jack to ask if he ever had had any difficulty with Momo around the chapel. Jack confessed that he had to deal with Momo on various occasions.

Now he went through the little speech Bud had taught him, suggesting Momo take the booklet home. He need not have bothered. Just as Bud predicted, Momo was entranced by the pictures.

The doorbell rang again.

Jack went over to it, nearly faint with hope but still unbelieving.

"I didn't know if I ought to come," Molly Galan said. "I know you have had a death."

"Oh, but visiting isn't until tomorrow!" Jack cried. He held the door wide, but didn't offer his arm. Molly Galan explained that she was a little breathless from having walked over from the motel. Then Jack remembered Momo. "This is Momo Friesman," Jack said. He went over and stood near

The Dignity of Life 103

Momo's knees. "Momo is going to zip up his jacket now and take his book home, before it gets even later and colder."

"I want to stay here," Momo said.

"Let's see your book," Molly said.

"You give that back," he told her.

"I promise," she said. She sat down beside him, turning the pages.

"And now you must take it home with you, Momo," Jack said. "But first you must zip up your jacket because it is much colder again now."

Jack realized that in one minute Momo would be out of there, and the thought made him so joyous he nearly danced the man into his zipper.

"I don't want to go," Momo said.

Jack thought, I could just strangle him until those eyes jump clear out of his head like twin pale spheres careening out into space and then I could pick him up and throw the whole mess of a man out the door. As soon as Jack noticed what he was thinking he backed further from the sofa. Anyway, he thought, retreating to the desk, what did he care if Momo chose to stay the evening? What good would it do *now* to have an evening with Molly Galan?

Oh yes! he cried to himself. Look at that flushed face of hers! And that lively look in her eyes: that isn't from hiking over here in the cold! And her wonderful smile! That smile was turned toward Momo, but how could such a smile be for Momo? Women of fifty did not look like that except when love was so recent the body itself still remembered it. Jack's anger narrowed and cooled and felt permanent. And anyway, he added to himself, all this is just a job of work for a woman

Carol Bly

like her. She was hired to tutor adult extension students in the humanities so she tutored adult extension students in the humanities. She had agreed to meet in his office probably because that arrangement was simpler than anything else.

He said aloud, "Well, if Momo wants to stay, that would be all right, wouldn't it?"

She looked at Momo and said, "Of course. Momo, you can read your book and we will work on ours."

"And afterwards I will pay my respects to Svea," Momo told her.

"Not tonight," she said. "When I say it's time you will zipper up your jacket and you can walk home with me."

In the meantime, Jack walked rapidly back and forth between his lighted desk and the sofa. Perhaps Molly Galan was going to open her copy of the red humanities workbook over there, on the sofa beside Momo. She might do that, he supposed.

But she didn't. She came to his desk and sat down in the conference chair. She picked up a bronze marker stamped CANON CHAPEL and laid it back quickly. She said, "The Extension people would like to know which subject we're going to work on, and they want us to write an evaluation as we go along. This is a kind of pilot program, you see." She smiled at him. "They want to know what your expectations are."

How could Jack tell her his expectations? All week he had planned how she was coming and he meant to tell her part of his life story. Shamelessly, he had meant to. Jack had meant to tell her how all his life he had wished to be serious, not just solemn as he must be at his work, but serious. He wanted to tell her how here in St. Aidan, where he practiced a trade he had never wanted to practice, somehow he could not rise over the chaff and small cries of daily life into some upper ring of seriousness. He imagined this ring of seriousness, like Saturn's rings, almost physically circling the planet—but he couldn't reach it because he was caught down here, blinded in the ground-storming of old jokes, old ideas, old conventions, which no sooner were dropped than they were picked up again like snow lifted and lifted and dropped and lifted again by blizzard wind, blowing into everyone's face over and over.

Molly Galan smiled at him. She had placed the four fingers of her right hand between five pages of the humanities notebook, and she held these pages apart as if for ready reference; he saw the lamplight through the spread pages like a nearly translucent Eastern fan, collapsible, of course, but taking up its space as elegantly as sculpture does.

Jack thought, How can it be that anyone with such hands spent last night with Marlyn Huutula? How can that be, when Marlyn Huutula all his life had never done anything admirable except play halfback for St. Aidan in 1936?—and Jack saw, as sharply in his mind's eye as he had ever seen it, Marlyn's sweaty hair as he removed his leather helmet.

Now Jack bent toward Molly under the beautiful lamplight and shouted at her, "What I want to know is, why did you ever do it? How could someone like you go and, go and, oh how could someone like you for the love of God go and spend the night with Marlyn Huutula? How could you *do* it?"

I know I did not just say that aloud, Jack told himself; I know I did not. Nonetheless, that is what I just did. However,

Carol Bly

I must not have really said that aloud because men in their sixties do not ask humanities consultants why they spend the night with whomever they spend the night with. Yet it was my voice that said that.

Then he thought, In one minute she will simply rise and leave without another word. She will go over to the couch and pick up her coat where she left it near Momo and she will leave. I shall offer her a ride home because it is so cold again and, oh, Christ, she will refuse even that!

However, the ladylike fingers did not fold up the fan. Molly Galan shouted at him, "I don't know! I don't know why I did it! And what do *you* care, anyway?"

"I don't care! I don't care what you do," Jack said.

"Well," Molly shouted, "you just don't know how dumb it all is!"

She burst into tears.

Very far inside himself, in a place really too dank to nourish a spark of happiness, Jack felt a tiny warmth: "What do you mean, 'dumb'?" he asked. But then the snarl came back into his voice. "So what's that supposed to mean, *dumb!* What is that supposed to mean, 'How dumb it all is!' Anyone can go around shouting things like that!"

"You don't know what it is to be lost in the dumbness of it!" she shouted, still crying.

"You chose it! You chose it!" he said. "You chose Marlyn Huutula!"

Suddenly then her hands fell simply, faintingly, like snow onto the booklet in her lap. Her face and voice suddenly were completely serene. "Yes," she said, pausing. "That's right," she said in an agreeable, logical tone. "Marlyn Huutula. Now he really *is* dumb." She added in an even more peaceful tone, "That is a fact, you know. He is really *very* dumb."

"The dumbest person I ever knew!" Jack said. But then he leaned forward and said, "What do you mean exactly?"

He felt a hope taking fire in him too quickly. He did not want to lose his proper anger in this hope. Already, he noticed that Molly was sitting with her head tipped to one side, nearly daydreaming at him, and he, too, on his side of the lamplight, was tipping his head at the same angle. They regarded each other like two birds, with that great concentration and that great natural stupidity of birds.

Hope kept rising rather weakly in Jack, like a hand rising from a lap, with the fingers still fallen from the rising wrist, the fingers flowing downward like an umbrella.

Momo meanwhile had approached them, and now wavered, his face turning from one to the other of them.

Jack whispered, "Well, will we go on with the course, do you think?"

Molly said, "Of course we will."

Jack said briskly. "It is too cold for you and Momo to walk home. I will drive you both. Momo, it is time for you to zip up your jacket now."

The telephone rang. It was the sheriff. "Jack, I thought you would like to know. The Huutula family read Svea Istava's will early, and you know what? She didn't have two cents to her name! After all that fuss! So what we'll do, Jack—the Marrow Lake patrolman and I will kind of keep an eye out the next couple of days, and we'll make sure the news gets around, so you shouldn't have any crowd-draw to the visitation hours. I expect you'll just get the usual for an old woman like that." In the background, Jack could hear the sheriff's puppies barking.

Jack and Momo and Molly all sat in the front seat of his car. The night had dropped below zero, so their breathing frosted the windshield and the side windows as well. The defroster opened up only a small space in the windshield directly in front of Jack; he had to hunch down to see through it. He guided the car gingerly through the cold town out on the north road toward the Friesmans'. The black woods were not wrecked, but they were nearly wrecked. The greater trees had been cut over. The earth under the forest was not wrecked, either—but it was staked out. Here and there, invisible to ordinary people, were concrete-stoppered holes where the uranium prospectors had pulled out their pipes and left only magnets so they could find the places again. As the car crawled along the iced highway, Jack thought of the whole countryside, nearly with tears in his eyes. He kept peering through the dark, clear part of the glass, with his whole body shivering and his skin cold in his gloves and the whole of him beginning to flood with happiness. His own life, Jack thought—It wasn't wrecked completely, after all! It felt to him, since he was sixty-three and much was over for him— or rather, had gone untraveled—that his life was nearly wrecked. But not completely. He began to smile behind his cold skin. He started driving faster, feeling more jaunty and more terrific every second.

The patrolman from Marrow Lake, who had just left the St. Aidan station, happened to see the car tearing along Old 61 where it crossed the north road. He thought, Oh, boy! Travelers' advisory or no travelers' advisory! Nothing stops some people! Car all frosted blind like that, tearing right along anyway! Behind the car's pure white windows he did not make out the local undertaker and a comely woman and a middle-aged retarded man.

Carol Bly

STORIES FROM

The Tomcat's Wife

The Tomcat's Wife

The Galls had not been in Clayton two weeks before my husband, Furman Hastad, got a crush on Tom Gall. The first I suspected it was when Mrs. Beske, a woman in our church, told me something while our Circle was putting together the spread for the Dollum funeral. We were making up the usual funeral spread—ground-up roast pork, ground-up roast beef, two onions chopped, three boiled egg yolks ground up, and Miracle Whip. Mrs. Beske said she was trying to get a deal on some chicken starter and oyster shells at the elevator. I believed that much straight off.

She told me my husband, Furman, was hunched over his desk on the telephone the whole time, so she had to talk to one of the girls there instead. The girl said there was one price for small lots of starter and she couldn't give discount. Mrs. Beske asked if Furman was ever going to get off the phone. She had to shout to get herself heard over the sudden noise of the blowers when one of the men opened the office door and brought in a sewn bag from the machine. The girl shouted back that Furman was pretty much on the phone recently. Then the door shut, which made the office suddenly quiet. The man balancing the feed on his shoulder, the office girl, and Mrs. Beske all heard Furman say, "I guess this has to be good-bye for now, Tom."

I didn't pay attention to it, because in our town Mrs. Beske wasn't much. When she wasn't trying to clip Furman at the elevator and all the businesspeople on Main Street, she was complaining that the interim pastor was perverted or crazy or senile. Everyone knows you don't criticize an interim pastor. She always angled to cause trouble, and her one kid, LeRoy, was as ugly-minded as she was.

In the next week, Furman started having long telephone conversations with Tom Gall from our house. Tom had been hired as Clayton's first school psychologist. He invited Furman to go with him when he drove down to Grand Rapids or over to Bemidji or even all the way to Duluth for psychological conferences. Until Tom Gall came to town, Furman was an ordinary, nice man, a good father to our Freddie and Faye. After the Galls came, Furman asked me to be especially nice to Mercein. I agreed it would be hard to be new in town. Furman said, "It isn't just that: it's that Tom has told me that Mercein has many serious problems, things that blocked her from being happy like a normal woman." Then I knew there was some kind of new situation here: Furman and I used to talk about a lot of different things, but they weren't about someone being blocked from being happy. We talked about the kids' artwork at school and the Clayton football team and ordinary incidents at the elevator and work around the farmstead—Furman part-time farmed our eighty, as well as working at the elevator.

Carol Bly

By the middle of October, Furman joined the Jaycees, which he had never been interested in before. I was glad, because I thought he could have more ambition than he had. Then I found out he joined the Jaycees because Tom Gall was offering a business psychology course to them on alternate Monday noons and nights. Furman also asked me to arrange going to the PTA and Artmobile and other doings at the same time Mercein and Tom Gall would be there.

We were shaking hands after church with the interim pastor, and Furman told him he had always wanted to sing in the choir but he guessed he was too shy to ask. The interim pastor told the choir director to get Furman in there.

Next Sunday, there was Furman in a navy blue robe beside Tom Gall, with the tenors. Tom Gall could read parts, so Furman said he kind of got the note from Tom and then bellowed it out because they needed more sound from the tenors and Furman's voice was all right. When you have lived with an ordinary man for fifteen years and know him, it is a peculiar feeling to see him decked out in those navy blue robes up there. And instead of coming right back to the farm on Wednesday nights after practice, Furman went for coffee with Tom.

Mercein had a five-sevenths appointment to teach art at the elementary and help Grayzie, the Artmobile director, with the exhibits. She had time on her hands. She and Tom hadn't any children, the way Furman and I and all our other friends had. None of us people in Clayton, even the ones right in town and definitely those of us living in the country, really ever hung around with the high-school teachers. Since Furman asked me to hang around with Mercein because it would mean so much to Tom, I got to know her all right but also I got to know Grayzie, a twenty-seven-year-old art teacher, who was famous for being someone the kids really liked. He was gay, but he never made passes at anyone in our town or in any of the six other towns where he took the Artmobile, so we all trusted him. He was a slow-moving bear of a man. He and Mercein could do British accents together, not just ending every sentence with "Old son" and "Old chap," which even our Freddie could do, but real-sounding ones. Grayzie was kind, too. He told me not to worry about Furman and Tom. Furman wasn't going to be homosexual, he said. Tom wasn't homosexual. Grayzie said Furman had longed for a mentor and now he had one. Give it a year and it's gone, he told me, patting my shoulder with his big, soft hand.

Day after day in October and early November that year, Mercein drove fast into our farmyard around two o'clock, promising to get me back to the farm before the school bus dropped off Freddie and Faye. Then we drove fast into town, the half mile of township road, the three miles of Minnesota 73. She parallel parked the Chevette very snappily alongside the football field. There were other cars parked along there, too. I never paid them any attention until Mercein told me they were doing the same thing we were doing.

Mercein was opening her box of charcoals and settling her sketch pad against the steering wheel.

"Now, that much I know isn't true!" I said with a laugh, but it was a nervous laugh, because even though I was one hundred percent sure those other women in those cars weren't making charcoal sketches, I always turned out to be

Carol Bly

wrong when I disagreed with Mercein about anything. Worse than wrong: I always turned out to have said something that had been acceptable before Furman and I met Mercein and Tom but now was either false or shabby sounding. Mercein was the first human being I had met who didn't lie about anything.

"I know those guys are not sketching," I said.

"Neither are we," Mercein said, throwing her head back. She had long black hair, with some silver very noticeable in it. Her facial skin was unusually white, and there were dark circles under her eyes. Her face was finely made. She had shadows under her cheekbones the way women in comic strips have—the ones who smoke cigarettes in long holders and lead astray men like Steve Canyon or Rex Morgan. That was another thing: she smoked hundreds of cigarettes every day.

Mercein was drawing the football team members' legs.

"You are too sketching," I said.

"No," Mercein said in her languid way. "No—no. I am doing the same thing you are doing. I am looking at the butts of the boys when they bend over for the huddle. Yup," she said leisurely. "Looking at how those silvery pants made of that snaky stuff draws tight against their incredible butts. However, nothing in life lasts forever. Soon they straighten up and go running off to their line. Then I sketch for a while."

She checked the rearview mirror and all around the car. Then she loosened the fifth of Vat 69 wedged between the hand brake and the passenger seat. She offered me a swig in her mannerly way. I always took a small sip. In 1975 it was not yet OK to turn down an alcoholic beverage, even if you were getting to think the person offering it was on the way to alcoholism. While the whiskey I had taken made me shudder a little, I daydreamed that I was an intense person like Mercein. I dreamed I had not married Furman because he was uncomplicated and I thought I could trust him.

A few snowflakes swung down. They were scant, but it was the first snow of the year and I had the whiskey inside me, so I felt something. I felt special. Mercein had told me just the week before *never* to talk about anything or anybody being "special," but the fact is that snow looked that way to me. The boys struck each other in the scrimmage: we heard the creak and thunk of their pads across the cold field.

Mercein said, "Yup, that's right, fellows, go to it, all you junior Einsteins. Men have been doing that since the Lascaux caves," she remarked. "One! Two! Hike! Everyone hit everyone else as hard as you can."

I was just about to say, "I guess you don't think too much of football, then," but I could tell it wouldn't have the right tone. In my few weeks' friendship with Mercein I had learned from her, and from Furman indirectly after he got it from Tom: if you haven't got any particular opinion or feeling about something, don't say anything. Don't say, "That's the way it goes, I guess" or "If there's one thing that doesn't change, it's human nature." Whenever I said things like that to Mercein she said, "Christ, Cheryl" or "Jesus, Cheryl." That was another thing. Literally no one else in Clayton, no other women I knew of, said "Christ" or "Jesus" to each other about anything. I don't expect anyone else said anything that brought it on.

Mercein lighted a cigarette. "Here's something f.y.i.," she said. "See how the boys' socks fall down when they bend over

Carol Bly

like that? See that? What happens is, the pants tighten up behind their knees, and the lower leg, the calf part, bulges, so their socks fall down. OK. Notice how their socks lie around their ankles in those messy, chaotic rings?"

I have to say one thing: if I had to be thrown together with Mercein so much of the time, at least it never got boring.

"Folds," she said slowly, drawing quickly with her charcoal. "Folds and shadow in them. No matter whether you're working in charcoal or crayons or oil or anything, whenever cloth folds it makes shadow. After you draw in the shadow, you take and wipe a thin rim clear around the outer edge of each fold, so it shows how it picks up light because it is uppermost and outside."

She did it awfully well. Her drawing looked exactly like those boys' socks and legs.

She glanced at me and smiled. "Yes," she said, as if agreeing with whatever was in my face. "A good drawing is a wonderful thing, let's face it."

She added, "So if someone comes up to the car and knocks on the window and says, 'What are you two nice ladies doing sitting out here staring at those young fellows' behinds, anyway?' I would instantly show them this drawing."

I said, "You really *are* an artist, though. Everyone in town knows that already. Grayzie says without you the Artmobile would go total zip. And even my little Faye loves the drawing lessons with you."

Mercein rolled her eyes. "But that is not why I am studying those boys."

"Why are you, then?" I said. "You mean you don't really study those boys the way an artist studies things?"

The Tomcat's Wife   119

"Jesus, Cheryl," she said. "Next you'll be telling me a doctor doesn't see a woman patient as a woman."

I thought of all the prenatal examinations in the state of Minnesota alone, including the sixteen of them I had had for Freddie and Faye. Then I thought of all the Pap smears in the world, not just those in the past but those in the future. I was thirty-four then, so if I had one every two years and lived to be seventy-eight or eighty, that would be twenty more Pap smears still coming up just for me alone, and people live longer these days, so I might get to be ninety-five, even.

"Jesus, Cheryl," Mercein said, tossing back some more whiskey. "Next you'll be telling me a psychotherapist doesn't see his women patients as women."

I told her, "You're the one who's lived in the Twin Cities and Grand Rapids and everywhere and knows all this stuff. How would I know any psychotherapists?" Back then we didn't even have a mental health center anywhere near Clayton.

"Well," she said slowly. "You know Tom. Of course, he isn't a real therapist yet, but he has sat in on a lot of workshops and he looks forward to taking on some clients. He's going to talk to the Lutheran Social Service guy about sitting in on some of their sessions here too."

Then the coaches blew their whistles. The tinny windblown sound of it came across the fields to us. We watched the boys, hulking under their pads, drift away in bunches, like dark clouds.

"Mind you," Mercein said, in the foreign accent she sometimes got when she had drunk a lot already that day, "to watch those boys, now . . . it makes your heart stop, actually."

"Why?" I asked. "I like watching them OK."

Mercein matter-of-factly wedged the bottle back into its place and started the car. "Yup," she said. "I like watching them, too. They look wonderful. And fortunately from here we can't hear anything they are saying. But if we were closer we would hear all their stupid remarks and their stupid jokes, and it would remind us that they will grow up to be really pointless. They look good—right now—from here. In three or four years they will mostly be idiots. Makes your heart stop to think of it."

Then she said, "Cheryl, how about just driving around another five minutes?"

We went through this every time. "Take me home, please, Mercein. You can come in, though, when we get there. The kids are always glad to see you. You can talk to me while I start supper."

She laughed. "Jesus, Cheryl. Next you'll be telling me that mothers are thrilled to get home in the late afternoons so they can start supper for the kids and show an interest in their schoolwork and sit around the kitchen table and praise their art projects!"

I felt ashamed, because I was feeling just the way she supposed I was feeling. As she drove down 73 I made a mental picture of me already home, cutting up green pepper and onions, melting butter, and then frying all that a little. Then adding chopped raw potatoes and the better part of a can of Carnation milk, then coarse pepper, and then putting it in the oven for about a half hour. I could not decide one way or the other about browning hamburger to go in. I half wanted to, but sometimes it is nice to have a dish that has not got any

The Tomcat's Wife

browned meat in it. Also, since Furman had been talking to Tom Gall so much, he had this new idea that he would go vegetarian.

Mercein took her eyes off the road to glance at me. "I see you *are* looking forward to seeing your kids." She gave me one of her deep-voiced laughs. I looked into my lap.

Back then, people always smiled when they had their pictures taken. Ordinary people had the idea you looked prettier when you smiled. We would all put on a full, open-mouthed laugh for our pictures.

"You don't like my laugh," she said, looking at the road, making the turn onto the township road. "Never mind. Tom says that people in pain always have ugly laughs. Also, the rich have ugly laughs. That's why they always pose for pictures very sober."

With a person like Mercein, there weren't a lot of places where I could jump into the conversation with confidence. She knew more. She analyzed things. I never analyzed anything before the Galls came to town. People were what they were. They knew what they knew. Whenever there was a chance for me to tell her anything I really was sure of, I would try. Now I said, "People always smile when they pose for pictures."

"Not the rich," Mercein informed me. "They—the women— know it is shallow to spend your whole life improving your tennis backhand or your parallel turn, so they put on sad looks in photos so you will be struck with how classical and womanly they are. If they are all that sad and classical and womanly, they should slit their wrists," Mercein said with one of her laughs.

Mercein was remarkable-looking when she wasn't jeering

Carol Bly

at herself or laughing. That word, "remarkable," got going around the Jaycees when the Galls came to town and Tom Gall started the course in business psych. When Furman took to Tom that much, he started using his language, which is how I got used to it. Tom had told Furman that Grayzie was remarkable. He said Mrs. Beske was remarkable. I didn't see the sense in either of those remarks. Mrs. Beske was extra poor and extra stingy. She slept with not one but both of the drivers who carried the bus service up from Minneapolis to Clayton. The buses stopped overnight in Clayton, because we were so near the Canadian border. Next morning, the drivers drove the morning service back down to the Twin Cities. When they changed drivers on that route, everyone in our church said, "Good. Mrs. Beske can keep her pillowcases cleaner now." Then she started sleeping with the substitute driver. All that was interesting and got talked over at Circle meetings, but I couldn't see it was remarkable. I didn't think Grayzie was remarkable, either. He was unique, being the only gay whom no one even thought of running out of town, but basically he was overweight for a person in his twenties, and lazy. A lot of his Artmobile exhibits, including I am sorry to say the recent one called "Ancient China and Her Arts," were really boring, even for us people who didn't exactly expect Mona Lisa to step off the bus at our Jack Rabbit station.

Furman started saying that things and people were remarkable. When he watched football with Freddie, our thirteen-year-old, he would say, "Here, hand her over here a second, Freddie," and Freddie would hand over our Mother Cat, who was allowed in the house on Sundays and at special times. Furman told the cat, "You are a remarkable animal.

Also very pregnant." I felt two things at one time: I was happy I had a husband who enjoyed his family life and was a sweet-tempered father. I also felt doom, because all that September and October and part of November he said words and whole sentences he got straight from Tom Gall.

When we got home Mercein followed me right into our house. She did what lonely people do: they learn quickly the customs of your home and then they pour into any space you don't physically lock them out of. Mercein thoughtfully brushed the new light snow off her shoes and then sat in a kitchen chair and leaned both elbows on the table. She was nice about not smoking. I started to cut up vegetables.

"Do you have time to talk now?" she said from behind me.

The school bus was due in four minutes.

"Oh, well," she said. She started going on about how well Faye drew in class. I didn't listen much because the chopped pepper smelled strangely fresh; although the snow was settling down to serious fall outside, this quavery smell of pepper coming up to me from the knife was like a pang of summer. Someone in my Circle at church once said she was cutting an orange in August and the smell brought her a pang of Christmas, like pine smell. I am not saying that the kind of feeling is deep or remarkable or anything like what Mercein was talking about from behind me, but it gave me a feeling, so I stopped listening to Mercein and thought about the pepper smell. Anyway, I wasn't used to listening to anyone hours on end the way Mercein seemed to want me to. Grayzie said, "Oh, one more motormouth won't break the town wide open."

Now she said more loudly, "I wanted to tell you something

Carol Bly

Tom said last night, but I suppose Freddie and Faye will be home in a second, won't they?"

"They get a kick out of it when you're here when they get home," I said. I quit cutting peppers and went to onions. "Especially Faye when you look at her pictures and help her."

"I can tell Freddie would rather get home and find just you here," she said.

"You know kids," I said from my repertoire of things to say when nothing you say is going to do it. Every day when Freddie got home he followed me around, whatever I was doing. He had not gotten his height yet. He was a fine-made boy, with huge hands hung at the delicate wrists like upside-down parachutes. Every day he was hassled by a bully on the bus, Mrs. Beske's rotten kid, LeRoy. LeRoy teased him on the way in to school, and then on the way home. Freddie was nervous about it all the time.

"Freddie is always real tired when he gets home," I said.

"Tired, shit," Mercein said. "Jesus, Cheryl, can't you see that when people act tired what they are is distressed?"

"Well," I said, not trying to be pleasant since I didn't cotton to being told I didn't understand my own children. "There's such a thing as making a—"

She interrupted me with her ugly laugh. "No! No! Cheryl! Don't *do* it!" she shouted. "Don't tell me not to make a mountain out of a molehill! Aaagh!"

Right away I felt hot.

Mercein said in a quieter voice, "All the molehills are mountains, Cheryl. I got news for you."

That was another of Tom Gall's phrases: "I got news for you." Furman said it all the time.

The Tomcat's Wife 125

Mercein said, "Christ, Cheryl, next time you'll be telling me that if a person just looks on the bright side . . . Shit, I don't even want to finish the rest of the sentence."

Then the children came swooping in. Mercein greeted them and did not sound especially drunk. She and Faye leaned over one of the construction-paper drawings Faye laid on the table. Freddie came over to me and jammed himself between me and the trash can beside the stove. "You can stir," I told him. "Mother Cat keeps trying to get in," I told him. "I think she's having those kittens pretty soon now. She scratched at the kitchen storm door all morning."

Freddie said, "Yeah, Mom, she did? She did? Mom, what do you think? You know what happened last time! You remember, all right! All those little kitties except the one?"

Around our country, the tomcats never stayed on the farms. As soon as a male kitten grew up, it wandered off and joined a pack of wild tomcats that roved around from farm to farm, living wild. The females stayed if you let them, and became what we called good farm cats—that is, they kept the outbuildings free of mice. What they didn't care to eat they killed, anyway, and brought up to the kitchen door to show you. Our Mother Cat left all her kills on the iron-grate boot mat. Whenever our Mother Cat had new kittens, she had all she could do, night after night, to fight off the roving tomcats. The toms systematically went around from farm to farm, biting new kittens in the neck. I had handled the situation in two ways. The first time the toms killed a litter, the children wanted a funeral. They dug a mass grave south of the machinery building. They found a Bidding Prayer in the front of the old red hymnal. Faye said the prayer, and Freddie pushed the shoveled dirt down onto the crowded little shoulders and heads. The next time we lost a whole litter to the toms, I didn't tell the children at all. I said, "Something must have happened to the kittens, I guess." Anyway, the church stopped using that hymnal with those ancient prayers in it.

"So, Mom? So, Mom?" Freddie said.

"You fix her up someplace either in the cellar or in your closet, but she doesn't get the run of the house. She can be in the living room during television, but someone has to be watching her. I don't want the house smelling of cat's business."

He was gone fast as light.

Mercein wanted to know if I could walk her out to her car. On the way out we passed Freddie coming in, with his arms full of Mother Cat. His face was all grins, hers very cool. I said to Mercein, "I am always surprised how cats keep their cool. A human being can be all the way excited about something, but a cat just keeps its cool." Before Tom and Mercein got to be such good friends of Furman and me, I didn't say those observations if I had them. *If* I had them. I could hardly remember if I thought about things before Tom and Mercein came to town.

"Cool! Christ, Cheryl," Mercein said. "cats aren't *cool:* They're inimical!"

I got sick of asking Mercein what different words meant that she used, so I decided I'd wait and look it up later. Inimical. What I mean to say is, it was something new in our lives to have such interesting people around. Ask Furman, who was always trying to get to any meeting he thought Tom would be at. And offering to drive Tom to the out-of-town psychology things he went to, in case Mercein needed their car or anything. The interim pastor said Tom Gall was stimulating. What I mean, though, is I didn't want to be stimulated all the time. I wasn't used to it. Sometimes I just wanted to live the way I lived before, doing the things adults do when they are married and raising kids on an eighty near an OK little town and their husband runs the eighty and also the elevator.

We stood outside in the falling snow a moment. Furman had put in one of those yard lights that knows to go on as soon as it gets dark. Now it cracked on with its blue-green glow. Mercein leaned against their dirty Chevette and took out a cigarette. What went through my mind is, Now she will have to send that raincoat to the cleaners.

"Wait a minute," she said. She bent into the car and came back out with the Vat 69.

"You?"

"I got the kids home and all," I said.

Mercein said, "Last night here is what Tom said. It was just last night, and he said this. Now, what he said was. . . . Let me see now. Let's see," Mercein said. "I need to get this right. What he said. . . . Well, what he said was, the reason that we didn't. . . . Christ, Cheryl, this is going to be worse than I thought."

She took a huge drink, which I thought she didn't need.

"What he said was, the reason that I didn't have kids is that my vagina is frightened and so it has turned to steel and iron and it is locked out of fear."

She drank again and then smiled. "Yup! That's it!" she said. "That's it! Other people's vaginas are made of blood and skin, and mine is made of metal, and it's locked. Locked out of fear of womanhood. Yes—that was the last part: locked out of fear of womanhood. I nearly forgot that part."

We both looked out to the edge of the driveway, to where the yard light didn't reach. It just barely picked out the tassels of the headland corn, which Furman always picked last. My problem was whether to act surprised that Tom said that. I had heard that he knew all about locked wombs and vaginas before, because he had told Furman, and Furman had explained it all to me. Once I remember we were lying in bed, and I said, "That's hard to believe," and Furman said, "Well, the remarkable fact is that the truth is always hard to believe. The real, inner truths are, but once you learn to believe them," he added, "'Tom says life is never the same again because you are alive in ways you never were before." It sounded like something to think about, all right, but it had to wait, because we were both tired, and I know I fell asleep then.

I didn't know what to say to Mercein. Who wants to be told, "Oh, I didn't know you had a iron womb!" Finally I decided to say something not completely loyal to Furman. "I don't guess I believe that, Mercein," I said. "I guess if it was me and I wanted children, I'd go get tested or whatever they do."

After another minute or so she climbed into the car. We arranged that both couples would meet at the Artmobile at seven o'clock the next night. Grayzie and Mercein had finally closed down the exhibit on ancient China and Her Arts and were starting "Artists Look at Our Life: Our Kids' Art." It was expected to be a success. No one had gone to the China exhibit except the people who support all community efforts at anything. "Artists Look at Our Life" was present times at least, and even if kids can't paint well, they're just kids, so you can allow, especially when it's your own kids.

On the way back into the house I figured out the rest of the hot dish and decided to brown some hamburger and dump it in, after all. Tom and Mercein had argued Furman into being a vegetarian, but it didn't completely take. Furman explained to me about three thousand times that if you ate lightly—vegetables, not hamburger—you will have remarkable insights flying in and out of your head, but I noticed that when we had hamburger, Furman put his elbows and forearms on the table and he ate as much as Faye and Freddie. As long as I didn't use the actual words "Do you want seconds of meat, Furman?" he would help himself to more. One insight I had before the Galls ever got to town was that if you don't use actual words about what they're planning to do, people will do pretty much whatever they've always done.

When the hot dish was in the oven, I went upstairs. Freddie lay on his bed with Mother Cat. She was absentmindedly clawing up tufts out of the chenille bedspread.

"Do you think she will have kittens tonight, Mom?"

I said, "You'd think all the years we've had that cat around, I'd know. But I can't tell." I sat down and we both petted the cat a while. I lifted the claw that was tearing up the chenille; old Mother Cat instantly drew her claws in. I pressed the pads though, and the sharp tips stuck out again.

Freddie and I talked about where cats get their purr.

After a few minutes, Freddie said, "That sucker told me

Carol Bly

that if he felt like it he would push me all the way out of the bus some day."

"The Beske kid," I said.

Freddie told me three or four cruel things LeRoy Beske had said, right in front of all those girls who rode that bus and the little kids up front.

Finally I said, "Here is this mean kid giving you a bad time, while his mother is always hanging around the elevator trying to skin Dad in some deal. She always wants money off everything, even though she's the tiniest customer he's got. Her with her half a pound of chick starter and then could she have some oyster shells thrown in? Anyway, she is losing her farm, it turns out. My Circle's serving that auction on Saturday."

"Mom, you won't say anything to anyone about LeRoy pushing me around?"

"No."

Freddie said, "Maybe you could poison the barbecue at the auction, and he would die a very painful death. They would think it was suicide."

"Yeah, that's right, Freddie," I said. "They *would* go around saying it was suicide, but you and I would know it was murder but we would never let on." I gave Mother Cat a last scratch under her ears. "I would have to spend the whole day at the auction trying to keep other people from eating the poisoned batch of barbecue mix."

Freddie said, laughing, "They'd say, 'Mrs. Hastad, how come you don't let us have any of that wonderful-smelling batch over there in the crock-pot? How come, Mrs. Hastad?'"

I left Freddie talking aloud to himself: "So then you'd say, you'd say, let's see, you'd say . . ."

The best way to get through a kids' exhibit at Grayzie's Artmobile was to do it on a double date. Furman and I met Tom and Mercein, who were standing around smoking in the lighted area beside the trailer. The Artmobile trailer was a project of Minnesota Citizens for the Arts and a whole lot of other organizations, mostly located in the Twin Cities. When Grayzie had it in our town it would be parked on the far edge of the football practice field, and everyone who had anything going for them in community leadership made sure they were seen checking out every new exhibit. There were men standing around breathing smoke, with their blousy Hollofil jackets open, delaying going in. Their wives would be inside the Artmobile, pretending to be as interested in other women's kids' artwork as they were in their own. We all stood around, stalling before going up the little staircase.

Mercein said that the Artmobile would be the perfect place to hide spent plutonium rods. I had to ask her what spent plutonium rods were, since I could see Furman didn't know, either, but would feel foolish to have to ask. "They could paint two or three thousand trailer rigs like this," Mercein explained, with one of her laughs, "white, with 'Art' or 'Culture' written in Caslon Bold on the sides big as life, and then pick up the rods in Charleston harbor and drive them wherever they like in the countryside and just park them in some schoolyards. No one ever goes into any culture site unless they have to because the town is behind it. All that

Carol Bly

radiation could just sort itself out slowly over those school-yards for the next fifty thousand half-lives."

Tom turned to Furman and said that when women got into what sounded like animals but was something he called animus, they got sharp opinions on every subject that came up. The way you could tell, he went on, that they were in their animus was that their opinions were always unpleasant and were designed to make people listening feel just slightly more miserable than they may otherwise have been feeling.

Furman said, "Yeah, Tom . . . I think I get the sort of thing you mean."

I did not marry Furman Hastad for his brains, and he never said he was Einstein, so I told myself there was no reason to feel hot when he pretended to understand things he probably didn't.

Now Grayzie shouted to the fifteen or sixteen of us standing around in the half dark, "Welcome, everybody! Welcome, folks! Come on up now! Welcome the true art done in your community! Hi, everybody! Come on, Tom and Furman, lead the way! Hi, Mercein—come on, Cheryl—all right, everybody! This is something special!" We all went in.

People in Clayton envied Mercein and me because our husbands went into church affairs and art affairs without being herded. The other men in town would drive their wives there, all right, but then they would hang around outside in their thick jackets, making jokes. "Yeah, you got a deer license, Orrin? You need a deer license like you need a hole in your head," and then someone else says, "What *you* going to do with a deer license, Merv? Use it to prove you're old enough to quit drinking, or what?" and everyone haw haw haws. I never could figure out the humor in men's jokes. Furman told me that October that Tom had explained it to him: The jokes did not have to be especially funny; the point was to keep up a jeering level to prevent self-pity.

Mercein said, "That is why the boys are so cute in football practice. They haven't got the joking perfect yet. But every locker-room shower session takes them closer and closer. Makes your heart stop to think of it."

Finally a whole group of us were slowly going around the U-shaped aisle of the Artmobile. Clayton Elementary School kids' drawings were matted and hung on the walls, and flat projects of various kinds covered the long, narrow center table. Grayzie had followed us in, and now he stood on a housewives' stepladder at the rear. "Your attention for one second, folks!" he called to us. "Welcome to art of the present! Now, we had art from the far past, and starting this coming Monday we will be having a very special look at things *future*—but for the weekend, here it is: the present, and best of all, your own children's interpretation of it. As you walk around, of course you want to find our own kids' work first and admire it! After all—it's the best of the bunch!" This got a laugh. "But then I suggest you go around and say, 'Well— here is how kids see the world around them. Here's some- thing they're trying to say.' Now—have fun, everybody!" And Grayzie let his large body down, his hands outward, deli- cately balancing as he came off the step.

Freddie's "America at Night" project lay on the center table. It was a wide, shallow box, whose lid was a dark blue painting of a United States map, with tiny flashlight bulbs at each of the capitals. On one edge there were forty-eight halves

Carol Bly

of tongue depressors on springs. Each had a state name rub-off lettered onto it. Wiring ran from the depressors under the map to all the capital cities' locations. Since Freddie had used paper clips for part of the electric wiring, you had to be careful when you touched the project.

Furman hung over the map a second. I could see he was pleased with it, but Furman never shows much. He was about to continue on around the trailer, when Tom Gall gave a shout. He gathered us all around the map. "This is one hell of a wonderful project!" he shouted. He pressed the Minnesota lever, and not just St. Paul lit up: Grand Rapids and Clayton and St. Cloud and Duluth lighted up too. "Look how bright the cities are at night," Tom said, smiling down at the map. "Then look at all the countryside asleep in all that navy blue darkness!"

Freddie's project looked better now that Tom explained it that way. I imagined all the unlighted millions of farmsteads like ours.

Tom turned to Furman and me. "You can be proud of Freddie," he said. "They always assume a boy gets his abilities from his father, but some of it *definitely* comes from the mother—don't let them tell you different."

Then I felt sorry I didn't believe some of the things Furman told me Tom had said.

Mercein had walked over to one of the walls. She said, "Look. Here is someone in pain." She said it quietly so no one but us four would hear.

The drawing showed two semis that had just struck each other on the interstate. Every detail of the trucks' brake lines and spare-wheel carriers showed. The interstate sign was

The Tomcat's Wife

drawn exactly. Some black crayon lines radiated from the trucks' smashed engines; the words "Pow!" and "Smash!" appeared in clouds at the outer ends of those lines.

Tom jerked one shoulder and said lightly, "That's not pain. That's just TV imprinting. Imprinting on a kid's mind is all. Who did that?" He bent his tall body so he could make out the signature. "Oh, yes! That kid! No," he said, "that's just your regular old USA violent-culture imprinting."

Furman said, "Cheryl and I have cut down on the amount of TV Freddie and Faye get to watch."

"That's very good, Furmy," Tom said. "Very good! A strong stand like that, especially from the man, makes a difference."

By then our group had made its way all around the trailer. Grayzie asked us to go down the front little staircase so the next group could come in the back. Mrs. Beske came running up. She looked rapidly over Furman and Tom and Mercein, as if to see if she dared interrupt. "Do you have a minute?" she said to me.

She took me by the elbow over to the parked cars, out of the street lighting.

She said, "I wanted to tell you I heard about how your Church Circle didn't want to serve lunch at my auction."

"We *are* serving your auction," I said. "My Circle is the one that's doing it, Mrs. Beske."

"I heard that," she said. "I heard you were the one made them do it, too." She went on in her slaty voice: "I heard people talked. . . ."

She heard right. Every month, the Stewardship Committee and the Circles met in the Fellowship Hall. I happened to be chairperson in 1975, so I was at the meeting. They planned all the weddings and they planned a schedule for the funerals, so when anyone died, each Circle knew if it was their turn to serve the funeral. Then they planned the lighter-weight stuff, like serving barbecues at farm auctions. We never even baked for those: we bought the doughnuts at the two bakeries, the Catholic one and the Lutheran one, so there wouldn't be feelings. We used the same barbecue recipe that had been thumbtacked inside the custodian's closet for as long as I had worked in that church at all, which would have been when I was in Luther League. It was a pretty good recipe; kind of a big sugar hit, but it tasted good at a freezing-cold auction.

At the end-of-August meeting, someone said that as a Christian Circle chairperson she didn't feel she could ask her Circle members to serve at a whore's auction, and she was very sorry but you had to draw the line somewhere.

When I rejoined Furman and Tom and Mercein, Tom was explaining to the other three that Grayzie was most likely unconscious of his own sexuality. Tom said, "In an unconscious little town like this, it is perfectly possible for a homosexual to be absolutely unconscious that he *is* a homosexual. Very likely the case with Grayzie."

Furman agreed, doing the nodding-several-times thing he had picked up from Tom.

Furman knew perfectly well that Grayzie was openly careful to have his social life in some other place. Two years earlier, some people had gotten juiced at the VFW and beaten up someone they said was homosexual. At an Artmobile meeting the following week, Grayzie had said cheerfully, "Probably get me next time!" and we all assured him that he was perfectly safe and very well respected. We told him that because he was originally from Grand Rapids or the Twin Cities, he didn't understand how the very small towns work: nine-tenths of the time men said they were going to straighten out some gay at the edge of town, they never got around to it. Furman knew that Grayzie was not unconscious of being gay, so I felt cross that he went along with Tom's remark.

On the way home I said, "How come you went along with Tom about Grayzie when you know better?"

Furman kept his eyes on the road. "I don't know," he said finally.

The next morning was very cold. Two distant relatives of Mrs. Beske's set up a cylinder-shaped gas blower-heater for us in the tools building of Mrs. Beske's farmyard. Mercein and another lady and I tied our price list to the stringer behind us. We plugged the crock-pot of barbecue mix and the two coffeepots into the drop cords and then spread our tables with white roller paper. We had twelve muffin tins for the nickels, dimes, and quarters. We kept the dollars and fives sticking out from under a breadboard, the way children keep their Monopoly money during a game. The blower roared and sent old hay wisps flying, but the feeling came back into our feet as we stood waiting for trade. Mrs. Beske herself came in and of course asked for a freebie. Since we were ready a quarter hour before anything really started, we took turns going out and walking around the flatbeds full of junk for auction, keeping our arms crossed over our chest, the wind lifting our aprons. Returning to duty, we discussed how none of the pillows or sheets would go, not even the old ones

Carol Bly

from the 1950s, when people embroidered them for wedding presents. We figured that about one hundred times that day people would say you never knew who slept on *these* and how many at a time. I saw Mrs. Beske's son, LeRoy, go by, dragging a rolled-up carpet. I took his measure and realized he would be a handful for Freddie, all right. He looked at least five foot ten.

Grayzie wandered in and ate a barbecue. "I love auctions," he said, keeping us company for a few minutes. "I always pick up old satin and velvet dresses. Oh, don't look so shocked, Cheryl. It's not for drag; it's for costumes for the kids' art projects and all."

Then, just when the crowd started coming and we had our hands full, Mercein said to me, "I have to go home, Cheryl."

"Oh, no!" I said.

"Don't discount what I say," she snapped. "I said I have to go home. That means I have to go home. I think I'm coming down with something."

That afternoon Furman was going along with Tom to a Psychological Outreach to Rural Communities session in St. Cloud, so I didn't see Mercein again until Sunday in church.

She looked even paler than usual in the navy blue choir robe. When they all stood for the anthem, Mercein in the second row with the other altos, Tom and Furman in the tenors' row just behind her, I could see she wasn't paying attention to the director. I still didn't worry about her, because everyone is absentminded some of the time, my guess being those deeper-thinking types are like that even more than us others. I don't know that; it's just a guess. Still.

I didn't pay much attention to the sermon because we still had just the interim pastor. We didn't know him very well. He didn't know us. You can't get terribly interested in people who obviously aren't going to stay in town. As we shook hands in the doorway, I told him thank you for the interesting sermon.

The first part of that afternoon was happy. Furman and Faye and Freddie all sat on the living-room floor. They were going to watch the Vikings play the Steelers and told me to watch if I wanted to see something good. Freddie explained that I couldn't go out in the kitchen and expect to be called when there was a Bradshaw-Swann pass, because a pass situation comes up so fast it'd be over by the time I got back to the living room to see. I had things I wanted to do in the kitchen, but I remembered how Mercein was always telling me, "Put people before things, Cheryl." People before things. I told the family I'd watch the first quarter, then.

The game had just started when the telephone rang. It was Grayzie. He was at the hospital, because Mercein Gall had tried to commit suicide an hour before, and did I know where Tom was? I explained he was back in St. Cloud, at the wrap-up of yesterday's conference.

"Furman!" I called into the living room. "We need to reach Tom. Where is that conference at? Mercein's bad."

Furman called back, "I wouldn't bother Tom at that meeting."

Finally Furman got the idea I wasn't going to shout what was wrong over the children's heads. He came and stood near me at the telephone. He took the receiver then and told Grayzie he should call the Sunshine Motel in St. Cloud and ask for the school psychologists' conference.

Furman followed me to the far end of the kitchen. "That was really a hostile thing for Mercein to do," he said. "What a terrific guilt trip to lay on Tom! To do a thing like that when Tom's away. Boy, that's hostile."

"Hostile" was a word like "remarkable": I wasn't just sure about it, so I didn't say anything.

Freddie gave a whoop, so we both went and stood in the kitchen doorway. On the television behind him I saw a player rise up way above the others like an acrobat: his arms clenched around the football up there, and then he fell down amidst a crowd of players on both sides.

"That's your Lynn Swann!" Furman said. "That's him!"

Furman decided to wait at home with the kids. He thought Tom might telephone and he could stand by him—go with him to the hospital if he wanted.

I certainly was not much at prophesying. As I drove from my healthy and happy farmhouse to town and the hospital, I thought sure I would get depressed when I got into room 101, which was where they put all the emergencies. I imagined Mercein lying there with her wrists all bandaged up, looking pale the way she always did anyhow, and me trying to say something appropriate and her scarcely answering, and Grayzie stalking around the waiting room feeling miserable and helpless.

It was not like that at all. For one thing, the moment I got outside 101 I remembered how back when Faye was born someone in 101 had moaned and cried aloud, rhythmically, nearly all the night. The maternity wing was just east of the nurses' station; 101 and 102 were just west of it, so we could hear across. When they brought me my fresh-juice ration at around two in the morning, I asked about who was crying and groaning. That was a stroke victim, the nurse explained. They do that, she said, in a reassuring voice. Then she added, This one needs to die. Don't think about him, she said. Drink your juice. I'll get your little girl in a sec.

All the rest of that night I had off and on thought about having a baby and then perhaps forty or fifty years later coming back to the same hospital and trying to die.

Now the memory returned. I pushed open the door of 101. Mercein was sitting on a wooden chair near the window; Grayzie was standing. They were laughing. Only one of Mercein's wrists was bandaged.

Mercein was telling Grayzie that she was the only person she knew who had tried to commit suicide who wanted to have the theme from *Masterpiece Theater* at her funeral. "I know you don't get to choose the music for your funeral if you have done a suicide attempt," she said. She and Grayzie both laughed.

"You can have any music you want," he told her. "You just can't have it *now*. You have to live a while. I wouldn't mind having the *Masterpiece Theater* theme at my funeral, now you mention it."

They were very high without drinking anything. I partly felt left out. I had prepared to say something like "I am so sorry, Mercein," but then I got into the room and there was all that hilarity. Finally I sat on the edge of the bed and smiled, because that's what both of them were doing.

They talked about *Upstairs, Downstairs* for a while. I couldn't join that, either, because no one in my family liked it. It just seemed like a soap with the wrong accents, we thought.

Carol Bly

"I live in some other world for about two hours after each episode," Mercein said.

"I have a fake British accent for two hours each time," Grayzie remarked. He gave Mercein a friendly smile. "I say," he said. "Mind *you,* that fellow looks a proper sod if ever I saw one."

A nurse came in and sang, "Time for temperature," as if Mercein were there with a head cold.

The interim pastor stuck his head in, looking shy. "You can come in," Grayzie said respectfully. "She has a thermometer in her mouth."

"Well, I just wanted to give you God's blessing," the pastor said.

We all lingered around a while, but there didn't seem to be anything to do or say. The hospital was keeping Mercein for the night.

"I suppose Tom is on his way?" she said to me when I picked up my jacket to go.

"He should be here soon," I said.

When I left through the waiting room, Tom came through the revolving door, his cheeks brilliant and red from the cold or from hurry.

"Don't leave," he said to me. "I want to talk to you."

"Mercein's been expecting you," I told him.

"Just a second," he said. "You see, Mercein has a lot to bear. She has a lot of real sadness to face. Frustration and anger. I knew that, but I didn't know she was this depressed."

We sat down on the plaid-covered chairs. Tom leaned toward me. "You see, Cheryl," he said, "she isn't in touch with what a woman is, the way you are. She has to face the fact

The Tomcat's Wife

she hasn't had any children. She definitely must be feeling that she has failed in some deep, horribly sad way. She's got to be feeling that. How else could she feel?"

I felt off center, somehow—from so many surprises in the last hour. An hour earlier, I was trying to understand how a ballet dancer could turn into a wide receiver. Then I was trying to understand how two good friends could be laughing and making gags in a hospital room right after one of them had made a suicide attempt. Now I was trying to understand whatever this point was Tom was making. I spoke up sharply, to my own surprise.

"I don't know how much Mercein feels about having children," I said.

Tom gave me a soft look. "Ah, Cheryl," he said. "You are a good loyal friend to her. But you mustn't get into denial about it, you know. She and I have openly talked about her feelings of failure, dozens of times."

That dumb waiting room with its dumb plaid-covered chairs and the beat-up magazines showing macho men dressed in sports clothes was not a kind of place to have a big personal-discovery experience, but that is what I did. I suddenly hated Tom. I stood up.

"She's been waiting in there for you, Tom," I said. "You're this big psychologist. Why don't you go in and talk to your wife once?"

When I got home, Freddie had the large cardboard box he had fitted up for Mother Cat on the living-room floor. Mother Cat kept lying down in it, then standing up, arching her back, turning around, and sitting down again. Then she would lie down for a moment or two and stand up again. On the

Carol Bly

flannel-covered bottom of the box were her new kittens. They needed another week to get cute-looking, but they already had the wonderful quality of kittens: you couldn't keep your eyes off them.

Furman wanted to know how Tom was bearing up. Then Faye came out of the kitchen and started drawing kittens, so Furman and I were distracted and couldn't talk.

All night I felt changed. It was certainly a new experience for me. In recent years there had been some prayer groups in our church, since prayer groups spread all across the United States in the late sixties and early seventies, so I had heard people in town going around saying they were changed, and they could tell you the exact moment they got changed. I didn't pay much attention, because most of those people who did all that religious changing were the lightweights around town anyhow, and besides, I had Freddie and later got pregnant with Faye. Just recently Mercein had told me there is a moment, now and then, when your life comes to a dead stop.

Next morning, the snow still covered the ground. After Furman and the children had left for work and school, I went around turning off all the lights they had left on: the yellow of the electric lighting gave way to the blue and gloomy snow light from outside. The house was shadowy. I sat down at the kitchen table without even looking at the dishes. I suddenly decided a lot of things *fast*. I decided I was a happy woman and I would live my life to the end, although I was in the middle of a somewhat boring marriage. I decided that although my marriage was a little boring I would stay in it. I decided I was a little bored with Mercein, too, no matter how insightful she was about everything. I decided I admired her honesty a lot but not completely and I was going to go back to saying things people around Clayton always say, since it didn't do any harm. I decided Tom was a mean man. I decided Grayzie was a human being to be taken seriously.

Grayzie! It brought me to the fact that in an hour or so he would be working on his new exhibit in the Artmobile. I decided I would drive into town and look at it.

He opened the trailer door with one of his fake-gallant bows. I peered into the darkness. "Come in, my dear, come in," Grayzie cried in one of the various accents he could do. This one was what he called his Basic Fulbright foreign accent, a kind of Transylvanian-blood-drinker-plus-Parisian-lady-killer accent. Grayzie was wearing a French Foreign Legion-style hat, with the visor in front and the neck flap in back, the whole thing made out of what I recognized as a blouse of Mrs. Beske's. I'd know that pink-and-light-green rayon plaid anywhere. He looked wild, but inside the shadowy Artmobile he had done something that knocked me out.

He had plastered the entire inside ceiling and walls of the trailer with brown-and-gray dirt—or plaster made to look like brown-and-gray dirt. Uneven strata of metamorphic rock stuck out here and there. Some roots and twigs hung from the ceiling. In one rounded, dark corner, two bright eyes looked out from an absolutely black hole. It was hard to see, since I had come in from the snowlit football field: in here everything was dark. Grayzie had laid old straw and some gravel on the floor. On the center table stood three lighted globes of the earth.

"Grayzie, how did you do it? Who helped you?" I put a finger on one cave wall: the substance of it was still wet.

Carol Bly

"It took me all last night," he said. "Isn't it wonderful? I have been dreaming of it for ages. I know we all long to go back to the cave times. I know it! I know it! So I have been dreaming it up, in bits and pieces, for years. Then I had this meeting set with Mercein for yesterday afternoon to do the center-table stuff," and he pointed at the lighted globes.

"We were going to plan the earth in the past, the earth in the present, and the earth in the future." He went on, "I got to her house at two-thirty. She had just done it," he said in a low voice. "She had just done it, Cheryl. Not five minutes before."

He brightened. "Well, so all last night I couldn't sleep! I thought I might as well work, so I came over and decided to get the whole thing done myself. It's a kind of present to her and to myself, too."

I went down the aisle to see the globes. Each one was lighted at its center, then painted with stained glass paint. In the first globe you could see the fiery gases of zillions of years B.C., already some molten and premetal, the crust still showing cracks full of fire; the seas were beginning, but they were seas the way Freddie and Faye free-drew the world when they tried to show Furman and me how much they knew of geography. The second globe was our world now, in its mantle of blue-and-white cloud, the way the world looks behind TV weather anchors. Tom Gall told Furman and Furman told me that some famous psychoanalyst had nearly died once, and when balanced between life and death he dreamed he was flying away from the globe and that it looked heartbreakingly beautiful in its blue-and-white winding cloth of cloud.

From the rear Grayzie called, "There's going to be sound effects, too. Here it is. French horn. Elgar. What do you think?"

Under the final globe, a plaque read: OUR EARTH, A.D. 65,000,000 YEARS. California was half gone. The Aleutians were too prominent. The East Coast was underwater. Other things were wrong. The midwest, my country, didn't show, because Grayzie had positioned blue-and-white clouds above it, but I knew it would be changed, too.

Grayzie now came over and stood next to me. We listened to what he called Elgar. I would have called it "Pomp and Circumstance," and I thought it was beautiful. I kept staring at the lighted earth.

"We'll all be dead by then," I said, not even caring if that was a dumb remark, because I was still in my strange new mood.

"That's my idea," Grayzie said. "The very thing I thought to myself."

I looked at him to smile. I saw now he was wearing a dickey of white cotton with handmade embroidered flowers on it. I knew instantly that he had bought a pillowcase of Mrs. Beske's at the auction and then sewn it so the embroidered part would show under his open shirt at the neck. He gave the plaid visor a soldierlike yank down. "Right!" he said snappily in the working-class one of his British accents. "All the shit that is going round now will be ended by then."

When I got outside I drove up to the hospital, but the nurses told me Mercein was sleeping and they didn't want her disturbed. They were going to keep her at least another night for observation. They added, "She's pretty anemic, you know."

I went home to wait for the children. I decided to make them a treat so I would get to feeling less strange.

"Cocoa!" they shouted, pleased.

Carol Bly

"Yeah, but listen," I said. We all sat at the table. "I have been thinking about that little drip LeRoy Beske."

"*Big* drip LeRoy, you mean," Freddie said, but he looked respectful and interested.

"I've been thinking about him," I repeated. "It's going to take the two of you, I figure. So here's the idea. Tomorrow morning, Freddie, you go to school but don't take your book bag. Take your books loose. You get into the bus, as usual. You sit halfway back, as usual. And Faye, you sit where you always sit.

"Now, as soon as the bus gets to the school grounds, let the little kids off first, the way you always do. Then, Faye, you hurry those sixth-grade girls. Tell them anything. But once they get off, don't let them start for the school building. Keep them around there."

"This is weird, Mom, " Faye said. "What do I tell them?"

"Just lie," I said. "Now, Freddie, you will have to hustle so you are down on the ground fast. Take each of your books and hand one to each girl and look her right in the face and say, 'Hold this for me, will you?' They'll take the book because people don't think fast. Believe me, kids, take it from your mom: people do not think fast. Then, Freddie, you'll see that the girls will stand around in a half circle. They may say a lot of negative stuff, but don't pay any attention."

"Will they *ever* say a lot of stuff," Faye said richly. "Words you hear only on school buses, Mom. They'll think it's really weird."

"But they'll stay around to see what's going on," I told her. I turned back to Freddie. "Freddie, now you turn around to face the bus doorway. When LeRoy Beske comes out and has one foot in the air but not on the ground and the other foot still bearing his weight on the lowest step, then you say very loudly, 'I forgot to tell you I don't like your tone of voice,' and you slug him as hard as you can just where the nose meets the forehead. If you get a second chance, hit him on just one eye. You need to get blood fast. Don't count on the second chance, Freddie. I looked over that kid at the Beske farm auction. So, as soon as you've hit him, once or twice, don't get smart and decide to stay for more. Turn around and walk up to each of those girls and thank each one for holding your book for you. Take the books and go up the sidewalk to the doors. Don't turn around, whatever you do."

"Mom, that is a very dumb idea," Faye said. "LeRoy will go right after Freddie and hit him from behind."

"If I get *that* far," Freddie said. "I'm thinking about it, though, Mom. Things sure can't go on the way they are."

"They won't," I said. "Nothing's going on the way it was."

The three of us went over the plan again. Freddie modified it some. Faye decided to call up each girl that evening, not tell her what was going to happen, but tell her that *something* was going to happen, so they would be geared up. Then she started drawing fists. She rested her own left fist on the kitchen table and then drew it, freehand, without looking at her drawing, the way Mercein had taught her. She put shadow between the knuckles.

In the next weeks our lives changed. Mercein had always told me, "Never, ever say, 'You just never know how things will turn out,' because it is such a boring thing to say." I felt like saying it a thousand times during that next week, however.

The local hospital staff didn't get in touch with the mental

Carol Bly

health center psychiatrists, but they did arrange some chemical-dependency counseling for Mercein. They were going to arrange for Mercein to see a social worker from Grand Rapids, but Tom reminded them that after all he was a trained psychologist: Why drive down to Grand Rapids on all this new snow and get killed on the road? The hospital staff said Mercein should get psychiatric care. All right, Tom told them, he was all for it, but not this very minute. All right, they told him back, but they wanted to do a complete physical for both of them, because she seemed upset about not being able to have a child.

The test indicated that Mercein could bear children perfectly well. Tom's sperm count was five percent of normal.

The following Sunday afternoon, Tom and Furman went off to a retreat for school psychologists and intake officers in St. Cloud. Grayzie had the Artmobile on the road that weekend, so after the police found Mercein and took her to the hospital, they called me. She had slit both wrists this time. She succeeded in dying.

After that, attendance at Tom Gall's business psych class dwindled. Even Furman missed some times, and right after Christmas he said he guessed he had had enough of singing with the choir. In April the school did not renew Tom's contract, and he moved out of town in June.

I never forgot all the interesting conversations I had had with Mercein. In the years following 1975, Grayzie and I often reminded each other what a wonderful exhibit he had made in the Artmobile, with those three globes lighted at their centers—especially the last one, showing the earth sixty-five million years from now.

The Tomcat's Wife

I also remember the details of Freddie's fight with LeRoy Beske outside the school bus.

He and Faye did everything by their plan. When LeRoy came off the lowest bus step, Freddie slugged him one. Freddie decided fast not to try for a second hit. He turned around and started thanking each girl for holding his book. Then, he told us, a semitrailer hit him in the small of his back. He felt himself caving. As he went down, another semitrailer hit him in the back of his neck.

Next he lay on the concrete sidewalk, face up. Snow was falling. The remarkable thing about it was that all of the snowflakes were angled straight at him. Some came from straight above, but also some came at him at a slant from left and right, and some from above his wet eyebrows and from below his chin. Then he noticed that in a ring all around that gigantic gray sky were the faces of little girls. They were all looking down at him. He saw the baby fat under their chins. The girls were cheeping and crying his name. Freddie could see they looked very respectful. As I listened to him, I thought: Maybe they'll grow up to be dull or dispirited like the football players, but for now, as Mercein would have said, they were enough to make your heart stop.

Carol Bly

After
the Baptism

The Benty Family had a beautiful baptism for their baby—
when a good deal might have gone wrong. It is hard to run
any baptism these days: of all the fifty-odd Episcopalians
in Saint Aidan's Church, not to mention the two Lutheran
grandparents, who really believes much of what the young
priest says? No one with an IQ over one hundred actually
supposes that "baptism could never be more truly, truly relevant than it is right now, in our day and age." People may get
a kick out of the rhetoric, but that doesn't mean they believe
it. If Bill Benty, Senior, the baby's grandfather, tried any of
that proclaiming style of Father Geoffrey, if he tried anything
like that just once over at the plant, he'd be laughed out to
the fence in two minutes.

At least Father Geoffrey was long enough out of seminary
now so he'd left off pronouncing Holy Ghost Ha-oly Gha-ost.
His delivery was clear and manly. When he took the baby
from her godparents, he took hold of her in a no-nonsense
way: her mussed, beautiful white skirts billowed over his arm

like a sail being carried to the water. But the man was vapid. A frank, charming midwestern accent can't bring dead ideas to life. He had been charming about agreeing on the 1928 baptism service, instead of the 1979. Bill's wife, Lois, loved the beautiful old phrasing. Beautiful it was, too, Bill thought now, but on the other hand, how could any realistic person ask those particular three godparents "to renounce the vain pomp and glory of the world"? Where would that crew get any glory from in the first place?

The middle-aged godparent was Bill's long-lost first cousin, Molly Wells. Thirty-odd years ago she had run away to North Carolina to marry. After almost no correspondence in all those years, Molly had shown up widowed—a thin, sad woman with white hair done in what Lois called your bottom-line, body-wave-only permanent. Neither Bill nor Lois had met her husband. Bill had mailed her dittoed, and later photocopied, Christmas letters, as he did to all his relations, giving news of Lois's work in Episcopal Community Services and whatever of interest there was to say about the chemical plant, and young Will's graduations and accomplishments—Breck School, Reed, the Harvard B School, his first marriage, his job with the arts organization before the snafu, his marriage to Cheryl. Molly and her husband had no children, and her responses to the Bentys' news were scarcely more than southern-lady thank-you notes.

Then in July of this long, very hot summer, she announced she was now widowed and would visit. Here she was, a house-guest who kept to her room, considerate enough not to dampen their family joking with her grief. Today, for the baptism, she wore a two-piece pink dress, gloves, and a straw-brimmed

Carol Bly

hat. Since one expects a young face under a broad-brimmed hat, Bill had had a moment's quake to see Molly when she came down the staircase that morning. Molly had frankly told them she had not darkened the doorway of a church in thirty years but she would not disgrace them.

The other godparents were an oldish young couple whom Will dug up from his remaining high-school acquaintance. Bill had warned Will that you had to give these things time: when a man has been caught embezzling he must allow his friends months, even a year, to keep saying how sorry they are, but the fact is, they can't really ever look at him the same way again. For a good two or three years they will still mention to people that he was caught embezzling or whatever, but in fact they have no rancor left themselves. In about five years, they will again be affectionate friends but never as in the first place. It was only a question of having the sense not to ask them for help getting a job the first two years—and then simply to wait.

Probably Will was lucky to have found this couple, Chad and Jodi Plathe, to stand up for his baby. They were not Episcopalians. They were meditators, and if not actually organic farmers, at least organic eaters. When Will and Cheryl brought them over to Bill and Lois's for dinner earlier in the month, it had been fun to goad them. Each time Chad mentioned an interest of theirs, Bill had said, "Oh, then it follows you must be into organic eating." Or "Oh, then it follows you must be into horoscopes." "Into Sufi dancing, I bet." They were—into all the philosophies he brought up. They looked at him, puzzled, and young Will said, "Very witty, Dad—oh, witty." Once Chad said something hostile back, Bill forgave him everything. In one sense, Bill had rather listen to a non-Christian fallen-away Bay Area Buddhist who is man enough to take offense, at least, than to this Father Geoffrey, with his everlasting love for everything and everybody.

Now Chad and Jodi stood at the front, their backs to the grandparents in the first row and all the congregation in the next rows. They wore their eternal blue jeans, with the tops of plastic sandwich bags sticking out of the back pockets. They wore 1960s-style rebozos with earth-tone embroidery and rust-colored sewn-on doves. Their shoulder-length hair was shiny and combed. At least, Bill thought comfortably, very little evil in the world was generated by vegetarians. He saved up that idea to tell Chad if the conversation dragged at dinner.

Early that morning, Bill had taken his coffee happily out into the little back-kitchen screened porch. The wind was down, and the ivy's thousands of little claws held the screens peacefully. Like all true householders, Bill liked being up while others slept. His wide lawn lay shadowed under four elms the city hadn't had to take down yet. The grass showed a pale gleam of dew and looked more beautiful than it really was. Across the avenue, where the large grounds of Benty Chemical started, Bill had ordered a landscaping outfit to put in generous groupings of fine high bushes and hundreds of perennials. He ordered them planted on both sides of the fence. Now that it was August, and everything had taken hold, the grounds looked lavender and gentle.

"You can't make a chemical factory look like an Englishman's estate," Lois had told him last week. "But, darling, darn near! Darn near! If only the protesters would wear battered stovepipe hats and black scarves!"

Carol Bly

Bill told her that he had heard at a Saint Aidan's Vestry meeting that the protesting or peace-demonstrating community of the Twin Cities definitely regarded Benty Chem as a lot more beautiful place to work around than any one of Honeywell's layouts. "And they should know," Bill added with satisfaction.

At seven-thirty, the usual Sunday contingent of protesters weren't on the job yet. It was generally Sue Ann and Mary, or Sue Ann and Drew, on Sundays. Bill learned their first names automatically, as he learned the first names of new janitorial staff at Benty Chem. Now he gathered himself, got into the car, and was out at Northwest Cargo Recovery on Thirty-fourth Street in good time. He signed for the lobsters. They were moving around a little, safe, greenish black, in their plastic carrying case. "Hi, fellows and girls!" he said good-naturedly to them. He felt the luggage people smiling at him from behind their counter. Bill knew he was more spontaneous and humorous than most people they dealt with. "For my first grandchild's baptism!" he told them.

When he got home, the caterers had come. Lois was fingering along the bookcases, looking for the extra 1928 prayer books. Molly sat, cool in her silk two-piece dress. "I do believe it's threatening rain," she said in her partly southern accent. "Oh, and rain is just so much needed by our farmers." Her "our farmers" sounded false, feudal even, but Bill said, "Darn right, Molly!"

Now he relaxed in church. He flung an arm around the bench end, a little figure carved in shallow relief. Some Episcopalian in Bill's dad's generation had brought six of these carvings from Norfolk. They all cracked during their first winter of American central heating. Bill and a couple of other vestry men glued the cracks and set vises; then they mortised in hardwood holes against the grain, to make them safe forever. Each bench end was a small monk, with robe, hood, and cinch. The medieval sculptor had made the little monks hold their glossy wooden hands up, nearly touching their noses, in prayer. The faces had no particular expression.

Bill sat more informally than other people in Saint Aidan's. He had the peaceful slouch of those who are on the inside, the ones who know the workings behind some occasion, like cooks for a feast, or vestry men for a service, or grandfathers for a baptism. Bill had done a lot of work and thinking to make this baptism successful, so now his face was pleasant and relaxed. He was aware of the Oppedahls next to him, the baby's other grandparents, sweating out the Episcopal service that they disliked. He thought they were darn good sports. He leaned across Lois at one point and whispered to Merv Oppedahl that a strong Scotch awaited the stalwart fellow that got through all the Smells and Bells. Merv's face broke into a grin, and he made a thumbs-up with the hand that wasn't holding Doreen's hand.

All summer the wretched farmers' topsoil had been lifting and lifting, then moving into the suburbs, even into St. Paul itself. Grit stuck to people's foreheads and screens, even to the woven metal of their fences. But inside Saint Aidan's, the air was high and cool; the clerestory windows, thank heavens, were not the usual dark and royal blue and dark rose stained glass imitations of continental cathedral windows—full of symbols of lions for Saint Mark and eagles for Saint John, which a whole generation of Episcopalians didn't know

Carol Bly

anything about, anyway. Besides, they made churches dark. Saint Aidan's had a good deal of clear glass, and enough gold-stained windows so that all the vaulting looked rather gold and light. It was an oddly watery look. In fact, the church reminded Bill of the insides of the overturned canoe of his childhood. It had been made of varnished ribs and strakes; when the boys turned it over and dove down to come up inside it, madly treading water, they felt transformed by that watery arching. It was a spooky yellow-dark. No matter that at ten their voices must still have been unchanged; they shouted all the rhetoric and bits of poems they knew. They made everything pontifical. They made dire prophecies. They felt portentous about death, even. Not the sissy, capon death they taught you about at Cass Lake Episcopal Camp, but the death that would get you if a giant pried your fists off the thwarts and shoved you down.

Now Father Geoffrey was done with the godparents. He put his thumb into the palm oil and pressed it onto the baby's forehead. Then he cried in a full voice, "I pronounce you, Molly Oppedahl Benty, safe in our Lord Jesus Christ forever!" Tears made some people's eyes brittle. They all sang "Love divine, all loves excel-l-l-ling . . ." using the Hyfrydol tune. Then it was noon, and they could leave.

Everyone tottered across the white, spiky gravel of the parking lot. They called out unnecessary friendly words from car to car: "See you at the Bentys' in five minutes, then!" and "Beautiful service, wasn't it?" "Anyone need a ride? We can certainly take two more!"

The cars full of guests drove companionably across the tacky suburb. People felt happy in different ways, but all of them felt more blessed than the people they passed. They may have been to a sacrament that they didn't much believe in, but they at least had been to one. Ten years before, all these streets had been shadowy under the elms. Now, though spindly maple saplings stood guyed in their steel-mesh cages, the town showed itself dispirited in its lidless houses that human beings build and live in. The open garages, with here and there a man pottering about, looked more inviting than the houses. The men tinkered in the hot shadow, handling gigantic mowing and spraying equipment parked there. No one could imagine a passion happening in the houses—not even a mild midlife crisis. Not even a hobby, past an assembled kit.

Another reason everyone felt contented was that all their troubles with one another had been worked out the week before. Unbeatable, humane, wise, experienced administrator that he was, Bill explained to Lois, he had done the best possible thing to guarantee them all a great baptism Sunday by having Will and Cheryl (and little Molly) over to dinner the week before. There were always tensions about religious occasions. The tensions are all the worse when most of the religion is gone while the custom lives on. Each detail of the custom—what's in good taste and what's the way we've always done it before—is a bloodletting issue. Now, there were two things to do about bloodletting issues, Bill told Lois.

"Yes, dear?" she said with a smile.

"If the issues can be solved to anyone's satisfaction, just solve them. But if they can't be solved at all, have the big fight about them a week ahead. Then everybody is sick of fighting by the time you have the occasion itself."

Carol Bly

Lois said, "Makes sense. What can't be solved, though?"

He gave her a look. "Our son and our daughter-in-law are not very happily married. They started a baby two months before they married. And you and I will always just have to hope that it was Will's idea to marry Cheryl and not Merv Oppedahl's idea at the end of a magnum. Next: Cheryl wanted the baby to be named Chereen—a combo of Cheryl, for herself, and Doreen, for her mother. Our son thinks Chereen is a disgusting idea. Next: Cheryl puts a descant onto any hymn we sing, including—if I remember correctly, and I am afraid I will never forget—onto 'Jesu Joy of Man's Desiring' and Beethoven's Ninth, whatever that one is."

"'Ode to Joy,'" Lois said.

"'Ode to Joy,'" Bill said. "Next: The Oppedahls are probably not very happy that their daughter has married someone who did two years at Sandstone Federal Prison for embezzlement. Next: You and I are not happy about Will's marrying Cheryl. She is tasteless. He is mean to her. Are you with me so far? Then next is the choice of godparents. Good grief! It is nice that Will wants to honor his first cousin once removed Molly Wells by asking her to stand godparent, but she hasn't gone to church in thirty years. And Cheryl wanted a young couple, not an old second cousin, for her baby's sponsors. It is obvious Will chose Molly because she gave them seventeen thousand dollars by way of a nest egg. Very handsome thing to do. *Very* handsome, considering Will's record."

Lois said, "Oh, dear, must you?"

"All these things are on people's minds. It's best to have it all out ahead of time. Just because a rich relation gives someone money is not a reason for having her stand godmother—

especially when the baby's mother obviously doesn't want her. Next: The Oppedahls aren't going to be comfortable with the Episcopal church service, but they'd be a sight *more* comfortable if we used the modern language of 1979—but the baby's grandmother on the other side wants 1928."

Lois said, "Oh, dear. I thought I was going to come out of this clean."

Bill laughed, "No one comes out of a family fight clean. Next: Mrs. Oppedahl is a horrible cold fish who doesn't like anybody. She doesn't even like her own daughter very well. In fact—poor Cheryl! Do you know what she told me? She told me the first time she ever felt popular, as she put it, was at Lutheran Bible camp, when all the girls discovered she could harmonize to the hymns. Suddenly it made her part of the group. When they all got back from camp, the girls talked about her as if she were someone who counted, and the boys picked up on it. She was OK in high school after that. She told me that just that one Lutheran Bible camp gave her more nourishment—her word—than she'd ever got from her parents."

"You're a wonder, dear," Lois said. "What about the other godparents?"

"The holistic birdseed-eaters? They know perfectly well that the only reason Will chose them was to override any chance of Cheryl's having some couple *she'd* choose. They know that I think their knee-jerk Gaia stuff is silly, and they will feel awkward about the service. I don't know what to do about them."

Lois said, "We will have lobsters. That's not meat! Then they won't bring their plastic bags of whatever."

"Boiled live lobster. Great idea. They will eat it or I will shove it down their throats," Bill said. "I will offend Doreen Oppedahl by offering Merv a strong drink. It'll buck him up, and she's hopeless, anyway."

"Have we thought of everything?" Lois said.

Bill turned serious a moment. "I am going to tell Will he can't speak cruelly to his wife in my house."

Lois said, "Well, poor Will! Do you remember how when we were all somewhere at someone's house, suddenly there was Cheryl telling everyone how she and Will met because they were both at the microfiche in the public library together and they both felt sick from the fiche?"

"Nothing wrong with that," Bill said. "Microfiche does make people feel like throwing up."

"But she went on and on about how nausea had brought them together!"

Bill said, "I remember. Will told her to shut up, too, right in front of everyone."

The week before the baptism, therefore, Will and Cheryl and little Molly joined Bill, Lois, and their cousin Molly Wells for dinner. They aired grievances, just as Bill had planned. Then he glanced out the window and said to his son, "Come on out and help me with the protesters, Will."

Everyone looked out. The usual Sunday protesters had been on the opposite sidewalk, near the plant fence. They looked flagged from the heat, but determined. Bill saw it was Sue Ann and Polly this time. They had their signs turned so they could be read from the Benty house. IT IS HARD TO BE PROUD OF CHEMICAL WARFARE was the message for that

Sunday. Now the two young people had moved to this side of the avenue, doing the westward reach of their loop on the public sidewalk but taking the eastward reach on Bill and Lois's lawn.

"Not on my grass they don't," Bill said, smiling equably at the others. "We'll be right back."

Father and son went to the lawn edge and stood side by side, waiting for the protesters to come up abreast of where they were. The women, in the house, could see their backs but couldn't hear what was said. Presently they realized nothing violent seemed likely. They made out the protesters smiling, and Bill turned slightly, apparently calling a parting shot of some civil kind to them. The protesters moved back over to the Benty Chemical side of the street, and Will and Bill came across the lawn toward the house.

Bill had used that time to speak to his son. "I can't stop you from treating your wife rudely in your own home. But in mine, Will, don't you ever swear at her again. And don't tell her to shut up. And stop saying 'For Christ's sake, Cheryl.'"

"Dad—my life is going to be some kind of hell."

"I bet it might," Bill said in a speculative tone. "It well might." Just then the sign-bearers came up to them. One said, "Good afternoon, Mr. Benty," to Bill. The other of them said in a very pleasant tone, "There must be some other way human beings can make money besides on contracts for spreading nerve diseases that cause victims five or six hours of agony," and they made to pass on.

"Off the lawn, friends," Bill said levelly. "Sidewalk's public, lawn's private."

Carol Bly

"Agony is another word for torture," the first protester said, but they immediately crossed the street.

As Bill and Will came back to the house, Bill said in a low voice, "Go for the pleasant moments, son. Whenever you can."

All the difficult conversations took place that could take place: all the permanent grievances—Will's and Cheryl's unhappiness—were hinted at. People felt that they had expressed themselves a little. By the end of the day, they felt gritty and exhausted.

A blessed week passed, and now the baptism party was going off well. The caterers had come, with their white Styrofoam trays. They set out sauces and laid the champagne crooked into its pails of ice. They dropped the lobsters into boiling water. There was lemon mayonnaise and drawn butter, a platter of dark-meat turkey—damper, better than white meat, Lois Benty and the caterers agreed. It is true that as she made her way around the Bentys' dining-room table, loading her plate, Doreen Oppedahl whispered to her husband, "It'd never occur to me, I can tell you, to serve dark meat on a company occasion," and Merv whispered back, "No, it never *would* occur to you!" but his tone wasn't malicious. He had spotted the Scotch on the sideboard. That Bill Benty might be pompous, but at least he was as good as his word, and Merv wasn't going to be stuck with that dumb champagne, which tasted like 7-Up with aspirin. An oblong of pinewood lay piled with ham so thin it wrinkled in waves. The caterers had set parsley here and there, and sprayed mist over everything; they set one tiny chip of ice on each butter pat. "Those caterers just left that chutney preserve that Mrs. Wells brought right in its mason jar," Doreen whispered to Merv.

He smiled and whispered, "Shut up, Doreen." She whispered back, "If you get drunk at this party, I will never forgive you."

When all the relations and friends had gathered into the living room, Bill Benty tinkled a glass and asked them to drink to his grandchild. After that, people glanced about, weighing places to sit.

Then the one thing that neither host nor hostess had foreseen happened: no one sat in the little groupings Lois had arranged. Nor did people pull up chairs to what free space there was at the dining-room table. They gravitated to the messy screened porch off the kitchen. The caterers obligingly swept away all their trays and used foil. People dragged out dining-room chairs; other people camped on the old wooden chairs already out there.

The morning's breeze had held. Some of it worked through the gritty screens. People relaxed and felt cheerful. They kept passing the baby about, not letting any one relation get to hold her for too long. Father Geoffrey kept boring people by remarking that it was the most pleasant baptism he could remember. Suddenly Lois Benty pointed across at Chad's and Jodi's plates. "Don't *tell* me you two aren't eating the lobster!" she screamed. "Lobster is not meat, you know!"

Both Chad and Jodi gave the smile that experienced vegetarians keep ready for arrogant carnivores. "Well, you see," Jodi said with mock shyness, "we asked the caterers—you see, we did ask. The lobsters weren't stunned first!"

Father Geoffrey said pleasantly, "And delicious they are, too. I've never tasted better."

Jodi said, "They were dropped in alive, you see. . . . So it's a question of their agony." Then Jodi said in a hurried, louder

Carol Bly

voice, "Mrs. Benty, please don't worry about us! We always bring our own food, so we're all set." She reached into her back jeans pocket and brought out two plastic bags of couscous and sunflower seeds. "We are more than OK," she said.

Lois asked people if she could bring them another touch of this or that—the ham, at least? she said, smiling at Mrs. Oppedahl.

"Oh, no!" cried Mrs. Oppedahl. "I've eaten so much! I'd get fat!"

By now Merv had had three quick, life-restoring glasses of Scotch. For once he felt as urbane and witty as Bill Benty, even if he wasn't the boss of a chemical industry.

"Fat!" he shouted. "Afraid you'll get fat! Don't worry! I like a woman fat enough so I can find her in bed!"

He looked around with bright eyes—but there was a pause. Then Bill Benty said in a hearty tone, "Oh, *good* man, Oppedahl! *Good* man!"

Quickly, the baby's second cousin said to Jodi Plathe, "Those little bags look so interesting! Could you explain what's in them? Is that something we should all be eating?"

Bill said, "Go ahead, Jodi. Convert her. That's what I call a challenge. If you can get Molly Wells to set down that plate of lobster and eat bulgur wheat instead, you've got something there, Jodi!"

Jodi gave him a look and then said, "No, you tell *me* something, Ms. Wells. I was wondering, why were you crying at the baptism this morning? Somebody said you never went to church at all, and yet . . . I was just wondering."

"Oh," Lois Benty said, getting set to dilute any argument, "I bet you mean during the chrism."

Molly Wells happened to be holding the baby at that moment. Above its dreaming face, hers looked especially tired and conscious. "My dear," she said, "that is a long story. I just know you don't want to hear it."

"Let's have the story, lady," Mr. Oppedahl said. "My wife is always so afraid that I'll tell a story—but the way I look at it is, people like a story. You can always ask 'em, do they mind a little story? And if they don't say no, the way I look at it is, it's OK to tell it. So go right ahead. Or I could tell one, if you're too shy."

"Never mind!" cried Bill. "Out with it, Molly!"

Father Geoffrey said gently, "I know I for one would surely like to hear it!"

Molly Wells said, "I have to confess I was mostly daydreaming along through the service, thinking of one thing and another. I never liked church. Unlike Bill here—Bill's my first cousin, you might not know—I was raised in the country, and my dream—my one and my *only* dream—was to get out of the country and marry a prince and live happily ever after.

"The only way I could think to escape at seventeen was to go to Bible camp. So I went—and there, by my great good luck, I met another would-be escaper, Jamie Wells. We cut all the outdoors classes and then used those same places where the classes met to sit and walk together when no one was there. We met in the canoe shed. We sat on the dock near the bin of blue and white hats, depending on how well you swam. We met in the chapel, even, during off times. Wherever we were, we were in love all the time. I recall Jamie said to me, 'There is nothing inside me that wants to go back to the old life, Molly. Is there anything inside you that wants to go back

Carol Bly

to the old life?' There wasn't, so we ran away. Away meant to stay with his parents and sister, who were at a resort in the Blue Ridge Mountains that summer. We told them we wanted to be married, and they were kind to us. We married, and we lived in love for thirty years.

"It was so pleasant—in the little ways as well as the big ones. Jamie found a hilltop that looked over the valley and across to two mountains—Pisgah and The Rat. He told the workmen how to cut down the laurels and dogwoods and just enough of the armored pine so that you couldn't see the mill down in the valley but you had a clear view to the mountains. We spent hours, hours every day, sitting on our stone terrace. We even had Amos and George bring breakfast out there. I remember best sitting out there in March, when the woods were unleafed except for the horizontal boughs of dogwood everywhere! They looked so unlikely, so vulnerable, out there among all that mountain scrub! The ravines were full of red clay, and the sound of the hounds baying and baying, worrying some rabbit all the time. I remember how we always made a point of taking walks in late afternoon, and I would never stop feeling dazzled by the shards of mica everywhere. And Jamie did have the most wonderful way of putting things. He said mica was bits left over from the first world, back when it was made of pure crystal, when it was made of unbroken love, before God made it over again with clay and trees, ravines, and dogs. I recall when he said that kind of thing my heart used to grow and grow.

"Nothing interrupted us. Now, Jamie's sister, Harriet Jean, always wanted me to do social work for her, but she forgave me when she saw I wasn't going to do it. I expect she understood right off from the very first that I loved her brother, and all a maiden lady really wants from a sister-in-law is that she should really love her brother. We three got along very well. One day, on Amos and George's day off, we had a copperhead on the terrace. Harriet Jean was over there in a flash, and she shot its head right off with her twenty-gauge. She was so good about it too: I remember she told us very clearly, 'I want you and Jamie to just turn your back now,' and she swept up its head and slung its body over the dustpan handle and carried it off somewhere. She had a good many projects with the black people, and she would have liked me to help her with those . . . but after a while she said to me, 'Molly, I see that you have your hands full with that man, and I mean to stop pestering at you,' and she was as good as her word. Different occasions came and went—the Vietnam War, I certainly remember that clear as clear. It was in the paper, and when Amos and George came out with the breakfast trays and brought that paper, Jamie said, 'There is a time when a country is in a kind of death agony, the way a person could be,' and I felt a burst of love for him then, too. No one in my family could ever observe and think that clearly."

At this point, Mr. Oppedahl said in a loud but respectful voice, "I didn't just get what you said he did for a living."

Molly Wells said, "Oh, that. He had a private income—that whole family did. Of course, he had an office he had to keep to tend his interests with—but it was private income." She shifted the baby, and seemed to rearrange herself a little as she said that. It didn't invite further comment.

She took up her story. "Everything went along all those

Carol Bly

years, except of course we just wept uncontrollably when George died, and Amos never was so springy serving us after that.

"Then one day we found out that Jamie had inoperable cancer of the lung."

There was a little pause after she said that. They could all hear the footsteps of people on the sidewalk, outside. The wind had cooled a little.

"They wanted to do radiation on Jamie, because there were some lung cancer cells in his brain. Well, so we had the radiation treatment. I drove Jamie all the way to Asheville for that, twice a week. It was a very hard time for us: he was often sick. When he wasn't actually sick, he felt sick.

"They managed to kill those lung cells in his brain, and gradually, after many months, he died, but not of brain cancer.

"Well, now," the middle-aged woman said. "Three occasions all came to mind during that baptism service for this beautiful little girl this morning. First, after I had been married not two months, I noticed, the way you gradually get around to noticing everything there is about a man, that the flesh in his upper arm was a little soft, just below the shoulder bulge. I could have expected that, since Jamie just wasn't interested in sports at all and he didn't do any physical work. But still I remember thinking: That bit of softness there will get a little softer all the time, and after twenty years or so it might be very soft and loose from the muscle, the way the upper part of old men's arms are—which kills a woman's feeling just at the moment she notices it. Right away, of course, if it is someone dear to you, you forgive them for that soft upper arm there, for not being young and handsome forever, but still the image of it goes in, and you feel your heart shrink a little. You realize the man will not live forever. Then you love him even better in the next moment, because now—for the first time—you pity him. At least, I felt pity.

"The second occasion was when he was sick having all that radiation. He vomited on our living-room floor. It was Sunday evening. We always let Amos go home to his own folks on Sundays, so there wasn't anyone to clean that up— but Harriet Jean was there, and she offered to. Suddenly I remember almost snarling at her—I just bayed at her like a dog. I told her to keep out of it. I would clean up my own husband's mess. Of course she was surprised. She couldn't have been more surprised than I was, though. That night in bed, I went over it carefully, and I realized that the only physical life I had left with Jamie was taking care of him, so his vomit was part of my physical life with him. Not lovely—but there it was.

"The last occasion was about a half hour after his death. The hospital people told me I had to leave the room, and I remember I refused. Finally they said I could stay another ten minutes and that was all. Now, you all may know or you may not know that they have their reasons for taking people away from dead bodies. I laid my forehead down on the edge of the bed near Jamie's hip—and then I heard a slight rustling. My mind filled with horror. I lifted my head and looked up to see a slight change in his hand. It had been lying there; now the fist—just the tiniest bit, but I wasn't mistaken—was closing a little. When a person looks back coolly from a distance on a thing like that, you know it is the muscles shrinking or contracting or whatever they do when life has left. To me,

Carol Bly

though, it was Jamie making the very first move I had ever seen him make, in all my life with him, which I had nothing to do with. He was taking hold of something there—thin air, maybe—but taking hold of it by himself. Now I knew what death was. I stood up and left.

"This morning, in church, I was daydreaming about him again. It's a thing I do. I was not going to mention it to any of you.

"I told you about this because I was so surprised to find how my life was not simple at all: it was all tied up in the flesh, this or that about the flesh. And how is flesh ever safe? So when you took that palm oil," she finished, glancing across at Father Geoffrey, "and pronounced little Molly here safe— *safe!*—in our Lord Jesus Christ forever. . . . Well, I simply began to cry!"

She sat still a moment and then with her conversational smile looked across at the younger godmother. "Well, you asked the question, and now I have answered you."

In the normal course of things, such a speech would simply bring a family celebration to an absolute stop. People would sit frozen, still as crystal for a moment, and then one or another would say, in a forced, light-toned way, "My word, but it's getting late. . . . Dear, we really must . . ." and so forth. But the Benty family were lucky. A simple thing happened: it began to rain finally, the rain people had been wanting all summer. The rain fell quite swiftly right from the first. It rattled the ivy, and then they could even hear it slamming down on the sidewalks. Footsteps across the avenue picked up and began to run.

They all noticed that odd property of rain: if it has been

very dry, the first shower drives the dust upward, so that for a second your nostrils fill with dust.

Then the rain continued so strongly it cleaned the air and made the whole family and their friends feel quiet and tolerant. They felt the classic old refreshment we always hope for in water.

Carol Bly

An Apprentice

I cross most of St. Paul to take my violin lessons. Then I drive slowly around Georgia's half block, along Hemlock Avenue, and through the north-south alley. I locate the regulars. They are of two kinds—the four men who generally are on their feet, laughing, shouting, dealing, waiting for the Hemlock Bar to open at six; and the three men who sprawl, elbows propped, right on the four low steps leading from the sidewalk up the low slant of Georgia's lawn. These three are more languid than the crack pushers: they lie at ease and blow their smoke straight up, pursing their lips at the sky.

For my first two lessons, I gave those men the stairs: I climbed up the grass slant, keeping a good ten yards between them and me. But by the time I was learning the third position and could do "Go Down, Moses," with harmonics on the G string, I thought, If Georgia Persons doesn't give way to these guys, neither will I.

So I make myself pick a way between them up the concrete stairs. They never move an inch, but they always stop talking, and their eyes creep over my black plastic Hefty bag. Inside it, my mother's old violin case does not bulge the way garbage would. I have my music-stand top, since someone, when breaking into all the apartments of Georgia's building, went off with one of hers. I have my chin support, the Friml and Kuechler and Handel sheet music, and *A Tune a Day,* my violin lessons text. I am nervous that the smokers think, Why *not* knock over that sturdy, timid-faced woman of forty-one? Why *not?* She might have a ten or a twenty in the chipped shoulder bag, even though she wears her grubbies. And they must think, Whatever's in the Hefty isn't garbage. Who'd bring garbage to 4303 Hemlock, where there are generally several sacks of it on the front-porch floorboards, not to mention the sacks left in the downstairs hallway for weeks at a time. I step through these men prissily, lifting my bag over their pot-fragrant skulls. I imagine their brains as indeterminate magma. Whatever thinking they do, the thoughts haven't cooled enough to be distinct, the way the central metals of our planet aren't yet quiet, reliable rock.

Georgia has opened the screen-and-torn-plastic door a couple of inches as soon as she has seen my car, so I will know she is there to let me in. She and the other tenants of 4303—the born-again on the ground floor and two men a flight above Georgia—have decided that the usual mechanical voice-check and relay lock aren't safe enough: they arrange for their guests' arrivals by phone. Then they crouch on the unlighted staircase inside until their guests' heads show through the scrim of door curtain.

Now Georgia opens the door wide for me. I bound in, taking the Hefty sack safely past her. She gives the street and

Carol Bly

yard a last wide scanning, like a bridge officer just leaving the conn. "I see the Boy Scouts have their troop meeting on my steps today," she says in her friendly, sardonic tone. "Good fellows that they are," she adds, "they invited a goodly number of policemen to their meeting in the alley yesterday—yes, they did—and finally the policemen invited a goodly number of them to a picnic somewhere; at least, they all climbed into two vans together! Very nice! Very nice indeed!"

Her ironic style restores my humor. It seems right that a disciplined artist should use archaic phrases and should nurture indignation against slobs. I follow Georgia's huge behind up the stairs. She always wears print dresses with dark backgrounds and large flower patterns: in the unlighted stairway, the white peonies and hydrangeas on her skirt lead the way.

Georgia is only ten or fifteen years older than I am, but her face is full and soft from her having taken prednisone for a year and a half. She has temporal arteritis, and drugs saved her eyesight in the first weeks. Now the doctors keep lessening her dose: they consider her much improved. Georgia wears hearty makeup—eye shadow bright as poster paint, paste rouge on each huge, viscous cheek. I try to draw her out, since I am interested in serious illness, but she explained the symptoms, the diagnosis, and the regimen to me once and refuses to go into it further. On what I have to guess are her bad days, all her makeup—shadow, rouge, and lipstick—looks lightly positioned, temporary, like an airplane parked. It might easily lift away.

She won't complain, even when I deliberately, hopefully, model complaining for her. I think of myself as someone coming to her only to learn the violin. I ought to be glad of having this discrete task as an escape from the rest of my life, but I have the slack-focused habit of dropping personal anecdote into our talk. I tell her about the first, even the second, laser vaporization I have had, a procedure for treating precancer and cancer of the cervix. Georgia waits through my talk. I try to intrigue her with bits of lifestyle at the In and Out Surgi-Center at Saint Alban's. When I stop talking, she says, "If you will hand me that Strad of yours, I'll tune it for you."

She turns sidewise to me and whines my violin strings with her thumb while striking her piano's A, E, D, and G keys with her free hand. At one of our sessions I told her I had not practiced very much because my ex-husband had asked the eldest of our children to tell me to have the younger children clean and well dressed for his wedding that week. Old friends of mine were going to the wedding without a qualm. When I was through talking, Georgia said, "It is impossible to have a good lesson if you do not practice." She added, "Impossible." Then, after a little pause, she said, "Men are repulsive. As always."

She is a martinet of a violin teacher—the only kind, I decide. At first I thought she wore her makeup and her rayon, floriate dresses for her one other adult student—a dentist. But it turns out that she despises him because he wants to learn the Handel immediately and will not do any of the exercises in *A Tune a Day,* which Georgia assures me is the definitive violin study book, better even than the precise exercises of Wohlfahrt. During my first few weeks of lessons, she told me how little the dentist practiced. By the time I was in the third position, and starting the third position and learning the languid, swooping vibrato of beginners, I heard no more of the dentist. I expect she has dropped him. Now she has only me and her several dozen Hmong and Laotian children, many of whom do not speak English. I imagine her extending her arms like fat bridges to them, pressing their half- and three-quarter-sized fiddles to their necks, and pouring all her theory of bowing and fingering, in English, into those full, black eyes. Once—*only* once—I exclaimed, "How good you are to them! What wonderful patience you have!" Georgia promptly jammed her violin into her throat. "*They* do not have trouble with atonal music. *They* are not hobbled by preconceived ideas about where *do* should be," she said.

I vow to be her best student. Sometimes, when I have mastered something difficult, like sliding thirds cleanly across two strings, Georgia says, "That's *very* good. *Very* good. Also, it is pleasant that you do not ever tell me that your mother forgot to put your *Tune a Day* into your bag. And that your mother forgot the rosin so you could not practice." At long intervals I get hints about the rest of her teaching life. "Ah! You've practiced very well!" she says, looking at me from the center of her serious, drug-changed face. "Why have you practiced so much? Have you only just now arrived from the boat and therefore haven't learned yet that there's welfare and you needn't do a lick of work, ever?"

It sounds like such a friendly opening, I pick it up quickly. "Then are the earnest Asian people learning to rot in America?"

But Georgia is back to my bowing. "Wrists! Wrists! Wrists leading lightly," she says. "You needn't get revenge on the violin. Play it gently. *Especially,* be easy on that tiny, slender E string."

At other times she notices I am doing something right when I least expect it. Several times, when I have thought she wasn't listening but was putting her feathery handwriting under my country-day-school manuscript printing in the assignment book, I find she has been listening. "Ah! Lovely! Very nice sound, that! Very!" she murmurs, still writing. "You must always do good work. If it sounds bad, go back and get it right. You must play at concert level all the time." Then she gives her small laugh, drops the assignment notebook onto the piano bench, turns to accompany me with her own violin. "It is just a question of time now! Before Memorial Day, I would say!"

She drops her soft chin onto the chin support; the spidery fingers, so thinly hung to the flesh of hand and wrist, make their hummingbird-speed vibrato. One good violinist can make another violinist sound better: in fact, you can have three or four indifferent players playing, provided at least one of them can do the uncompromised bowing and vibrato that thin a string's sound to its lyric bone.

But I am too curious to continue. I stop and ask, "Before Memorial Day, what?"

"Oh," she says. "The Saint Paul Chamber Orchestra, of course. They will call, probably at midnight, wanting you for concertmaster, and of course, like Cinderella, you will have to go. Naturally you will mention to them that I am your teacher."

Georgia wanted to charge me four dollars a lesson. I told her that was absurd. "But I don't need more," she said. "I have my salary from the school"—where she teaches the Hmong and Laotian children—"and I have another private student. I have Minnesota state employees' health coverage."

I tell her that other violin teachers assure me that any musician of musical integrity must charge starting students twelve dollars. Each month I hand her a check for forty-eight dollars.

"This will pay for your lessons through the 1990s," she says each time, dropping my check into the little velvet lining of her violin case. I envy that velvet lining, with its blood-colored fur and its neat little zipper. I would buy one with part of a child-support check, but I am loyal to the ugly case I inherited from my mother.

"Now the Handel," Georgia says briskly.

It is in E major, but the first movement is adagio, so I have a little chance. From somewhere under the cry and grind of my efforts, I begin to hear Handel's lilt. It isn't pathos that makes Handel so tuneful: it is character. Under my fingers and crimped bowing, his beauty is only beginning to show. Even so, I can hardly believe I don't live in a state of gratitude all the time.

Georgia refuses to play it all through once so I can hear the full beauty. Fat arms go up—but drop. "No, no," she says. "You make it beautiful yourself. The first time you hear it all through and it sounds beautiful will be when you yourself do it. And now," she says, "that is enough for today."

She looks ill. I put everything away as fast as I can.

"I will let myself out," I tell her.

"No, no!" she says, in her singsong ironic tone. "I will see you safe into your car," and she follows me down the stairs.

Of course it is a relief to get away from one's teacher. No matter how good a teacher she is, it is a relief to escape. Once I am in the car, I daydream of going back to smoking. I daydream of stopping for some greasy fast food. I sing a descant, which, like Girl Scout camp descants, rides its resolute third above the melody without break, ruining any music it attaches to. I want to feel the *easy* emotions: I drive along in my car, leaving behind slatternly Selby Avenue and Hemlock Avenue and Dale Street, and I sing "You Want to Pass It On," a tune from twenty years ago, when I was a born-again Christian. My thoughts get silvery and loose like fish. I think of my mother, who died when I was a kid. I was not allowed to have violin lessons. She said it was ridiculous: I had no gift. Why give lessons to someone with no gift? Right, I think, without rancor, and I start humming "Abide with Me," imagining the fingering for the key of D, key of G, key of E. I do an upside-down vibrato on the left side of the steering wheel.

I have been home two hours when a man calls and asks who I am. Then he asks, "Are you a relation of Georgia Persons?"

"She is my violin teacher. Why?"

"I am a policeman, at 4303 Hemlock Avenue," he says. "Is Georgia Persons a close friend? Just your teacher, or what?"

Right now my children are my close friends, but I am trying to ease them more and more away, into their father's care, just in case. I make it a point to think of them only a few quarter hours a day. Old college friends are close friends, but right now they avoid me because divorce might be catching. And whatever makes people have surgery once and then surgery again and even again might be catching too. Sometimes

Carol Bly

on the Hardanger plateau, in its endless landscape of scraped stones and freezing creeks high above the treeline, you see a walker in the distance walking another path, which won't cross yours. The other walker may stay within view for as much as two hours. You feel an affinity for him or her, because you are engaged in the same energetic project. The people who feel like friends to me at the moment are Georgia and the nurse-anesthetist at Saint Alban's.

"She is a close friend," I tell the policeman. "You had better tell me what is going on." I am now recalling Georgia's pallor.

"We will send someone around to pick you up," the man says. It is clear that Georgia Persons is dead.

I always wore the shabbiest jeans and tees to take my lessons from her. I meant to give the impression of someone without a nickel, so the alley and sidewalk folk would leave me alone. Now I put on a silk orange shirt, a silk jacket, and a flowered silk skirt: it is full and has the huge roseate flowers of spring 1990 styles. I put on stockings and a new pair of yellow high-heeled pumps. "Well, Georgia," I say as I dress, "it's for you, since you won't get to hear me play for the chamber orchestra, after all. Do not feel bad," I say, trying for her exact ironical note. "Everyone in the Saint Paul Chamber Orchestra may not have musical integrity, even though we have to admit they sound as if they have."

The policewoman's car is astir with air-conditioning. We ride in great comfort to Hemlock and Dale. "It was assault, and she died," the policewoman tells me. At Georgia's house, not only are all the regulars there, on their feet for once, collected into a little group, with two policeman watching them, but the alley types are standing around on the grass. Three police cars are parked askew in the street, with blinkers going. All around and in neighboring bits of yard, people hover in groups, not a single person smoking anything.

"We're using his apartment for now," my cop says, jerking her head toward a man standing beside a policeman on the porch. I realize this is the born-again Christian.

In his apartment, three people approach me and stand close around. Was I there two hours ago? Yes. My lessons started the better part of a year ago. Was anyone else ever in Georgia Persons's apartment when I was there? Whoever stole her music-stand top, I think. I decide I had better mention that. They listen, as they do to everything I say, taking no notes. I mention the dentist. Yes, they have his name already, but he refused to come. He said he was not a friend and had quit taking lessons from Georgia because she did not "address his needs." All the while we are talking in the middle of the room, I must have seen that there is a slightly raised stretcher on the floor, but I avoid the idea, thinking of ways I will insult the dentist someday if I live so long. I will find time to insult the born-again Christian, too. It turns out that a first-rate violinist was assaulted and killed and her body left drooping over his pileup of garbage bags in the staircase landing. I tell myself how much the author of Ecclesiastes would disdain the born-again Christian. Of course none of that does any good: The policewoman takes me gently over, and I am shown a three-cornered opening to Georgia's face. The fine craft of her brain, whatever of her that can fly, clearly has got away.

The following week, I am to have two laser vaporizations

Carol Bly

and one small ordinary surgery done at the same time. All three procedures can be taken care of in the In and Out Surgi-Center, as before, but I feel like a girl at the Scout meeting who is a little too old and really should join the serious organizations of adulthood. I know that any future surgery they have to do will be in the main, serious part of the hospital, where patients survive or they don't.

As before, they hand me my papers, a folder called "Welcome to the In and Out Surgi-Center," and a zipper bag long enough for my clothes. I undress in a cubicle and emerge to claim a comfortable lounge chair in the waiting area. There are several of us, our chairs spaced informally about. We all have our angel robes and light blue dressing gowns over them. We are mostly graying or white haired or bald. We look so much alike it is a reminder that our insides—cervixes, kidneys, veins—are more alike than not.

I note how kindly each of us is treated: white-dressed people lean over to drop a word; someone brings a magazine. It crosses my mind that if the Saint Alban's In and Out Surgi-Center were part of a gigantic lab experiment in human outcomes, we would probably be the control group—the ones you handle kindly but don't give any of the hopeful treatment to. None of us has eaten in twelve hours, so we give one another shy, starving smiles. We doze in the marvelous chairs. From time to time, a nurse wakes one or another of us to go to a curtained area, where we get anesthesia on a gurney.

In my curtained area, I find the same nurse-anesthetist I had last time.

"Oh!" she says with a laugh, entering the IV. "I'd know you, all right! You're the one who is learning the violin! It isn't everyone you meet who studies a tough instrument like that, I can tell you!"

"I remember you, too!" I crow back.

Now she tells me in a triumphant tone, as she disappears around behind the drip stand, "I remember that you're fussy about what we do for you! You told me to give you something that would leave your brains in good condition, that would kill pain but leave you conscious, because you wanted to experience the procedure—and you didn't want sodium pentothal, which we don't have anyway, because you were afraid you would use foul language. You thought I'd *forget* all that?"

I tell her, "I also remember that you told me the ordinary dose of fentanyl is one cc, and I told you I wanted half, and you said, 'Oh, just relax'; you had already entered the full dose into the intravenous. Tricky, I thought."

"I know," she says in her gentle, nurse's tone. "And I have done it again."

She has come back to my side. "How are the violin lessons going?"

"Very well," I tell her. "I have one of the best teachers in the city, it turns out. It is important to study with the best, especially if you yourself are not particularly gifted."

"Gifted schmifted," the nurse says. "What's gift?"

Now the tremendous boost of the fentanyl, not to mention the sugar hit of the glucose drip, comes into my elbow. After its overnight fast, the body is pathetically grateful. "I feel my IQ not only not *dropping* but actually going up," I tell the nurse.

"Could it go up?" she says with a laugh. "I didn't know

Carol Bly

they got any higher than what you came sashaying in here with."

It is precisely the tone in which Georgia Persons had told me that the chamber orchestra would need me by Memorial Day of 1992 if not 1991, no question.

The drug makes me every second more airy. I like to keep everything in a kind of bullety focus, so I monitor the drug working in me as sensibly as I can. Yes, you are getting smart-ass with the drug, I think, but *intraveno veritas,* I think, too, and I notice I am dissolving into smart-ass peacefulness. The world looks unrealistically softened, but the scrim over everything looks like wise scrim, and I raise myself up to lead my bow hand gently with my wrist, not sawing, not vindictive, gently taking the right wrist forward and back down right, upward and left again. I keep the left elbow bent in the required, absolutely unnatural position under a violin, with the wrist bent the other way so the fingers can work.

"What's going on?" cries a cordial-enough male voice.

I hear the nurse explaining that I am demonstrating how much more difficult it is to hold a violin than any other instrument—than a cello, for instance. Anyone can hold a cello without tiring. You are working at it against your knees. One can nearly droop above a cello.

But now I am a little lost and notice only that other people in white or green go drifting by outside the furry edge of my cubicle. One of them is my surgeon. It crosses my mind (though now I am wafting a good deal) that if he loses me in the end, it might hurt his career. No, I reply to myself, coming to sense by main force of will now, nothing hurts anyone's career. People continue to do whatever they now do. The Hemlock Avenue Boy Scouts, as Georgia called them, will continue to smoke mild dope and sell serious drugs. The born-again Christian will go on explaining to new tenants at 4303 that the last thing in the world he would do is take credit for God having chosen him, rather than someone else, to work through with His gifts. The born-again Christian will continue leaving his garbage in the tiny hallway and on the front porch. And at Saint Alban's, the nurse-anesthetist will go on letting patients ask for .5 cc while she administers 1 cc.

And I will go on being afraid of death all the months that lie ahead of me, even though I have had Georgia Persons as a teacher of courage. Now I imagine her as hard as I can, because the nurse is wheeling my gurney into the actual icy surgery itself, where a crew of people dressed up in green insect costumes are engaged in bee tasks here and there. And now I remember what it is that lifts us above the flower patch of our fears: It is our good teachers, of course, but behind them it is the artists themselves—Handel or Friml or Kuechler, doing their work. Georgia was right: men are repulsive. And women are repulsive, as well. But there are always a few artists ghosting around who invite us to do the work of beauty, and who give us back our humor when we are terrified.

Carol Bly

The Tender Organizations

Nature is so rife with life that tender organizations can be
serenely squashed out of existence like pulp. . . .

—HENRY DAVID THOREAU

There is a natural, satisfying enmity between ecstatic people
and practical people. The Marthas of the world know the
Marys are goldbricks. The Marys, smiling at their gurus'
knees, would never trade their numinous excitement for
housewives' depression.

Where we go wrong is in supposing that it is the ecstatic
people who find the practical people boring. They do, of
course—but not nearly so boring as the practical people find
the ecstatics. Of course anyone skilled in bread making and
other kitchen work gets irritated by the ecstatic people's
pouring oil over the mentors' feet or at the way the ecstatics
wait silent until their mentors stop speaking, and then give
off an odd singsong trill of admiration. All that is merely irri-
tating: what drives the practical people to exasperation, and

finally drowsiness, is the way ecstatic people can't get hold of a project and do it simply. In parish churches all over the world, not just in Clayton, Minnesota, practical people go straight to sleep while the ecstatic people cry, "Oh! Oh! How *shall* we get people to *feel* the loving-kindness in our beautiful universe!" The practical people simply drop off to sleep, right there in the Lady Chapel or the Guild Hall or the Fellowship Room.

Sally Thackers, the Episcopal rector's wife, was a methodical sort. She was twenty-eight, a healthy-faced woman who went about in a Hollofil vest in the wintertime. In the summer she was a raiser of perennials; in the winter she planned to develop beds of the sparer flowers: she planned where she would put Carpathian harebells, and how to present their slight flowering as delicate, instead of simply scant. She was pleased to spend a lot of time in the kitchen—rather more pleased to be there than participating in her husband's discussions before the rectory hearth. She had nothing striking about her looks: her hair was already turning pale, and her healthiness seemed just that: healthy, rather than decorative. Her plainness was not all bad. She found it easy to slip from the rectory living room to the kitchen, with a deprecating wave—"There is the bread to be looked after"—hiding in her persona of Jack Thackers's practical wife.

In the last week before Saint Andrew's Feast, she hovered at the kitchen window, listening to the hushed sleet tick on its panes. She half overheard the men's conversation in the living room; she half sang a nursery rhyme to her unborn child. She sang sotto voce its violent plot. She sometimes pretended that life was as it had been before these seven-and-a-half weeks of

Carol Bly

her pregnancy. She pretended she was a freestanding person, at liberty to be lost in the universe. She wished that her husband's few, slight failings—his fear of dogs, his belief that God answered personal prayers—struck her simply as touching, the way they had before her pregnancy. Now that she was to be a mother, she saw him as the loved, honored father of her child but also as a man not one hundred percent reliable. She would have to stay on tippy toe.

She and Jack had a slightly older friend, an oncology nurse named Mercein. Mercein's brother Dick had come to the rectory this morning to share with Jack that he had laid out the fleece for God, and God had answered. Dick must be forty-two, Sally thought, old enough to know better. Dick had told God that if God wanted him to move from Clayton down to the Twin Cities, as Dick's wife wanted to do, God was to give a sign. If no sign was given on the designated day, the man would know it was all right to stay in Clayton, where life was so pleasant, with the mixed forest to hunt in and all the calm, low-paying jobs. Dick went hunting up around Route 6 all day. He checked out the little lakes near Emily, and Outing, finally standing in a blind on Lawrence Lake, but he never got a shot. When he got home he told his wife, and she agreed what it meant, even though she had wanted to be in the Twin Cities so much. Now Dick wanted Jack to know that he had spoken to God, and God had spoken back. It was OK to stay. Dick gave Jack and Sally a Williams-Sonoma bowl.

Sally listened a little from the kitchen, her lip curled. When she went into the room with a tea tray, she saw Jack nearly weightless on his seat, his body bent toward Dick. His face was guileless and vacuous; he prompted Dick's story nearly in a whisper. Sally had trouble even thanking Dick for the bowl. Born-again Christians would never just give you something. They never said, "Sally, here is a bowl." You had to listen to their rhetoric as well. "Sally and Jack, I really feel as if you two are really Servants of God, you know? I feel as if I can really tell my feelings about God to you—here is a bowl."

It was hard for the Thackerses to find a whole morning, or afternoon, or even a whole evening, to be alone with each other. Two days after Dick's visit, Jack brought in an armful of the dry ash firewood from 1988 and announced that they were going to spend the morning hanging out. Since Sally felt nauseated, he would make the tea.

The wood came from an eighty just north of Carolyn's animal hospital, straight across from the regular people's hospital. Two summers ago, George, Carolyn's husband, who had the Super Valu store in town, and Carolyn, and Mercein, and Norma, the new UCC minister, had taken down eleven trees. The following January they stood in the snow, brushing against the spiny redwood bushes, and swede-sawed up all the trunks. Now the wood was perfect.

Just as Sally and Jack settled down to waste the morning, Mercein called up to say that the Otto Schlaeger situation had become intolerable and would Jack please get on the stick and use whatever clout he had with the Schlaeger family's pastor to intervene. And also get the daughter home. The man was dying fast.

Aloud, Sally said to Jack, "You can have him over." To herself she said, Good-bye, hearth, for *this* morning.

Carol Bly

A disadvantage of clerical life was that Jack couldn't use the statement so handy to people in the women's movement: *Sorry, I need to do something for myself*—so would you please take your problems with the Schlaeger family somewhere else? Jack's twenty-four-thousand-dollar-plus package deal made him a professional, the way the president of Merrill Lynch was a professional.

"Too bad," Jack said, lingering in the kitchen doorframe. "I really thought this time we could just drink a lot of tea and get nervous and enjoy the fire. Now we have Kurt instead."

He dutifully dialed the Missouri Synod church number. Sally heard him say in a full, open-throated voice, "Sally's baking something with raisins in it that smells wonderful! How about making it over here in a half hour or so?"

Kurt would come. He was a huge, comfortable man, whose body dropped fast into any inviting space. He always took Jack's recliner when he visited the rectory. If the chairs were unevenly drawn up to the fire, he inched his forward until it was fair. He was interested in the arms buildups of all countries—not just of the big ones. He knew, for example, that Afghanistan rebels had repulsed Soviet helicopters with their mix of rifles, even old Enfields, as effectively as they would have with SAM Sevens.

Sally said, "I had better go ahead and bake something with raisins that smells delicious, then."

Jack looked apologetic, and then smiled. "How is the baby?" he asked.

They had not told anyone they were expecting a child, so it was still a mysterious happiness and pathos of their own. Sally imagined the baby somewhere on the wall of her vaulty, blood-colored womb. She imagined the egg and the seed still so newly joined they were curious to have found each other: they were binding themselves together as fast as night. She imagined the baby hanging on for dear life, now in November using only the tiniest part of the space reserved for it. The womb must feel very rangy to the baby.

She and Jack found their rectory a little rangy, too. There it stood in their town of 2,242, a fake-half-timbered-English house rough in its sleety grapevines, in the police catchment area of St. Cloud, in the hospice catchment area of their friend Mercein, in the mental health catchment area of Mora, in the Anglophilia catchment area of the Episcopal church. Its walls were hung with British servants' hall hangings, in the way that Missouri Synod Lutheran parsonages have Dresden flower stollen plates, or barn owl steins made in West Germany.

In Jack and Sally's house the kitchen hanging said that any servant caught feeding dogs under the table would be fined threepence halfpenny. Any servant coming to dinner without his jacket would be fined twopence. "It's not evil—it's just silly," Jack said to Sally. "Any object from a revered place feels *holy* to people. People revere England, period." He no doubt recognized the expression on her face: he said firmly, "We are *not* either just a museum piece of Anglicanism."

Now they clung together a moment. "I am singing to the baby every day now," Sally told him. "And using less bad language. Today the music is the Magnificat, half *tonus peregrinus* and half faux-bourdon, and the nursery rhyme is 'Three mice went into a cellar to spin—Puss passed by and Puss looked in.'" She added, "On with the raisins and white dough."

A half hour later, she shamelessly eavesdropped as she spread an ironed piece of old Fair Linen on a tray. Jack was explaining the Schlaeger situation to Kurt.

"There's old Otto Schlaeger in horrible pain now, from the cancer, and apparently Vi is secretly not giving him his painkillers. She *tells* Mercein she has given it each time, but when Mercein shows up, Otto is often in outright agony. Apparently Vi is skipping the every-three-or-four-hours' morphine dosing. Mercein says the idea is to give the meds at exactly the same time intervals. Vi isn't doing it."

No sounds for a moment.

Then Jack's voice again: "If you skip one of the scheduled times, the pain gets so out of control it takes a shot to bring it down. Shots are not the idea," Jack went on, obviously relating information exactly as the hospice nurse had recited it for him. "Oral meds is best. Then suppositories. Third, injection."

"Yeah? Suppositories?" Kurt's full, friendly voice.

Good, Sally thought, taking out the white-dough-and-raisins muffins. Kurt is taking an interest.

Kurt's voice again: "Suppositories, huh? I would hate to have to have a suppository."

Jack's voice: "So Mercein said to Vi, three days ago, that she absolutely must *not* fail to give Otto his meds. Vi told Mercein to get out of the house. Mercein couldn't even get back in this morning. So that's where we are with this now," Jack wound up.

Kurt said, "A difficult time of life for those two—very, very hard going, I know. I remember when my dad got his cancer. . . . Well, now—Otto and Vi Schlaeger. Much to be said on both sides, Jack . . . much to be said on both sides.

That isn't a marriage that's always been easy. I don't think I am talking out of school when I say that."

Jack's voice: "Easy marriage! Easy marriage, Kurt! Holy shit, Kurt! Otto's been beating Vi for twenty-six years! The grown daughter won't even come home!"

Kurt: "These things are so darn difficult to judge from the outside. Naturally I've heard some about this, and I'm not at leave to pass all of it on. But I will say that Vi came to me twice, saying how hard he was on her."

Jack's voice: "Just twice?"

Kurt gave a small laugh. "She wanted me to look at a mouse she said he'd given her. Both times. Same thing. My feeling was then and is now that I'd want to hear both sides of these family things before I moved on it."

Jack: "So did you hear both sides?"

Kurt: "Otto never came complaining to me, so I figured they'd worked out something. I know that I sure gave them focus in my prayers, for quite a while there. Well, Jack: it does take two to tango, it really does. I know Vi is supposed to be a wonderful homemaker—all that canning and gardening and all—but there isn't any rule says a woman can't put on a spot of lipstick once in a while, or get herself done up a little."

Sally carried in a tray of the muffins and coffee. Kurt smiled happily and took two. She went over to Jack. They mentioned the sleet and how it would freeze soon and Interstate 94 would be a mess. Sally knew they would keep making small talk until she left the room.

"Schlaegers have a wonderful dog," Kurt remarked. "Airedale bitch. It'd be fun to have a really smart dog like

Carol Bly

that along for hunting. I'm not one of your hunters who has to have a dog to *work* all the time! I'd just like to have it for the companionship. A lot of people forget that hunting is supposed to be recreation and that goes for the dog, too. They treat it as if it were just work, work, work."

Sally slid back into the kitchen and regarded the sleet out the window. It lay in shining fur along all the basswood branches.

In the kitchen closet, Sally found her Hollofil vest and a sou'wester hat and let herself out the back door. She drove very carefully down Main Street and then over to Seventh Avenue to George's Super Valu.

The frozen-foods manager told Sally that George was out back somewhere. A shelf stocker told her to try the office, all the way back, past all the crates in the warehouse part of the building. Sally barged along the huge, shadowy warehouse aisles, where the air was snappy and smelled of old ground. She knocked at George's little ply-and-bare-studs office door. Inside, it was all bright light, sudden heat from the electric strip, and George's work spread out on a desk—claimed coupons, bad credit notes, truck vouchers. He poured Sally a cup of boiling water with a beef-flavor cube in it and listened to her story. He made a telephone call. Mercein, he told her, would be there in five, and thank God someone was doing something.

George and Sally made negative, catty small talk as they waited. They and their group—Carolyn, Jack, Mercein, and Norma, the UCC minister, and even George's frozen-foods manager, who was also VFW post commander—had too high profiles to gossip in the usual places—at coffee parties on

Eighth or Ninth Avenues, or at the VFW, or during dish-washing at Men's Fellowship or at Guild. Therefore it was delicious for them to assess and criticize when they could. George told Sally that as far back as he knew, the Schlaegers were the worst family in town. They weren't the worst in the conventional sense—that is, they didn't live in an AFDC addition and they didn't miss church because of hangovers. They were quite respectable. In fact, Otto was the one who first proposed that everyone on Eighth Avenue mow their lawn on the same day of the week so that the grass height from lot to lot would match. Once he had gone around to Mercein's brother, Dick, and told him to set his mower height lower because it wrecked the look of the whole street. The Schlaegers were middle-class, but everyone in town was sixty percent sure he beat his wife whenever he had three beers, and for all anyone knew, the kid as well. That would be his daughter, George said, looking up, thinking: who must be something like thirty-five now. Gone away to the Cities.

Sally offered, "Beaters are beaters." In the Episcopal church, the wife-beater was the guy who made sure they ran up the flag of Saint Andrew every November 30. Sally said, "How is Carolyn?" George told her he didn't see much of his wife this time of year, when the rich went to McAllen or Waco to get away from the Minnesota winter. They left their domestic animals in Carolyn's kennel.

Sally and George gave each other the superior look of people who stay through the winter. Then Mercein burst in, bright from the cold.

"What're you two hatching up?" she said. "I could tell

Carol Bly

from your voice on the phone." She gave Sally a fast appraisal. "How are you, Sally Thackers?" she said.

Sally instantly saw that Mercein knew she was pregnant. So much for that secret, she thought.

George said, "We have a solution for the Schlaeger problem. You move in, Mercein. Nights. Tell Vi that Otto needs round-the-clock nursing care."

"Tried that," Mercein remarked. "As soon as I saw Vi was trying on purpose to make him suffer. For revenge! I told her I would move in, but she threw me out."

Sally explained the fine points. "We force her," Sally said. "We threaten to call a psychiatric social worker from Mora if we have to. That ought to work."

Mercein heard them out. "OK," she said. "But I don't go over there alone. This last time she offered to set that Airedale on me."

George said, "Sally and I go with you."

Sally said, "No—I go with you. George stays here. George, we save you for *heavy metal* if we need it later. And our backup plan is to haul in the whole ministerium if we have to."

George said, "That's right, and we can't use Norma, either. She's had that UCC job less than a year, and she can't get in trouble with breaking and entering, in case Vi goes to court. Speaking of clergy, Sally, are we telling Jack about this?"

Sally said, "Jack needs to not know. If Vi calls him, he can draw a complete blank. It'll have to be just us, Mercein."

Sally thought, as she and Mercein moved out through the drafty warehouse, past all the piled vegetables far from wherever they were grown, This is an untoward business for the baby. On second thought, though, she decided the baby was still so very small—only a scant eight weeks old—it couldn't be paying even the most unconscious, most inchoate attention to her projects. Still, she felt that the activist flavor was not right for in utero people. She would counteract the tone of all this with some bland song the moment she got free.

Mercein and Sally stalled outside the Super Valu window. "We had better take both our cars," Mercein said. "I may need to stay a while, if we ever get in there today. By the way, this might get tough. If it gets tough, Sally, you do exactly what I tell you to do, and you do it right away."

"What nonsense," Sally said. "I am stronger than you, and I've seen grievouser and worse things in the world than you ever thought up in a bad dream." The moment she had said it, however, she couldn't make a mental image of one grievous thing she had seen. She felt like a faint, ridiculous child, brought up in a childish way, helping other people live childish lives, and now carrying a still fainter and more childish child inside her. It all seemed rather wonderful, if stupid.

Mercein said, "People who are expecting should stay out of fights."

Sally felt as if she were watching a flare slowly sink down above her.

Mercein said snappily. "For goodness sake, I am a nurse. I know you are pregnant. I can tell a birth or a death months ahead."

"How nice to be a prophet," Sally said.

Mercein said, "You know we're stalling, don't you? We're both scared to death. Let's go over there and get it over with."

Carol Bly

Each got into her own car and drove through the new slush to the Schlaegers'.

Mercein stood to one side of the storm door; Sally rang the bell. The moment Vi Schlaeger opened the inner door to see who had come, Mercein whipped around and put her foot in the storm door opening. She was an old hand: she put her boot in so that when the home owner slammed the door on it, it hit the soft part, not the anklebone.

Vi was a German-American immigrant's grandchild. She had the remarkable horizontal eyebrows and forehead width of thousands of northern faces. The eyes were gray-blue, with handsome dark eyelashes; the mouth was wide. The straight, abundant hair, now gray, was drawn back. Every single feature was handsome and powerful, yet the overall effect made your blood run chill.

"Told you before, I'm telling you again: you get out, and you're not coming here anymore. He don't need you, and I don't need you," Vi said to Mercein. She ignored Sally.

Mercein said, "I am moving in. Otto needs round-the-clock nursing, and that's what he's going to get."

The infuriated wife cried, "He don't need no round-the-clock nursing, period!"

Sally geared up for her lines and said them. "Mrs. Schlaeger, I am here as a witness. If you refuse entrance to the oncology nurse, I will act as witness. It is your legal right to know that."

Vi Schlaeger did not know much about American justice, but she watched the American average of six-and-one-fourth hours' television each day. She knew that words like "witness" and "your legal right" had grave muscle. She opened the door.

Vi's bit of living room was dark and heavy, like the inside of a cave. Sally was aware of dreary lampshades, their bulbs unlit, of at least a dozen plants with wide, drooping leaves hanging above the clay rims.

Otto Schlaeger lay curled on the sofa, legs pulled up, his whole body rocking frantically. Mercein went over to him immediately. When she said his name, he jerked his head around and he cried, "For Christ's sake!"

The nurse was on the floor by the sofa, bag open, fixing her syringe. "Better in two minutes, Otto," she said.

Sally hovered a few feet behind her. She heard Vi mutter, "Hurts, does it, huh?" When Sally swung around, Vi looked back at her, steady as a column.

Sally then paid attention to everything Mercein did, interested in the earmarks of a new trade. "Just like a hobbyist," she then told herself, "learning how people do what they do— give medicines, bake bread, run stores, decorate churches. Why don't you just live your own life?" Only a part of her mind said that, however. Another part went on watching how Mercein kept her hand on the man's forehead and kept talking to him, waiting for the morphine to take. Mercein also talked to the patient's wife, in a friendly, Scout-leader tone. "Vi? Let me show you this. Say you're going to put an afghan on a patient. That afghan on the chair. Would you bring it over?"

Mercein said a little louder, "Vi, bring over the afghan."

"He don't need an afghan. He's all sweaty anyhow."

"Sally—you bring me that afghan, would you? Now. You pull it up not just *to* the shoulders but all the way over, because that's where the chilling gets in. And Sally, would you

Carol Bly

bring my bag in? And Vi, would you tell Sally where to set my things so they will be out of your way? Bad enough to have houseguests without they don't leave their stuff around!"

Mercein kept up everything in a singsong. "We'll keep Otto on these meds, every four hours, day and night, so the pain never gets ahead of us. The three of us can manage perfectly well. And if Otto needs it, he can have a bump now and then."

"A bump!" cried Vi.

"Extra morphine," Mercein said. "Everyone knows you take pride in your work, Vi. All that canning. All your housecleaning. Well, I take pride in my work, too." She kept talking.

Presently the dying man's knees relaxed. Sally thought, He doesn't look so much like a cause now. He simply looks like an ugly person asleep, who is neither interesting nor kind when awake. There must be millions, millions, of men like Otto. Sally told the baby, It's bad luck, someone like Otto. But your luck is already better.

Suddenly Vi said, "Now you get out, you the one that's not nursing or anything."

Sally said, "I *am* going home now. But Mercein is going to stay. And if you give her any trouble I am going to call the psychiatric social worker from Mora, and you know what I'm going to do, Mrs. Schlaeger? I will tell her that you live at 314 Eighth Avenue instead of 312 Eighth Avenue, so the social worker will knock there first, and explain who she is, and ask where you live."

Vi's cheeks shook. "You get out, or I'll set Hoffer on you."

Sally now realized that a large dog lay behind the vertical

leaves of the dining-room table. Its head arched forward about two inches above its paws. It kept one eye squeezed shut, or perhaps the eye was missing. Sally thought, Not just a bad thing for the baby, bad for me. Although she was only half as frightened of dogs as Jack was, she was still frightened her full half share. The Airedale, however, didn't move when Mrs. Schlaeger spoke its name.

Sally said, "If you try to kick us out, we are going to call the police, Mrs. Schlaeger. Not the police which is that fellow that goes to your church, either. The real police. In St. Cloud."

"You can't call the police," the woman said, but her voice wobbled, and Sally, with one eye on the dog, now felt that everything would be all right.

"I'll walk you to your car," Mercein said.

The translucent sleet was turning to real snow. In the quarter hour—which seemed like hours—that Mercein and Sally had been inside, the snow had been disposing itself in its own tendrils and handsome ganglia along all the ash and maple trees.

At Sally's car door, Mercein said, "Now listen to me. Here is how you look at this. You keep your mind on how really peaceful and painless old Otto looked on the couch. That's *all* you think about. You remember this, Sally: in all the rest of his life—one week, ten days—he isn't going to feel any pain ever again. You understand that?"

Mercein paused a moment. Sally thought she was about to comment on the weather, because she looked about her, at the little street full of cold lawns and trees and some cars parked. But Mercein said, "Forget Vi. All her life she has had a mean husband, and her daughter ran away and never writes home,

Carol Bly

so she's mad. But the mean husband is dying, so her problems are over. I will go back in now, and talk to her some, and also try to find out where the daughter is. I'll be in touch."

In the next ten days the weather deepened. George's Super Valu staff greasepainted the front store windows: REMEMBER LAST SUMMER? WELCOME THE MOISTURE! HAPPY HOLIDAYS! Sally recovered from morning sickness and went on a whole-grain baking binge. Outside her kitchen window the snow did the one thing we want snow to do: it turned the twentieth century back into the softer nineteenth century. In this softer, quieter landscape, the snow said, technology is nothing, industrialization is nothing; surely the hole in the far south sky will heal . . . everything can be managed.

This is your first snow, Sally told the baby—since how would it know, otherwise, hiding in there, as it did, self-centeredly growing its brain, its nervous system, its stomach, still keeping its beginnings of hands curled inward.

Jack said, "Kurt just called. Of all things, he called to say that God has answered our prayers about Vi Schlaeger."

Sally heard the "of all things" as Jack's willingness to join her in a small jeer at the Missouri Synod Lutheran pastor. She also saw that Jack leaned a little springily in the kitchen doorway, his elbows sticking out, one hand touching along the back of the other in front of his stomach. "Did you know—" he went on, "perhaps you didn't know—that Kurt and I agreed we'd each pray that Vi would find it in her heart to let Mercein take over the care of old Otto?"

Sally felt Jack's mind alternately flaring and shrinking in front of her, wanting her to agree to this mysterious outcome, that something had come of two men's prayers. He wanted her to agree to it, of course: worse, he wanted her to feel wafted away, as he seemed to feel. Once, in their five years of marriage, she had pretended to get more pleasure in bed than she had felt at the time. It was a February night, as clear as stars in her memory. She had gone to sleep early, exhausted from housecleaning the whole rectory. She had made herself get through all the cleaning, knowing that once bathed and in bed, she could look over the new garden catalog. She had her pen and paper and a clipboard lying alongside her, on Jack's side. She carefully drew all the flower plots and drew some brick layouts. She planned how to keep something white and something blue in bloom throughout the summer. She liked flowers that had a good deal of green, with space between the blooms, rather than crowding flowers, like daisies. She wanted Carpathian harebells.

Jack's lovemaking had not distracted her from her thoughts. Therefore she had lied a little. Now, looking toward him from the kitchen worktable, she lied again: that is, she gave him a smile, but she squinted her right eye, hoping it would make the smile into a kind of twinkling, good-natured grin.

Jack then said, "Funny fellow, Kurt. He calls me up to tell me about the Immanent God, but the next minute he gets onto deer hunting, deer hunting, deer hunting."

Nearly five hundred of Clayton's two thousand and more people sat in Saint Paul's for Otto Schlaeger's funeral. The great, bluff pastor told them that Otto Schlaeger's father had come to America so he would not have to serve in the Kaiser's

Carol Bly

army. Kurt's sermon went on, quietly, undeniably giving its own kind of consolation. It connected the little town with the great world outside. It connected the past of Germany and America with this death. If that German had not emigrated, Kurt told them, he might well have dressed in field gray, and he might have shot at our Clayton, Minnesota, men who met Germans at Château-Thierry. That man's son, whose life among us we celebrated today, might never have served as a rating on the USS *Mississippi*.

As Kurt began to maunder, Sally let her thoughts shift here and there. She told the baby she would teach it history, because learning history—it was a simple fact she had not thought of before—makes people happy. She daydreamed about that idea for all the rest of the service. It spared her getting irritated when Kurt got lost on one of his hobbies: he was now listing Navy ordnance options to this funeral audience. It spared her feeling sardonic at the grave, when George's frozen-foods manager and a young guardsman stretched and yanked corners of the flag, put it roughly into its triangles, and then took it, a pad of cloth now, and marched, squaring imagined corners across the undertaker's green cloth and the snow, to Vi Schlaeger. The post commander presented the flag to Otto Schlaeger's widow on behalf of the president of the United States. Clearly the widow didn't know what expression to arrange on her face. She seemed to try two or three. In the end, she settled on the expression of people returning to their pews after they have taken Eucharist.

As they came away from the graveside, Jack put Sally's gloved hand into the crook of his elbow. "Tomorrow I am going to make a fire and we are going to sit around our house, *alone,* all day. There's no one in the hospital. No one is getting married."

"I will bake whole-wheat rolls with oat bran in them," Sally said. "On the other hand, there is something really depressing about oat bran."

"That's true," Jack said in a happy voice. "Oat bran sucks."

The next morning, however, someone banged their door knocker before ten o'clock.

It was an energetic-looking woman in her early thirties, with springing hair, glittering eyes, an expressive mouth; she was made up fully—there was something of everything: shadow, liner, mascara, blush, and lipstick—yet the woman's focus was so strong, even aggressive, that the makeup couldn't gentle it.

"Mrs. John Thackers?" she said loudly. "They said over at the church that your husband was home today."

She jammed her way in past Sally. That was close, Sally said to the baby. She felt cheery. Whoever this visitor was, Sally meant to throw her out after fifteen minutes. Sally had been a good rector's wife: she had gone to the funeral, even out to the cemetery, instead of waiting in the Saint Paul's basement with the old, the pregnant, and the greedy. Now this was her and Jack's day off. Besides, the woman had thick, strong hair. She probably had a coarse nature, Sally decided.

"I don't guess you'd know who I am," the visitor said. "I'm Francine, Vi Schlaeger's girl."

Jack came in with an L. L. Bean canvas full of fireplace wood.

"This is Jack Thackers—Ms. Schlaeger," Sally said.

Carol Bly

"We didn't know you'd got here for your dad's funeral," Jack said.

"I wouldn't come for his funeral!" Francine said with a laugh. "I drove up from the Cities this morning. Just to pick up my mother and take her to stay with me a week or so. Just to put the dog down and get the stuff out of the refrigerator. But then, on the way up, I had an experience. A direct relationship to God."

Jack motioned toward the chair Sally usually sat in, by the fire. Sally started to ease on out to the kitchen, as she always did as soon as people started talking about having a direct or personal experience of Jesus Christ. She did so not so much to spare herself the thrilled, self-congratulatory voices but because people having a religious experience always want to tell it to someone in authority—a clergyperson—not to a spouse who happens to be there.

But Francine called after her. "Don't go away! I won't be long! In fact, my mother's waiting out in the car!"

"Waiting in the car!" both Jack and Sally cried, going toward the door.

Francine raised and dropped one shoulder. "She wouldn't come in," she said. "She doesn't want to hear about the way God spoke to me! I don't know why I'm surprised. She wouldn't even listen to ordinary-life things I tried to tell her as a child. And things I tried to tell her about. . . . Anyway," she said. "Anyway. And I couldn't go to Pastor Kurt, because of course he's gone hunting or trapping. And anyway . . . there was some nurse that took care of Dad hanging around the house this morning; she said to come to you."

She stopped, giving Jack a look.

"Now," she said, "I hope you don't *mind* hearing about a personal religious experience?"

You're in luck, Sally thought, looking at the woman. It's too late for *me* to get out of the room, but Jack not only does not mind personal religious feeling; he likes it very much. Sally felt like a Martha who has been told she absolutely may *not* go out to bake the loaves: she *must* stay, like Mary, and pour oil and be admiring.

Francine had driven out of Minneapolis very early in the moring, before full light, if you could call any daylight in December full light. She was half asleep on Interstate 94 when a voice said, very clearly, "Keep a sharp eye out for animals on the right side of the road." Now, Francine was very surprised, since she thought the only person who heard voices was Joan of Arc, a Roman Catholic. Francine didn't particularly *want* to hear voices. This voice persevered. It insisted she watch for "beautiful animals on the right." Well, all right, she told the voice, but I don't expect anything out of this. Now Francine said to Jack and Sally, "I expect very little of God and very little of people of God, too. The one time I ever went to the pastor in need, he told me I should be a good girl and not go around carrying tales about my dad."

She'd kept driving and presently whizzed past a crow, which stood right beside a fair-sized carcass, a dog or something that size. As roadkill goes, it must have been very fresh. It was a cold day, but the entrails, some of which hung from the crow's beak, were still bright red and flexible. The crow was so pleased with its find it scarcely budged as the powerful car shot by.

Carol Bly

Francine then said to the voice, "If that is your idea of 'beautiful animals,' forget it."

The voice said monotonously, "Keep watching for beautiful animals on the right."

Another ten or fifteen minutes later, Francine's car fled across the Rum River bridge. There, far on the right, with their skinny black legs silhouetted against the white ice, stood a buck and several does. The bridge noise startled them: they pawed once, and the buck bobbed his head so Francine saw his full rack.

Now her face, under its no-nonsense permanent, was bright. "So you see? . . . You see?" she nearly shouted at Jack.

Jack said steadily, "That is a wonderful, wonderful story."

He spoke in a companionable, respectful, calming tone, but Sally felt his excitement as well. And his right foot went lightly pigeon-toed and back several times.

Eventually Jack let Francine out of the doorway. Sally heard him say, ". . . something to hang onto for a lifetime."

Sally told the baby, Well, your father is an extraordinary man. He would be delighted to have such an experience himself. He always nearly comes out of his chair when someone tells such stories. But he never, at least not ever that Sally knew of, let on how much he wished *he* saw visions or heard voices or got any proofs of anything numinous.

By the time Jack had closed the door, Sally had her Hollofil vest on. "I'm off for just a half hour," she told him. "Then I'll be back, and we will still have the whole day."

He held her shoulders. "Where are you going?"

"Out," she said ironically. "You don't want to know where."

Then he said, "Don't slip. It melted last night and then froze up again this morning."

Carolyn's animal hospital and kennel were at the north end of Clayton, past the flower shop, past the nursing home and hospital. As she drove by it, Sally gave a respectful glance at the hospital's maternity wing. A part of her fate had already moved in over there: it was much the way a part of her fate had moved into the rectory when Jack first showed it to her, before they were married.

She found Carolyn examining a cat. The vet kept one hand on its breast and reached for things behind her with the other.

Sally said, "We just got a telephone call from Francine Schlaeger, of all people. She said she'd been trying to reach you, but the line was busy."

"It wasn't," Carolyn said briefly. "I've been right here, working on this fellow."

Sally relaxed. "I suppose she had the wrong number. She asked me to tell you she has changed her mind about that Airedale of her dad's and she wants you to give it to me. Along with a leash and a couple of days' food. Then she will call me and make other arrangements later."

Carolyn said, "She wanted me to put that dog down, I thought. She said it was vicious."

Sally said brightly, "Well, she's changed her mind."

"She has, huh?" Carolyn said. She molded her hands around the cat and laid it in a small cage. She went out back and reemerged with a one-eyed animal, which Sally recognized as Hoffer, the dog under the Schlaegers' dining-room table. It looked huge. Could it have grown in two weeks?

Carol Bly

Carolyn took a leash from the wall. "Now, you want to be careful with this one, Sally. She's been knocked around some. Ill-fed, too. My guess is, if you feed her and water her a lot, right from the first, she'll make her home with you. Don't move fast around her at first. Did Francine Schlaeger tell you what to do with the nine-dollar check for the Nembutal?"

"Oh," Sally said, "she certainly did. She absolutely wanted you to keep it, in return for your trouble."

Carolyn grinned and said, "Yeah, she did, huh? Well, here's enough dog food for until Ms. Schlaeger decides to relieve you of the dog. Now . . . in case she changes her mind *again* and doesn't relieve you of the dog, bring her back in so I can give her some shots and check her over for you. Airedales are Airedales. I thought you were scared of dogs, hey."

Sally thought, If I put the dog in the backseat, it might bite me in the neck as I'm driving. Also, I would see it in the rearview mirror and get scared. But if I put it beside me, as a passenger, it might leap at me. Life, she told the baby, is made up of the greater evil and the lesser evil. She put the dog beside her.

At the rectory, Jack took Sally's vest and hung it on the visitors' coat tree. He also took the leash and said, slightly in his falsetto, "Hello, big fellow. Welcome."

"Big girl," Sally said. "Her name is Hoffer."

Jack dragged the fifty-pound feed bag to the kitchen. He came back with the Williams-Sonoma bowl, filled to the top with dried dog food. He made another trip and returned with a bowl of water. He set the food and the water between their two chairs before the fire. The fire reflected a little in the water.

Then Jack and Sally sat down, leaving the dog at the back of the room.

"You see what a first-rate husband I am?" Jack said. "Do you hear me asking any questions? No. And after a while, when I recover from the cold sweat that animal put me in, I will go to the kitchen and make cocoa. Then we will not have any more adventures all day."

Sally and Jack heard a series of thuds. They turned to see.

Hoffer had lain down bonily, with the idea of thinking everything over. She knew that eventually she would creep forward; eventually she would do that, and eat some of that food and drink about half of the water, if that's what that was in the other bowl. She also knew she would kiss the hands of these human beings, the male one and the female one, who had left their fingers hanging off their chair arms, in full sight. She would do that, although they were nearly strangers. She had seen and scented the female only once before, and the male not at all.

Life doesn't offer perfect choices. When Hoffer had lain in a pile of puppies, her mother had told them all: Look, you either *adore people* or you live your whole life in the Great Emptiness. You take what people give you, kisses or blows or both, because if you don't, you know what you'll end up with? The Great Emptiness—that's what! The puppies didn't know what that was, but it sounded execrable.

Hoffer obeyed her mother. She spent about two-thirds of her life being beaten by the male of her people, sometimes by the female. Once, even, the male of her people had set upon the child of her people, and Hoffer had had to make the only decision of her life: her nose had raged with the scent of the

Carol Bly

same blood on both sides as they struggled, and Hoffer, in terror, elected to save the child of her people. She leapt upon the male. In return for her trouble she lost one eye. Then the child went away and Hoffer went on being beaten by both of the others, but less and less frequently. A sorry business.

Now then, these new people: Hoffer's jaws were already wet with her plan. She meant to creep forward and thoroughly kiss their hands, between all the fingers and up to the sweater cuffs. She decided on the female of them first, then the male. She had a notion, which she knew she couldn't get across, but she had the idea, anyway. It was that she would explain with her tongue how close to death she had been; she meant to explain with her tongue how life always looks much more ordinary than it really is—how its dangerousness, and its ecstasy, scarcely show.

A Committee
of the Whole

Since her middle-aged daughter had died before she did,
Alice Malley expected only sorrow, increasing solitude, and
eventual decrepitude. Instead, she found herself in the midst
of twenty-three friendly people enthusiastically bent on any
number of projects, one right after another. While Linda was
alive, Alice had paid no attention to the other residents at
Saint Aidan's: they were simply vague background—people
you saw greeting one another at the elevators, people accus-
ing each other of cheating at checkers or hearts, people forever approaching with smiles, handing her computer graphics
called "Housekeeping Update" or "Our Week's Events" or
"This Week in the Duluth Area."

There was a happy, rather drunken couple among them,
Charles and Martha. There was a loner, who kept himself to
the one third-floor room Saint Aidan's had. There was the
community paranoid, LeRoy Beske, who had a strange conviction that all the world was divided into the lucky Shattuck
School graduates and the unlucky, who were principally

LeRoy and his grandson. When Charles or anyone else tried to explain to LeRoy what a small part of the world's population was made up of Shattuck graduates, he snarled, "You can call 'em what you want—Andover, Saint Paul's, whoever—they're all Shattuck in my book, with their feet on the neck of the poor!"

As long as Linda was alive, Alice Malley's world shook and woke itself at the moment when Linda swung into her room, grinning with her great fair fifty-year-old health, her bluff manner, her armfuls of organic-gardening manuals. In the spring she generally had a cardboard box or two of cuttings or bare roots. The last time Alice saw her, she had brought dwarf-pear stock to espalier on the parking-lot wall. Meals, nights, walks, were simply the distance between Linda's visits. Sometimes Linda telephoned from K.C. or Atlanta to explain she was stuck. She told Alice exactly when she could get home and visited Alice exactly at the time mentioned.

One day Petra, a woman who lived next door to Linda, came. It happened to be a Wednesday morning, when Saint Aidan's residents were gathered in the Fellowship Lounge, so Petra sorted her way through people folding up chairs, finding canes, taking turns using the elevators. At last she found Alice trying to drive a beanpole firmly into the gravelly soil of the residents' garden. Petra told her that Linda's plane had struck another plane.

After that, Alice stopped keeping herself apart from her surroundings and the others at Saint Aidan's. She had grown up in Duluth, so Lake Superior, with its spit of land making the harbor, was familiar to her. But now the landscape touched her as it hadn't before: she took in everything—the

Carol Bly

queer aerial bridge, the cold water strung across with white-caps, the harsh, curiously medieval rooftops of the West End. She saw everything inwardly. Alice made herself join everything going on at Saint Aidan's. She saw that people pretended to be much more interested in one another than could possibly be true. They smiled at each other a good deal. They were patient with LeRoy Beske. Linda had been killed in late spring: by midsummer Alice was secretary of the group that a social work student convened each Wednesday. She donated her daughter's library to the Seamen's Mission. By autumn she joined the protests against the Saint Aidan's manager's various schemes to remove the residents' privileges.

Nearly all meetings and programs were well attended. Everyone except Jack Laresstad went to everything. A few people, especially Martha, who drank in the mornings, nodded off during slide shows of third-world countries, but they politely woke themselves during the question period and tried to have eye contact with the speaker. Mr. Binner, the manager, brought in a good many fourth-rate speakers for them. Each one was introduced as a "very, very special person," whom they were lucky to have right there, as a rich resource person. Someone told them how cruelly used the third-world sailors were on oceangoing boats. A marine biologist told them what could live and what could not live at the deepest levels of Lake Superior.

Each Tuesday Mr. Binner held house meetings, which he liked to call "Housekeeping Updates." Everybody tried to pay close attention at the updates, in order to spot and forestall any planned loss of privilege. LeRoy Beske was sure that Mr. Binner invested their monthly payments, as well as the grant money Saint Aidan's got, in gigantic firms whose fingers went deep into all the money pots of the world and delivered the booty into Mr. Binner's personal account. Each Wednesday they had "Group." Nearly every day they had a cocktail hour of sorts, in Charles and Martha's room, where Malcolm the minibus driver left off cases of vodka and beer, wrapped in Eddie Bauer camping bags. They had parties, everyone holding a toothbrush glass or a glass taken from the Fellowship Lounge. Charles called their parties "celebrations." They celebrated defeating the manager in his attempt to plow over their gardens. They celebrated defeating the manager in his plan to authorize Malcolm to drive them into downtown Duluth only twice instead of three times a week. They celebrated after the Housekeeping Update in which they voted that Mr. Binner take the sunflower seed for Saint Aidan's ten bird-feeding stations out of his operating expenses instead of insisting the residents pay for it themselves. Charles was forever shouting, "Celebration, folks! Martha and I want you all to come to our room! Five sharp!" as if life were a succession of marches under the Arc de Triomphe.

Their recluse, Jack Laresstad, mainly stayed in his third-floor room, monitoring the harbor with binoculars. They had one bellicose member, LeRoy Beske. Like most paranoids, Beske made strong use of *Robert's Rules,* bringing them in even when the meeting was not formal. "Call the question!" LeRoy would shout. "Call the goddamned question!" in just the mix of fury and expertise to waken even Martha, who generally had her head on Charles's shoulder throughout any meeting. She would raise herself gently, like a mermaid trying

Carol Bly

the air. She would cry out charmingly, "Yes—oh, yes! Call the question!"

"We need to adjourn the goddamned meeting," LeRoy said. "We need to reconvene as a Committee of the Whole!"

"So the chair can't stop you from talking? Not a chance, my boy!" Charles said with a laugh.

"I am sick of being pushed around by a bunch of snobbish old Shattuck grads!" LeRoy flung back at Charles. "My grandson's trying to get started in business, and who cheats him clean? Gentlemen! Shattuck graduates who think they're so good they don't have to pay their bills!"

Everyone knew about LeRoy's grandson. Everyone knew about everyone else except for Jack Laresstad.

Alice, amazed at the folly of her life, took part in everything. She did not cultivate a friendship with Jack, because he was solitary. He was the only chance of a serious friendship, so she saved him for last, whatever last should be. The grief of Saint Aidan's was that you ran through any one person's repertoire of wit and wisdom in two weeks. You knew the names and circumstances of their relations, you knew whether or not a harsh wind of Lake Superior would make them complain or talk about neuralgia. You knew of all the blizzards they and their friends or family had nearly died in. Alice was saving Jack, therefore, so there should be something other than LeRoy Beske's tantrums to differentiate each day.

She knew Jack had taken it in that she was now among them all, in a way she had not been before. He greeted her, and she responded, in the affected raillery that Saint Aidan's residents used with each other: it was a slightly unnatural formality, which seemed to say, At some point in my life I lived a little more elegantly than I do now, and the elegance remains inside me.

At the elevators Jack said, smiling, "Madam!"

"Sir!" Alice said.

"May I ask what your energetic group have on for this frigid, blustery day?" he said. The elevators of Saint Aidan's did not go to the third floor, where his room was, so he had come down a flight of stairs and now waited with Alice to descend to the Fellowship Lounge for breakfast. He was very neat in his white shirt, open at the neck, not a lumberjack shirt. He had just a bit of white hair. He had the habit of bending toward anyone he spoke to, actually seeming to listen.

She told him, "We constantly fight against crime. Last week it was Mr. Binner's crooked deal with some landscape company that wanted to do away with our gardens. Today we have to save Helen's job."

Jack said, "Who's Helen?"

"Our social worker. She helped us fight Mr. Binner about the landscaping, so he left in a temper. Now he has asked her supervisor to come be at our meeting. We know he intends to disgrace her. She is doing something called a 'practicum.'"

"You garden, don't you?" Jack said. The elevator slowly lowered them.

Alice turned the conversation away from gardening. Her instinct was not to talk about the subject of greatest interest.

"What's out on the lake so far today?" she asked him.

"Something big moored sternwise to us, sailing under a Libyan flag. And fourteen hundred gulls at last count."

No sooner did they emerge on the main floor than Charles

Carol Bly

came rapidly forward. "Oh, Alice!" he cried. "Hello, Jack. Oh, Alice! LeRoy is saying he won't go through with it!"

She had to follow him over to the window, where a few of the residents had set their trays. Beyond their heads the November day looked rather bright, whity, and fragile: there was a slight frosty lick on the rock outcropping just below Saint Aidan's, a slight shine to the steep-pitched roofs on the hillside. The lake still lay motionless under its morning fog.

LeRoy looked up. "I'm not going to do it," he said. "It's goddamned humiliating. Besides, it's blackmail. What do I care if Helen loses her job or her practicum or whatever it is? Lots of people lose lots of things! Look how many people have cheated my grandson!"

Charles tapped LeRoy's hand with his fork. "We know about your grandson, you know. Cheated by Shattuck graduates!"

"Sneer all you like!" LeRoy shouted.

One of the maids came over. "Can I help with anything, Mr. Beske?" she said.

"Oh, hell!" LeRoy said. "Why should all you city slicks care about one poor kid trying to make a living at a wrecking business?"

Alice said, "Doing our best, LeRoy. *You* work this morning, *we* all work to help your grandson this afternoon. We do care!"

People always went to their rooms after breakfast. Then the elevators clicked and clicked over their safety catches as the residents returned in twos and threes and fours to the Fellowship Lounge for Group. Helen Pool, their young social work student, got the chairs set around in a circle. This morning a sensible, kindly faced woman of fifty or so stood talking to the manager near the Fellowship Lounge doorway.

When everyone sat down, Helen said in her terribly young, not particularly resonant voice, "Before we *check in,* I would like to introduce a very, very special person to you."

The Group waited, unaffected.

"This is my supervisor, Ms. Dietrich," Helen said.

Charles leaned over and said to Alice, "This is it!"

Alice couldn't decide whether she felt pleasantly excited at the adventures they had planned for the day or if she felt depressed at the stupidity of all their agendas. Since Helen had introduced Ms. Dietrich to Group, they were to go with Plan B. LeRoy was very red in the face, but he swung into his first speech.

"Hi, Ms. Dietrich!" he shouted.

"Good to have you with us," Charles said.

"Before we *check in,* can I say something Helen?" cried LeRoy. Now he was on his feet.

"You know you don't have to stand up to speak out at Group, LeRoy," Helen said.

LeRoy sat down. "Helen," he said very loudly, "I want to say what a difference it makes that you come have these sessions with us. Before you started Group with us, we never shared any of our personal concerns. We had negative feelings and nowhere to go with them. We acted out. The bottom line is, we didn't bring anything out into the open."

LeRoy paused. Alice heard Charles say very low, "I know that I myself had trouble with . . ."

LeRoy manfully took it up: "I know that I myself had trouble with how I conducted myself in this room. I would

Carol Bly

feel angry that my grandson Terry didn't visit me more. Or I'd feel angry the way this place is run. It always seemed crazy to me that people accused me of cheating at checkers when I always felt that Mr. Binner, over there, was cheating the residents here in any way he thought he could get away with. Of course, that was just a feeling of mine. I had angry feelings."

"It is OK to have angry feelings, LeRoy. We've talked about that," she said.

LeRoy was grinding forward. "I'd be still feeling angry that someone had cheated my grandson—see, Helen, there is this optometrist downtown that cheated my grandson—"

Helen cut in: "We've talked about the optometrist, LeRoy."

LeRoy cut back in: "And I'd think about that and have angry feelings, and if the person I was playing chess with got up and went out, sometimes I would move one or two of their pawns off. If the person was a dumbbell or if they were some rich Shattuck School type, I'd try to slide their knight, maybe, off, too, and then stand it up with the other pieces which had been taken."

Charles did not forget his cue. "You cheat, LeRoy! You cheat! That was my knight you took, and when I said so you denied it, and in front of the whole Group, too!"

Helen said, "Did you want to respond to Charles, LeRoy?"

LeRoy said, "So I cheated sometimes. In hearts, too. If there were three, I could look at the kitty. I think I was under a lot of pressure but didn't realize it."

Charles: "Why are you telling us all this *now,* LeRoy?"

Martha, who had no assigned part, suddenly said very clearly, in a silvery voice, "How come LeRoy Beske is wearing

a tie when he never wears a tie? I think it looks very sweet."
Her head slid back down onto Charles's shoulder.

LeRoy said, "Helen makes it possible for us to work out
this kind of stuff," he said. "Somehow I feel so much more
in . . . in control of my life now."

Charles said, with his hand steadying Martha so she didn't
sink into his lap, "I must say, I feel the same thing, Helen.
I feel as if we can all get together and make the changes we
want to make in our lives. I used to get depressed. Now when
I feel depressed by something, I let it have its space, but I
don't let it climb all over me."

"Like all my cursing and dirty language," LeRoy said. "I
am cutting down on it, making a track record like you said,
Helen. But I am going to need help with this. So the rest of
you can help me."

The ten who were in on the project kept a straight face,
but a few of the others looked stunned. One woman, who had
firmly slept through every Saint Aidan's program ever offered, was not only wide awake but on her feet, half her
weight square over the four points of her cane. She studied
the face of each speaker.

Alice Malley thought, Well, it stands to reason. When you
are nine years old a skillful liar can fool you. But when
you've lived another eighty or ninety years you have heard a
good many people lie in a good many different kinds of circumstances, so most likely you can tell when you wake up in
a room where four people are lying steadily.

LeRoy had one more speech, if Alice recalled the rehearsals
right, then Charles, then she herself was to say, "I don't know
if I can take in anything more right now, Helen—I think I'm

Carol Bly

winding down!" and then Martha was supposed to follow the two social workers out to the parking lot to overhear their reactions to everything. But Martha obviously had not obeyed Charles's request that she not drink anything just this one day when they had so much to do. Alice decided she would go to the parking lot herself.

She got past LeRoy, who was shouting at Charles, "How'd I do, big boy? How'd I do? Now it's *your* turn, big boy!"

It was bright and cold outside. Alice found Helen and Ms. Dietrich leaning against one of their cars. They had lighted cigarettes and were laughing and talking, not, Alice noticed, bothering to make eye contact. Eye contact was a bloodletting issue at Saint Aidan's Group: people hated being told by the twenty-three-year-old social worker they must make eye contact.

They smiled as she came up. Alice was delighted when Ms. Dietrich shook hands with her. She caught herself just in time before saying, "You remind me so much of my daughter—I noticed it all through Group! You remind me so very much of her! How much you remind me of her! It is the same rather hearty, frank face! I should not mention this, perhaps—but you remind me so much of Linda! Did you know that my Linda was killed?"

She did not say any of that.

Helen, who had a trick of not just looking at people but rather pouring over them, said, "Don't cry, Alice: it came out all right this morning! Really it did!"

Ms. Dietrich, still holding Alice's hand, smiled. "I have been telling Helen here," she said, "that she must be doing something right in her practicum. I have overseen a lot of practicums, but I have never yet seen a whole roomful of people lie themselves blue in the face in order to make a Master of Social Work degree candidate look good in front of her supervisor!"

They all laughed, and Alice wiped her nose.

"I gather Mr. Binner is a jerk," Ms. Dietrich offered.

They talked about the sleazy manager for a while, they shook hands again, and Alice spent a couple of minutes studying the parking-lot wall. She would need to furr out from the stone, with bamboo or other sticks, so she could progressively train the pear-tree branches as they came along. Now the little roots of them were curled, spineless still, safe under the gravelly dirt and mulch.

After a while she went in: for a half hour she had been lost in thought about the baby pear trees. She felt happy about it.

Charles caught her arm in the hallway. "Bad news," he said.

He led her over to the checkers table, away from people who were beginning to line up for the luncheon trays.

"LeRoy is very sick. Right after Group he apparently sat down on the carpet by the elevators and wouldn't get up. People thought he was having one of his paranoid tantrums. It turned out he was in a coma, and they've taken him to Saint Mary's."

Charles paused. "I guess that's the end of the afternoon plan."

Alice said, "Nonsense. Let's go ahead with it!"

"But what good will it do? What difference will it make to LeRoy? He's probably had a stroke! We'll go downtown and make fools of ourselves—and all for nothing!"

Alice said, "It's true we will make fools of ourselves. Let's go through with it, anyway. If LeRoy recovers, think how he'll feel!"

When the Special Committee of Ten gathered by the minibus, Malcolm checked their names on his clipboard. "LeRoy's not here yet," he said. They explained he was sick.

Alice went around to each person and made sure he or she had the right typed sheet: half the sheets had little else but figures on them; the other half had a couple of paragraphs of neat typing. Mr. Binner's secretary had let Alice use the copier, but she had had to pay fifteen cents for each copy because Mr. Binner had told her if they ever let the residents start making copies free, next thing everybody would do a whole book.

Malcolm drove them sedately down the Skyline Drive, then down one of the steep avenues to Superior Street, and then east.

"I'll be right here in an hour!" Malcolm told each person climbing out. To Alice, who got out last, he said, "Don't spend everything you got in one place!"

Alice had not lived in a jovial community for two years for nothing. "Spend all *what* in one place!" she jeered back in the right tone.

"Come on," Charles said. "We're on."

The man who owed LeRoy Beske's grandson $215 was Dr. Royce Salaco, an optometrist with an office facing Lake Superior on one side, the ground-floor lobby of a business building on another, and Superior Street on the north. Charles and Martha and Alice had been past it so many times they felt as if they knew it inch by inch.

No one wanted to get started: all nine clustered together on the windy sidewalk, longing to be like the passersby—just private citizens not committed to some dreadful project.

Charles whispered, "Keep your spirits up! Here we go! Big celebration afterward in Martha's and my room, OK? OK! Let's go! OK, Alice."

With Charles hanging a few feet behind, Alice went into the foyer of the building and turned left into Dr. Salaco's office. Out of the corner of her eye she saw the residents divide themselves into those who were to stay on Superior Street and those who were to stand about in the building. Charles waited at the office door, without coming in.

Throughout both rehearsals she had found Dr. Salaco to be simply another Scandinavian-looking Minnesota optometrist: he had rather coarse, neat, pale hair, expressionless eyes behind the rimless glasses. Now, as Alice crept over toward his counter, with its swivel seat for customers being fitted, Dr. Salaco looked like a film-version Abwehr officer—pale, blond, gigantic, with the snappy look of someone with life-long skills in doing evil.

He said, "Can I help you this afternoon?"

"I've come about your account with Terence Beske," Alice said.

"How's that?"

"I've come to regularize your account with Terence Beske," Alice said.

"Lady, I haven't got the least idea what you're talking about!"

"Terence Beske," Alice explained, "is the young man who pulled your car out of the ditch you put it in on August 16,

Carol Bly

1987. It was three-fifteen in the morning. Then he drove you and your lady friend to where you needed to go. He did it as a personal favor, charging you only for the gas, although you promised, at the time, to make it worth his while. Then, as contracted for by you, he replaced your Michelins with some old tires, since you told him that was all right with State Farm. He presided over the assessment by the claims officer. He has sent you a total of four billings since then, which—"

"Lady," Dr. Salaco said, "I don't know who or what you are talking about, but I'm afraid I am going to have to ask you to leave. As you see, I have a busy day, and there is a customer waiting."

Alice did not look back. "The man in the doorway?" she said. "He's with me."

As Alice and Charles had planned it, there would be nice sass in the scene if she did not even look over her shoulder to check if it *was* Charles who had come in. They had reckoned that if someone else happened into the doorway just then, that person wouldn't hear Alice's "he's with me" and, if he or she did, wouldn't believe it had any application. If worse came to worst, Charles could elbow in front of someone.

"Yes," Alice said, actually drawling now, warming to the part. "He's with me. And those ones out in the street now— if you'd look. Those people out there passing out sheets to passersby? They are handouts explaining how you didn't pay your bill to a twenty-year-old entrepreneur. And the people in the building lobby now . . ."

Alice waited while Dr. Salaco spun around and glared through the lobby window of his shop. A few people were waiting for the elevators. Four senior citizens were handing sheets of paper to the others. A man stooped over the water fountain: when he straightened up, an old person smiled at him and handed him a sheet.

"Those people," Alice now said, "are handing out just the figures—billing dates, a breakdown of Terry's services to you. We thought people who do business right in the same building with you should know the level of ethical unconcern you operate on."

Alice moved over to a wall full of tiny shelves: each little bracket held a model piece of eyewear. She ran her hand over a few of the nose sections, then picked up one of the frames and put it on. There was no prescription, of course, which gave her an odd feeling: when she put the frames on, even though she *knew* they had no glass in them, she unconsciously expected to see better.

She wandered over to the window that overlooked the harbor.

"You're good at your trade," she said, loudly, so Dr. Salaco would hear although she was looking at the lake. "With these glasses of yours I can see so well I can see right into the portholes of that ship way out there. Libyan, I see she is. Right—and lying on the bunk is a guy from some African country who has been 220 days aboard and can't even go ashore here because one of the ship's officers cheated him. You know," Alice said conversationally, "it is amazing how if someone doesn't have someone to look out for them, they get cheated by the rich. That poor sap in his bunk there, reading some book he probably got at the Seamen's Mission—yes—wait a second!" Alice took the glasses off and tipped them in front of her eyes, as if to sharpen the lenses' angle. "Yes," she said. "A

Carol Bly

book on land stewardship, how do you like *that!* Anyway, third world, no union, no ombudsman—no advocate!"

She came back over to the middle of the shop. "What surprises me is that someone of your luck and prestige and wealth should decide to cheat a helpless young person! Now, why would that be?"

She could feel Charles fidgeting in the doorway.

Dr. Salaco went around behind the counter. "How much do you want?" he said.

Alice thought fast. "Your account with Terry is 215. If I were you I'd make it 250. You've given the man trouble."

The optometrist handed her the check and said very levelly, "I want both of you out of here in one second flat. Get out."

Alice turned to go. There stood Charles, with his raincoat collar up, looking pleased as punch, exactly like the kind of man who explains to traffic cops that he is with the CIA. She felt happy as a girl that the whole job was over. She spun around and said, "Do you want us to explain to the people out there on Superior Street that you decided to pay up and be fair, after all?"

"That's all right, Doc," Charles said. "We're leaving."

Alice escaped from the celebration in Charles and Martha's room. When she knocked at Jack's door he called "Come in!" but turned to look at her with his binoculars still up to his eyes. It made her feel as if she had entered a tree shrew's apartment—and this ancient, owly creature was welcoming her.

"I understand all your day's projects went very well," he said. "Would you like some insty-pot tea?"

Yes, she would.

They drank the hot, mindless-tasting stuff.

Jack looked at her carefully. "There's lots to be depressed about," he said. "I understand that LeRoy Beske is seriously sick?"

She told Jack what she knew about LeRoy. She thought of him in the brilliant lighting of an intensive care unit.

Jack said, "I only know two tricks against feeling sad. And neither one of them works perfectly. Here's the first: What you do is, you shut off the lights in your room at this time of day." He got up and turned off his lights. "Most people try to brighten up the dusk—great mistake! Turn the lights *off*, and then the lights and everything else from the outside will come *in*."

They looked at the shadowy, chilled city. The last of the afternoon sun still lighted the lake some: it gave its surface a rounded, smooth look, as if the very surface of it were strong enough to support life. Alice and Jack couldn't see the slight chop that reminds one of what lies on the bottom of even inland seas.

"When the light outside is stronger than the light inside, you aren't so aware of yourself," Jack said. "All you have is nature, so to speak. . . . OK so far?"

"Better than OK!" said Alice.

"Then here is the second idea," he said. "Let's say a person feels the life leaking out of them. Day by day, here at Saint Aidan's. Now, here is what you do: You had better go on imagining the leak, all right, like imagining yourself a leaky cup. But instead of imagining your life leaking out of the cup, what you do is, you imagine the universe out there slowly, slowly leaking into you."

Carol Bly

Alice nodded. "Those are two very, very terrific ideas," she told him.

"I think so, too," Jack said. "I think they're terrific. But they don't work completely. I have been going around and around about it," he said. "There are a couple of things that just keep coming and coming and coming, and you can put all the philosophy you like up against them, they still get through like dust. One of them is death, of course, and then the other one is just pure idiocy. That's what it is, just pure human idiocy."

My Lord
Bag of Rice

When Virgil had been healthy and mean, Eleanor had loved him; now that he was dying, his pain grinding his shoulders and hips into the bed, she sometimes found herself day-dreaming: if Virgil died this week instead of next, I could start everything that much sooner. "Do you feel guilty?" B.J. at the Women's Support Group said. "You have a right to your own life." It sounded 1980s OK to have a right to your own life; it did not sound so good to say, If Virgil Grummel would only die this week instead of next, or tonight instead of tomorrow night, I could inherit the farm and the engine-repair service all the sooner. I could sell it all and take the $180,000 cash that their neighbor Almendus Leitz said it was probably worth. She would start a boardinghouse in St. Paul and never, never again hear cruel language around her. *Never,* she thought, patting Virgil's ankle skin.

It was three in the morning, the hour when she usually visited Virgil at Masonic Hospital, because then the drugs didn't cover the pain. She also drove over from St. Paul during the day. Sometimes, like tonight when she walked right into the hot, wide doorway of the hospital, no one sat guard at Reception. The flowers leaned on their stems in the shadowy glass cooler. The crossword puzzle kits waited motionless in the gift case. Someone could perfectly well walk in and hurt people, and steal things, and trot back out into the August night. Eleanor always walked past the dark counters to the elevator and came up to floor three.

Despite his morphine, Virgil once again was awake and in pain. He wanted to talk about the good old days. His agonized, liquid eyes watched her as she cut in half each sock of a new woolen pair. Then she slipped the toe half over his icy feet. Whole socks didn't work because of the Styrofoam packed around Virgil's insteps to prevent bedsores.

In his wispy, pain-throttled voice, he said, "Do you remember how we went to Monte to get you your stone?" Dawson was their town, but Montevideo was the town that counted, the place for buying major things like wall-to-wall carpeting and diamond rings. Eleanor smiled down at Virgil's face in the shadowy hospital room, but she was thinking how he had never called the ring an engagement ring; he called it a "stone," just as meals were "chow" and making love was "taking your medicine." One day their older neighbor lady had come to the house, Mrs. Almendus Leitz, and told Eleanor how Almendus was always telling her to "just roll over and take your medicine." Mrs. Leitz was sick of it. She and Eleanor stood on the stoop, both of them with their work-strong arms folded, looking out over Virgil's steaming acreage of corn and beans. It crossed Eleanor's mind at the time that the whole breathless prairie was full of farm places at half-mile intervals where

Carol Bly

men were telling women to roll over and take their medicine, but she didn't dwell on it. "Yes, but you *should* have been thinking about it," they all said firmly, down at the Women's Support Group she now belonged to in Minneapolis. Not just B.J. said so. All of them. B.J. said she fervently hoped now that Eleanor was in the Twin Cities she would become sexually active. Eleanor let her talk.

As soon as they were married, Virgil put in a bid for the old District 73 country school and won it. He dragged it over to their place on a flatbed, laid down a concrete floor for it, and set it down. He never even yanked the old school cupboards and bookshelves off the walls: there were dozens of Elson-Gray readers and some children's storybooks. Eleanor found a book of Japanese fairy tales: she took it up whenever she had a moment. Now Virgil wanted her to recall how he'd be repairing machinery out there in the shop, and he'd call her on the two-way to come out, and how they worked together out there. "Do you remember," he whispered, "how you'd quit whatever you was doing in the house and come on out and help me in the shop?" She remembered: The two-way crackled and growled all the time in the kitchen. She could hear the field hands from Almendus's west half section swearing because they'd dropped a furrow wheel or a lunchbox out in the plowing somewhere. Then, very loud and close, Virgil's voice would cut in: "Hey, Little Girl, this is Big Red Chief; get your butt out here a minute," and he would go off without waiting for her to answer. He had fixed up both the laundry area and the kitchen for radio reception so he knew she'd hear him, wherever she was, canning or what. She would go out to the shop, arms crossed across her breasts:

My Lord Bag of Rice   239

if it was cold, running; if it was summer, looking out over the fields past Almendus's place toward Dawson Mills. Virgil was fond of the radio. Sometimes he wanted to make love in the shop; he would lay out the hood drop cloth on the station wagon backseat, which he never did get back into the station wagon—when the wagon finally threw a rod, the backseat stayed in the shop. Each time he was through making love, he said, "This is Big Red Chief; over and out," and gave her head a little slap on the temple.

Eleanor knew she was lucky. All her childhood, her father had gone on every-six-month beating binges. He beat up her mother, and then he forced her sister. "You don't have to look so owly," he told Eleanor when she stood dumb, watching. "Your big sister is a real princess." She was so lucky to be married to a good man like Virgil, who didn't drink much. It was boring helping a man in the shop, though. Much of the time he would say, "Don't go away, little girl; I might need you." He didn't care that she had quart jars boiling in the processor. So she gave his feet a glance (he had dollied himself underneath someone's Buick now) and she carried the Japanese fairy-tale book over to one of the old schoolroom windows. Virgil's FARM AND ENGINE REPAIRS sign creaked outside, the corn tattered in the wind, and Eleanor found a story that she had read over and over.

"Hey," Virgil shouted from under the Buick he was fixing. "Get that V-belt and hand it to me." Then he said, "No, dang it all, not that one—the other one!" Then she would open the book again.

"Hey, get your ass over here," Virgil cried. "Hand me all this stuff when I tell you, one by one in order."

Carol Bly

She wiped the grease off her hands and went back to the story. A young Japanese hero had a retinue of servants. Watercolor illustrations showed him mustachioed, with slant eyes and nearly white skin. All his servants wore thin swords tucked into their sashes. They looked a little like middle-aged, effeminate Americans in dressing gowns, who had chosen to arm themselves. Eleanor couldn't keep her eyes off the pictures. The hero was traveling through Japan, looking for adventure, when he came to a high, rounded bridge over a river that ran to the sea. As he began to cross it, he saw that a frightful dragon slept at the top of its arch. The dragon's scales and horns and raised back ridge were everything a child would count on when it came to dragons. No one was around to sneer at a grown woman reading a child's book when she was supposed to be helping her husband.

The young Japanese started to step right across the dragon, and it suddenly reared up. His servants dropped back, aghast, but the hero held his ground. Then the dragon took the form of a beautiful woman, who explained that she was the ruler of a sea kingdom under the bridge. Each night, a centipede of gigantic size slid down from the mountain to the north (she pointed) and ate dozens of her subjects, who were fishes and sea animals. They realized they needed a man—but not an ordinary man. "You can imagine what fright an ordinary man would feel," the sea princess said.

Dusk was falling. She pointed again to the mountain, which now showed only its black profile before the green, darkening sky. Some sort of procession of people carrying lanterns seemed to descend the near slope of the mountain.

"Those are not people," the sea princess said. "Those are the eyes of the centipede."

"I will kill it," the young Japanese said simply.

"I think you are brave enough," the princess said. "I took the form of a dragon and placed myself on this bridge, pretending to sleep. You are the only man who hasn't fled at the sight of me."

The hero drew a light green arrow from the quiver on his shoulder. He sent it at one of the centipede's eyes. That eye went out, but the monster kept coming. He fired another arrow—a pale pink one this time—but it only put out another eye. Then he recalled a belief of the Japanese people: human saliva is poison to magical enemies. He licked he tip of an arrow the color of a bird's egg and sent it off into the thick dusk. It went true. It put out the creature's foremost eye— and then the princess and the hero were joyous to see all the eyes darken to red, then gray, like worn coals.

The princess clapped. "Wait, O hero!" she cried. She clapped again. Fishes dressed in silk robes like men and women rose from the river. They carried gigantic vases from earlier, greater times. They brought hundreds of years of hand-embroidered silks and linens. They handed everything to the hero's servants to carry.

Then a sea serpent not changed into human form brought a large plain bag. In the watercolor illustration it was light brown, like a gunnysack gone pale. The sea princess said, "The other gifts are for you and your court, since obviously you are a prince. But this bag is for your people. Even if famine comes to your country, your people will never be hungry. This bag full of rice will never empty."

Carol Bly

"Then I will carry it myself," he told her. But before raising it to his shoulder, he bowed very low, and the sea princess bowed low back to him. Then she faded.

When the young man returned to his own country, he was known forever as My Lord Bag of Rice.

In the first year of her marriage, Eleanor Grummel read through all the books left in the District 73 schoolhouse. She would hand Virgil what he needed—the snowblower sprocket, the fan belt, the lag screw, or the color-coded vacuum tubing—and then lean against the wall or sometimes sit on the old station wagon backseat and read. She read all the books, but returned over and over to "My Lord Bag of Rice."

Now, eighteen years later, she held Virgil's hand while he whispered to her, his memories blurred by drugs, getting the times wrong, getting the occasions wrong, his eyes weeping from illness and recollection. Eleanor saw herself again standing at the old schoolhouse window, sometimes glancing out at the fields, sometimes studying the illustrations in the fairy-tale book. Now she thought that she had read in an enchanted way, because she had been too unconscious to know she lived in misery.

Twice each day, throughout Virgil's dying, Eleanor drove happily from Masonic, a building of the University of Minnesota hospital system, back to Mrs. Zenobie's boardinghouse in St. Paul. On the night run, she recited aloud in the car whole passages from the King James translation. Aloud she cried, "And the darkness comprehendeth it not!" or she shouted in the car, "And none shall prevent Him!" She remembered to add "Saith the Lord" after any pronouncements she could remember from Genesis.

August changed to early fall; she still drove with the windows open. The air was dusty and smooth, its blackness so thorough that she felt that it lay all over the Middle West—as if even the Twin Cities, a polite place, hardly made a pinprick of light in all the blackness. Of course the Twin Cities were not really a polite place—Mrs. Zenobie, the landlady at her boardinghouse, was not polite—but politeness was possible.

In the normal course she would have lodged nearer the hospital where Virgil was dying. The university volunteer explained that all the special housing for people like Eleanor happened to be full. Mrs. Zenobie was not the greatest, she explained—and Eleanor would have to drive across to St. Paul— but the price was reasonable. The volunteer gave Eleanor a map and highlighted her route from I-94 to Newell Avenue, St. Paul. She urged Eleanor to join a certain Women's Support Group, since she was under stress and was new in the city. Eleanor was allowed to visit her husband any hour of the night or day she liked.

The night runs brought her back to Mrs. Zenobie's at about four in the morning. No matter how quietly Eleanor turned the key and tiptoed past the roomers' coat hooks, Mrs. Zenobie would always wake and come out from behind the Japanese room divider. She slept downstairs, she told Eleanor, because of the crime. If crooks ever realized no one was on the ground floor, especially when it was a woman who ran the household, they would take advantage. And once they robbed a woman, they'd rob her again. The police right now were looking for LeRoy Beske, the lowlife who had owned 1785 Newell, three

Carol Bly

houses over, and then sold it to someone who never moved in. "You got to learn these things," Mrs. Zenobie told Eleanor, "if you're serious about wanting to start a rooming house. Also I wanted to say I'd be the last not to be grateful you have brought us so many doughnuts from the bakery, but I can't give you anything off the rent for that."

"I didn't expect it," Eleanor said.

"It doesn't matter how many men boarders you got," Mrs. Zenobie said. "It doesn't do any good. Crime is crime."

Mrs. Zenobie had five elderly male boarders, four of whom were not so polite as Eleanor hoped to find for clientele whenever she finally got her own house. Her idea was to have a five o'clock social hour: they would all gather in the living room before dinner and she would give each boarder some wine or cider, so it would be like home. Eleanor herself had never seen a home like the one she had in mind, but the image was clear to her.

Eleanor started up the staircase, exhausted.

"If you're serious about wanting a house," Mrs. Zenobie whispered fiercely up after her, "I heard that 1785 is for sale again now. It'd be big enough." Mrs. Zenobie's eyes glared as steady as bathroom night-lights. "I wouldn't feel you were cutting into my prospects," she said. "There's so many people wanting boardinghouses these days, there's enough for everyone."

Eleanor slept well all that late August and early September. She felt the grateful passion for sleep of people whose lives are a shambles. Only sleep was completely reliable. She dreamed. Every morning, she woke up haunted and mystified by the dreams.

In the mornings Alicia Fowler, a realtor recommended by B.J. at the support group, picked her up. Eleanor felt cared for in Alicia's car. They ignored the big sun-dried thoroughfares—Snelling, Cleveland, Randolph. Alicia knew every house in St. Paul or Minneapolis and what it likely was worth. Eleanor said, "My idea is three storeys, homey, decently built. I can't afford Summit Avenue, but I don't want a dangerous part of town."

After the morning's searches with Alicia, Eleanor took Virgil's car over to the hospital for an hour or so. If Virgil was sleeping, she daydreamed beside his tubings. Once a technician came in to get Virgil ready to wheel down for X-rays. Eleanor realized that whatever the X-rays would teach Virgil's doctor, these trips were not for Virgil's sake but for other patients after Virgil's death. She pointed out that it was painful for Virgil to be moved onto the stretcher table and off again. The technician said he was only following orders. Eleanor did not dare oppose the doctor's orders. After they wheeled Virgil down, she thought of how she should have protected him from that extra pain. Her fist shook as she held his drip stand.

After an hour she left and drove courteously home on Oak and Fulton streets, onto 94, and east toward St. Paul. She waved to let people from parking lots enter the column of cars. She was delighted to be courteous to strangers. For eighteen years she had shrunk in her seat while Virgil gave the finger to anyone who honked when Virgil crossed lanes. On their few Twin Cities junkets, he pulled ahead two feet into the pedestrian crossing when he had to wait for a stoplight. It forced pedestrians to walk around the front of the car. When

Carol Bly

a pedestrian gave Virgil a hostile glance, Virgil would gun the engine, which made the pedestrian jump. Eleanor looked out the right-hand window in order not to see Virgil smile. Now she enjoyed driving under the speed limit; she played at imagining other drivers having their lives saved by her carefulness. She even formed a mental image of those in the oncoming traffic saying to themselves, "At least *there's* a car not driven by some natural killer!" as they whipped past their side of the yellow line. When Virgil was caught speeding, he would not look up as he passed his driver's license out the window to the officer. While the man asked him a question or told Virgil his computer reading, Virgil steadily stared at the steering wheel and kept both hands rugged on it, as if to drive off. His face looked full and stung with blood. The moment the officer turned away, initialed the citation, and wound up the invariably courteous request to keep it down, Virgil came to life. He snarled, "I took your number, fellow! If you ever, like *ever,* try to drive through Chippewa or Lac Qui Parle Counties, I know the right people that'll put you up so high, by the time you hit the ground eagles will have made a nest in your ass!"

Eleanor now went to Saint Swithin's Episcopal Church confirmation class on Tuesdays. There were three men in the group, and an innumerable, changing roster of women—all of them older than Eleanor. One of the youngish men spoke either wrathfully or weakly about one issue or another. Two of the women kept saying, "I'm not sure this is relevant," a remark that caused the young priest to tremble. Eleanor felt at odds with all of them, since her aim in church instruction was not relevance but beauty. She wanted to learn polite ideas, whatever they were. She memorized a good deal of what Father said. Once—only once—she repeated one of the phrases she had memorized. The group looked astonished and then disgusted. She stayed on but only because the group met in a room called the Lady Chapel, where the royal and navy blue stained glass windows pleased her.

On Thursdays she had the Women's Support Group. They were people so different from herself that she didn't like to think about it. B.J.—all of them—had been sympathetic when she told them about her father's abuse. When her thoughts grew more and more centered around getting a boardinghouse, they turned indifferent. Anyone in pain was a priority: in October a woman who had recently been sexually assaulted joined them. After that, Eleanor felt unseen. She knew these women were more intelligent than she was; on the other hand, she felt stung when they wouldn't rejoice with her over having found a house she could buy.

In the week of Virgil's death and the weeks following it, Eleanor had so much to think of that she forgot to tell B.J. and the others that she was widowed at last. When they found out, B.J. threw her arms around Eleanor, crying, "You are so wonderfully centered!"

Eleanor blushed. She felt stupid. People had emotions that meant nothing to her; they used words she never used— "centered" and "on top of your shit."

Eleanor stayed on at Mrs. Zenobie's. There was no social hour before dinner, as Eleanor planned for her own boardinghouse, but now and then Mrs. Zenobie's niece brought in a group of Sunday-school students for what was announced as

Carol Bly

a very, very special occasion. One October Saturday, the children came to explain some small kits to Mrs. Zenobie's boarders. If the boarders would be good enough to assemble these kits, the children would pick them up on Saint Andrew's Day.

Eleanor perked up a little at hearing "Saint Andrew's Feast" since memorizing trivia about saints was a favorite part of her new church life. Each kit was a plastic sandwich bag, in which lay two tongue depressors, a plastic twister, and a plastic baby poinsettia. The idea was to use the twister to attach the tongue depressors at right angles to make a cross, then jam the poinsettia's stem into the twist as well. It made a good Christmas present for shut-ins, and then you could trade the poinsettia for a lily and, presto, you had an Easter symbol, too, which was the kind of thing that shut-ins could relate to.

Eleanor backed around the room divider as discreetly as possible and made for the staircase.

Suddenly a man's voice said, "Oh, no, you don't, Eleanor! No one gets out of this!"—with a laugh. He came out to the hallway where she hovered. "I have seen many cultural atrocities in my life," he said to her—not only not lowering his voice but raising it slightly, and even, as she had heard him do any number of times at the dinner table, adding a slight British inflection—"But I think this one surpasses them all!" It was Jack Lackie, the retired Episcopal priest, a member of Mrs. Zenobie's household.

"The mystery is, what was he really?" Mrs. Zenobie once said, gouging a used Kleenex into her apron pocket. "Janitor, maybe. Not a priest. You get wise to what people used to be

and what they say they used to be. To hear it, I've had boarders who invented the atom bomb, and I've had CIA opera-
tives, and I've had a hundred of President Kennedy's cousins."

Eleanor had felt endeared to Jack Lackie because he never
once lifted his trouser cuff to show the ribbing of long underwear. Mrs. Zenobie's other men liked to explain that now
that winter had set in, they put on their long underwear, and
that was *it* until spring. Two of them shoved their wooden
chairs back, bent over, and lifted the bottoms of their trouser
legs in case Eleanor didn't believe them. Jack Lackie was the
only man not to do it, and Eleanor had made up her mind
that she would have him for a boarder in her home when she
got it.

Now she smiled at him. It would give a classy tone to the
place if someone spoke of "cultural atrocities."

She lay on her bed upstairs, hearing the children's voices
singing from below. Under the house, the ground throbbed
from a parked Amtrak train on Transfer Street; even the
house thrummed gently through the concrete basement and
wooden studs. Eleanor smiled in the dark: this was her favorite mood. She felt simple, full of plans, and not confused.
It was true that nearly everyone she talked to that day was so
different from her they could never be friends. She passed
quickly over the idea that she might be lonely the rest of her
life. She raced to make image after image of her boardinghouse. There would never, never be any church groups allowed into it. There would be a wood-burning stove in the
living room. There would be a wine-and-cider hour before
dinner each night. If anyone sneered or shouted, she would
ask that person to leave. There would be an outside barbecue.

Carol Bly

There would be climbing roses. She would tell Alicia the realtor that she definitely wanted 1785 Newell Avenue.

It seemed like a million years since Big Red Chief's voice crackled at her from the speakers in the farmhouse kitchen. Was it true that you needed to be widowed in order to lead a courteous life? She didn't pause to think that idea through but happily imagined the stained glass window at 1785 and thought how holy it looked even if it lighted a staircase, not a church. It made her feel holy and unconfused. Months before, Father had said, "It is always a risk to take your soul into real life!" The others nodded, as if wakened and strengthened by his remark. Eleanor made nothing of it, but she memorized it, another graceful phrase, even if "risk" to her meant only the risk of borrowing against her inheritance to buy a three-storey house. Her mind drifted back to the house.

On the third Sunday in November, Alicia hurried Eleanor to an office building in downtown St. Paul, where they crowded into a small room with a conference table and vinyl chairs. There were four other people. Alicia sat close by Eleanor, bending right over the papers in front of her, making sure she signed nothing that wasn't right. A man at the opposite end of the crowded table was being similarly coached by his real estate agent. Presumably he was the owner of 1785 Newell Avenue. Eleanor supposed she would shake hands with him at the end, but for now each avoided the other's eyes. The closing agent's dull, energetic voice kept explaining terms. There was some cloud on the title, but it was cleared. . . . The police had asked that if Ms. Grummel ever saw LeRoy Beske, to call them immediately: he had been seen hanging around several times since he sold the house.

Eleanor was in a dream. She looked affectionately at Alicia's permanented head: it was back-combed and sprayed as still as a howitzer shell. If you touched it, surely your hand would come away with tiny cuts. Eleanor had two feelings: affection for this tough person who had helped her get her life's dream, and the memory of her mother, who wore dark glasses when she went to the beauty parlor. Even if she had to cover bruises with pancake, she never missed a hair setting; the time she had three stitches in her right cheek, she postponed her hairdo by two hours. Eleanor kept signing in exactly the places where Alicia pointed a Lee press-on nail to show her.

Keys tinkled across the table. Smiles. The men stood up: people's hands reached across to shake. Then they were back out into the cold street. Alicia said, "Come on. We'll drive to Mrs. Zenobie's and walk to your new house."

Eleanor was learning the measured graces of the rich. They brought each other small but ceremonial presents. Women brought just a few rosebuds for other women when they had a meeting together; the support group people arrived with newspaper cones full of flowers to celebrate someone getting her shit together. Men brought a bottle sometimes—Father had some sherry for the confirmands at the end. Now Eleanor said, "We'll drink to the house!" She had a bottle of champagne in the backseat.

The previous owners had left a dining-room table and two chairs. Eleanor opened the champagne. Alicia lifted her glass. Then they both heard scrabbling in the basement. "Not rats," Alicia said quickly and firmly. "I checked that out before. No rats."

"I'm not afraid of rats," Eleanor said. "I'm a farm girl." She

Carol Bly

was about to tell Alicia about how Virgil would lift up a bale of hay; when the rats burst out she whacked as many as she could.

"Down we go," Alicia said, rising.

As they moved through the fine old kitchen, Eleanor realized with surprise that she had paid no attention to the basement. It was the third floor that had fascinated her: one finished room, churchlike, with steep eaves going up to the ridgepole, and a charming dilapidated balcony at the peak end. The other half of the third floor was not finished; boarders could store their luggage there. The second floor was like all second floors of abused houses: radiators with paint chipped off, smudgy windows, deeply checked sills and mullions.

Alicia turned on the basement light. They trotted about the basement, between the abandoned coal room and the laundry room, around the monstrous octopus of a furnace, spray-painted aluminum, like ship's equipment. Behind the work-table, there sat against the wall a very thin, old, dirty woman. Her awful eyes gleamed. One skinny hand plucked at her blouse buttons.

Alicia said, "OK, both together . . ." They raised the woman up. "Nope—she's too weak to stand." Alicia paused.

"Let me," Eleanor said. She bent down, her back to Alicia. All that farm work. "Just put her on my back." They got the woman upstairs and laid her on the floor in the living room, which had carpeting.

"Police first," Alicia said.

"I'll run to Mrs. Zenobie's," Eleanor said.

Mrs. Zenobie herself frankly listened while Eleanor called 911. She rubbed an elbow and smiled. "You're getting into the problems of running a rooming house even faster than I did! You haven't been there even one night, and already you got a nonpaying-type tenant hiding in the basement! Gosh!"

Eleanor riffled through Mrs. Zenobie's directory. She ordered one chicken-onions-snow-peas-and-rice and gave the address.

"Unsuitable tenants is the second greatest pain next to taxes," Mrs. Zenobie offered.

The police car was already parked at 1785 when Eleanor ran back.

"It's Saturday, so the only social workers are Primary Interventions. We'll just take her to jail for the night," one of the two young men explained.

Alicia said she had to beat it, since the situation seemed to be under control.

Eleanor said, "I'll keep her for the night." She added, "I run a boardinghouse."

"Doesn't look like one yet," the other young cop said. "We've been kind of keeping a watch on this house. There was a real bad-news type here. This lady probably needs a doctor. We'll take her, and we'll get a social worker around to you tomorrow."

The policeman looked down at the old woman. "Can you talk, lady?" he said gently.

He waited a second. "OK. We'll wait for the ambulance." One of them went out to radio.

"This the kind of customer you going to have in this house?" the remaining policeman said with a grin.

There was a knock. Eleanor paid the Oriental foods delivery man and brought in the little white paper buckets with their wire handles.

Carol Bly

The policeman got the idea. He and Eleanor knelt on the floor. "If you can eat, lady, it's the best thing you can do," the officer said. He said to Eleanor, "Show it to her."

Eleanor said, "We're going to help you lean up against the wall." She opened one of the packets, and the old woman suddenly dug her whole hand into the rice. She put a palm full of it into her own face and begun to chew slowly. She reached in again and again.

"She needs chopsticks like I need chopsticks," the young officer said comfortably. Eleanor leaned on her heels. The woman finished all the rice. Eleanor offered her the chicken. "This is going to be a mess," the policeman said. He stood up and ambled into the kitchen. "Someone at least left you some paper towels." Together they wiped the woman's face. Then Eleanor wiped her neck where the Cantonese sauce and a few onions had run down. The ambulance came. The policeman left a number to call if there was any trouble. Eleanor walked over to Mrs. Zenobie's for the last time. Tomorrow night I'll homestead, she thought.

The social worker came the next day. He introduced himself as Rex, from Primary Intervention. Rex told Eleanor that none of the women's shelters had any room for a new person. Eleanor and he sat at the dining-room table, while he explained that there used to be an office especially for cases like this woman's. Now there wasn't the dollars. Rex thought this woman was named Eunice something: she was a victim of the second-to-last owner here, a LeRoy Beske, who'd run a racket diverting old people's welfare checks to himself. Then Rex looked at his hands.

"I don't know how you'd feel about this," he said. "I don't

know what kind of house you want to have, but if you could take care of Eunice on a temporary basis, we could offer you the Difficult Care rate. That is, we'd pay you twenty-two dollars a day to feed and shelter her. The hospital says she is OK. She's just in mild shock and can't talk. They don't think there is anything organically wrong except she's nearly starved to death. If you wanted to take her in four or five days . . ."

Eleanor said to herself fast, I could still get five or six courteous people who would have polite conversations at the table. It shouldn't be too hard: It'd still be a house where no one told anyone else to get their butt over here or there.

The truck finally came from Dawson with the furniture. Eleanor bought three more beds from Montgomery Ward. She interviewed prospective tenants. She put Mercein, Mrs. Solstrom, Dick, Carolyn, and George on the second floor. She put Eunice in the room she had imagined for herself, behind the kitchen on the ground floor. She slept on the sofa for several weeks. She kept the third-floor bedroom untenanted until the second floor was filled.

"Here," Mrs. Zenobie said. "They've got that racket on the TV so loud I can't hear myself think. Come in the kitchen."

She watched Eleanor with eyes blazing.

"Have I got this straight?" she said. "You want to trade one of your tenants for one of mine? What kind of crap is that?" She paused. "I don't want to get tough with you. I know you are mourning your husband. But you're in business, too, and you and I are doing business on the same street. So naturally I am looking at everything carefully. Let me just give this back to you, and you tell *me*. You want me to take someone

Carol Bly

named Mrs. Joanne Solstrom into my house, and then you want Mr. Jack Lackie to move to your house? You're going to pay them one hundred dollars each for the inconvenience?"

Eleanor nodded.

Mrs. Zenobie looked at her fingernails with the finesse of an actress. Since they were cut to just below the quick, there couldn't be much to discover about them. "I never paid any money to have some man move into any house of mine," she remarked.

There are some things you can't explain to some people, Eleanor thought. You can't tell your support group that you're *not* going through "the grief process" for your husband but that you are furious at the state of Minnesota for chipping tax out of your late husband's engine-repair service inventory before you inherited it. You couldn't tell Mrs. Zenobie that you wanted a retired Episcopal priest in your boardinghouse because he talked about history and culture and you did *not* want a perfectly nice woman named Mrs. Solstrom because she sneered during wine-and-cider hour that if that Tommy Kramer couldn't learn to move his butt out of the pocket, he deserved every sack he got.

"I don't get it," Mrs. Zenobie said. "She pays her rent? She's clean? OK. But if you think you're going to get any help out of that Lackie, think again. He's retired. He never picked up a leaf in the yard; not around this place, he didn't."

Their lives went smoothly through the winter. Eunice still didn't speak, but everyone fed her. Mercein and Dick brought her Whopper burgers, Carolyn brought her doughnuts, George brought her take-out Italian food from a place near his plant.

Jack brought her cans of Dinty Moore beef stew and helped her stack them up in the unfinished part of the attic. She grew fat. The social worker, Rex, thought it might be months before Eunice could speak again.

She followed Jack everywhere; he talked to her all the time. Eleanor began to feel happy. She moved Eunice to the north end of the second floor: she herself took the downstairs bedroom. Jack arranged his few possessions—his oddly old-fashioned clothes, his complete set of Will and Ariel Durant's *The Story of Civilization,* in the third-floor room. Jack took over laying and lighting the fire in the living-room stove that Eleanor bought at an auction on Fulton Street. Each late afternoon, they all watched the dull, comfortable flame through the isinglass while Jack served the wine and cider. Whenever he rose to refill someone's glass, Eunice stood up, too. If he left the room, she followed him. He had to turn directly to her and say, "No" when he wanted to be alone.

The other tenants were grateful that she followed Jack instead of driving them crazy. Eleanor was glad because she needed the hour before dinner to cook, she needed the hour after dinner to plan the next day's work, and she liked to sit alone in the kitchen at night. The dishwasher chugged through its hissing cycles. Eleanor wrote out lists of repairs needed, hardware to buy, meals for the rest of the week. She could hear Jack's voice rising and falling in the living room. He was telling Eunice everything that ever happened in human history.

As the weather warmed, Jack took on some outside chores. He renailed the rose trellis to the house while Eunice passed nails up to him. He sorted through the loose bricks lying in the backyard, dividing wholes from brokens. Whenever he lifted a brick, Eunice picked one up, watching his face. When he set his down, she set hers down. When her hands were free, she ate. There was always food in her jacket pockets— a wrapped ham-and-cheese or mushroom-and-Swiss from Hardee's. Sometimes Jack let her into the third-floor storage area to count her cans of stew and soup. She arranged and re-arranged them into pyramids, straight walls, squares. Her eyes lost the terrible glint they had at first. The boarders decided that probably she was only sixty or sixty-five, not eighty or ninety. She bathed, dressed, cleaned her teeth, and followed Jack everywhere.

In March, on a Saturday, it was Eleanor's turn to manage the food shelves at Saint Swithin's. By now she was a con-firmed church member.

Just before she left home, someone outside threw some-thing through the first-floor stained glass window. Glass and wood splinters were scattered all over the base of the stairs. Sharp, normal sunlight broke in. George, Eunice, and Jack had been clearing the breakfast table. Now they stood still. Then Eunice moved toward the mess of glass and smashed sashwork; she bent and picked up a brick. Jack immediately took it from her, in case there were glass shards stuck to it. Eleanor called the police.

"Go ahead," Jack told her. "I'll sweep this up, and George can go outside to see if anybody's around."

Like most people who have done plain labor in their lives, Eleanor could separate events at home from those at the job. All that day she worked hard, instructing volunteers, making quick judgments about clients. She knew now who were the few people who picked up food and sold it later. When they showed up and explained what they wanted, Eleanor looked them right in the face, with a deliberate smile, and said, "I'm so sorry; we're fresh out of that." If the person pointed angrily to where that very item stood on the shelf, Eleanor smiled and said, "I know it looks as if we have it. The funny thing is, we're fresh out."

That afternoon, she was happy to get out of her car and start up the sidewalk to her boardinghouse. Since it was still March, Jack would have lighted a fire, and they could all gather as usual and speculate about who had broken their stained glass window.

Her neighbor from across the street called, "Big trouble, huh, Eleanor?"

He was coming after her to talk. "In a way, I'm glad that happened, Eleanor," he said in a kind tone. "I know it doesn't seem like the right thing to say, but at least now that guy'll get what's coming to him."

Eleanor said slowly, "LeRoy Beske, you mean."

"That creep," the neighbor said. "Hanging around here. Trouble whenever he shows up. I'm sorry it had to happen at your place, Eleanor, but all of us along the street feel relieved." He paused. "Cops came, of course," he said. "They wanted to talk to you and said they'd be back around now or so."

Then a last word from the neighbor: "That Jack Lackie, that tenant of yours! I'll say one thing for him: If a job needs doing, he does it!"

Eleanor looked and saw that the paper toweling she had suggested Jack stuff into the broken window wasn't there.

Carol Bly

The whole window was reglazed, although only in clear glass now.

Inside the house, the living room was empty and dark.

"Hello?" Eleanor called up the staircase.

"Hello!" Jack called down, in an odd tone.

Eleanor turned back to the door, since someone had rung the bell. It was the two policemen Eleanor remembered from months before.

"Finally you got home," one of them said. "We've knocked and rung your bell, but no one would let us in."

Both policemen came right in.

"I hated losing that stained glass window," Eleanor told them.

"That's the last window Beske'll bust in a long time," one man told her. The other loped over to the staircase and called upstairs: "Everybody down! Police!"

"Well," Eleanor said, preening a little. "I think it is very nice of you men to be so concerned about a broken window."

Then they told her what had happened. LeRoy Beske had thrown the brick through her window, all right. Then he had hung around, and the boarders had seen him go around to the side of the house. They heard a sharp cry. Dick and George ran outside and found Beske bleeding severely from a head wound. A blood-splashed brick lay near him. They glanced around a little—and then upward at the little balcony off Jack's third-storey room. There was no one there. Both men hurried into the house to call the police. They both noticed that neither Jack nor Eunice was in the living room, where the other boarders began to huddle, overhearing the telephone call to 911.

Eleanor thought to herself, her boardinghouse, her polite structure, had fallen into violence just as quickly as any other household in a crime-filled country. The very man she had designated cultural leader had assaulted someone right in her own side yard.

One after another, the boarders denied any knowledge. Jack's turn came. Eleanor nearly shuddered. His voice denied knowledge just as flatly as the others' voices had.

"Now this lady: your name is? . . ." The policemen were now looking at Eunice. She was forty pounds heavier than when they had seen her three months earlier.

George said, "That's Eunice. We can pretty much answer for her, officer."

The officer said, "She'll have to speak for herself. Eunice," he said, "what did you see and where were you?"

Eunice opened her mouth. Her voice croaked and squealed like equipment long unused; phlegm caught in her throat and stopped a vowel now and then, but Eunice talked. When she started in, Eleanor remembered "My Lord Bag of Rice" and how the hero helped the sea princess. For the moment, Eleanor forgot that her reason for having Jack in her boardinghouse was that he should provide cultivated conversation. Now she believed that she had intuitively spotted Jack as a kind figure who would stand guard when they needed him. She thought, Well, well! Now he'd done it. So she had been canny. Her mind felt large and nervous.

But Eunice was not ratting on Jack. Eunice said, "In the beginning the human race needed strong leaders. The Jews in Egypt needed a leader to get them out. When medieval farmers had their lands stolen by the church or the state or by

Carol Bly

their landlords, they needed brave people to get them their freeholds."

She kept talking. When Eunice got to the Reformation, she switched to Chinese history. She explained that the Chinese invented watertight doors for ships, so that no enemy could rake through the entire hold and sink a ship. Any leader knew it was devastating for a man to be trapped in a watertight compartment with the sea pouring in. Nonetheless, a leader told men on the other sides to secure the watertight doors. They heard the doomed man's screams, but the leader could save the rest. A leader could do desperate acts while others froze.

Then there was a brief pause, in which Eleanor could see that Eunice was going to switch to another culture. She explained how painful it was to learn that the world was not terracentric—so painful a truth thousands couldn't bear it.

"OK, lady, OK," one policeman said.

"For now, that's enough," the other said to Eleanor. "You all have your dinner. We'll come back tomorrow, and anyway they will know by then if LeRoy Beske is going to live or not."

Before the door had closed behind them, Eunice had begun again. She explained that in every age of bullies, a leader shows up to give the people respite. She told them about John Ball, a sixteenth-century agricultural reformer. She explained the odal law of Norway. Jack declined to have wine with the others, and Eunice followed him upstairs, telling him about how Captain Cook used psychology to induce his men to eat sauerkraut. It saved them from scurvy.

Those down below could still hear her hoarse, unaccustomed voice, less distinct, as she and Jack rounded the landing

My Lord Bag of Rice

and started up the reverse flight. They heard her close the door of her room. Jack's steps continued up on the third-floor stairs. Then they heard Eunice speaking to herself in her room.

Eleanor lighted the stove, listening to the boarders' various exclamations. Gradually they told each other their versions over and over, more and more quietly. After a while, Eleanor put the crock-pot of stew on the dining-room table. She called to Jack and Eunice. Everyone sat quietly, whispering now and then—"Would you please pass the rolls?" "Would you send the carrot sticks down here?"—with a good deal of glancing at Eunice.

Her face was full of color. She looked fifty now, not sixty. She kept facing Jack and telling that nineteenth-century Chinese grandmothers were certainly sorry to see their granddaughters' feet bound the first time. She described how the mothers and daughters cried as they removed their clogs at night, unwinding the bloodied cloths from their toes—yet they, more than the men, made certain the practice was kept up.

One by one the boarders finished eating, nodded to Eleanor, and left the room. Eleanor and Jack and Eunice remained at the cluttered table.

At last Jack rose. Eunice followed him immediately, in her usual way. She was explaining what the Marines did in Mexico in 1916. Eleanor set the dishwasher growling over its first load. When she went upstairs, she heard Eunice, alone in her room behind her door, saying that the Michigan National Guard helped Fisher Body's Plant Number 1 defeat union workers in 1937. Eunice's voice, getting exercise, sounded smoother now. Eleanor paused on the landing, decided to go back downstairs to bed, then noticed Jack sitting on a stair on the flight above.

"You're listening," she whispered to him, going up a few steps. They regarded each other in the weak night-light.

"How can I help it!" he said in a whispered laugh. "Amazing! Amazing!"

Eleanor said, "She's not so amazing! It isn't her! *You're* the one who's amazing!" She didn't mind if her enormous happiness showed in her whisper. She felt out of her class, somehow—but this much she knew: it is amazing when a man uses all that violence that's in men to help people instead of just pushing people around! Virgil would never have dropped a brick on a friend's enemy. Her father never defended anyone. She realized that sometime between dinner and this minute, she had decided to lie for Jack if she had to. She would say what was necessary to keep the police from cornering him. It would be something new for her: she had not even been able to prevail on the X-ray technicians to leave poor Virgil in peace. She had underestimated Jack, admiring only his ability to talk courteously.

Now she whispered, "You have actually saved her life!"

He said, "You don't even know what happened."

Eleanor ignored that idiotic modesty and whispered, "What's more, she half-saved yours, too. When she rattled on and on all that history to the police, they obviously decided she was out of her head, and they got up and went home! Of course," Eleanor added, feeling very sage, the way bystanders do when they second-guess the police, "they had been looking for that awful LeRoy Beske for a long time, anyway."

"She didn't save my life, either," Jack now said.

Behind her door Eunice was moving away from Max Planck and introducing Marilyn French and Ruth Bleier.

Jack said from his stair, slightly above Eleanor's, "I want you to listen now. I did not—repeat: did not—drop or throw a brick onto LeRoy Beske from that balcony. You know who goes around this house carrying cans of beef stew and books and bricks."

Eleanor was still. "I don't believe you," she said then.

Jack said, "LeRoy Beske swiped her welfare check for over two years. At the end, he hid her and then nearly starved her to death and dumped her in your basement when he couldn't figure out anything more convenient. She was mad at him. Then he made a mistake. He was drunk when he came around here this morning. For the fun of it, he tossed a brick through your window. He didn't figure Eunice right—she was on the balcony when he ambled by a few hours later. He shouted, 'Hi, little girl!' to her when he saw her. People on the other side of the house heard him. He probably didn't recognize her. He shouted, 'Hi princess!' She had a brick with her, because she and I were going to build the barbecue today. She was so mad she got off a fast, accurate shot. Anyway," Jack finished up in a satisfied, brutal way, "she got him good."

He whispered down at Eleanor, "Another thing. I am not a retired priest. I am a retired janitor. What you have here is a retired janitor who has read a lot of history."

By now Eunice's voice had almost the lilt and ease of ordinary women's voices. She said that Eskimos' teeth had caries from eating American-made candy bars. She said Eskimos were listening to reggae up there, on the ice floes. She described the hole widening in the Antarctic ozone.

Eleanor and Jack sat on for a few minutes. Eleanor imagined the Eskimos looking out over the ice-filled water. She

Carol Bly

also remembered the watercolor illustration of the hero with his huge bag of rice: it weighed on one shoulder; he was looking out over water; his robe was painted in baby colors—pink and light blue and dusty yellow—and the Sea of Japan was pale green, a shade you might choose for a child's nursery.

New Stories

Renee:
A War Story

Renee was the sixth-grade softball batter no one jeered at. Vern, the main bully of our class, leader of all the bullies, the natural hater of girls, chose Renee first for his team. Then boys, alternately with the other team captain until they used up the boys and started choosing girls. Vern rolled his eyes up and groaned over each girl's name, while the already chosen kids—*in,* safe, superior—leaned against the woven backstop fence. When Vern sighed, they sighed. They closed their eyes in fake pain as each girl's name was called out. Alice, a friend of mine, and I were invariably last. When it got down to us, anyone could see each team captain had to take one of us. Alice was no worse at bat than I was, but she had been what was called "socially promoted" from fifth grade last spring. Vern took me before he would take her, adding, "I guess," to show that he had no ownership in the choice. Neither team captain bothered to name Alice. They just pointed. By then all the kids would be walking to their positions.

All of that humiliation took place below Renee's world.

Her concentration was perfect. At bat she looked at nothing but the ball. She was the only one of us, boys or girls, who classically sagged her knees at bat. She was sprung like a daddy longlegs, her skinny chest vaulted so airily over the base. Her face was still as rock. Her eyes burned lovelessly toward the pitcher. Nothing he could send, her gaze said, nothing, not even anything the terrible Vern could send, would ever unsettle her.

That Renee rarely missed was all the more surprising because she swung at every pitch. If the ball came way inside, she would cave back fast to save her life, yet somehow she would give it a slug at the last moment. If the pitch was way outside, she would lunge across the base and then some, and bash it clean and hard. She batted pitches so high that she looked like someone using a baseball bat to serve at tennis. Since none of us, not even Vern, pitched very well, we were grateful to Renee for swinging at everything. Our school recess was only sixteen minutes. That meant a couple of fussy batters could fritter away the whole period. We glowered at fussy batters. They made us feel like people tied down while someone let our lifeblood out right in front of us. We were eleven and twelve years old. Most of us weren't allowed to swear or talk back or bust up stuff: these morning and afternoon recesses were our serious explosions of freedom.

I was too insecure a kid to love anyone much, particularly someone always picked first for softball when I was always picked next to last. Still, Renee, right from the first, touched me. I noticed her and noticed her. She didn't look like an athlete. At twelve, she had a serious home-kit permanent, with the usual pompadour above her forehead. Dark circles went

Carol Bly

round her eyes. Sometimes those circles were so pronounced you could see a clear circumference between their darkness and the rest of her facial skin. Surely she stayed up far past what my parents called a decent bedtime. On the days when Renee positively looked like a raccoon, Alice, my slow-paced but loyal friend, estimated that Renee had been memorizing away at the Old Testament until three in the morning. For all we knew she might even have started on the New. There wasn't anybody in our Sunday school who knew anything about the New Testament.

It was an amazement to me how someone at only my age could be wonderfully pale, waxy, thin as a page. Renee was the only friend I had who looked like the *before* part of an Ovaltine ad. We all admired her, but I did not admire the same things that Alice and the other girls admired. I did not admire the upsweep of hair, making her look like a Brownie 620 snapshot of a USO girl. I came from an agnostic family, a dreadful secret that I lied about. I would vehemently agree with Alice and the others that it was just plain very nice how Renee had memorized so much of the Old Testament. We girls walking home from school together were agreed on a number of other reasons why Renee was wonderful. She was a real good leader, Alice would say. But I could not casually add, "Well, actually, what I admire is that she is so unhealthy looking. I bet she gets to stay up late. And listen, you guys, I bet she will die young just after meeting a man who really loves her. She will be so ill that they will not even be able to consummate the marriage." In my fantasy I threw in that part about her being too ill to consummate the marriage a little insincerely. In our grade we were very big on consummation of marriages. Actually, I admired Renee for some dark future I felt would be hers. I knew deeply and sadly that I was bright as tinsel compared to her.

Renee had described for us her parents' smooth, white, leatherette-covered Bible. Her father's fingers sank into its soft, padded front when he led the family devotions. My parents and even my older sister and I had a lot of books, but none of them were plumped out like that white Bible. And though Alice's parents owned a gigantic shortwave radio with something called a Police Span, they had no books at all. "I can just *see* that Bible of theirs!" Alice would exclaim.

I could not tell Alice that I envied Renee the fact that her parents drilled her on Sunday-school memory lines. My father and mother thought my older sister and I were a gas. They would egg us on to tell funny stories from our eighth-grade and sixth-grade lives. They belly-laughed when I complained about the class bully.

But when I repeated one or another particular insult Vern had handed me on the softball field, they turned solemn. My dad would turn to my mother and my older sister. "We have to put our heads together on this," he said. "We have to figure out a way she can straighten out that little sawed-off bully once and for all." Then he turned to me, while rising to carve seconds for everyone. He said handsomely, "OK, honey-bunny-rabbit, now hear this! Now hear this!"—he was in the navy reserve—"We . . . are . . . all working on it!"

He was captain enough for my little ship. I knew I didn't have enough armament for the wars life might take me to, but I had my parents behind me. I would glow then, while he carved and passed seconds for us all—but always, always, at

Carol Bly

school during the week, and at Sunday school, I pretended to the other kids that, boy, if I didn't get my Sunday-school memory lines right my dad would go straight up.

Renee's most remarkable quality had nothing to do with either softball or bad health. It was her addiction to teacher-surprise parties. She would slink around to us sixth-grade leaders; me, Alice, other girls who had been elected monitors, any boys who had been elected police boys, anyone whose parents weren't on WPA. She would whisper, "The class is getting up a teacher-surprise party." In our dim intuitions we knew that only *she,* Renee, was getting it up. We knew we were the first few she had told, but when she whispered to us and regarded each of us from the center of those cloud-encircled eyes, we felt that the party was a fate brought on by powerful, absent forces, and Renee was simply the harbinger. We could no more stop that teacher-surprise party from happening than we could stop *My Weekly Reader* from showing up at three every Wednesday afternoon.

Renee got permission from the principal. He advised her to choose Wednesdays for all surprise parties, for the very reason that Wednesday was *My Weekly Reader* day and therefore the party would not interrupt any real curriculum. Renee would briskly put together a girls' food-buying committee and a boys' committee to soak everyone for a nickel each. Even the WPA kids had to ante in, but Renee made sure to collect from the WPA kids herself. Years later one of those kids told me that she used to stare them right in the face and tell them to quit whining: they had to pay up like anyone else but they could have three months' credit. As far as this kid knew she never dunned anyone for any of those many nickel loans.

At last, on the given Wednesday, Renee and two accomplices, usually Alice and I, crept down to the principal's office at three o'clock to pick up the apricot-glazed white rolls and the cupcakes that we had helped her stash there at first bell. Alice and I had all we could think about just to keep the big trays level on our arms so as not to lose the twenty-six cupcakes with stiff sugar flowers punched into their frosting. But Renee was already an organizer. She had thought to order an extra cupcake for the principal. Nor was her tone supplicating the way we girls talked to him whenever sent down to his office. Under the shopgirl permanent, Renee's grown soul sang out small talk—thanks and good-byes—to him.

When we got upstairs, Renee would fling open the classroom door and shriek, "Teacher surprise! Teacher surprise!"

First, our classmates would all look up at us. Next, everyone eyed the teacher's face. If she showed any signs of real surprise or of real ecstasy, I was willing to love her, but only for a few minutes. The fact was that teacher was dull. I would grasp her blackboard demos about fractions and decimals and percents only to be left for quarter hours on end to daydream about life lived with polar bears, and about mass killings that just started up spontaneously in cities larger than Duluth but would sooner or later come to Duluth too.

Renee wished on us more teacher-surprise parties than we wanted. If we demurred, she overrode us with her glassy philosophy. "The teacher works so hard for us," she said. "She gives us so much." I couldn't see that she gave us anything. She didn't even have to ante in five cents for the food.

I felt daunted by Renee's altruistic love of this teacher—and her love of the one last year, too. She had even liked the

Carol Bly

fourth-grade teacher way back. I could not imagine myself loving a teacher, even for the reward of a cupcake with its frosting of mortar. But Renee already traveled far into the outer space of adults. She was galaxies outward from the rest of us. She cajoled us to support her celebrations; anyone on her surprise-party team lived briefly in the glow of her leadership. I was happy to do anything Renee got us doing, but I also felt, heavily, how superior to mine her character was. I half-wanted to resist. At base, I was a contented slob. I had my slob-kid's life—reading books and daydreaming—I couldn't fathom altruism.

Once, only once, Alice and I saw Renee's home. One Thursday morning, Renee had come to school with the darkest of dark, raccoonlike rings around her eyes. She seemed distant, vacant. I felt moved. For once her permanent did not look tacky. Her pallor was beautiful. Renee lifted her desktop, and her free hand hovered like an angel's over the pencils and workbooks. We other kids rummaged when we couldn't decide what we wanted. Not Renee—not that day, at least. At last her fingers floated quiet as snow down onto her copy of *My Weekly Reader*. We were supposed to write something about the world news lesson we had had the day before.

Just at the end of morning recess, Renee keeled over onto the playground gravel.

Since it happened in 1942 no one looked for a cause. Someone said, "I guess she fainted." When Renee came to, the teacher, in a no-nonsense way, assigned Alice and me to walk her home.

Our school stood in one of the last ordinary neighborhood blocks at the northwest corner of Duluth. We all believed that the woods there were not just woods, but solemn forest that led to Hudson's Bay. I daydreamed that in some millenium that forest would move back over our city.

Renee kept saying, "You kids don't need to walk me home. I'm just fine."

I replied in a principled tone, "We are walking you home because we promised to." My real reason for being so keen was that her house lay a good two blocks' length outside the city. By the time it got to her house, that street stopped being called a street and became a road. I wanted to get outside the usual civilization.

"Well, anyhow you wouldn't both have to come," Renee now said to Alice.

"I'd like to see that beautiful Bible your folks have," Alice said.

Renee's house had a wringer washer on the porch, rusted solid from mangle release to hose clip. We reached the porch steps.

"I'm OK now," Renee said. She said, "You guys wouldn't have to come in."

Alice said, "We're supposed to see you safe into your house."

Not a sound came from inside the screened door.

We all went in.

Renee's father, not her mother, sat across the living room from us. He looked like any man out of work, in his sleeveless undershirt and his bib overalls. He did not get up from the huge chair. The May issue of *Detective Comics* magazine lay in a double curve over his knees. Even from across the room I recognized the tiny bright squares of violence. Clearly, Robin swung on a rope and stuck one yellow-gauntleted fist into

Carol Bly

some bad person's face. It was very interesting to me that both Batman and Robin got around by swooping down from ropes that hung from a hook far above the full moon itself. There was never a half-moon, either. It was always the real thing.

Few men wore deodorants in the early 1940s, probably no poor men. All the way across from where he sat we caught the swift tang of this man's sweat.

"How come yer home?" he said.

Renee brought out a gauzy tone I had never heard. "It's nothing, Dad."

"Must be something yer home," he said. "If yer in trouble—" He half-rose from his chair.

Then he paused. His face swung toward Alice and me. "You girls can just leave now," he said.

I got up my nerve. "She fainted during recess," I said. For a second I felt I had put myself between Renee and some obscure danger. My usual style was a combination of my own cowardice and a lot of admiration of people who were brave, so I now felt a little high.

But her father only glared. Then he turned back to Renee and repeated, "Oh, so she fainted in recess? She fainted in recess?"

Then he grinned at me, and this time repeated in falsetto, "Oh, so she fainted in recess, huh?"

"It's nothing, Dad," Renee sang, like a bodiless star.

"You girls could leave now," her father repeated, still in his falsetto.

We nearly flew.

Everyone gathered around us in the lunchroom. Even Vern, who generally avoided any table with girls at it.

Lunch was three cents unless your dad was WPA or out of work and you had a note from the principal. Both the richest kids and the poorest kids knew enough never to ask what anyone's house looked like, but the medium-rich and medium-poor kids were openly curious.

"You seen in Renee's house then?" they asked. They leaned toward us over their trays.

"It is beautiful!" I said. I slowly shook my head, a gesture of bemusement and sharing. "They have that Bible all right, the one with the soft white-leather cover. And a real fireplace, with the smell of birch logs burning in it, too."

Now Alice raised her face ponderously, infinitely slowly, to mine. For a split second her face looked blank yet illumined, like a marquee that they haven't put the movie-title letters onto yet. Then she said, "A real fireplace."

Alice was not a quick type of kid. She paused. Then she said, "And Renee's mother is so pretty . . . so pretty."

I took it up. "They have a gigantic radio. They get stations from all over the world. Her dad happened to be home from his office, too. He was listening to Germany. It is like magic how clear it came in. As if we were right there."

"Germany!" Vern exclaimed. "How could he be listening to Germany? We're at war with Germany! Even if some radio *could* reach that far, what Americans would listen to German propaganda—all that mean stuff they believe in— *might equals right.*"

Just the day before we had had an article in *My Weekly Reader* about the Hitler Youth being taught that might equals right. Of course those German kids would grow up to be hopeless bullies. Everyone knew all about that.

Carol Bly

But all that spring Vern had jeered at me because I couldn't ever bat myself to first base. So now I held out against him.

"Her dad was listening to Germany all right," I remarked. "Beethoven, if you want to know. They may not have the Bible over there but they got Beethoven and Renee's dad was listening to it."

Kids lost interest. Even Vern didn't stay to jeer any further. Boys and girls rose and drifted off as soon as they finished their trays.

I said to Alice, "I liked her mother's dress. I liked how there were flowers on the bodice. And those silver high heels. Not the unrationed kind with straps either—*real* high heels. Solid silver leather."

Alice and I steadily drank our soup. On that day we tipped the spoon edge into our mouths instead of shoveling in the whole spoon. In between spoonfuls we each regarded the other. We each nodded at everything the other said. We were like two lighthouses on the same promontory, whose beams gladly shone straight at each other.

I said, "I liked the way Renee's mother ran that hot bath for her. Those piles of thick towels."

"Those towels were scented," Alice said with some snap. "And she wrapped Renee up in an afghan and brought her a tray."

"With apricot-glazed rolls. And cupcakes," I said.

Alice said, "Those kind the frosting doesn't get hard."

Renee: A War Story   281

Chuck's Money

Leona Singer liked going to Einar's Motel to do his books.

Einar was a gracious-looking fellow, an absolute fool, but he gave kind little speeches, and his well-combed hair, long since gone white, was so beautiful that women paused to listen to him. He seemed to pick up on that little pause and would say just a bit of agreeable rhetoric, whatever occurred to him at the moment. He always had the manner of someone presiding over a meeting of kindly disposed people. When the motel office needed vacuuming and Cheryl, who cleaned, had done one of her many no-shows, Einar would clean her units for her—not just vacuuming, but reciting his thoughts over the howl of sound. When he had time, he hung around the Dearing, Minnesota, courthouse. He looked more like a judge than Judge Meyrens.

Einar had long since gone broke trying to run that twelve-unit motel, but a cunning motel chain executive in Hibbing knew Einar made a warm presence. The chain picked up the motel, hired Einar as manager, and left the name of the business as was: Einar's Motel. Tourists took it for a mom-and-pop business and stayed there for the ambiance. As Einar swung around the registration pad for them to sign, his avuncular dignity suggested that the reading lights would be 100 watts, not those whorehouse 40s, and the televisions, in their fake wood-grained cabinets, would be color and cable. The management company did insist, however, that Einar hire a bookkeeper and he get a cleaning woman who would really show.

So Leona Singer, fresh from her six-week bookkeeping course, came to do his books. As for getting a decent cleaning woman, Einar did not take the management people seriously. It was true that Cheryl was unreliable, but he wasn't about to fire her. She had the curious habit of muttering and growling to herself as she cleaned. Einar once crept into one of the units while she was cleaning and heard an unbroken stream of obscene epithets and threats to enemies. But he noted that Cheryl's enemies were the usual choice of enemies in Dearing—a powerful businessman named Mincesky, and the football coach, a few others, the Lutheran parish education secretary—the recognized town bullies of both sexes. Einar withdrew quietly, lest he disturb her. He did not mind her language. Cleaning women work alone in the rooms.

Local Dearing businesspeople knew at one time or another that Einar had lost his business and now only worked there for a chain, but he presided with so complacent a smile behind the registration counter—with the office radio set to Minnesota Public Radio, not some USA junk station—that people forgot. They began to believe that Einar magically owned the place once again. He had even become a kind of

Carol Bly

revered town leader. People thought he was an ombudsman or a legal entity of some kind. One often saw him shaking hands with plaintiffs in the courthouse hall. He could neither add nor subtract, but he was elected church treasurer three times running. If you hung about after Sunday services, you saw him and Charles Mincesky hunched over the little table in the narthex anteroom, counting the collection. Handsome men, both, and the room looked so nice now they had the new carpeting. Einar had the gift of praising others. He also had the gift of not disturbing people when they were doing his work for him.

One Saturday forenoon, the morning after homecoming, Leona Singer arrived at the motel to do the books. If nothing unusual came up, she expected to be done in time to drive a car pool of church women to Duluth.

"Ah, Leona!" Einar cried. "Right on time as always! As always, Leona, as always! It is so good of you to work me in when you have such a tight schedule this weekend—and Allen down with flu, too—you're off to District, aren't you?"

"Going to District" to a football player meant his team was progressing through neighbor-town playoffs—a thing that never happened to the Dearing High School fellows. When you said "going to District" to a Lutheran, it meant attending the women's regional church conference, complete with car pool, gossip on the road, overnight accommodations in Duluth, workshops, and dinner out, with luck a few drinks on the sly.

"You are looking far too gorgeous for a whole day of church work," Einar observed.

Leona was wearing her going-away suit for the millionth

time. In the one year of her marriage so far, the pale suit had dropped from top dress to out-of-town-travel in her gradually shrinking wardrobe.

"I am letting you have everything," Einar added, waving his arm. "The whole office. I can do my telephoning from Reception. And Leona, I have moved the copier out of the office into the TV console in 12. It is nicer without it in the office. Here, the key to 12. Which reminds me, where is that naughty Cheryl? She should have been here and done all the units by now! Oh well! Maybe the homecoming game was too much for her! There you go, Leona—it's all yours!"

Only Einar, of all Leona's customers, made you think he was doing you a gigantic favor when he cleared some space for you to work in. And as for removing the copier—!

Like all natural-born speech givers, Einar believed in a humorous touch. "I am going to put up a sign some day," he said. "'Brett Favre slept here.'"

"Really?" said Leona. She took the master guest book from him.

Einar said, "No, but we did have a quarterback in 12 last night. Chuck Mincesky."

"A nice boy, but not Brett Favre," Leona said.

She carried everything she needed into the back office.

Here it was again, the unmistakable pleasure she felt when she opened up someone's books. People's accounts were always mysterious, either in the actual transactions people got into, or simply in the wondrous ways people chose to record their negotiations. You never knew. People told her, you are a natural at number crunching. She was glad of the reputation. Less than three years into her career, she already did half the books in town. She was beginning to feel she would be able to support her husband all right. She settled happily to the job. Einar's boss company wouldn't let him give credit, so there were no statements for Leona to mail out. Most P and L program users could have done it themselves. Quicken should have served. But just as Einar, in his role of church treasurer, enthroned in the little anteroom off the narthex, could not figure out how much the church collection came to each Sunday, he could not figure out where he was with the motel.

Leona said to herself, Done soon. Then she would pick up Coralie Ann, the sheriff's wife, and the other carpoolers. She saw that Einar had tried to fool with his accounts, entering items wrongly. Leona reentered everything to suit herself. She forgot that she was sitting in a wool suit, stockings, and heels, that her husband was only starting to recover from the flu, and that she was sorry to be leaving him alone overnight. She forgot that she herself felt nervous because she had to give the opening meditation at District. She lost herself in Einar's work.

She was ready to use the copier in only a half hour. She opened the door that communicated between the back office, where she had been working, and unit 12.

The motel room was dark, so Leona went across to the curtains and let in the noontime sunlight. On the bed lay a queer sight: a white forehead and nose profile, rocky like the top of a small mountain range. But it was a human being, clearly dead, because on its other side, as Leona saw when she crept closer, the right side of the face lay spilled open like once molten, now stiffened lava flow.

Leona was a practical person not given to trembling. Still, she decided to sit down. She backed gingerly toward the desk and sat on its edge. She saw that the dead boy was Chucky Mincesky, the son of her least favorite person around town, Charles Mincesky. A nice enough boy. The nice son of the bullying father. The smiling son of a gray-faced, unsmiling mother whom Leona couldn't stand because she always tried to take both your hands and say some soppy thing.

The room smelled. Not of breathing and human skin, the way motel rooms smell so often, but of blood. Perhaps of brains. I am smelling Chucky's brains, Leona thought. She began, then, to shake but told herself, Oh for goodness sake don't shake. She stopped.

Next she noticed that a large envelope leaned against the upper part of the TV console where Einar said he had stashed the copier. She tottered over to it. "To the Maid," the envelope said, "or Whoever Finds Me."

Leona tottered back to her perch to read. There was a wad of twenty-dollar bills and a small sealed envelope inside. *To whoever finds me,* the note read, *here is $340 in cash. Sorry I don't have more. Don't tell Einar. This is for you because it is not very nice to find someone who has blown their brains out. Put this large envelope and the money and this note into your pocket. Then put the little envelope up where you found this one.*

The top of the smaller envelope read "To Whoever Finds Me." Leona went back to the TV console and set the note up.

I will give myself two minutes, she said aloud in the room with its fragrance of blood. Two minutes before I call Einar. Before whatever else happens. Jerry the sheriff. A doctor. Whatever.

There was a great silence in the room. This silence reminded

Carol Bly

her for some benighted reason of the noise just after her own wedding service. She and Allen had got out of the church ahead of the others, he in his rentals, she in her dress from Duluth, made of white satin and pretty good imitation Belgian lace. The little church tolled its bell above them. The sound crashed down upon them, loud and pointless. The late afternoon sunlight felt harsh after the dark narthex. They paused.

There he was, then. Her husband with the limp, pretty hair, tall, not taking her arm determinedly enough. A moment's rage for her, then. Is this how this whole marriage is going to go? she thought. He was thinking some thoughts of his own, apparently.

Aloud she snapped, "It is pure chance we got married, wasn't it?"

As soon as she spoke, she remembered that it wasn't true. She had married for love, just as she had told his father the year before.

Leona had had the idea she would get to know Allen's father and stepmother. They were people who kept clear of cold winters, now that they were middle-aged. Leona had supposed that since it was only October, a mild fall, they might hold off returning to Florida a day or two. Leona would get to be friends with them.

Allen said, "Chances are, that won't work."

Leona said, "You mean, they won't like me?"

"Won't either like you or dislike you. They're busy. They don't either like or dislike *me*, even. I'm just here. They're just there."

They invited Leona over to dinner, which was cooked by

a recently divorced, financially strapped mother of three, a member of Leona's church. The food was wonderful. Jackie Scree had done them chicken, of course, like every meal you ever got anywhere, but this chicken did not make you feel as if you were eating grandmother flesh. Way to go, Ms. Scree, Leona thought: Leona knew the look and mannerisms of a hungry person who packages together an income out of separate one-shot jobs. She had had about a tenth of her present accounts back then, but those books had already taught her how tough it was to make a living on any cottage industry. She took it in how Jackie Scree smiled energetically each time she came through the kitchen door to freshen their coffee. Guts, Leona thought, and good business sense: business-wise. There's no money in looking brave and sad, not in business anyhow. You had to be all hustle even if there were dark circles under your eyes.

The caterer brought them coffee.

"Well then!" Allen's father said. "Now tell us, Leona, whatever do you see in this son of mine that makes you want to marry him?"

That was a joke so everyone laughed.

The stepmother smiled around vaguely. This family, the man's son by the other marriage, and now his girlfriend—clearly she was indifferent to all that. She was waiting to return to Florida, where no doubt they conducted something they felt was their real life.

Just after everyone laughed there was a short silence. Leona thought, You can't tell your future father-in-law that you are marrying his son because of something that happened in confirmation class six years ago!

Carol Bly

"I'd need days to tell you," she said conversationally. "Do you two have to leave so fast? The weather is holding all right, isn't it?"

They could not delay even a day. The stepmother, who hadn't spoken before, now spoke in a rush about their commitments on Marco Island.

Allen explained to Leona later that his father needed to be out of Minnesota more than a half year or they could not claim Florida residency and exemption from Minnesota income tax.

Leona's own parents were easier to manage. Her mother exclaimed, "Such a nice face!" She seemed to mean it. Starting as a teenager, Leona had ridden all over northern Minnesota in carpools from Dearing to Hibbing and Duluth and Chisholm, for debate, and sports, and Luther League. In a female carpool, "he has such a nice face" wasn't much compliment to boy or man. In a carpool of girls or women, when a man had a nice face it meant he was incompetent in school or business, or he lacked any horsy energy. Sometimes it meant that whoever made the observation knew much, much more about the man, all of it far too lewd or business spoiling to mention. But Leona thought her mother meant to compliment Allen.

Her father said, "Leona, you've been around some, you know. What with that summer job for the senator and all. Washington, D.C. And you easily could have gone to college, too. Might still, honey. Honey, are you sure about this young man? He knows so much less of the world . . ."

Leona said, "Dad, being a page and stapling a thousand brochures an hour in the Hart Senate Office Building one summer doesn't count as knowing the world much."

Chuck's Money

Her father made a last remark. He wondered where the two of them would go, no college and all. He said it was only that he couldn't see just where Allen was headed.

Leona reminded him that she had taken six perfectly good weeks of bookkeeping.

Her father had smiled immediately. She could see he had decided not to quarrel with her choice.

Her father would seem to have been right. Allen was not going to go anywhere. Leona couldn't see that she was, either. Dearing had its complement of boy-men who put on long faces and told you they were going to get it together to go back to school as soon as they'd worked some more.

Allen Singer didn't even reach up into that crowd. For one thing, Leona was horrified to discover that he couldn't get a price for his work. She had no reason to hold it against him. He never said he was good at business.

She first began to go with him when he was thrown out of the confirmation class. Even back then he was the only kid left in Dearing who would mow lawn for five dollars. The other fourteen- and fifteen-year-olds were already getting at least ten. Well, he felt he couldn't jack up prices on single mothers. He couldn't charge Mrs. Scree anything much. Leona knew that "anything much" meant he worked jobs for her for free. The others knew if someone was an old woman, especially someone with arthritis, you could raise the prices all the faster.

After their high-school graduation, Allen, along with two broke dairy farmers around the area, contracted to mow alleys with his International cub and sickle bar. He did the whole of Dearing for sixty dollars, whereas the other two, when they took their turns, charged and received seventy-five.

Carol Bly

When he and Leona got married, he rented a house at the west edge of Dearing, a wreck of a place, where they were happy. Allen found old paving brick behind the courthouse where the county had some construction stuff going. He laid out a brick walk going around the side of their rental house to the back porch doorway. But Leona found out that their landlord, Charles Mincesky, would not give Allen anything for this permanent improvement. Leona sometimes took up with Mincesky about one thing or another.

Mincesky said handily, "If I had wanted a hand-laid brick parquet sidewalk up to the door I'd have hired it done by an expert. You or Allen should have asked me ahead. And as for the cellar and your complaints about the floor giving way—if Allen's so handy, he can put up a pole with a jack."

Allen was not put out when she reported that conversation. He would like to jack it up, he said. Leona thought they should move. There were other better rental houses around.

But Allen dug in, with an expression on his face she had first seen in confirmation class. "I love this place," he said. "I like the way it's on the edge of town."

She contemplated his face. A man being stubborn is almost, almost, as fascinating as a man being heroic, she thought. She thought he was being stubborn, hanging to a stupid idea like spending time and money on a rotten house they didn't own—but the stubborness glowed in him, making the lock of straight hair look swept like a seaman's—as she imagined a seaman, of course, having seen only one CPO who wandered through the Senate office she worked in one summer.

Their rickety porch gave out to the west. Across McCabe Creek, a disused pasture was beginning to come up in willows.

On the far edge of the pasture a ring of fir forest made the skyline. Well, she liked it all right herself.

It was beautiful, Allen said. He had gathered Leona tighter against him as they looked out.

In his arms Leona thought, OK, everyone is going to clip Allen whenever they can. That's what people do in this town. Well, she bet they did it in Washington, too, even if the particular senator she'd worked for that one summer didn't clip any people so far as she knew. OK, then, she said to herself, *I will be the income person. I will do books for everyone in this town. I will get to know all the businesses and I will keep high visibility in church work and I won't make any mistakes and people will trust me. I will keep my mouth shut at all times. That'll be worth about fifteen thou per annum all by itself. I'll support us OK.*

Just having made up her mind to it relaxed her; out of simple resigned feeling, she moved closer in Allen's arm.

He read her gesture his own way. He said, "I'm proud you trust in me, Leona."

To please him she said, "That's a very beautiful river and meadow, anyway." But she hadn't much feeling for nature.

On their honeymoon they had by accident established a style of intimacy neither could have guessed at ahead of time. Allen had proposed they go camping in the Lake of the Woods somewhere. Leona said, well yes, they could, she supposed. They could, of course.

Allen heard her tone. If not camping, what would she like?

She had thought to see some sights. Like Iron World, that museum in Chisholm, where she'd heard there were Events. And people serving ethnic foods. And then they could camp,

Carol Bly

too. Mrs. Preck, the parish secretary, recommended a place where she had very much enjoyed a spiritual-journeys conference. One of Leona's first jobs was going over the church books every fourth Monday, so even back then she knew Mrs. Preck was as crooked as as an auger shaft. But Allen and Leona hadn't any ideas of their own about resorts, so when Mrs. Preck mentioned the name of a particular lodge, Allen and Leona reserved a week there.

One day they went to Iron World and were served German pastries by a young woman dressed in German national costume. This woman told them she was proud of her German grandparents and of all that Germany had done for Minnesota. There were ten German Americans for every one of all the other ethnic groups put together. So, she laughed with a certain brilliance, "we Germans can take a lot of credit!" The next day the same woman went around the Iron World grounds wearing Norwegian *nasjonaldrakt.* She grinned but this time cried *"God dag!"*—and offered them *smørbrød,* the *egg og ansjøs* looking so good that Leona and Allen each took two. Their server told them that her Norwegian grandparents had come from the Jutenheim, which had made a huge contribution to the population and culture of Minnesota. She may have seen something quizzical in their faces, for she gave Allen his change quickly and turned away. They heard her gaily crying, *"Vaer så god!"* and *"Takk skal De ha!"* as she moved about with her tray.

Then they went into a little building near the edge of the old Hull Rust pit, from which 65 percent of the world's mined iron came. Chairs had been set out for twenty people or so. A black-and-white film said that the mining operators were largely Englishmen and Americans of English descent. The miners themselves were of central European and Finnish stock.

Allen and Leona knew that the mine operators had fought every possible improvement to the lifestyle of their workers. They left the film once they saw it wasn't going to deal with the subject fairly. They felt a little forlorn, yet—it was so difficult. Leona felt, they were supposed to be happy on their honeymoon, weren't they? She half-hated public issues of any kind.

Their unhappiness led to their pattern of lovemaking. They had retired early to their tent. Outside, two loons made a wonderful racket. A bobwhite called. But they began to talk about the girl who lied for her job at the museum. Then they talked about how the mining operators of English extraction had not been interested in housing or health arrangements for the workers. It is true they paid enormous taxes, so the Chisholm schools were rich. Allen said, it is hard to bend your mind around, though. A few hundreds of thousands of dollars would have made all the difference in the workers' lives.

They talked to each other quietly, dispiritedly, feeling bad that their wedding trip was so lackluster. Allen had much the smaller self-confidence. "It's hard for me to think what made you marry me," he said, not even looking at Leona, but up at the tent roof. They heard other families talking in low voices in their tents. They were relieved and comforted that these voices seemed to belong to older people and people with small children. They dreaded hearing any newlyweds who would seem happier than they were.

Carol Bly

Leona said, "I know perfectly well why I married you, and I've told you a thousand times, too."

"Better tell me again," he said, laughing—a little falsely. "Really tell me," he said.

"Well," she said, "there we were in that confirmation class, minding our own business and nothing going on."

The ELCA pastor must have been fifty-five if he was a day, because that was only six or seven years ago, and he was well into his sixties now. He had set the kids before him in two semicircles—seven in the front, eight in the second curving row. He smiled at them. He reminded them that every single Christian mother was already cooking the cakes and cookies for confirmation Sunday. Those who could had ordered special cuts of meat to be ready on the Friday. Generally it was agreed that lamb was the Christian meat, but no one in Dearing ate lamb. Perhaps some of the summer people who stayed at Charles Mincesky's lodge north of town, but none of the real people did. Any kid whose mother, like Allen's mother, wasn't excited about confirmation, kept his mouth shut to protect her from scorn the others might feel for her.

On the rehearsal day, the boys sat back with their new length of legs thrown forward as if to say, none of this affects me much! The girls crossed their arms, partly to diminish the look of breasts, but partly to protect them from intense ideas of any kind. These people, including Allen and Leona, had been in school together since kindergarten. They were arranged not only in these two curved rows but also in invisible groupings, like medieval principalities and devils, with perfectly clear divisions in status between each group. Leona was not in the top group because everybody already knew that she was not going to a liberal-arts college or the university, not even the one in Duluth. She meant to have a business career, however. Never even in girlhood had she answered, when asked what would she be when she grew up, "Oh, a mother I guess." So she was in the next-to-top group, but not on the bottom.

She had never known Allen Singer very well. He was squarely in the bottom group right from the first. No one explicitly blamed him for being such a scanty little boy, and, later, ragged teenager. Still, his parents left him alone two or three entire winters, and the disgracefulness of their negligence misted onto him.

When it first happened, Allen was eleven. He kept quiet about it, but somehow the sheriff found out. Since it was a small town, the sheriff ambled quietly over to the little boy's house. He found it neat. No dirty dishes in the sink. Refrigerator had fresh food. Eggs. Whole wheat, not white bread. Borgaard's jack cheese. Jerry later eased over to the grocer to find out where the food came from. The minimarket owner said, "Allen? He comes in once a week with a list of stuff his mother said for him to get. Wait a minute," he said. "I get what you're getting at. His mother's not here, is she? Or him either? The kid pays in cash."

Jerry said, "Well. . . . I have to do something."

The grocer said, "Ask the judge. He's smart. And he keeps his mouth shut."

"Or the pastor," Jerry said.

"Like I said, the judge is smart. Try him," the grocer said. "He'll think of something."

It came about that Judge Meyrens hired Mrs. Scree, a

Carol Bly

single mother, to look in on Allen twice a week. She vacuumed the living room. She asked no questions. She upped her visits to three or four afternoons a week; Allen would find the house full of the smell of cake baking. She stayed long enough to ask him if anything interesting happened at school. She told him she did not do very well at school, herself. He said nothing, which made her decide he got straight As and that he probably wanted her to go home. She went.

Once the telephone rang when he had come home and Mrs. Scree was still there. "Just fine, Mom," she heard him say. "Everything's cool, Mom."

Now the pastor began at one end of the confirmation class's first row. "Do you," he asked each candidate, "take the Lord Jesus Christ to be your Lord and Savior?"

Each kid muttered or mumbled yes. The pastor then leaned over the first-row communicants to the back row. Did *they,* each in turn, take Jesus Christ to be their Lord and Savior?

Everything was all right until he reached Allen Singer, that kid at the end with the lank hair and the terrible clothes.

"I don't think I can say yes to that," Allen remarked in a muffled voice, but looking directly at the pastor.

There was a moment of heavy silence.

"Now whoa," the pastor said. "Let's just take this very slowly. Just slow down. Don't get excited. Just quiet down— all of you." His face bloomed red. No one had said anything. No one had moved.

"Let's get real quiet, and there's no need to feel anxious," he said.

Another moment passed.

Chuck's Money

Then he said, "Allen, let's take this again. Do you or do you not take Jesus to be your savior?"

This time Allen said fairly loudly, "No, I can't say I do."

The pastor, looking at him intently, put a foot up on one of the girls' chairs in the front row, and rested an elbow on his knee.

Next, he stood up and went over to the window.

"Already the parents have sent out their invitations for our confirmation Sunday. The smells of cooking are filling the houses, where your parents—your parents, all your parents, and not just your parents—the whole congregation!—are looking forward to welcoming you into the fold of Christians. Look, I'm not saying that we are a perfect fold. We are a community of sinners. But we are a community, for our lives and forever. No matter how far away you move, you will always belong to each other." He had been saying this much facing out the window, but he was one who knew how to project his voice. No one missed a word.

The pastor returned to stand before the candidates. "Plans are made. This occasion is for others as much as for yourself. Let me ask you again, Allen, because this is no time for quibbling."

But the speech about cooking smells was ill fated. It had apparently given Allen Singer time to gather himself.

He said, "It is no time for lying, either. I don't believe the things that you want me to say I believe."

Everyone looked down. The pastor even looked down. He again lifted a foot back up onto the girl's chair. She moved her blue-jeaned thigh slightly away to make room.

"All right!" he said. "Into the sanctuary, everybody. I see

Mrs. Preck has come and is ready for us. You come, too, Allen, because there is still time to change your mind. We'll run through how everybody will come in, where we stand, how it will be on Sunday. Mrs. Preck is here to help. And by the way, kids, your instruction in our church is over now. You could give Mrs. Preck a vote of thanks. No Mrs. Preck, no church-education records all these years!"

Dutiful clapping.

They trooped out of the Sunday school room and into the nave.

Leona lingered, to see if Allen Singer was going to join them after all. "I knew right then," she said.

"Knew what?" he said deliciously, turning toward her. They kissed and listened to the mosquitoes singing outside the No-See-Um tent screen.

"I knew right then that I was going to go with this boy, the only one who did anything at all that the others weren't doing." She added, "So, it wasn't just luck, this business of us getting married."

She didn't tell him how strange she had felt once he spoke up in confirmation class. Until then she had thought of herself as simply a practical person. Someone who would not be taking advanced placement to get into college, but a business course. When he said he did not take Jesus to be his savior she felt dropped clear outside herself, looking back.

In the first year of their marriage they followed that pattern of talk and love from their honeymoon. They would lie down beside each other and talk over all the tiny, soul-smirching events of their day. Confirmed or not, Allen had been made a church usher, paired to the town's big shot,

Charles Mincesky. Too bad you couldn't have been paired with just about anyone else, Leona remarked. Allen explained that the church secretary, Mrs. Preck, had brought in a facilitating team who told the pastor always to have one low-class person paired with one town leader in the usher teams. So they had put the funeral director with that new bank teller, Gloria, who came from out of town. They put Mincesky, the richest man in town, with Allen. Wait a minute, Leona said, her arm going around Allen. They couldn't have said that, could they? A low-class person with an upper-class person? They said that? Allen told her how the facilitator team had explained that the church membership needed to seek commonalities. They said that Christ would have wanted commonalities among diverse populations in any church. Since everyone in that particular church happened to be white, and all the ushers were males, the only identifiable diversity was income level. Mincesky was rich. Allen was poor.

Mincesky told Allen not to start up his aisle with his plate of money and envelopes until Mincesky had started up the other aisle.

Allen reminded him that both ushers should go up at once. Exactly at the moment when people were rising and singing "All things come of thee, O Lord."

"Just wait until you see me nod. I will nod and *then* you go," Mincesky said. "And see this tie, the stripe? I think you should wear a coordinating tie."

Allen said, "Did the pastor actually say that?"

"Well, Allen," the man had said, smiling, reaching across to touch his arm. "If it costs too much I'll be glad to spring for the tie."

Carol Bly

Leona said slowly, "I did see you bought a tie. Was that why?"

Allen said then, as he said several times later, "Did I get taken, Leona? Did I get taken?"

Before they were married a week she had decided to protect him. She never gave it further thought. Therefore, without hesitation, she held him tight and said, "Listen, Allen, no one expects an oak tree to know which way a snake is going to move. It isn't oak-tree thinking. Oak trees don't get it. You're like that."

She said, "Actually Mincesky is really, really crooked." She did not tell him her own adventures with the man. In theory, any bookkeeper is the creature of the business that hires her. Confidentiality is what is expected, not whistle-blowing. Now and again, though, simply in the course of doing the job, the bookkeeper is forced to bring something forward.

Leona went over to the church on Mondays. She took the treasurer's accounting of Sunday's earnings, and all other checks, all notations, all memos from Mrs. Preck, and docketed everything. The Monday before Allen told her about obediently buying a tie, she found that there was no item representing the Scree Family Fire Fund, which the pastor inaugurated when Mrs. Scree's house burned down.

Leona saw, while checking Judge Meyrens's third-quarter records, that he had written a check for two hundred dollars to the church, with a memo that it was for the Scree Burn-Out Fund. She told Allen about it. Nice of a big shot judge like that, they agreed.

They were sitting on the porch to watch the lowering sun.

Chuck's Money

They ate tunafish sandwiches with too much mayo, and too much sugary chopped pickle. They were delicious.

"You make the greatest tunafish sandwiches of anyone," Leona observed.

"Gourmet cooking," Allen said.

His idea of making food good was to make a list of the things in the recipe that were bad for you and then double them. Double the butter in desserts, double the sugar in stir-fry sauces, double the mayo and chopped pickle for the tunafish.

The following Thursday, they were doing the same thing—eating a supper of tunafish sandwich, mayo, sugar, and chopped pickle. Allen had cleared some junk off the porch and swept the rotting boards. It looked much better and Leona said so.

"We should give to that Scree fund," Allen said. He handed over the church newsletter. "They've got only forty-five dollars in it so far."

Leona remembered Judge Meyrens's check for two hundred dollars.

Next morning she called the judge. She said she might have made a mistake—could she have another look at his paid-through checks?

"The day you make any mistakes," he said, "is the day I quit the bar for not knowing human nature when I see it."

They set a time. She found his check stamped by the church, paid through. When she got home she said, "Where'd we leave that church newsletter, Allen?"

He looked chagrined. He had dumped it.

That was all right. She only wanted to confirm that Einar

Carol Bly

was still treasurer this year. She was trying to envision who the current two people were who took the plates into the little room off the narthex after church. They had to add up everything and give it to Mrs. Preck.

Allen was serving as usher with Charles Mincesky, so he knew that Mincesky stayed late after the service to sit down in the little room off the narthex to check plates with either Einar or another church officer. Mincesky was assistant treasurer.

Next morning Leona called the pastor. She explained that a check intended for the Scree fund had shown up in general operating income.

He couldn't believe that would happen. He would look into it.

Then he said, "May I ask how you came across this information?"

"Sorry, Pastor," she said. "I can't answer that. But Ms. Scree is in awfully poor shape, financially speaking. If I happen to know of one check designated for her that ended up in gen op, how many others might there be, if, Pastor, if one of your people is simply dumping these checks into the main church fund?"

"You can relax," he said promptly. "This is something for me to take care of."

"I agree," she remarked.

The rest of that day she worked for Genuine Auto Sales and Mickey's Pantry and the Funeral Parlor. Each of these local businesses had contributed fifty, one hundred, and two hundred dollars, respectively, to help Mrs. Scree. She noted the dates in her mind, because she never took away written notes from anyone's records even if she needed to check something.

All three contributions should have shown up in the Scree fund.

The pastor called her. "You can relax about that Scree fund problem," he said. "The whole thing has a simple explanation. All such checks were put into gen op, as you noticed, being the good accountant that you are—and don't think we aren't grateful. Then a record is being kept of the earmarked checks. At the right time, then, a single check will be deposited in Mrs. Scree's bank account directly."

"What's going to be the right time?" Leona asked.

"When she really will be needing it," he said. "And when the committee feels she can handle it."

Leona said, "In the meantime, those people who wrote her a check thinking it would go to her and *she* would decide what she needs or when—are those people being told that the church is borrowing that money from them and from Ms. Scree without paying interest? Without any definite date of handing her over any of it? And pastor, whose idea was this?"

He was soothing: "Leona, you're good at figures, and bank accounts don't worry you. Not everyone is a natural numbers cruncher. A person like Mrs. Scree needs to have things made simple. I think it was a wise move on the part of the treasurer."

"Einar," she said.

"Einar? Well, no, actually," he said.

"Then Charles Mincesky?" Leona said.

The pastor said, "It is a much less clumsy arrangement than us going to her with a ten-dollar check here a ten-dollar check there. It was a decision of the Worship and Growth Committee."

"I believe you," she said. "That makes not one but two

wise moves on the part of Charles Mincesky: One, to delay giving the money people wanted Ms. Scree to have to alleviate her suffering; two, not to mention a word about this arrangement with the parish. I will need to see the list of donations to that fund. They should have been left for me to go over. Pastor, who prepared the newsletter this past week? I know, Mrs. Preck. Anyone else, too?"

"I know you mean nothing that isn't in the interests of accuracy, Leona," he said. "I know your intentions are kind. But I do have a meeting in five minutes, and I need to get set. You're one of our District women's delegates. You of all people know how rushed a person can be right in front of a meeting."

"OK, pastor," she said. "But you need to think about this. That newsletter was mailed out, U.S. mail. It said that the Scree fund stood at forty-five dollars when in fact there has been, to my knowledge, a minimum of $450 subscribed to it. For all I know so far, there may be a couple of thousand dollars in it. This is fraud through the U.S. mail, Pastor. Please get this straightened out. Give the money to Ms. Scree immediately. Correct the figures in next week's newsletter."

"I'll have Charles get on it," came back his voice, weakly.

"I don't know that I would leave Charles with it," she said rudely. She slammed down the receiver.

Quietly, quietly, she and Allen talked it over that night. "Poor Mrs. Scree," he said. "She took care of me sometimes, when I was little."

The next day Leona was still mad. On the following day, less mad.

When she got home at six, Allen said, "Mincesky was here to see you."

Chuck's Money

He added, "He is making us still another offer on buying the house. He's improved the offer. Better than last time."

Leona laid her jacket across the porch railing. She saw that Allen had pulled out a silver-plated filigreed cocktail tray that they had been given for a wedding present. He handed her a ginger ale from it. She felt a little doom at the sight of the tray, because it suggested he was going to urge something. He was acting celebratory. She sighed.

Allen heard her sigh. "Well, but Leona," he said. "He did point out one thing. Something I wouldn't have thought of. He said you can figure it costs a clear three thousand dollars just to move out of a house and into another one, so if you have *any* thoughts at all of staying where you are, you save three thousand right there. Darned if I would have thought of it. I know he is crooked, but I had to see the sense of what he was saying." He said, "I know you say the house is no good, Leona, but I like it so much. I love sitting here. I love the quiet of it. Just before you came home, a whole string of geese landed on that meadow. Geese, Leona. They are so nice." He shoved his chair back, so that, tipped against the house wall, it was almost as comfortable as a rocker. "The house isn't everything," he remarked floatingly, as if it didn't matter whom the comment went to. "House schmouse," he said with resolution. "Some of it is just plain universe around you."

"That's not what they taught me in bookkeeping school," she said.

They drank their ginger ale peaceably. After a while she told him that the city engineer had tried to make Mincesky take a cat to three of his rental properties, including their house. Those structures were so poor, he said, they shouldn't have roofs lying across the tops of them.

Allen looked so struck, she forebore to tell him the rest of the conversation, which the engineer had laced with some theory of footings and basements and water movement in subsoil. All she needed, Leona thought later, lying in Allen's guileless arms, was for him to be convinced that the house wasn't worth buying. She didn't need to horrify him. She hated when he looked at her nearly round-eyed as a boy and said, "Did I get taken, Leona?"

Leona told Allen how Mincesky had the county assessor evaluate his own house—with its three baths tiled in ceramic, not plastic, its two full floors, its two open fireplaces—at fourteen thousand. Someone at Mickey's Pantry was indignant and said he ought to take a swipe at Mincesky, when the rest of them paid so much property tax. Oh yes! Do that very thing! someone else had said. Mincesky was six feet four. The other three men started jeering at the man who had said he wanted to hit Mincesky. Leona leaned over to him and said, "Is that right about his assessment?"

Leona and Allen did not drop the pattern of intimacy started on their honeymoon. They would lie close in each other's arms, but both gazing off a little. They would tell each other the little repertory of low-level cheating and crime that they had witnessed during the day. They would go over it together, trying to figure it out. This thinking about bad ways human beings treated each other—it took Leona and Allen further and further away from what was left of their own youth with their parents, Allen's step-parent, and their recent catch-as-catch-can life in high school. As they talked to each

Chuck's Money

other they finally got clear of everything around them, and they felt as though they had migrated from the world of others and landed together, simply, like birds with a flight pattern mapped tiny in their brains. By the time they began to make love to each other, they felt alien and delicate, oddly lugubrious. They gave each other only the lightest kisses until they were near, until they knew they had no business with anything else of the world.

Leona came back to the present. It was a fluke that she, not Cheryl, found this dead boy in unit 12.

Leona was sick of how people pretended to be more involved in a death than they really were. "Funny thing," they would say, between mouthfuls of funeral bun, "the way it worked out. I mean, I was one of the last people to see so-and-so."

Leona therefore said to herself, Poor Chucky Mincesky, poor guy, but I didn't know him, and therefore I should be businesslike and report his body to Einar.

Chucky's death meant nothing to her, she said to herself. She stopped her legs from trembling. She left the room, went into the front office of the motel, where Einar was giving one of his little speeches to a departing motel guest. Both men were laughing evilly.

"No, my friend!" Einar said. He clipped the man's credit card printout to his bill. "I sympathize with all the petty criminals you put up with, but my sympathy starts, bottoms, at eight hundred dollars per annum. Yes, sir! Eight hundred dollars a year in stolen towels, not including the towels people wipe off their air circulator top with."

Carol Bly

Dollar figures, frankly mentioned, tend to bring people closer. The guy had been shoving away from the counter, stooping for his weekender. Now he came back and pushed his hand out toward Einar. He laughed and shouted, "Next time I come tell you a sad story it'll be about eight hundred dollars' worth of chiseling!" When he finally left, Leona spoke.

"Trouble, Einar," she said. "Trouble in 12."

Some people have an instinct for rhetoric. No sooner does any novel event take place than they make a pronouncement. Einar was magisterial as he peered at the quarterback.

He said softly, "Yes, sir. Yes—that's Charles Mincesky Junior all right, sleeping off a big one I bet. Well, now. Poor guy. If I'd passed a football the way he passed the football last night I would tie one on, too. Leona? Leona, if you'd just open up that cabinet and start the copier, that'll wake him up anyhow."

But then Einar got round to the end of the bed and saw the other half of what had been Chuck's face.

Now Einar clasped his hands. Then he said softly, "There lies a nice boy. What a shame—and what a shame to die just because of a football game." Then, still more quietly, and his voice as full of respect as if he spoke to death himself, he kept saying, "Yes, sir. Yes, sir."

"There's a note," Leona said with some croak in her voice. "On the TV cabinet."

Einar opened it so as not to make a tearing sound. He read aloud, "To whoever finds me: I don't think I will ever do anything right. And if I did my dad wouldn't think it was right anyway. I love you, Mom. Chuck."

Einar said, "It really is a shame, you know. All for football, and football only a game, too." He went on, speaking gently, saying how curious it was, too, since Chucky had been losing football games in their town for two, three years and it hadn't seemed to bother him. Well, now, he must call Jerry. And Jerry would get in whichever doc had coroner duty this term.

When the sheriff came, everything went off according to the rules of little-town life. One of the town's two doctors arrived. Coralie Ann, the sheriff's wife, arrived but did not come inside because she was not official. Instead, she held court in the front drive-up area of the motel. Word had got round. People respectfully moved one foot or the other so they wouldn't smash Einar's drying chrysanthemums in the turn-around area. Coralie Ann told everyone that the son of the richest big shot in town had committed suicide in the motel. The ambulance finally came. Two people carried the wrapped stretcher out, and Coralie Ann stood upright beside the police ribbon, out of respect.

The cleaning woman finally arrived, noticing nothing since she used the back entry near where Einar parked his car.

She narrowed her eyes at the sheriff. "What do you mean where have I been," she snarled. "You want to know where I've been? I've been in bed, with a hangover like a ValuJet. Why? Why did I have a hangover? I had a hangover for the same reason everybody in the world gets hangover, why do you think? Too much to drink is why. And why did I drink too much?"

"That's OK, Cheryl," the sheriff said.

Carol Bly

"I drank too much because that stupid quarterback who never should have been the quarterback lost us one more game, when if the coach had eyes to see the last three years he would have used my boy for quarterback and none of this would have happened!"

"None of what," the sheriff said a little narrowly.

"None of the last three years of lousy football at Dearing, that's what!" At last she stopped. "What's going on?"

After a while, at about the time Leona finished with his books, the proprietor himself came out. A few people still hung about. Einar opened his arms wide, like a child making an angel. Einar said he understood their grief, but he told them they must respect the parents of their dead townsman—

"Townsman!" Leona exclaimed to herself. Just like Einar to come up with fancy language in the presence of death. Nobody had used that word since Nathan Hale and he hadn't used it either. You must respect the parents, Einar was saying, and disperse now.

Leona thought, More to the point. Disperse because it was getting on for twelve-thirty, one o'clock, and Einar would want the motel back to normal for Saturday business. Leona eased on over to Coralie Ann.

"You set to go?" she said.

Leona and Coralie Ann found the two women from Ely exactly where they said they'd be, parked at the funeral parlor lot. Everyone used it for car pool pickups because it was easy to find and almost always empty.

The trick to carpooling was to keep your mouth shut. At twenty-two years old, Leona had already driven any number of car pools. Middle-aged women, half-interested in their lives, half-bored with their lives, would lean forward, so their heads blocked her rearview mirror vision, and say earnestly, "This is something I want to share, and I feel safe with all of us here"—while Leona would think, Safe! Safe with *these* motormouths!

She once said, "Actually, this may not be so good a place, or good a time as later, so-and-so," but was halted by the other three in the car. They crowed, "Of course you may share, so-and-so! It will stop right here, dear." It seldom did. It takes character to keep your mouth shut.

The car pool this Saturday got started all right. Leona began to relax. As you went down the road, the trees looked healthy enough, and the fact that they were dying back from the highway fumes didn't get rubbed in your face. The oaks were amber, the maples still in leaf and red, and among all that brilliant color, Minnesota's conifers, red pines and jacks and white spruces, looked dark and fine.

Leona began to quiet down. She knew that she must re-envision poor Chucky Mincesky's body over and over until she harbored no feeling about it. Chucky was no particular friend of hers. She wanted to get free of the horror so she could return to her own life.

The women in the backseat were comfortably engaged on a safe topic—the fact that that rural family north of Dearing, someone named Scree, got burnt out three weeks ago and of course, word was, what with her being a single parent, there was no insurance, so now she had virtually nothing. Leona called out, making eye contact through the rearview mirror, that her church had, in fact, started a disaster fund for the

Carol Bly

Screes, mother and children. "Oh that is just swell, then," said one of the women in the back, but her voice sounded let down. The radio came on with the sudden-breaking news that a high-school boy in Dearing, Minnesota, had died in a motel. The county sheriff was investigating. The women in Leona's backseat had a good deal to say about that. Neither Coralie Ann nor Leona joined their pronouncements about Christians taking lives sacred to God. Then, at the cutoff, Minnesota 33, the women in back turned to other disasters, disasters for which there was no known cure. The miles whipped by.

At last they all saw Lake Superior. Coralie Ann and the other two exclaimed about how blue and how beautiful the lake looked. Leona was always surprised by how people got a thrill out of Lake Superior. No matter how many times they drove down from Dearing or Ely or Hibbing, and if you lived on the Iron Range you were always driving to Duluth about one thing or another, they would always ooh and ahh over the lake.

Leona didn't get the point. But then, she didn't do nature. Allen seemed to like it all right. He always wanted her to watch the sun go down from the half-wrecked porch of their house. In the night they sometimes heard wolves. She felt Allen smiling in the dark beside her—"Wolves, honey," he said softly. "There they go again!" He was breathless as a little kid. The two of them hadn't camped since their wedding trip.

They didn't do spirituality about nature, either. Allen didn't do men's spirituality when that fad came through, and Leona didn't take any of the all-day women's spiritual journey retreats that the parish secretary made such a brouhaha

Chuck's Money

about. Last June, the Worship and Growth Committee had got in someone to lead the journey for a Saturday at church. Since Leona was responsible for overseeing the church books, she knew that the parish paid the spirituality lady fifteen hundred dollars for 10 A.M. to 3 P.M. The evaluations indicated that she gave everyone a breath of new life—that was what they said—but Leona thought then and thought still, it seemed like such a big wad of money being spent on something that didn't show.

"You're awfully quiet, Leona," Coralie Ann said in a low voice not intended for the women in the backseat to hear. "You feel bad about what happened today at the motel, I guess. You're not worried about giving the opening meditation are you?"

But the women in back heard that phrase, opening meditation.

One of them laughed. "Opening meditation is nothing to worry about!"

Leona wanted to be sociable. "I know," she said. "Wrap-up is what's hardest."

There was a little pause.

The skinny, proud little houses of West Duluth went by. The car was coming down the escarpment.

One of the Ely women in back said, "Well, what's so hard about giving the wrap-up?"

Coralie Ann swiveled around to face the backseat. She said, "Wrap-ups are hard because you have to say it was an exciting conference and that we all sure are going to go home all fired up with a feeling of being renewed, when half the time the conference wasn't very interesting and no one said anything that

Carol Bly

you hadn't heard a hundred times, and you were going home not feeling renewed but just worn out, and for what?"

Leona gave Coralie a grateful glance. The sour remark suited her mood.

The woman in back said, "I don't guess I have ever felt that way and I guess I wouldn't go to a conference if I thought it was going to be all that bad."

Coralie Ann still did her hair in the old way. Now she peacefully took baby-pink curlers out of it and poked them into a plastic bag. "That's all well and good," she said loudly so it would carry into the backseat, "but you can't tell ahead if something in church work is going to amount to anything or not. Or life either, now you mention it. Take this conference. It may sound exciting ahead of time; what doesn't? High-school proms? Marriage? Having kids? Then you get into it and some of it is so dumb you can't believe it's happening to you. If you are doing the wrap-up you have to lie and say it was very renewing and all that."

Leona laughed coarsely.

The woman in back said, "I don't know about you two."

Coralie Ann winked at Leona. She turned around to face the two in back again. "Look," she said, "I'm just a sheriff's wife. What do I know, huh? Chill, OK? Chill. Don't take me seriously. The one time I ever had to do a wrap-up I was so scared I wrote it up ahead. Can you imagine? Writing up the wrap-up of a conference you haven't even been to, ahead? Talk about crooked."

Leona looked in the rearview mirror. The woman Coralie Ann had been talking to had gone red. Her soft cheeks trembled, though that might have been from the car's joggling.

Chuck's Money

"Oh," cried the other woman in the backseat, "it is such fun to get away! Such fun, such fun! I'm not saying I don't love my hubby, but a person sure needs to get away! This is just plain fun, if you ask me!"

"Yes, fun! You're right," said the other woman. "That's one of the things people sometimes don't understand about Jesus. He will never ask us to do something that isn't fun."

Coralie Ann and Leona shrank iron-still in the front seat. One of the things that can go wrong with a car pool to a District church meeting was having a freshly renewed or fundamentalist Christian in the car. It meant you had to pretend to be glad about everything in the world and everybody walking around you and regard them as a blessing and you had to pretend to be cheerful when in fact it was depressing to have the humor sluiced right out of every conversation.

The woman in the backseat said, "His love is everywhere about us, and it is for each of us, no matter how much we have sinned."

Leona decided to get through the Saturday and most of Sunday by daydreaming. She herself had never experienced anything she would call the love of Jesus or of God, and she instantly disbelieved anyone who said they had felt such love. Clearly it was wrong to suspect all those people of just making up a secret pal called Jesus. She was only a bookkeeper. She told herself, just because *you* don't feel something, it doesn't mean *they* don't. But then she went back to thinking they were making it all up again.

The car was maneuvering its way, getting lane-locked, getting free again, with a lot of tourist traffic on Canal Drive, the made-to-order drag that led out along the spit making the harbor of Duluth.

The two women in back now sat on the forward edges of their seats. "Oh let's take a walk!" one said. "So we can see the boats coming in, and watch the bridge go up, if it does."

The other said, "It would be a healing thing to do. I feel as though we need to heal. I know I feel kind of criticized. Kind of bruised, actually. We need to process."

Coralie Ann said, "Well OK, but if we're going to process let's do it walking along the canal—look, where those others are."

People ambled along the concrete channel walls. On the far sides, the lake smashed against the walls and sent up spindrift. I know there is something the matter with me emotionally, Leona said to herself. I can't even guess what that woman feels bruised about, and I don't feel much of anything—well, that's not true. I feel sorry I ever came to this conference.

Then, having decided deliberately to lose herself in day-dreaming throughout the conference, she brightened up.

She told them all, "Why don't we go to the motel, get settled, and let's do the opening session. Then let's skip the fellowship hour, which is dry, walk along the canal, and then eat Vietnamese together."

The opening session went much as Leona had forecast. The two hundred women were welcomed. They listened to the housekeeping remarks. Leona tripped up on the opening meditation because she had chosen the Ecclesiastes passage about a time to live and a time to die before going to the motel that morning. As she read aloud now, Chucky Mincesky's profile, like the white top ridge of a mountain heavily shadowed, filled her mind's eye. Snow filled the deep coll where his mind had been. Her voice shook but she got through it, glad to back away from the little hand-grenade of a microphone.

She returned to her seat in the front row. One of the women from the car pool whispered in her ear, "I could feel the moment when the Spirit came into you! Oh Leona! Right in the middle of your reading, too! That is so much the way the Spirit operates! Just when you least expect it!"

There followed a speech by someone brought in from Albany, then a prayer, then a reminder about the evening plenary session, and the promise of a good dinner before it.

The four carpoolers walked along the concrete bulwark. Behind them loomed the aerial bridge, with its clean triangles of steel. Ahead lay the great lake, cooling for winter.

The other three women regaled one another. For them this was an outing. They nearly skipped along. Coralie Ann had reserved a dinner time for them at a Vietnamese restaurant where they could order wine.

At the end of the pier they turned back. Coralie Ann said, "Listen, everybody, two minutes until drinks!"

The others laughed. Leona noticed, as they returned, nearing the bridge, how in their rows upon rows the rounded tops of the rivets went up the steel beams. The honorable little rivets, in their rows, doing their job, heavy, not good for much, just good for one thing, holding the space forms. Leona thought of Allen and turned around to walk backwards, now gaily, so she could talk to the others as they kept moving toward her. Leona grinned and cried, "What do you think of this idea? We leave right after the last break-out

Carol Bly

sessions tomorrow! How about we skip the plenary session and the wrap-up and just go home!"

The others—even Coralie Ann—actually stopped walking.

"Can't," Coralie Ann said. "I promised to report on the final keynoter to my circle."

Their church was fearful of hurting people's feelings. For some years there had been one keynote speech maker, usually timed to follow after the housekeeping announcements, in the first plenary session of any conference. But then people were hurt when asked to be the final speaker. "Oh," one of them had said a little too brightly, "this'll be a first for me. I guess I am used to doing the keynote." Some ingenious administrator had pounced on that. "You are a keynote, that's what we want from you. We have the opening keynoter and the closing keynoter. You're the closing keynoter. Your talk is the one that leaves people with their final impression." Word got around, and soon two speakers were always designated as keynoters. One year there were four: opening keynoter, opening *theme* keynoter, discussant keynoter, and closing keynoter. Then sense prevailed again. None of the district or regional meetings Leona had been to had more than three keynote speakers per conference.

"Well," Leona said, "right after the final keynoter then! At least we could skip the wrap-up!"

"Skip the wrap-up?" the especially Christian woman said. "We oughtn't to do that! We have other people's feelings to consider, after all."

Coralie Ann shook herself like a dog. "I don't know. I like the idea," she said. "Skipping the wrap-up."

Leona thought, Home by four instead of home by five or six.

Chuck's Money

She said aloud, "I don't see any harm in skipping it. We will have already been to the whole conference. We either got the point of what the different speakers said or we didn't."

"Well, we can't, that's all," the especially Christian now said. She said, "I'm the one doing the wrap-up, I may as well tell you. Something else, too. I've spent a lot of time writing it up, too. All that work would just go to waste."

Coralie Ann slowly turned around to her. She said, "How can you write a wrap-up ahead?"

The other woman turned red but held her ground. "I know what's right," she said. "And I know my limitations. I wouldn't be any good at listening to a bunch of speakers and then trying to figure out what they meant. I know I couldn't. But I know something else. I am not the only one who knows I couldn't."

That is the f-word truth, Leona thought coarsely.

But the woman said, "God knows my limitations and wouldn't expect anything of me that I can't do. God never asks you to do what you can't do. I know how He wants me to serve. So I wrote it up as well as I could and I feel that is the best I can do."

Her face, a moment ago red and creased, now shone without shame, like milk glass. Everyone smiled.

Leona turned around forward again and they hurried to the restaurant. The place smelled placating and kindly thick with garlic. But even though they each had two glasses of wine instead of just one, they couldn't pull together. Their several dishes came, with the beautiful stained glass glittering vegetables, the glistening beef and shrimps, but the women did not pass them around. Each simply ate her own, and took rice only from the particular stiff mound set down by her plate.

They drove home at dusk the next day. Dearing was under two degrees of latitude north of Duluth, but as the women went north autumn paled in the woods. They seemed to drive into winter. Each day of October made its difference. Many more leaves had dried and fallen from their twigs since the day before. The birch forest showed its skimpy, upright bone. Against the sky the treetops revealed showed the dendritic pattern of everything that is—the branching of twigs, the branching of stress-playout in rock, the branching of each river at both its rise and its delta, the branching of brain neurons.

There are women who in a car pool always say it is wonderful to get away from home and it sure is wonderful to be getting back, too, because they were really beginning to miss their hubbies. One of the Ely woman said it just as they got to Dearing. The other agreed. Leona dropped them off in the funeral parlor parking lot. She and Coralie Ann waited to make sure their car started all right. Then Leona gunned the engine and went off to the police station. Jerry and Coralie, for convenience's sake, kept their mobile home in the lot right behind.

Coralie said, "Well, there go Barbie One and Barbie Two. Barbie One goes back to Ken One. Barbie Two goes back to Jesus. But they're right about one thing. It's great to be home."

Leona was still feeling coarse and cynical when she drew the car up alongside the house. Allen was at the car door immediately.

"You must be feeling a lot better!" she said.

"A lot!" he crowed. "And wait till you see!"

He steadied her bag onto his head like a nineteenth-century bearer. With the other hand, he nearly manhandled her through the rotting porch and into the house.

"Now!" he cried. "Now what do you see?"

Leona flung her arms around him. She was enchanted. "Flowers! Beauties, too! Roses, Allen—roses!" After all the sadness at the motel, and then the silly church weekend—roses! Every time she saw roses she found she had forgotten how beautiful they were. "Roses!" she cried again.

But when she looked up and took in Allen's face, she said, "What are we celebrating?" She fingered open the florist's little envelope, thinking with half her bookkeeper's mind, this one sale ought to liven up the P side of poor what's-his-name's, the flower shop guy's, P and L sheets. People in Dearing who bought roses were Mincesky, maybe the judge, maybe the guy who owned Genuine Parts, hardly anyone else. If she remembered rightly this would be as big an individual sale as any the florist had had the month before.

"Don't you see anything else?" cried Allen. He nearly danced around her.

She felt irritated by his boyish enthusiasm. He had done something nice for her, she supposed, and now wanted to be petted for it. He was such a baby. He had no idea that she had worried about him in the car, for hours, really, underneath and intermingling with her other worries. And she had made up her mind again, as she had to do every day, not to feel wistful that he bungled it every time he did business with

Carol Bly

anyone. And he usually moved slowly. He would never do anything with dispatch! Why didn't he? Wasn't that a man's responsibility? No—it wasn't. She was being a sexist. Still, one expected . . . no matter what she expected, she felt irritated because she had to make herself be patient, first about herself for being so upset by that Mincesky kid's suicide, then about Allen, then about those women in the car with their soapy, self-indulgent lying—she had forced herself to be sociable and nonjudgmental and cheerful. She felt gritty and heavy with her thoughts. She had longed for Allen. She realized that late Saturday and all during the daytime on the Sunday she had wanted to lie in bed with Allen. But she had wanted him in a slow, deep frame of things. She wanted him because he was quiet and he was what he was—not this ignited colt prancing about, begging her to be enthusiastic about something.

But all of a sudden he seemed to change his mind. "Oh never mind," he said. "Sit down."

The couch clearly showed he had spent restless hours on it. The afghan, a knitted wedding present made of acrylic yarn, was wadded up at the foot. The white-encased pillow she had brought from their bed yesterday lay piled on top of the ordinary sofa pillows, deeply dented by Allen's head. She thought he may have spent the night there.

"Wait till you hear," he said. He had fetched out their filigreed silver-plated tray, which he admired but she didn't. She never saw it but she thought of how she had made Allen write the thank-you note for it. Allen handed her a glass from it, filled right up to the top. It spilled over a little as she took it.

"Wine!" she said.

"We're celebrating!" he said. "Just you hear!"

He told everything, looking hard at her all the while, as if to make sure she didn't misunderstand his feeling of each moment.

He had been very sick with the flu before she left. He had been touched at how she fixed him up on the couch, with hot-water bag and kleenex and a large mixing bowl in case he had to vomit. When Leona's car had backed away from the house, stopped, and then gone down the street and he couldn't hear anything of its engine he felt lonely for a moment. In the next moment he didn't mind that Leona was gone. This surprised him, but he couldn't deny it. He was not in the mood for her brisk practicality. She was such a problem solver—well, and weakened from sickness, a little starving, really half dreaming, he didn't feel like all her common sense. He wanted just to moon around through his thoughts, lighting wherever his mind felt like it.

From the couch he could see the first of the oak leaves going. Allen lay half awake. He felt a little piteous, the way he had sometimes felt as a boy. As a boy he had fantasized committing suicide not for any wanting of death—he had loved life, actually—but for the sake of the delicious vision of how terrible his parents would feel. They would come home and find him dead, dead on a couch, just as he lay now. If only we had loved him more, they would say. Especially his father would apologize. His father would say to his mother, "And I am sorry for . . . sorry for everything else, too." Allen felt reminded of that boyhood fantasy now, but mainly only

Carol Bly

for the fun of it. Mostly he was glad to be getting over the flu: he felt affectionate and protective of his body as it went about healing itself. He lay there, contented enough, weak and full of daydreams. Out the window, a mist clarified itself here and there in the brome grasses and quack. He felt slack-hearted and yet moved by the brown sight outside. He dozed. He dreamed about his mother.

He woke shaken, unnerved, scornful of his own sensitivities. Outright scornful. He turned on the radio to clear the air of emotion. Someone announced that in Dearing, Minnesota, a young boy had been found, a case of apparent suicide in in a motel. Charles Mincesky Junior. Allen had sat bolt upright. Chucky Mincesky, not a kid he knew well, but the son of his landlord.

Then, fast as a mist, fear poured over Allen. Not altruistic fear, but fear for his own death. He knew better but got afraid of his own death anyway. He told himself, he was only twenty-three. Unless one is of a nationality that gets invaded and bullied to death by some other nationality, one doesn't die at twenty-three. He was helped by nature. A loon called in octave—that is, not the best-known, trilling laugh, but the full-octave squawk, which is their comfort sound as opposed to their fear sound.

Buck up, Allen told himself. Buck up. When Allen's death came it would come a long time from now and it would come slowly. He and Leona would notice it and talk about it, analyzing it in bits and pieces, in bed together, taking its measure, like other bad news they talked about. They would gradually wrap their minds around the idea of death and then they wouldn't be terrified.

Chuck's Money

Allen now halted his narrative to say, "Leona, did I ever tell you? My family never talked about *little* things. We never talked about anything except crises, and then my mother would give some little speech and my father would give a little speech. They'd both look at me and ask if I understood. I actually believed they wanted me to understand. Once I said, why did my father call my mother such bad words? He said, he would never call my mother bad words. She said, he didn't mean those bad words. Then they'd each give some more speeches. Always big-time stuff. And in between, them off to Florida. Same as with his present wife.

"So that's a wonderful thing about you and me," Allen said. "We talk about little things."

Thinking of how death would come only as quickly as he could manage it, and not for decades anyhow, he had got up from the couch. He felt refreshed. He thought he might even try to eat something. The kitchen, though, still smelled a little of vomit and he was afraid of being sick again. As he considered, pausing at the refrigerator, he saw someone outside the window. Of all people! He scarcely believed it. It was the landlord, Charles Mincesky, the man whose son, the radio said, had committed suicide at the motel.

Allen watched the man go past, going around to the back where the porch was. Like everyone, he knew that they used the porch door, not the street door. Allen was sorry it was Mincesky. It was never what you'd call fun to do any sort of business with the man. Even conferring with him about where to leave the plates for the treasurer after church was some sort of confrontation.

But today, Allen felt sorry for him. He held the door open.

Carol Bly

Mincesky was an enormous man, and he threw his weight from foot to foot, no matter how small a space he entered. You felt the pure massiveness of him. But today he seemed pale. Allen couldn't imagine what the man wanted . . . nor why he would be here on the day of his son's death.

Mincesky took a seat and looked around. "You two've made it very cozy here," he said slowly.

Allen waited.

The man said, "I suppose you've heard our news. Somehow . . . well, somehow I can't sit in my own house today. Everything in it reminds me of my boy."

Allen said sympathetic things; he didn't recall what exactly.

Mincesky said that he was having trouble getting it through his head that death could have come to his son before it came to him.

Allen, feeling a wave of weakness, said he had trouble sitting upright. He hoped Mincesky would not mind if he lay back down on the couch. He'd been pretty sick. He was better now, but it was hard to sit up.

Mincesky was really civil. He even sounded sympathetic. "And Leona had to go to a church conference in Duluth?"

It was like him to know everything that is going on. No doubt a harmless habit of big shots in small towns, a social style that seemed pleasant but made you feel measured and counted.

Mincesky said, "I know you and I run in different crowds, Allen, but at least we've been ushers together and what with one thing and another I feel I can talk to you. About real stuff. Serious stuff, I mean."

Allen felt so newly emerged from the daydream of death—

Chuck's Money

from the dread he had felt on waking—that he told himself, They are always saying in church how we should look for the Christ in everybody. Now Allen pulled up short. He had never looked for the Christ in Mincesky. He just figured Mincesky for a cheat and a bully. Well, Allen now felt remiss in that. Every man is horribly vulnerable. Here was this poor fellow, whom nobody loved really—suffering the death of a son, suffering alone. And the fellow had come to talk to Allen in trust. Damned if Allen was going to cut him off.

Mincesky said, "You know what's surprising, Allen, is how the really big things—I mean the passions, I don't mean just sex, I mean other major passions—lie just under the surface where you can't see them? I find myself just, just—well, just confused, that's all! I feel as if I were losing my balance on top of some huge horrible grief."

Allen tried to nod and cry, "Oh yes, I know! I know exactly what you mean!" Well, he felt he *did* know exactly. In fact, he remembered, it was odd he did, just then how he had refused to be confirmed with the others in his confirmation class. The whole thing came back to him! The pastor had said, Even as your parents have loved you, God loves you, and even as you love your parents and want to obey them, so you will grow in the love of God and you will want to obey Him. And you'll get better at seeing what he is asking of you, as you get more mature. You will be able to please him better.

Well! Allen had thought, way back then—and now, of all things, to be reminded in front of this bereaved father—he could hear his own fourteen-year-old voice refusing to say he accepted Jesus as his Lord, and he remembered that the reason he had said so was that his parents had abandoned him

Carol Bly

winter after winter. They had not loved him and he had not loved them.

He certainly didn't love Jesus either, who died long before he was even born, nor God the father, whom he didn't even believe in. He would have lied, like the others, those in the front row of the pastor's reading class, and those in the back row whom the pastor reached before he came to Allen. He would have lied except that someone, someone two or three kids over from him, had *hesitated* before muttering "I guess so." Stupid liar, Allen then thought. The pastor, too, heard the hesitation, and had said, after the boy said "I guess so," "You made the right choice, son!" That did it, as far as Allen was concerned. He heard the word *choice*.

Choice! he had never thought of it before. He had taken it for granted he must lie and say that he took Christ for his master. Why not? everyone else did. When drunk the other boys always admitted they didn't believe any of it. The girls, even when drunk, demurred. Allen supposed they were just preserving the status quo without thinking one way or the other about it. So he had said, "No," when the question was put: he didn't believe any of that . . . and that it was no time for lying.

So now, feeling half invalid, half compassionate to an old enemy, Allen gave Mincesky a gingerly smile. He said, oh, he understood all right!

He kept an encouraging expression on his face. He was glad enough to be kind. Inside Allen, a curling, dodgy little rat of guilt was twisting here and there, growing, twisting and curling along the walls of his heart. All these years he had failed not just in not seeing Christ in everyone, but in not even wanting to! He was always angry with his parents. He had developed a satiny way of speaking to them. It would have never crossed his mind to see Christ in them. And so . . . with this poor fellow, Mincesky, with his shoulders slumped, sitting in a plain wood chair, looking like any poor brother of anyone. How could Allen have just written him off all these years!

Mincesky was gazing out the window to the west. The sunshine still lay on the fir treetops, orange and cool. "Even the most strong-hearted people, the ones who pass themselves off as just practical," he was saying, "even they have passions. Passionate desires for things, but they never say anything because they're afraid of . . . afraid of I don't know what."

"Oh but I know!" Allen had cried. "They are afraid of sounding like fools. And afraid of not having self-discipline."

"I bet you're right!" said Mincesky in a level way. "Allen, I bet that's right on the mark!"

Then he gazed off again. "Everybody wants pretty simple things, really," he said. "A man wants to die before his son does. A woman wants a house. A child wants to be loved . . . we aren't very complicated, Allen. We talk big and tough . . . but at the bottom . . . we have simple passions."

They talked some more. Allen was curious to know more of how the man grieved for his son, but Mincesky was steering away from that. Even the most carefully educated people, he was saying—and he allowed to Allen that he met a lot of them—pretended they were cool-headed and down-to-earth businesspeople, but fact was, at bottom, they wanted simple things.

Carol Bly

The talk went on. Somehow Allen began to realize that his own wife was one of those people with a good business head. And what did she seem to want? Mincesky was talking about any woman wanted to own her own home. Oh, they might prevaricate, of course, and make up some rationalization or other, but they all wanted a home of their own—

Allen exclaimed silently to himself, And Leona would! She would! Even if she didn't admit it.

All this year, he thought, I haven't been really listening to Leona.

In the end, Allen wrote a check for two thousand of the $2,037 that he and Leona had in their savings account. The house was theirs. Mincesky had stood up shortly after that. He said, "You made the right choice, son." He handed Allen the purchase agreement.

"And Leona," Allen wound up now, "there it is!" He pointed to the top of the bookshelf.

He had framed it in a ten-cents-store diploma frame, the mitered corners of which met well enough.

Eventually Leona was able to speak. "Allen," she said, "didn't you wonder that he asked you for exactly the same amount for a purchase agreement as we have in our savings account?"

He looked at her. "No, we had $2,037." But he stopped.

He said, "What are you saying, Leona?"

"I'm saying that he knew I would be gone, because as Worship & Growth Committee chairperson, he knew the women had District in Duluth. So he looked up our account balance at the bank."

Chuck's Money   333

"You mean he planned this?" said Allen in a whisper.

"He planned part of it," Leona said. "He knew there would be the District meeting. So he had the bank tell him the account balance."

Allen: "But they can't do that! That's confidential information!"

"It's confidential," Leona told him, "but it is on the computers. So he could easily call up one of the women who's fairly new. Like Gloria, say. He calls her up and tells her he's Allen Singer and he'd like the balance figure. She says, 'Hi, Allen, of course. Let's have your account number.' 'Shoot,' he says, 'I haven't got it with me. Damn it, I'm up in Ely. Can we work this somehow?' She pauses, scared, but wants to please a customer with a savings account. Finally she says, 'Of course. One second please. Allen? Your balance is $2,037.' 'Thanks a lot, Gloria,' he says. 'I appreciate that a lot.'"

Allen stooped lower and lower, looking at the floor between his knees. "I don't believe this, Leona," he said in a low voice.

Leona felt terrible for him. But she still felt terrible for herself, too. She had told Allen a dozen times how rotten the cellar was. One couldn't jack up the first-floor beams because a water course went under the thin cement of the basement floor. The jack would drive itself right through the cement into the mud before it would raise the ground-level floor an inch.

"I may be wrong," she got out at last. "That may not be what happened. He may not even have planned to come see you and try to sell you this building. It may be that Chucky shot himself dead, there's all the family gathering, getting into town, people muttering and murmuring the way they do

334   Carol Bly

when there has been a suicide, and his wife wringing her hands, probably insisting it wasn't suicide, or at least trying to get the pastor to say it wasn't—suddenly he's fed up and he realizes he can come over here and talk sad and maybe . . . maybe he can talk you into a down payment. He'd get to kill two birds with one stone."

Allen murmured, "No, Leona. He had already filled in the purchase agreement. I noticed when I signed it."

He said, slightly louder, "So Mincesky conned me. Conned me again."

Leona got up. "Don't feel too bad," she said. "He has conned a lot of people. Even the tough coach. Think of it, Allen. For three years he has made the coach run *his* kid as quarterback and his kid can't play worth two cents, and all this time Cheryl's kid might have made a pretty good quarterback! Now that poor kid is in his senior year, too, so now he might never play quarterback in high school. Thanks to Mincesky. I don't think he even had to threaten the coach with anything. He just tricked him somehow. The coach is a tricky guy, himself, now, but Mincesky got what he wanted out of him. No, sweetheart," she wound up, "don't feel bad. People like Mincesky move through the grass toward people like you without even disturbing the blades."

Again they were quiet. Leona was thinking fast.

"Shit," Leona said after a minute.

"Shit what? What did you think of?"

"I was just thinking of how Mincesky even got around Judge Meyrens. Judge Meyrens wrote a check for two hundred dollars for the Scree family. That little family that got burnt out. You know."

Chuck's Money

"She used to take care of me," Allen said.

"Mincesky told the parish secretary to deposit everything that came in for Jackie Scree into the church's gen op. It's one of Mincesky's miracles, Allen. Head of the Worship and Growth Committee, he gets to decide to save the church interest payments by paying off interest and principle on that new narthex carpeting. You know what he did? He told the parish secretary that he wanted to offer financial planning to Ms. Scree before handing over a fund to her. He told Mrs. Preck—she was so proud of this—that she was a person who could handle finance and other complex issues in life, but the Ms. Screes of this world can't, sad to say. Mrs. Preck bragged about this to me, word for word. Then she told me she thought we were lucky to have the well-heeled people in town willing to share their financial expertise with the, well, you know, lesser kind of people. So what's the upshot? Ms. Scree *never* gets the money people thought they were giving her. Even Judge Meyrens got fooled."

Allen's jaw fell. "But what if she went and asked? Jackie Scree knew they had requested donations for her!"

Leona gave him a look. "You know the parish secretary, I know the parish secretary. If you were a very poor person, Allen, would you go give that woman a chance to tell you, looking at you from underneath the permanent and all, 'Well, honey, I'm so sorry, but nothing seems to have come in! Honey, I don't think it means people don't like you or trust you. I just think it means they're awfully busy.'"

"Oh Christ," Allen said. He regarded one of his squared hands on his knees, and then the other.

Leona made out his face in the shadows. All of a sudden

she brightened up. "That's what is so wonderful about you," she said. She went over next to him and sat on the couch. It was a cheap couch. As soon as she sat down the couch dumped their hips together in the sag. She put her hand on top of one of his. "You haven't got one crooked drop of blood in you," she said. "And you never lie. How come you never lie, sweetheart? Everybody else does. It's the way to make things flow."

"You don't lie either, Leona."

Instead she said, "You're like a big oak tree, tell you the truth."

He said in a bitter tone, "You're always saying that. Well, I'll tell you something. I am no more like an oak tree than a bowl of vomit."

"No," she said, because all the time he was talking she was secretly moving ahead with some planning inside herself, "no, it is true the house smells of vomit, but you are like an oak tree. All you do is breathe air, with your leaves, and drink water and minerals with your roots, and get more stature all the time. And you never move. You're where I know where you are. But with a snake like Mincesky—"

"I don't want to hear that snake and oak tree crap, Leona."

"A snake," she went on. "It never stays still. If it wants to be in constant motion it goes into constant motion. And the way it identifies its prey is by their warm hearts. And you have a warm heart, so that guy, Mincesky, just naturally goes for you. He sees you sitting at a football game and thinks to himself, 'I wonder if there isn't some way I could empty Singer's pocket a little!'

Chuck's Money   337

"That's how snakes think."

Allen said, "Leona, you really are awfully cynical. People really just plainly aren't as bad as you think they are."

Leona's church served its funerals on a rotation. Each circle took a funeral in its turn, now Eunice Circle, now Ruth Circle, now Esther Circle. Esther Circle had any funeral coming up this week. The system worked so well that almost all arrangements could be made by telephone in the last day or so—arrangements for bringing the food to the church kitchen, arrival times for the workers, making sure sandwiches stand covered with plastic wrap, setting up the coffee, questions of who could or would stay to clean up.

The chairperson of Esther Circle was out of town, so it fell to Leona to make the telephone calls. Seven women told her they would love to help but couldn't because they "worked." Leona called five older women, one of whom had broken her hip. She got a promise from two of the remaining four. Then she went back to two of the women who "worked" and asked if they could get off work. One said she'd try, but her tone of voice suggested that was the last Leona would hear from her. The other said, "Frankly, Leona, I am not too excited about serving this particular funeral."

Leona asked her what that was about.

That boy, the woman explained, has desecrated the holy life that God gave him. She didn't think his body should be put into the church cemetery and she didn't think Christians should serve a funeral for him in the church basement just as if he were one of them.

The woman added, "That boy's dad may think he's the

Carol Bly

cat's pajamas in town, and maybe he is, wealthy like that, but that doesn't mean his son hasn't broken God's law. Anyway, Mincesky may think he can shove us all around any way he likes, but he can't make me serve his suicide-kid's funeral and that's the end of it."

"You've got a point," Leona said.

Leona went into the church woman's occasional emergency mode. She called up the executive officers and asked them to serve the funeral because her circle wasn't coming up with enough people. Two agreed. The other four said they were working and couldn't get off midday like that.

Leona put down the phone and figured out how four, plus herself making five, people could serve that funeral. She sat at the kitchen table, with the phone line trailing over across the toaster and the microwave. The telephone rang. "Leona? I'm Jackie Scree. People say you can't find people to serve Chucky Mincesky's funeral. If you need me, I will."

Leona thought of Jackie Scree driving her wreck of a 1973 Chevette in from her farmstead. Leona had gone out there to help her fill out claims forms. The burned-down house ruins still stood bleak like a war photograph. Jackie and her children were living in an old mobile home that someone had dragged over for her. They had been kind to drag it over, but they hadn't asked her where she wanted it set. They left it in the middle of the driveway, with the jack under the stem— meaning that the moment Jackie Scree found some other arrangement they wanted to haul the mobile home back. Leona pictured the children going out to the end of the road to wait for the school bus. She pictured the other children,

Chuck's Money

looking out the bus windows from above. Those children might or might not recognize some of the clothes the Scree kids were wearing.

"I do need your help, Jackie," Leona said.

"All *right!*" exclaimed Jackie Scree's voice.

They talked together about the bars and the pork-cooked egg-beef-mayo mix for the sandwich buns. Leona added up to herself the difference between the combined price of sugar, chocolate chips, and flour, maybe buying the vanilla too, and the combined price of a small pork roast and a little beef roast. Into the telephone she said, "Jackie, we have people for the sandwich mix. What we need is bars. Either chocolate chip or lemon or brownies."

They talked over which Jackie preferred to bake. She would be there she said, Wednesday, at 1:30 with the bars.

Leona said carefully, "It's going to be a huge funeral, Jackie. We servers are going to park back behind the church kitchen door."

The funeral director had been known to ask people with old rusted cars not to drive in the entourage out to the cemetery. Leona now called him up. She explained that the funeral lunch servers would be parked out back behind the church, but that some of them might want to go out to the cemetery because a lot of people knew and liked Chuck Mincesky. So did he think he could possibly come into the kitchen before the funeral service itself and offer rides to the six women in the kitchen?

The funeral director said, "What's up, Leona?"

She said, "Otherwise we will drive the cars we have."

There was a pause. Then the funeral director said, "What's

Carol Bly

wrong with you and Allen's car? I like it fine. And you guys keep it washed and all. Who else you got serving?"

They went over the list. Clearly he knew which car everybody on that list drove. Makes, years—or rather amounts of rust and tendency not to be washed—were things he kept track of as part of his job.

"OK," he said finally. "This is a big funeral as you know. The trouble with a funeral for a family as important as the Minceskys is that the people who hate them will come as well as the people who like them. And people on food stamps will come for the food. But anyway, the out-of-town relationship will come and they don't want that cemetery procession to look like a solid landfill transfer station. OK, Leona, we will pick up your ladies in one of the stretchies."

All day Monday and Tuesday, the town lay quiet in its funeral frame of mind. Everyone was aware of the long boy's body lying in the funeral parlor. They knew the casket had to be kept closed. They imagined the destroyed part of his face. They made up reasons for his choosing to die. People felt torn. They knew that the father was a tough guy, but he was a town leader as well—and they hated to have moral objections to a leader. It made you cringe. You wanted your leaders to be all right. People went around saying things like "say what you like, human beings are basically good." Sometimes people mentioned the mother, Mrs. Mincesky. She was a colorless woman of forty-seven who could not decide on anything. For instance, it got around town that the Minceskys were putting up a lot of their relatives at the motel. Mrs. Mincesky went over to talk to the owner about reserving rooms. She was so undecided about how many units to book, Einar had asked her for the list of relations coming in. He gently confirmed with her who was married to whom and could be put into a room together, and so on. He made it clear to her that she was the one with the expertise about who needed to be put up at the motel. He also told the entire conversation over coffee to several interested people at Mickey's Pantry, and explained that he hoped he had made her feel better about herself.

Einar, very grand in a real suit—actually in shirt, tie, matching loden-colored jacket and trousers—went about town like death's own sergeant-at-arms. He had been drinking coffee on Main Street more than once on Monday morning, more than once on Monday afternoon as well. He was much sought after. People who didn't feel confident enough to ask if they could shove in with the others in Einar's booth at Mickey's Pantry would gaze at him from booths or tables nearby. People longed to hear about Chuck's body. Einar told his story, several sides of it, over and over, in a sober, harmonic voice. He went past mere facts. He explained to people there is something in a man hates the sight of a dead boy. One would be willing to die *for* the boy if it would save that boy's life. Each time he said that people looked startled, but when they regarded Einar's reposed, solemn face, they remarked, "I bet Einar just would, too. I bet he really meant that." Soon a few people realized that Leona, that young woman who did books for the motel, not Einar, had actually been the first to discover Chuck's body. Two middle-aged women approached her to ask what Chuck's head had looked like. The consensus was that Leona Singer might be a pretty darn good bookkeeper but she sure was tight about sharing with people. It

Carol Bly

took a man, a real man, like Einar, to have some feelings and share them in a non-snobbish way. Even people who hadn't gone to Chuck's football games had decided that everyone was in this thing together.

People didn't work much. They hung around in town, standing just outside the doors of the stores and the two cafes. People were a little better dressed than usual. Even the senior and junior cheerleaders, when they showed up to buy Danishes after school, wore slacks, not jeans. People noticed that even Mrs. Scree, a woman who had been burned out and supposedly had a church fund being raised for her, came to town wearing a dress.

People were kind to each other. Kids stood around in groups of seven or eight, and stopped jeering at other kids who had no groups. They let the lonely hang in their groups. Boys and girls who had love affairs going on held hands but didn't make out. A busload of older people came into town for the Tuesday giveaway drawing, as usual. People regarded them quizzically. The old people understood that look perfectly clearly. One of them, instead of this kid, might have died and no harm done, said the looks. All the while, focused and sturdy, the funeral director presided over the constant visitation going on in his parlor. He had memorized the names of the out-of-town Mincesky relations, and he bowed with special respect to them, when they showed up in twos and threes.

At last the funeral service was over. The smartest thing a small-town church can do after a funeral is the same thing the greatest churches and temples of Europe and Asia have always done: toll the bell. The Dearing bell slammed down its rhythmic crash, over and over. People blinked to come out of the dark nave and into the white, curiously empty afternoon light. They went quietly to their cars. Out back, the women designated to serve the lunch did not speak as they took turns getting into one of the funeral director's limos. The bell kept ringing and ringing. Inside the church, the old, the pregnant, those wounded in any way, made their way to the fellowship hall. They muttered quietly to each other, waiting out the burial to join the others at lunch. In the kitchen the only sound was the *pfut pfut pfut* of the three giant coffeemakers.

Everyone sat around a long time over that lunch. Over half the town was there. Leona and the other kitchen crew members saw the faces of fellow church members and people who had been financially used by Mincesky, people who had loyally gone to three years of high-school football games lost by Chuck Mincesky, faces of strangers who must be Mincesky relations. Then there were the people who go to any funeral they can get a ride to. Some came from Hibbing. Some even from Ely.

At last the last dishes went through the washer and the workers divided up the leftover sandwiches onto paper plates for themselves. Leona told Jackie Scree she had better take some sandwiches since she brought such good bars everyone ate them so there weren't any left to take home for the kids. Jackie Scree wanted to know if she was kidding about taking home a plate of sandwiches. I don't kid, Leona said. Here. She put some plastic-wrapped sandwiches into the 10 x 17 pan with its adhesive tape that said "Jackie Scree" in ball point. The workers all thanked each other, over and over.

Carol Bly

They were proud of themselves, because it really had gone off well. Everyone had had lots to eat. People had smiled at the white-aproned women offering them second and third cups of coffee where they sat. Leona told Jackie Scree that it was lucky for her (Leona) that Jackie had volunteered to serve. She had saved her life, you could bet, and Leona would never forget.

Jackie Scree said, "Well, I didn't just do it to be nice. See, you may not know, but I used to help take care of your Allen a little when he was a boy. I always did cotton to him—well, and here you are, married to him. So it was a pleasure."

The two women shook hands.

Leona said to herself that it was so wonderful that not everybody was a liar or an asshole.

But now she realized she had no more time for philosophy and church activity. It was time to go home, gear up, pick up the hotdish that Allen had said he would make, and take it over to the Minceskys' house. It was time. She had distracted herself with easy duties at the church. She was on, as they say.

Allen shouted from the kitchen that he was just now wrapping up the casserole in towels, how about she find a box to put it in for better handling? Leona hurried to the bookshelf top. She took the purchase agreement out of its frame, folded it twice, tore it neatly into fourths, put it into her pocket, and then went to the kitchen. "Mushroom soup in it?" she asked with a grin.

Allen said, "No, I went all the way. The real thing. Cream sauce, butter not crisco, all meat, no elbow macaroni, no can of mushroom soup. Hey. Let me." He carried it out to the car for her.

Chuck's Money   345

They stood together outside their beat-up car. Rust was beginning to scab and snake its way along the fenders and doors where the design strips imprison water and salt. Soon it would look like Jackie Scree's car. Soon they would start talking about how keeping that car in repair was nickel-and-diming them to death, while they both knew that replacing it with a newer car would thousand-dollar-bill them to death.

"In a way," Allen said, "Christianity really does suck. Here I am, sending over a casserole for that guy who keeps making an ass of me. God I hate it!" Leona got in and rolled down the driver's window. He leaned in and kissed her. "Don't be long," he said. "It's been such a dumb day. Come home. We'll do something intelligent together. Like go to bed, say."

They kissed again and she drove collectedly across town. It was a perfect October day. She would ask Mr. Mincesky to step out into his backyard. She knew it looked east, its far bounds being a farmer's barbed wire fence, with a still-unpicked cornfield behind it.

The place was full of relations, as she had known it would be. Mrs. Mincesky took the casserole and then took both of Leona's hands. She said she was very, very grateful for the hotdish. She said Leona would find *him* in the living room, last she'd seen him.

"Well," Leona said to Mincesky, "how about we go out back so we can talk for a second?"

Mincesky was surrounded by tall relations. They loomed above Leona. Oh yes, of course, Leona thought, that's why he ever got away with insisting his boy be the quarterback. Anyone so tall—how could they be a bad athlete? Well, she thought, that is like saying if someone is the head of the

Carol Bly

Worship & Growth Committee, how can they not be a spiritual person?

She geared up some more. She was on, now, she thought. Too late to turn back.

"Lead away, lady," Mincesky said, nearly flirtatiously. He grinned at the middle-aged men in the little circle with him. "I never turn down a beautiful woman or a tough bookkeeper, either one!"

Leona led the way to the barbed wire fence at the end of his yard. Mincesky tried balancing his wineglass on a fence post near him, like a boy seeing if a ball will stay balanced on an octagonal pencil.

"Something I thought you had a right to know," she said. "Chuck left a suicide note in the motel."

Mincesky sneered. "You think I don't know that? That's the first thing the sheriff told me about."

"A second suicide note," Leona said in a forbearing tone. "There was the one you saw, and then there was another one." She told him how it was she, not the cleaning woman, who had found Chucky. She told him how the other suicide note came in a large 4 x 9 envelope, enclosing the note he had seen in its smaller envelope. She told him she didn't see any reason why the contents of the outer suicide note should be talked about all over town, down at the Pantry, and maybe at the chamber. Or now she thought of it, at the sheriff's office. Why, in fact, should even the pastor and the parish secretary know what's going on in a man's perfectly private life? If a man wants to knock his wife around a little and do some psychological abuse on his kid, what business is that of everyone else's, anyhow?

They faced each other like two rocks. The only motion

Chuck's Money

347

was Mincesky's rubbing one finger slowly back and forth along the smooth wire between two of the twisted barbs.

"I don't know what game you're playing, Leona," he said finally. "But I don't believe you."

She felt in her pocket to make sure that only the envelope came out in her hand. She passed it over to him. "Chucky's writing, isn't it? You're the dad, you'd recognize it, wouldn't you?"

He read aloud in a choked whisper, "To the maid or whoever finds me"

"Nobody likes you," Leona said. She now took up the false, contemplative tone she had been rehearsing to herself for two days. She continued, "Then again, no one thinks of you as a wife beater and a child abuser. It's possible," she went on, looking at the fingernails on her right hand, "I suppose it's possible you don't care what people think of you. You've got everyone twisted around your little finger anyway. Though it would be hard to live in a town where people not only *suspected* that you drove your boy to suicide but where they *knew* you had. I think that'd be hard."

He snarled so deeply she jumped. The sound of his voice seemed to come from the man's very skeleton rather than from his throat. "Let's see the note, Leona."

She looked up. "Did you think I would bring it along? No," she said. "If you want to see the note, I will bring it to the church and read it aloud to you in the presence of the pastor, and the parish secretary, and the treasurer. I have to think of my safety."

He said, "What do you want?" He raised his finger off the wire. "You realize this is blackmail?"

Carol Bly

"Oh yes," she said in the languid tone she had planned in case he said that. "But very small blackmail. You know. Just the way small crime is not the same as great crime. Let's face it. Stealing from Ms. Scree's burn-out fund, say, is hardly the same thing as hiding Nazi victims' gold in Swiss banks. You're a cheap crook, Charles, and I am a cheap blackmailer."

"Shut up," he said. "What do you want?"

"A check for two thousand dollars," she said, "which you took from Allen for a purchase agreement on a house. I expect you night-deposited that check, so just write me one on your own account."

He placed his checkbook flat on the fence top and began to write. As he wrote he said in a conversational tone, "If I was a woman I sure would hate being married to a man so pussywhipped his wife had to hike over to get the sucker's money back!"

"Oh shit!" she exclaimed in an equable, conversational voice. "There went *that!*"

The businessman looked at her. "What do you mean?"

"I lost the bet is all," she said. "Allen and I had a bet whether you would say something like he was weak or pussywhipped or whatever and the so-called strong wife had to come over to get the money back. He said you would say that. I said no, there're a lot of things about Mincesky, but he wouldn't stoop to that old gouge. We had fifty bucks on it."

Mincesky handed her the check. Leona went back into her left pocket and brought out the four torn quarters of the purchase agreement and handed them over.

"Get out now," he said. "Get out. Go around the side of the house. Don't go back into my home."

Chuck's Money

But his wife was approaching. On her face wormed a sycophant's smile. Her spot makeup nearly covered the yellowing bruise that Leona had seen looking darker a few days earlier. Mrs. Mincesky took both her hands, "You and Allen are a real Christian couple," she said. "Will you tell him how much I appreciate the hotdish?"

The evenings were drawing in. As Leona drove west through town, the sun came below the visor in her car. She felt herself grimacing as she squinted. I did it, she said to herself.

She found Allen upstairs. "I have been thinking it over very carefully," he said. "Here's the plan. We go to bed. Then we get up at about nine o'clock tonight and we eat chicken casserole with cream sauce laced with sherry. Do you think I gave *all* that wonderful casserole to the Minceskys? Not a chance. And we open a bottle of wine."

"I have something to confess to you," she said in bed.

She told him how she had gotten the two thousand dollars back from their landlord.

He was openly appalled. They had been lying on their backs, holding hands, daydreaming. Now his hand opened and left hers uncradled. "It is awful to blackmail someone," he said. He added, "But how did you do it, anyhow? How'd you fake an envelope with Chuck Mincesky's writing on it?"

"It was real. He did leave a second suicide note." She told Allen what the note really said. She told him about the $340 the boy had enclosed, and how she had put it into her suit jacket pocket, where it stayed throughout the District church conference. All the money Chucky had had, she supposed.

"What if Mincesky had called your bluff?" Allen asked.

Carol Bly

But Leona was perfectly happy to answer his questions, because his interest now was in *how* it had gone off, no longer in whether she should or should not have done it. She felt let off.

"I don't know," she admitted. "If I was feeling gutsy I suppose I would have gone ahead and met him in the parish secretary's office, with the pastor and all. Maybe let him see me talking in the Pantry just ahead of that, so he would think I was spreading it around town. I don't know. I didn't think that far ahead."

"I think you thought pretty goddamned far ahead," he said lightly.

She faced the fact: he liked her less now.

But in the next moment he took her hand again. Oh good, she thought, he is a human being. He is in this just as much as I am. I am so glad. The hell with virtue, she thought, squeezing his hand. She moved against him gladly. I am so glad he is not going to be moral about this.

But they were like spent grass in October. They could not make love. They only lay close.

Just as she was falling asleep, Allen's voice said, "Leona, how do you *know* that Mincesky beats his wife?"

"She sometimes goes around with that Quick Corrector or something like it. I can spot that stuff a mile off. She's the only person I know uses it around one eye or the other. Other people use it for a last-ditch fix on blemishes and all. Sucks, as products go. Sweat, and it rivulets off."

He laughed in a desultory way. They were silent. Again she was about to fall asleep.

He said, "Leona, do you think that Chucky Mincesky *saw* his dad beating up on his mother?"

Chuck's Money

She said, "Somehow a kid would know. They'd hear it if they didn't actually see it. Woman once told me in a car pool, kids always know."

When she woke up Allen was gone. She leaped out of bed, very happy. The funeral was over, she had worked out an inch-by-inch plan to gouge that bastard Mincesky and get their money back and she'd done it, and now she was going down to the kitchen to make some dessert for them, something special that Allen didn't know how to make so it would be a treat. She knew that sooner or later nothing either of them cooked would surprise the other very much, but that time hadn't come yet, and she wanted to surprise him now. She clattered downstairs like a girl playing house.

Odd he was gone, but she remembered he had had the notion of dinner at nine. It was only eight-thirty. He would be home soon.

The telephone rang.

"Leona? This is Jerry, sheriff's office. I just wanted to call so you wouldn't worry, and tell you that we have Allen here and he is fine."

She asked what was going on. "No, never mind, Jerry," she said. "I'll be right over."

He cut back in. "Don't come, Leona. The judge doesn't want you to come over."

"Wait a minute, Jerry. You're holding my husband in the jail for some reason I don't even know what it is and I can't come see him?"

Jerry's voice, very steady: "Judge says absolutely not. Allen's supposed to be locked up for tonight and the court will arraign him tomorrow at ten o'clock. But you're not supposed to come over."

Leona found her voice. "Why are you holding him? Can't I talk to him?"

Jerry said, "Naw, Leona. He's made his one telephone call. Judge says, we're going by the rules. He made the right call, too, if you ask me. He called the judge. So the judge says hold him all night so it's a day in jail. Obey all the rules. So I said, Leona's got to know where he is, you know, and she's going to ask, what are we holding Allen for? And the judge says, tell her, but no visiting tonight. Judge says, he's arraigning Allen ten o'clock tomorrow. He said, tell you very clearly when the hearing is. People have a right to go to it. That's what he said. So Coralie Ann, she's been calling up different people. Leona, you and Allen, you got a lot of friends it turns out. Cheryl what's-her-name. She said she's calling everyone she knows."

"Yes but why are you holding Allen?" Leona said.

"Well," Jerry said, "apparently he went over to the Minceskys' earlier tonight. They were having supper and all, with all those relatives still in town. And Allen assaulted Charles Mincesky. So someone called the police, which is me, and I went over and picked up Allen. Then when we got back to the jail, Allen called the judge—Hey, Leona, Coralie Ann wants to talk to you, Leona."

"Leona? This is Coralie Ann. Listen, I'm taking care of Allen OK. Only light bruising and he didn't lose any teeth or anything. He has a shiner but we got ice on it. And Leona, normally, we hold someone here overnight. Normally what we do, we give them a choice of a TV dinner from the freezer— they can have the turkey or the veggie. I just wanted you to

Chuck's Money

know that I ran over to the minimarket and got a T-bone for Allen. Onion rings, too. Not as good as homemade but still, you know, onion rings are onion rings. And Leona, he is going to be fine. Jerry and I, we bandaged up his hand, he didn't break anything, and the eye'll be OK. I just wanted you to know."

"Christ, thank you very much," said Leona. "Thank you, Coralie Ann. But I thought Allen slugged Mincesky? Did Mincesky slug him back?"

Coralie Ann's tone was crisp. "Allen did pretty well," she said. "Pretty darn well considering. He got in one, I think. Jerry said he kind of missed but got him in the ear,"—here she turned half away from the phone and bellowed, "Jer, did you say Allen got Mincesky one in the ear?" The sheriff's voice in the background responded, and Coralie Ann came back to the phone. "Yeah, he says he did pretty good actually. I guess he was going for his chin or his eye but Mincesky turned so he got him in this one ear. Jerry says that ear's going to ring real good for him for a while."

Leona said, "OK but what about Allen? What happened? "Oh that," Coralie said. "Yeah, major dogshit. Well those brothers of Mincesky, we're talking major shit, Leona. One of those brothers or cousins or something from out of town, this one bopped Allen a couple. Great big guy with a long reach, like Mincesky."

Leona said, "Someone from out of town? Who didn't even know Allen? They up and hit him?"

Coralie Ann said, "Consider the source, Leona. You know what kind of people those Minceskys are. Look, if there's dogshit in front of the kennel there's dogshit behind it."

Carol Bly

Coralie Ann told Leona she had called up a lot of people to tell them about the hearing. And Cheryl what's-her-face, that woman that cleans motel and all? she said she'd call everyone she knew. Coralie Ann said that she was surprised that woman had such a dirty mouth on her. As soon as Coralie Ann mentioned Mincesky, that Cheryl came out with language that Coralie Ann had never heard before in her life, not even from people who came over from Wisconsin to be locked up for a night or two in their jail.

Leona and Coralie Ann talked some more and then hung up.

The Mincesky funeral had been well attended, but the Dearing County courtroom was stuffed. The only time she had been in there, Leona had used the back bench row to collate some tax returns she had photocopied at the machine in the hall. She remembered laying the white pages down in their rows on top of the shiny oak. Oak has little scratchings in it that give it some of its beauty. She didn't know anything about nature stuff, but she supposed those were the marks where twigs had grown from. Anyhow, nice, formal-looking wood. And the courtroom was nice looking. It had been in Dearing since the great iron ore businesses first came to the Range towns and began pouring money into public buildings.

Today, though, coats and jackets lay hung over the entire length of every bench back, and people were talking and gesturing to one another. Leona felt shy. She paused in the doorway. Then Einar from the motel, in matching jacket and trousers, carrying a clipboard, waved over people's heads and wove his way toward her. Now he was in one of his favorite

Chuck's Money

roles—docent to the United States justice system. He took Leona by the arm and floated his announcement to those nearby: "Here she is! Here she is! Here, shove along, would you? Here's our Leona! Of all people *she* gets a seat!" People turned around and grinned at her. On both sides of the aisle people made sitting space for her. Now everyone was sitting down.

Leona peered between heads to see who all was up front. One of the sheriff's men was laying papers on the judge's desk. Leona recalled that he was that worthless lowlife who tried to claim he didn't have any income except his social security. When the feds got after him he had called Leona and asked her if she would just testify that she had done his taxes for the last three years and could attest to the fact he had just about zero per annum income. Now he was a sheriff's deputy. He went out a side door up front. Someone else, perhaps a bailiff, came in. Then the lowlife returned, this time bringing Allen Singer by the arm but not cuffed. They sat down at the defense counsel table. Charles Mincesky already sat at a smaller table between Allen's and the front row of audience.

Jerry, the sheriff himself, looking very spruce, with a visible press to his khaki shirt, now shouted, "All rise!" and everyone, combed or tousled, kempt or unkempt, got to their feet. He went on: "The Court of the State of Minnesota, Dearing County, is now in session, the Honorable John Meyrens, Justice, presiding."

Judge Meyrens appeared in a black gown. He went up onto the platform and took his seat. He said loudly, "You may be seated."

Then he looked around, as if he had noticed the filled

Carol Bly

courtroom for the first time. The people, on their part, now took in their judge, many of them for the first and perhaps the only time in their lives, dressed in the raiment of his profession. He still had, of course, the familiar curly hair and the same about-to-smile expression. This was the benign, middle-aged face of their friend. People recalled how he shouted unjudgelike things at their football games and liked him for it. He had even been reprimanded by the refs, just five days ago at homecoming, right there under the Friday bright lights in front of them all, for conduct unbecoming to sportsmanship. For that particular behavior, they not only liked but loved him. So here he was in his regalia and everyone settled down with wiggly smiles at their neighbors and watched. They hoped he would bring about some indecipherable but basically good thing.

Judge Meyrens said, "This is the case of the People of the State of Minnesota versus Allen Curtiss Singer, Docket number 68,547. Is the defendant present in Court?"

Jerry said, "Yes he is, Your Honor."

The judge then looked directly at Allen. "Mr. Singer, you have been charged with assault and trespassing. How do you plead?"

"Guilty, Your Honor," Allen said.

A single, almost lyrical sigh waved across the whole courtroom. Following that floating sound, total silence. Judge, bailiff, court reporter, sheriff, deputies, defendant and plaintiff, and the roomful of people—all were still.

The judge said, "Since neither defendant nor prosecution have elected to be represented by counsel, I will now ask Charles Mincesky to explain his position in this case."

Chuck's Money

Clearly, Allen Curtiss Singer of this county had entered the home of Charles Mincesky at 413 East End Avenue for the purpose of assault. He had struck Charles Mincesky. Guests of the household had called the police. The sheriff had brought Allen Singer to the jail and incarcerated him for the night.

In a polite voice, Judge Meyrens then asked Mr. Mincesky if he would be willing to tell all of his side of the story.

"Willing! You bet I'm willing!" snapped Mincesky. "He came right in, when my relatives and my family and I were grieving for our dead boy. He just came right in and said a lot of crazy stuff, and then tried to slug me, the dumbass."

The judge said, "Keep all language clean or I will have you fined."

Mincesky said, "He tried to slug me but he missed."

The judge said, "Are you saying that he missed? That he did not hit you?"

"I meant he missed my face. He's hardly an athlete. He just ticked my ear."

"Please show your ear."

It was red, oddly shaped, like a plantain leaf.

The judge looked at the recorder and said, "Record that Allen Singer landed a blow on Charles Mincesky's right ear." He looked back at Mincesky. "What did he say before he landed the blow on your ear?"

"Crazy stuff, Your Honor."

"Be specific."

"I don't remember that crazy stuff he said, shouting and crying, too. Yeah, he was crying."

"Please remember it," the judge remarked. "I will then ask Mr. Singer to confirm it."

Mincesky spoke quietly. His back was to the audience. The judge said, "Will you please speak plainly so everyone can hear."

Mincesky said, "He told me I was nothing but a cheat and a bully, but that he had not known before that I—Your Honor, I do not have to incriminate myself in a county courtroom."

The judge turned to Allen Singer.

Everyone in the room now looked at him. Leona's husband wore some stickplaster on one side of his face. The left eye looked out cheerfully from a wide, dark rim. His right fist was wrapped in so much bandage it looked like prizefighter's equipment.

Allen said, "I told him I hadn't known before now that he beat his wife. Your Honor, I told him that when I was a kid I never stood up for my mother. I was always dumping on myself about it but I couldn't make myself stand up for her, because I'd see her all bloody and a couple of times, my dad had knocked her teeth out, and I didn't want to lose my teeth. I just didn't want to lose my teeth, Judge! I just couldn't make myself reach up and slug him one. So I was always relieved when my parents left me to go to Marco Island, this place in Florida. The grocery store guy and all, they would be sympathetic to me, so I didn't let on I was happy because it didn't seem right, some way, to be happy your parents were gone. But those winters, your honor, they were the best time of my life. I didn't feel like a coward then. And Mrs. Scree would come over. I suppose she cleaned around some while I was in school, but the big thing was, she would bring me chocolate-chip bars and stuff. But the biggest thing of all, Your Honor. She didn't give speeches at me. I would tell her

Chuck's Money

different ideas I had. They were kids' ideas about life, but they were ideas. And she would sit there and I noticed she would take another cookie or drink out of her coffee while I was talking. And I didn't feel like a coward.

"So I said to Mr. Mincesky last night, I said, 'This one is for my mother. I guess it is for Chucky Mincesky's mother, too, but it is mostly for my mother. I mean, I know it is too late. My mother's gone now, but that's who it is for.'"

Someone far back in the courtroom moaned. People reached around for their jacket pockets to get Kleenex.

The judge said, "Has either one of you anything more to say?"

The courtroom was quiet.

The judge then said, "Allen, we can't have citizens going into other citizens' houses and striking them in the head because they think the other fellow deserves it. I sentence you to ninety days in prison and I fine you seven hundred dollars. I hereby stay eighty-nine days of the prison sentence. You have already served three quarters of one day in jail, and so must be returned under guard until six o'clock this evening. I stay four hundred of the seven-hundred-dollar fine, but you must pay three hundred dollars and a surcharge of thirty dollars, which is used for agencies statewide that help battered women, plus ten dollars, which goes to legal libraries. We keep these libraries open for Minnesota citizens so that they can apprize themselves of learned knowledge on their legal occasions."

Judge Meyrens gave the gavel a pound. The sheriff didn't seem to be in a hurry to take the defendant back to the jail, so people began surging forward.

In the hullabaloo it was impossible for Leona to get to

Carol Bly

Allen. She caught glimpses of him now and then, through all the heads with their seed-corn caps. She noticed that men were not actually talking to him much, but simply gathering close, and grinning at him. She caught and lost sight of his face. Then she would see him again. Even with the Band-Aid and black eye, he looked formal.

Allen was smiling at his townspeople. He was smiling oddly. His smile reminded Leona of a foreign diplomat she had once seen when she was just a kid, working in the Hart Senate Office Building as gofer. Her boss, an honest Minnesota senator, had brought in some big-shot statesman from another country. He introduced this gentleman to everyone in the room, by name—introduced him to all those people right down to Leona, who barely had the sense to turn off her electric stapler. That big shot from some other country came around and shook hands with everyone. He smiled at each one of them and he spoke perfect, friendly, American English. But she remembered thinking, even back then, that a person like that can talk to you gently and perfectly, but you can tell that they also know some very different language, a language that people speak in some country you may never get to in your lifetime.

CAROL BLY is the author of many books, including the short-story collections *Backbone* and *The Tomcat's Wife* and the essay collections *Changing the Bully Who Rules the World, Letters from the Country,* and *The Passionate, Accurate Story,* and most recently a memoir, *An Adolescent's Christmas—1944.* Her next book, which will be published in 2001, will be a book about creative writing. Bly teaches Ethics-in-Literature in the University of Minnesota's Master of Liberal Studies program. She has taught creative-writing workshops in the University of Minnesota's Split Rock Summer Arts Program, at the Vermont Studio Center, and in Northland College's Lifelong Learning Program. She lives in St. Paul, Minnesota.

Live at Five
David Haynes

Somebody Else's Mama
David Haynes

The Children Bob Moses Led
William Heath

Pu-239 and Other Russian Fantasies
Ken Kalfus

Thirst
Ken Kalfus

Persistent Rumours
Lee Langley

Hunting Down Home
Jean McNeil

Swimming in the Congo
Margaret Meyers

Tokens of Grace
Sheila O'Connor

Tivolem
Victor Rangel-Ribeiro

The Boy Without a Flag
Abraham Rodriguez Jr.

Confidence of the Heart
David Schweidel

An American Brat
Bapsi Sidhwa

Cracking India
Bapsi Sidhwa

The Crow Eaters
Bapsi Sidhwa

The Country I Come From
Maura Stanton

Traveling Light
Jim Stowell

Aquaboogie
Susan Straight

The Empress of One
Faith Sullivan

Falling Dark
Tim Tharp

The Promised Land
Ruhama Veltfort

Justice
Larry Watson

Montana 1948
Larry Watson

Interior design by Elizabeth Cleveland
Typeset in Old Style 7 and Wade Sans Light
by Stanton Publication Services, Inc.
Printed on acid-free, recycled 55# Miami Book paper
by Friesen Corporation